Laura Black
Castle Raven

Pan Books London and Sydney

First published in Great Britain 1978 by Hamish Hamilton Ltd
This edition published 1980 by Pan Books Ltd,
Cavaye Place, London SW10 9PG
© Laura Black 1978
ISBN 0 330 25932 6
Set, printed and bound in Great Britain by
Cox & Wyman Ltd, Reading

one

I was helping to dress my little half-sister, Malvina, for her appearance in the great drawing-room after tea. It was a lengthy business.

It was the custom in those days (I am writing of the year 1861) for young girls to be dressed in the full, elaborate style of their mothers. So Malvina, who was barely thirteen years of age, wore an afternoon gown of sky-blue silk in the last cry of fashion, hooped to an astonishing size at the hem; over the hoops of her skirt fell layer upon layer of silken flounces; her waist was nipped to an hourglass; her precocious bosom swelled a bodice as tight and smooth as an eggshell. Above, corkscrew ringlets of bright gold fell about her shoulders. Wilson, her personal maid, spent hours upon those ringlets.

Wilson, dressing Malvina, looked as out of place as I felt. She came from a small farm on the estate. She was a big, strapping young woman; I do not think she would have chosen to be a lady's-maid, but her father's tenant-farm was very small and barren, and the family needed her wages. If ever a woman did, she earned her money.

Besides Wilson and myself Malvina's governess, Miss Maitland, was helping to gild our miniature lily. She was a despondent female, tall, not unhandsome, with pale green eyes, and a passion for geography, and a passion for Malvina. She treated her charge with a sort of frightened deference, as though terrified of breaking her. It was curious to see such a tall gaunt governess so nervous and tentative with her pupil. Their lessons together were consequently quite brief, and included little of the drudgery of learning.

Mamma knew quite well that Malvina was not becoming highly educated. She was not discomposed. 'One bluestocking in the house is enough,' she said, glancing at me with the smile that bewitched half Scotland. 'Katharine may grow pale and round-shouldered, poring over her books, because that is what she likes. Malvina is different.'

Malvina was different, indeed.

She pirouetted before the tall triple glass, and dimpled at herself over her shoulder. Her smile was amazingly like her mother's. Looking at her, I glimpsed my own reflection beside hers. Two more different creatures could hardly be imagined. People often said it was amazing that Malvina and I were of the same blood, and they were right. I was thin and paper-pale, with straight black hair, and heavy straight eyebrows, and high cheekbones, and green eyes. I wore a snuff-coloured dress, without hoops or crinoline. Though her half-sister, I visibly belonged to a different species from Malvina.

I thought I was not precisely ugly, though my face was not of the kind that people admired. I thought I was not exactly stupid; I was certainly not ill-read. But there were things gravely wrong with me, with my mind and my nervous system. The doctors said so. As a child I had been desperately shy, miserable with strangers to an extent which was not normal or healthy. I understood that this was so when, later, I saw Malvina as a child; she was not shy at all; she loved meeting strangers, and talked to them confidently; she was undoubtedly healthy. So Mamma was worried about me, and great doctors came from Edinburgh to examine me. I do not know what they said to Mamma and Uncle Frank, but I know that ever afterwards I was a sort of invalid. I could be physically active, and I could read all the books I wanted, but I must be spared the excitement of company, the unsettling strain of social life.

From time to time the doctors came again, and asked me searching questions. I was still protected from hearing what they said, or seeing what they wrote. But I was still a sort of invalid.

It was violently annoying. As a child I had railed and stormed against the bitter ill-luck that made me 'different', that kept me from people and gaiety. At eighteen, I accepted my hidden ill-health, the frailty of my nerves, because one does not disbelieve great doctors.

So I was content – I made myself content – to help Malvina enjoy all that I could not have myself.

'Ye're as bonny as ye'll aye be,' said Wilson to Malvina.

'Your Mamma will be more than satisfied, dear,' said Miss Maitland.

'Will she, Katie?' Malvina asked me.

'Yes,' I said.

Malvina looked as though she expected me to say more: but I had no more to say. The women had said it.

Malvina and I went out from the sunny warmth of her bedroom into the great cold vaults of the upstairs corridors. When our grandfather built Ravenburn Castle in 1839, he was more concerned with his grandeur than with his comforts: and on a February afternoon one wanted a fur cape and a pair of mittens to go from one room to another.

We went down the marble stairs, and it was like descending a mountainside into a glen, for the great hall could easily have accommodated a cluster of ordinary houses. We crossed the hall, under a forest of antlers, coldly observed by a regiment of suits of armour. I opened the drawing-room door for Malvina and she danced in, like a bird of paradise taking possession of a garden.

There were cries of greeting, and there were cries of wonder and admiration.

I stood by the door, my hand on the knob. I did not want to irritate Mamma by leaving, if she required me. I vexed her all too often, by saying the wrong things, or failing to say the right thing. I vexed her by the way I looked, and by being the kind of person I was. I did not want to irritate Mamma yet again: but I did not want to bore myself to the pitch of madness by listening to Mamma's friends.

Malvina danced up to Mamma and kissed her, careful to disturb neither her own hair nor Mamma's. By chance, Mamma was wearing a sky-blue gown like Malvina's, and the likeness between them was more startling than usual.

'It's bewildering,' said Colonel Blair. 'It's impossible to believe that you're this fine young lady's mother, Lady Ravenburn!'

'Impossible!' cried Mrs Seton. 'Why do you not admit, Isabella, to your friends, that you have not a daughter but a sister?'

'A sister,' said Sir Malcolm Rattray, 'very little younger than yourself, by George!'

'Very little younger,' echoed Lady Wood faintly.

'Very little,' said her daughter, Miss Serena Wood, in a still fainter echo.

My stepmother was, in truth, only thirty-four. I felt strange, at the age of eighteen, calling so young and lovely a woman 'Mamma', but I had done so ever since I could remember – ever since she married my father when I was four. It was always done. Every stepmother was 'Mamma', every stepfather was 'Papa'; perhaps other stepchildren found it came more naturally than it did to me. I felt strange, calling her 'Mamma'; I felt yet stranger because by no freak of inheritance could I have been her daughter. She was all that Malvina promised to be – golden haired, gentle faced, dainty featured, pink and creamy in colouring, voluptuously curved, dimpled and rounded.

Beneath the skin, difference piled upon difference, between Mamma and me. She was happiest among people. Because of my nervous weakness, I had learned to be happiest alone. She sang like a nightingale. I made a noise, when I was obliged to sing, sometimes like a peewit, sometimes like a screech-owl. Her greatest joy was amateur theatricals, in which she blazed like a comet. The excitement of performing in public would have been (everyone agreed) dangerous to my uncertain nervous system. Above all, Mamma was content with the company of such people as surrounded her now. I thought they were dreadful.

Malvina curtseyed to Mrs Seton, who had been staying in the Castle since just after Christmas. She was the widow of an admiral, an unbending lady, so rigidly corseted that she could hardly move, a great admirer of Mamma and of Malvina and her brother.

Malvina curtseyed to Lady Wood, who had been staying in the Castle, with her daughter, since just before Christmas. She was the widow of an Edinburgh Law Lord, a lady as flexible as Mrs Seton was stiff, forever swooping and swaying, like a reed at the loch-side, and making faint cries, like a puzzled echo which has not quite caught the words it is supposed to repeat.

Malvina curtseyed to Miss Serena Wood, a young lady no longer young. She was like a chintz that has been left too long in strong sunlight; she either modelled herself on her mother, or had imitated her unconsciously, so that she was the echo of an echo.

Malvina curtseyed to Sir Malcolm Rattray, who had been staying at the Castle for a month. He was a widower of fifty, and though a very rich baronet (with coal-mines in Lanarkshire) he seemed always a little alarmed at the size of the Castle. He spent much of his time sucking the knob of a stick and gazing at Mamma, which she did not seem to dislike as much as I would have disliked it.

Malvina curtseyed to Colonel Blair, who had been staying at the Castle for a fortnight. He was not overawed by the immensity of the place. He was wonderfully glossy and fashionable, and often talked about his racehorses and pheasants.

Finally Malvina kissed the one other person in the room, my Uncle Frank Dundas: who was my uncle in the same sense that my stepmother was my Mamma. He was Mamma's brother, several years older than herself, a distinguished lawyer who had largely abandoned his career in order to look after the estate for her, after my father died. Uncle Frank was more reddish than Mamma, with sharp features rather than dainty ones; what in her was physical magnificence was in him simply plumpness. Yet they were very alike. He looked wonderfully placid, like her, and as though nothing would put him in a rage. Yet I knew how hard he worked, and how much he sometimes worried. He took everything upon his shoulders, including me. It was Uncle Frank who urged me not to attempt to be like Mamma, but to be myself: to be as solitary as I liked and spend my time with books, or with my spyglass, looking at the birds and animals of the loch-side. So he tried to make me reconciled to the life the doctors said I must lead. Sometimes he almost succeeded.

Sometimes, into Uncle Frank's blandness, there crept a look of irritation and even of disgust, at the inanities of people like Lady Wood, or the posturing of people like Colonel Blair. I knew fellow-feeling when I saw it. I wondered why he bothered with them – why he threw his life away at Ravenburn, instead of being an eminent Edinburgh Writer to the Signet.

The answer was the strength of his family devotion. In looking after Mamma and her children and me, he was doing the thing that mattered to him most. I knew this was so. But I thought it was a pity.

Uncle Frank kissed Malvina with great tenderness. He did not disarrange her hair. Like Miss Maitland, he treated her always as though she were precious and fragile.

Mrs Seton begged that Malvina would play for them. Lady Wood echoed her, and Miss Serena echoed the echo.

'But I cannot sit on the piano-stool in this dress,' said Malvina, 'and it would be a pity to change it. I could sing, though. I have learned to accompany myself on the mandoline. The mandoline is just here. Shall I do that, Mamma?'

Knowing what the answer would be, Malvina took her mandoline out of a cupboard. It was adorned with ribbons, and had come all the way from Venice. She had not truly mastered it.

I slipped out, and went upstairs to my room. I had helped Malvina to dress. That was enough. To listen to her piping was beyond the call of duty.

Going upstairs to my room was a weary journey. I was not sure how I came to have that room, but I had had it for a very long time, and I was thankful for it. I dimly remembered that, while Papa was alive, I had a different room, in a different part of the Castle – a big room, with great windows opening to the western sky, with a cheerful fireplace and comfortable furniture. I thought it was the room which Malvina now had.

After Papa died – not at once, I think, but soon – they said I would be happier off on my own, in a little room in the East Tower. I always accepted that they were right, for a young child accepts what grown-ups say as the voice of wisdom, as the voice of God. Perhaps my change of room had something to do with Uncle Frank coming to live at the Castle. Perhaps it had something to do with what the doctors said.

A governess looked after me, found by Uncle Frank in Edinburgh, Miss Anderson. She was like a white mouse. I loved her dearly. Because I loved her, and because I saw far more of her than of anybody else throughout my childhood, I took after her, more and more. I was a mouse, too. We squeaked together, Miss Anderson and I, in our little grey schoolroom, nibbling at books.

Miss Anderson was not deemed a suitable governess for Malvina; Miss Maitland came instead, and Miss Anderson went away. I was not deemed a suitable pupil for Miss Maitland – certainly not by Miss Maitland – so I became my own teacher, and read an extraordinary variety of ill-chosen books. The result was, that I knew a great deal about all kinds of useless and ridiculous things, and nothing whatever about anything useful.

I climbed the steep stone steps of the East Tower; I passed the door of Miss Anderson's room, which still stood empty, and of my own bedroom, and went into my schoolroom. Malvina and her brother had never used it; Miss Maitland had never, I think, poked her gaunt nose into it; it was mine. My books were there, which Uncle Frank found for me in Edinburgh, and the books

Miss Anderson had given me when she left, and the books I had brought up from the library: shelves upon shelves of books, so many of which I had ploughed through, so few of which I properly understood.

I looked at them with a sudden wave of hatred. Books, in the company of which I was supposed to be so happy. Books, of which I had had more than enough.

I had come upstairs meaning to read; but the thought of reading, of yet again spending an afternoon reading, filled me with weary disgust. I went instead to my bedroom, which was much unlike Malvina's. I opened the door of my wardrobe, which was much unlike Malvina's.

Of course, I could have had clothes like hers, if I had been a person like her. But when I was her age, and two years older yet, I had no figure at all: I was like a skinny boy: so that when Mamma dressed me up in fashionable grown-up gowns, off the shoulder, intended to reveal the swell of the bosom, the effect was absurd. Mamma was quite disheartened, and abandoned the attempt to turn me into a little lady. For my part, I was not at that age at all interested in gorgeous clothes, preferring things in which I could be active; so it was understood that I would dress to suit the person I was, and the life I led.

'It is silly,' Mamma said, 'to spend money and effort on something the child does not want, especially as she sees nobody. In any case, you are forever scrambling and crawling and climbing and falling into the burn, Katharine, and the sewing-maids and laundry-maids . . . I suppose the word for you is "tomboy". Do you not think so? A tomboy in a crinoline . . .'

Mamma often left her sentences unfinished. It was as though, by halfway through, she became exhausted, and relied on her listener to do the rest of the work, by guessing what she was going to have said.

I did not envy Malvina. I did not want, even at eighteen, to wear such hoops that I could not sit on a piano stool. I did not want three people to help me dress. I dressed myself in a few seconds, delighted not to be subjected to the agony of choice which faced Malvina whenever she opened her wardrobe door.

I did not envy Malvina? Well, I knew it was silly to do so. I was what I was; the doctors had said what they said. It was silly to envy Malvina. I tried to set my face against doing so, and sometimes succeeded.

11

The sun was declining, but it was still a bright afternoon, and I decided to go out. I pulled on stout boots, and took a cloak and a fur-lined bonnet. From its special place, in the drawer of my bedside table, I took my spyglass.

I went down back stairs, to avoid any slight risk that I might be seen and summoned to the drawing-room. I went out by a little side door, and crossed a stone footbridge over the burn that had been diverted to girdle the Castle. Then I walked briskly downhill towards the loch.

Half way to the waterside, I turned to look at my home. In the bright merciless February sunlight, it looked even more absurd than usual.

Our family, the Irvines of Ravenburn, had lived for centuries in a solid, sensible, fortified house set on the shore of Loch Chinn, in the Central Highlands of Scotland, at the mouth of the Raven burn, which curled down the flank of Ben Chinn. The estate was large, and included the whole north bank of the loch, a great area of hill, and rich farmland to the west. The Irvines were substantial lairds, and baronets of ancient creation, but no more than that.

Then my great grandfather married an Englishwoman, heiress of a moderate estate in County Durham. They found coal on the estate, one of the richest mines in the North; the whole property sat on coal as icing sits on a cake. My great grandfather became incalculably rich, and consequently – by a logic I never understood, but which everybody else found satisfactory – was created first Lord Ravenburn, in the Peerage of Scotland.

Lord Ravenburn's son, my grandfather, had a long minority, good trustees, and a million pounds in the funds; he decided that the family's new grandeur required a proper setting. He pulled down Ravenburn House, and further back from the lochside built Ravenburn Castle. He intended something magnificent, romantic, awesome. He achieved an oversized Manchester cotton-mill, but with towers and battlements, drawbridge and portcullis, stuck on, like so many gigantic afterthoughts, to turn the cotton-mill into a Castle.

My way southwards towards the loch rejoined the burn, which, after being contorted into a false moat for my family's false Castle, was here allowed to regain its original course. It chuckled among the mossy rocks, low now after a dry month, clear but peaty brown; later, when the snow melted from the high tops, it would rush and froth and boil, so that it seemed impossible that the little trout could hold their places against the icy onrush.

I once heard someone say that the snow-water in the burn was 'as cold as a stepmother's kiss'. They must have been speaking of a different stepmother. Mine never kissed me at all.

I came to the mouth of the burn and looked westward to where, half a mile away, a wall of granite a hundred feet high thrust out into the loch.

Near the inland foot of that cliff, on a slope of grass, a gaggle of grey-lag geese was feeding. I raised my spyglass to look at them, wondering how many my brother Jamie would try to shoot, and whether he would cry when he missed, or merely curse his gun, and the dog, and the keeper. The grey-lags were alert, shy, wary; though they were busy cropping the thin grass, they were vigilant too; any disturbance would fling them into the air, and send them out over the water. I did not disturb them. I was motionless, and wore drab clothes, and stood a long way off.

Though far away, I could see the birds with wonderful clarity, because of my spyglass. It was my greatest treasure. It was my only treasure, except for the miniature of my mother. It was left behind for me, by my older brother Tom, when he ran away: when he fled the country, after committing a murder.

I never used the spyglass without thinking of Tom; and often, all the old miseries and complexities flooded into my mind, and I had to wrench my attention back to the birds and beasts I was watching, or I should have sat down on the ground, and whimpered like a baby; and, when I was younger, that is exactly what I often did.

Like Malvina and Jamie, Tom was in truth my half-brother.

The way of it was this. My father married first, when he was quite young, a lady of a Lowland family. For all I know, they were sublimely happy, but I never heard one way or the other; I never heard her mentioned; I never even knew her name. But I think she must have had strange qualities, for she gave birth to Tom: and soon afterwards died.

Then Papa lived very quietly, in a remote place in the West Highlands, in a house which was lent him by some great man. He brought up his little son in that place, teaching him to be a

13

sportsman and a naturalist like himself, rather than a scholar. I think he was content, devoting his life to the child, and earning a reputation for the greatest kindliness.

Of this last, I can speak with certain memory. I have heard my father described as the kindest man in Scotland. Perhaps he was too kind to Tom; perhaps he spoiled him; perhaps that may a little explain the horrible thing that happened.

Well, by and by, he married a second time: a very young lady, who was Jean MacNeil of Glennie. It was an ancient family but a very poor one. I have heard that Jean MacNeil was gentle and shy, and shared my father's love of wild places and solitude. My miniature portrait of her showed a small pensive face, with straight eyebrows and straight dark hair. I knew no more about her, although she was my mother, for she died when I was a few months old.

So my father had two tragedies, and two children. His heart turned against the lonely lodge of Kilcraig, and he came from his western solitudes to the capital of the north, to Edinburgh. And he married a third time, the reigning beauty of the city, Isabella Dundas, who was called the Venus of the Lothians. She became my Mamma. Though only a few years older than himself, she became Tom's Mamma, too.

A year later, my grandiose grandfather died; my father inherited Ravenburn Castle, and became a lord and a millionaire. Within weeks of this event, Mamma presented him with twins, a boy and a girl, as fair as herself, known at once and ever thereafter as the 'Heavenly Twins'.

And so, for a full year, all of us were happy. I remember only fine weather, laughter, and birdsong.

I heard long afterwards that Tom was in that year becoming wild and difficult. Perhaps it was some unbalanced streak inherited from his mother; perhaps Papa had too much indulged him. He was almost expelled from Eton, they said; he made dreadful friends; he took to harebrained exploits, poaching the deer and salmon of neighbours. Of course, in my nursery, I saw none of this. I saw only a happy and audacious God, who was kind to me, and whom I idolized.

And then my father went out fishing, by himself as he preferred, in a boat on the loch, one August dusk. What happened, nobody knew. He fell somehow into the water, and knocked his head as he fell, and his body was found upon one of the little half-moon beaches, at dawn, after a night-long search . . .

If something had been wrong with Tom before, much more, it seemed, went wrong with him now. From that time dates my clearer memory; and I remember the long faces, the anxious conferences, the angry neighbours; I remember the patience of Uncle Frank, the lectures he read to Tom, the solemn warnings. I remember the sense of impending disaster.

I remember that awful night. Tom, wet, limped into my bedroom in the small hours. Just before I cried out in dismay, he put a hand over my mouth, to silence me. He whispered to me rapidly for a time, but I did not afterwards remember much of what he said. He told me he must run away, because a dreadful thing had happened. He put the little spyglass in my hand. He kissed me, and slipped out of the room.

In the morning, I thought I must have been dreaming. But the spyglass was under my pillow; and when the maid came in, her eyes were like saucers, and her tongue raced into wild tales of struggles and blows and bloody murders . . .

It was the shock of that night and morning, they said, which disturbed the balance of my mind, and obliged me to live a quiet life by myself.

This, I suppose, was natural enough. I know that I screamed and ran from the room when Tom's name was mentioned, because I could not rid my mind of that dreadful night, of Tom's despair, of my misery. This was apt to happen, unfortunately, when the Castle was full of company. When the family was alone, Tom was not mentioned. But outsiders sometimes, in kindness or in unkindness, would start to ask questions about the tragedy: and it was then that I screamed and ran. I remembered clearly this happening once. It was not long after Tom's disappearance. The questioner was a woman with a sharp nose and a cold half-smile. She lanced me with questions about Tom, each one feeling like a barbed and poisoned dart, until I could bear the torture no longer.

I remembered this single occasion. I remembered no others. I was told there were others. I was told I had forgotten the others, because . . . because I was what the doctors said I was.

It was a long time before I heard the whole story about Tom, for they tried to keep it from me, for the sake of my peace of mind.

Tom had been poaching in the night, on a stretch of the River

Chinn which belonged to Sir Campbell Stewart of Crossmount, a good neighbour and close friend of Mamma and Uncle Frank. Two of the Crossmount keepers had come upon him, and tried to catch him. Tom picked up a big stone on the river bank, and smote one of the keepers with it, hitting him full on the head. He smashed the poor man's skull, and killed him. The other keeper recognized the criminal.

Similar crimes – identical crimes – happened all over Scotland, every year. But this time it was a little different, because the poacher and murderer was Lord Ravenburn.

There was an investigation of the keeper's death, at which the other keeper, called Dickson Carmichael, gave evidence to the Procurator Fiscal. He did not testify at great length; he did not have to. Uncle Frank secured a copy of the Indictment, to help him in his battle to clear Tom's name; one day I found that copy, and read it.

It was the saddest and most horrible thing I ever read. Tom, my idol and hero, had without the slightest doubt committed a brutal murder, in order to escape arrest while committing another crime. Until I read the Indictment, I always cherished a tiny hope that some awful mistake had been made – that Tom was the victim of confusion, that the witness had not seen clear in the darkness. The hope died as I read, killed as surely by the evidence as the victim had been killed by Tom.

We heard of him again, two years later. He had worked his passage to Australia, and found work in a silver mine called Yellow Springs. There was an accident: a fall of rock: and he was killed.

I cherished another hope, that *this* might be mistaken identity, and that Tom was alive, under some innocent name, behind whiskers. But the body was dug out and identified. There was a man who knew Tom, an intimate friend, in whom Tom had confided his secret. This man swore to a statement, which was sent from Australia to Scotland.

The case of the murder was closed, for the Courts accepted the affidavit, Little Jamie became Lord Ravenburn, for the Lyon King of Arms accepted the affidavit. If I had been a boy, I should have inherited as Lord Ravenburn. I did not greatly care about being Lord Ravenburn, but I was very sorry not to be a boy. If I had been one, that terrible summer night might not have had such a dismal effect on me.

After Tom's death was reported, the talk at last died down, the ghoulish speculation, the secret glee of the envious, the hints of bad blood; and Tom's name was no longer mentioned. Everyone contrived to forget about him: except me: I could not: for I had his spyglass.

I wrenched my mind away from miserable memories, and looked through the spyglass, into the lemon-yellow western sky, and at the grey-lags feeding on the grass. And suddenly, to my astonishment, they were off, launching themselves all at the same moment from the ground, and winging their way out over the loch, honking in furious alarm. Something had startled them. A man or a dog must be thereabouts, a shepherd or gamekeeper. I swept the spyglass over the bare ground, and over the granite face of the spur beyond. It was all utterly empty. If a man was by, he was a very furtive man. What could a prowler be doing, in such an empty and barren place?

I was puzzled. So I set off, westwards towards the spur.

I passed the place where the geese had been feeding. There was nothing I could see that might have frightened them. I came to the tumbled rocks at the landward end of the promontory. I climbed easily up the broken ground, thankful to be light and thin, hard and active, even though Mamma would have preferred me so very different.

I breasted the top of the spur, and went out to the end, where the granite fell almost sheer into the loch. From there I could see the island, which was in the midst of a bay. Because of the spur, the island was invisible from the Castle and its policies. It lay four hundred yards from where I stood.

The island had a new-moon shape; it was perhaps three acres in extent. Once it had been inhabited, but it had been deserted now for three hundred years, since the massacre of its inhabitants, and it was completely wild. Part of its shore was precipitous cliff, part such a tangle of bramble and thorn that a snake could scarce have wriggled a way to land. For so small a territory, the island showed wide variation – for here it was bare granite, there gorges choked with birch and hazel, here mounds of smooth grass, there stands of gaunt pine trees. On the nearer horn of the crescent rose a half-ruined tower, once part of a considerable castle.

Sometimes, on summer afternoons, guests at the Castle (the new, Manchester-cotton-mill Castle) would be taken out in a comfortable boat, and rowed all 'round the island. Ladies of poetic tastes were deeply affected by it, and saw in the wildness and the ruined tower echoes of the historical romances of Sir Walter Scott. Ladies of sensitive disposition were apt to shudder with a certain delightful terror: for the island was said to be haunted by a throng of unhappy and malignant ghosts.

Miss Anderson had taught me the story of the island long ago in our schoolroom – for, though a lowlander from Edinburgh, she was a great student of Highland history and legend.

The island had been the stronghold of a small robber clan called the Hargues, a name as uncouth as were they themselves, who lived by raiding the richer nearby clans. The Hargues built the castle, but the island was already a natural stronghold almost impregnable to attack. From time to time over the years, one or other of the mainland chiefs would fill boats with his clansmen, and launch an attack on the island, to end the expensive irritation of the Hargues. Every one of these attacks was beaten off, with bows and axes and claymores, and great stones thrown down on the attackers.

At last, Irvine of Ravenburn lost patience, after the theft by the Hargues of two wagonloads of whisky, which was accomplished in broad daylight, with intolerable audacity, under the very walls of Ravenburn House. Irvine had a huge boat built, with an iron deck rising to a point like the roof of a house. Below this deck sheltered his men. The stones and arrows of the Hargues bounced harmlessly off the armour, the men landed with grappling-hooks and ladders, and, infuriated by the theft of the whisky, put the entire clan to the sword.

'Even the little children!' said Miss Anderson in the schoolroom. 'It shows, dear, the dreadful effects of whisky.'

All that Irvine brought back from the savage enterprise was the severed hand of the Chief of the Hargues. 'For,' said he, 'this hand was always in other men's sporrans, and I shall wear it as an example to all thieves.' And so he did, and the Robber's Hand became the crest over the arms of the Irvines of Ravenburn.

Since that night of slaughter, all the Hargues – men, women, and little children – remained on the island, desperate ghosts, filling the place (it was said) with hatred and terror, and still defending their stronghold against any intruder.

'I am an educated woman,' said Miss Anderson, 'as you,

dear, will be an educated woman – but I would not set foot on that island! I should be quite distraught with terror!'

Among some of the country people, it was firmly believed that anyone who set foot on the island would never return; but some believed that a person might return, but forever witless, a raving lunatic.

It was all very easy to believe.

As a result of the swarming ghosts, and indeed, of the extreme difficulty of landing, no one had put these beliefs to the test – no one had set foot on the island in living memory, and very likely, no one had ventured there since the night of the massacre. The Hargues, in death, guarded their own even better than they had guarded it in life. There was one consequence of abiding interest to me. Ravens nested there.

All wild creatures enthralled me, but ravens most of all. I cannot say why, entirely. They did not seem to me like birds, but like strange visitants from another world – strong, clever enormous, mysterious, sinister, clad in profoundest black, not crying, like other birds, but barking, like great dogs ... The shepherds and gamekeepers hated them, for they took young lambs and grouse: but they shot very few, for the ravens were cleverer than the men. The crofter women regarded the ravens with dread, as the familiars of witches, the ghosts of murderers, and such ...

All of which was also very easy to believe.

Still, the ravens had come to realize that no men ever set foot upon the island; and that there were no predatory four-footed creatures there, because they would not swim so far. Every year, a pair of ravens nested in an embrasure in the half-ruined tower, in full view of the promontory; and there, every spring, I watched them. Ravens had nested in that spot, people said, since the year of the massacre. So the island was called Eilean Fitheach, the Isle of the Raven; and the castle was called Daingneach Fitheach, which is to say, Castle Raven.

I looked at the birds through my spyglass. They were engaged in their courtship dance, rolling and somersaulting in the air, diving and soaring; for all their giant size they flew with the agility of fly-catchers. Then one bird went to the nest. I saw she was the hen, for she settled down on her great untidy bed of sticks and heather stems. The cock came after her, making a strange vibrating noise I had never heard before. Then, through the spyglass, I saw something wondrous, that I had never seen or heard tell of. The cock bird was caressing his hen with his beak, stroking her beak and crown. She raised her head, and he gently tickled her under the chin, as Uncle Frank had tickled Malvina when she was a baby. It was amazing to see these huge and sinister birds engaged in tender love-making.

Suddenly the cock raised his head and twisted it, as though he was listening. An instant later, he opened his enormous wings and threw himself into the air. She followed him at once. They soared and circled, looking downwards at their island.

I did not think a ghost had startled them. I thought a man must have done so. But that was stark impossibility. No man dared land on Eilean Fitheach. No man, practically, could land there. There could be no wildcat or polecat, marten or stoat. It was not I that had frightened them, for I stood still as death, in the cover of little trees; I made no sound, and my clothes matched the colour of the background.

At last the birds returned to their nest. They did not resume their love-making but seemed alert and uneasy.

I remembered the grey-lag geese, which had risen in panic from the ground, when there was nothing to alarm them.

I was alert and uneasy myself, as I walked home.

I was wet and muddy when I reached home, owing to slipping in a burn; I carried a little mud upstairs to my bedroom. As I was pulling off my boots, my maid came in, Flora Morran. She was not really my maid – not as Wilson was Malvina's maid – but simply a middle-aged housemaid, who as part of her duties looked after my clothes and room, and sometimes made an effort with my hair. No doubt I could have had my own lady's-maid – 'We do not grudge you a woman of your own, Katharine,' said Mamma, 'but if looking after you was all she did, she would scarcely . . . I mean, it is not as though . . . You can quite well pull on . . . But of course, I do not want you to feel . . .' Mamma's unfinished sentences looped about the room like ribbons, trailing and fluttering.

Flora had a wooden face, and big red hands like raw beef. She stumped and thumped through the room, and complained of the number of stairs. I thought she did not like me, which made it difficult for me to like her.

She cried out when she saw the traces of mud on the carpet.

'Wae, wae,' she grumbled. 'Wan I passit the isle, Eilean Fit-heach, an' spied wha' I spied, I kenned fine there waur ill ploys afut. Ay, ilka sichtin' o' yon puir ghosties gi'es warning' o' dire deeds an' fashments.'

'You went past the island today, Flora?'

'Ay. I walkit oot tae hae a crack wi' ma frien's o' Auchenlo-chan. Soonds an' sichts! Smoke frae a lum o' the auld cassel! Whaur nae leevin' fut hae trod three hunder' yair syne! Soonds an' sichts! An' the folk o' Auchenlochan, tu, hae spied an' harkit. 'Tis a' the clash o' the toon. Wae's me! I kenned fine there waur ill ploys afut, an' losh! Ye brang yon clods o' dairt intil the hoose.'

Sights and sounds of the ghosts on the Isle of the Raven were commonplace events. Hardly a month went by without some awestruck report. Disaster was always presaged, and over the years, a sort of system had been worked out – if a wife saw a man on the island, and heard singing, her cow would slip a still-born calf; if a crofter heard the clash of claymores, the revenue officers would find his whisky-still. Whisky, in fact, had as much to do with most of the sightings, as it had with the massacre itself.

Flora had seen smoke rising from the ruined castle. She expected disaster, and found it in a little mud on the floor of my bedroom. She did not look superstitious; she looked incapable of fancy; yet she totally believed in the ghosts of the Hargues, and in the ill omen of any sighting.

Since I had been brought up in that place, among the credu-lous country people, part of me believed with Flora. But I did not think a ghost had frightened the grey-lags, or alarmed the ravens.

In the morning I went down out of the East Tower, and along the cavernous passages to Malvina's bright room. She hated being alone; other people were often busy in the morning; so it was part of my life to keep her company. Malvina was sitting up, having her breakfast in bed: for Mamma and Miss Mait-land agreed that she was delicate, and must take her mornings gently.

Malvina's mouth was full. She offered me a cheek, which I kissed.

Mamma came into the room, swathed in a blue morning-gown, and looking like a young girl. Malvina no longer needed me, but she still wanted me.

Presently there was a knock on the door. Uncle Frank's voice called, 'Isabella?'

'Here, Frank. Come in,' called Mamma.

He came in, with a letter in his hand. He wore a frown, which was not like him.

'The old man's coming here again,' he said abruptly.

'What old man, Frank? It seems to me that dozens of old men, whether I ask them or not . . .'

'Cromarty.'

'The Duke of Cromarty?' asked Malvina from her pillows. 'I don't like him.'

'Of course not, my precious,' said Mamma. 'No more do I. But he comes to discuss things with Uncle Frank, so we must all . . .'

'It's only a year since he was here last,' said Uncle Frank. 'I wrote to him only two months ago, with a statement of the accounts.'

'When is he . . .?' asked Mamma, not quite completely, but adequately.

'Next Wednesday.'

'Ah. Then we have time enough to arrange . . .'

'Yes, of course. There is no problem. It is irritating and unsettling, and thoughtless of him, but a man like that feels entitled to make his own rules of behaviour. At any rate, I thought it best to give you the earliest warning.'

'Thank you, Frank dearest,' said Mamma, smiling like a contented angel. 'I will leave all the details to you, as I always do.'

I spent an energetic afternoon, going up the steep glen of the Raven burn. I wondered, as I climbed, about the Duke of Cromarty's visit. I remembered the name. He had come before to the Castle, several times. He had some connection with my father – perhaps simply friendship, although he was much older. He came to confer with Uncle Frank on matters of business. It did not concern me – I would not have understood it. I had not met the Duke, on any of his visits, and I was quite glad of that. He was an awesome man, of the utmost eminence – not simply as being a Duke, but also as being a Governor General in the Empire, and Chairman of weighty societies, and so forth. I had seen him, from a distance, through my spyglass, a year before. He was tall, very thin, a little bent, with white hair, and a black silk hat of astonishing height. He looked as alarming as he sounded. No doubt I was kept away from him, because facing such an awesome grandee would be a strain for my poor nerves.

I came to a slow pool below a waterfall, and tried to spy for trout. I slipped and fell, and got very wet and muddy, and my ears were full of the small thunder of the waterfall.

So I did not hear the party ride up – two gentlemen, and two ladies, on Highland ponies.

The first thing I heard was my name, called in a cheerful voice. I looked up, and was very pleased to see General Ramsay of Tulloch, who was always kind to me, and Lady Angela Ramsay, who was kind to me when she remembered. The General was about sixty, brown-faced and grizzle-haired; Lady Angela's face was almost as weatherbeaten. They were very active, sporting people, who went huge distances on foot when stalking deer or walking grouse; Lady Angela rode everywhere, never using a carriage for choice. Mamma thought she was quite mad.

The other two riders were strange to me. The gentleman had a face which immediately made me want to laugh. He was not ugly or grotesque, far from it, but – I think the word is droll. It was a round, open face, with twinkling grey eyes, and a thatch of untidy brown hair, which he revealed when he took off his hat. He looked as though he wanted to laugh at himself and at everything else.

The lady was in the sharpest contrast. She held herself extremely straight and rigid in the saddle, even though she was riding a stocky little pony, instead of a tall thoroughbred. Her habit was severe but beautifully cut; she wore a low-crowned top hat. Her face was like an eagle's, with a high-bridged beak of a nose, and very sharp, bright eyes, the colour of peaty burn-water, and thin bloodless lips.

If the gentleman made me want to laugh, the lady made me want to run away and hide.

'This,' said General Ramsay to the eagle-lady, 'is Katharine Irvine, eldest daughter of the palace you see below.'

'William's daughter?' asked the merry gentleman.

'Of course. Who else's daughter could she be? I am presenting you, Katie, to the Marchioness of Aberfeldy, and to Lord Killin.'

I curtseyed, keeping my footing with difficulty on the bank of the burn.

Lord Killin said, 'I knew your late father extremely well, Miss Irvine. In fact, he was my godfather, and no schoolboy could have had a kinder. I used to go and stay with him, you know, and he tried to teach me to be a sportsman.'

'We are about to call,' said General Ramsay to me, 'on your Mamma and your Uncle Frank. Do you think it will be convenient?'

'Oh yes,' I said. 'They are probably only listening to Malvina playing her mandoline.'

'Do you not care for music, then?' asked Lady Aberfeldy, looking down her eagle-beak nose at me.

'Yes, ma'am,' I said. 'And that is just why . . .'

I stopped myself from making an ill-natured remark. General Ramsay and Lord Killin laughed. They rode away, and presently I followed them.

It was more than ever desirable that I should slip in by my usual postern, owing to the callers, and especially the Marchioness. I knew I must be a very draggled and tattiebogle figure as I squelched across the footbridge.

I saw a still-room maid, and an under-footman, and a page-boy. The maid gave a little shriek when she saw me, like one of Malvina's shrieks. The footman tried to hide a grin, and succeeded pretty well. The page-boy tried to smother a laugh, and failed entirely.

Not until I got all the way to my room did I understand the shriek and the grin and the laugh. I saw my reflection. Most of my nose and right cheek were richly daubed in the rich mud of the burnside; I looked like a savage, in warpaint. Evidently, after falling, I had without thinking rubbed my nose, and the rest, with a very muddy hand.

And thus daubed, like an urchin in a Glasgow back-alley, like a tinker-child sleeping under a whin-bush, I had made my curtsey to the Marchioness. And I was eighteen, not eight. What might have been forgivable in an active young child, must be disgusting and laughable in a grown-up young lady.

Well, the calendar insisted that I was a grown up. So, for all its slenderness, did my body. I did not feel like one. At that moment, staring at myself with consternation in the glass, I felt like a childish idiot.

No one had ever told me that I was an idiot – only that I needed care and quiet. Perhaps they were sparing me. I wished very much that I could hear what the Edinburgh doctors really said.

Flora Morran came stumping in. She had a curious expression on her large face, startled, alarmed. I wondered if she had seen more ghosts on Eilean Fitheach, and what agonies they presaged.

She said something in a strangled voice, as though making an announcement in a foreign language; and then, to my intense surprise, the Marchioness of Aberfeldy came into the schoolroom.

'Your maid,' she said to me, 'was kind enough to pilot me to this remote anchorage. I should not have found it unaided. Do you use a compass, or have you a chart? Had I known how far the journey up here would be, I am not at all sure that I would have embarked on it.'

'I am afraid,' I stammered, 'that I am covered in mud.'

She looked down at me – she was inches taller than I – like a buzzard inspecting the carcass of a sheep, and deciding to leave it to the hoodies.

'Yes,' she said, 'you resemble a coal-miner, just emerged at the pit-head . . . I have been talking to your stepmother, child. I asked her if you were to be presented, as you should be, at Holyrood, and go to the balls and Highland Meetings, and take your place as an adult in society.'

'I do not think Mamma plans . . .' I began unhappily.

'I do not think she does. She tells me that the doctors . . . But I expect that is all well known to you. She recalls that, years ago, you were so afflicted with nervous misery, at a little party for children, that you were dreadfully sick. You have recoiled from parties since, from all social gatherings. She concludes that disagreeable consequences would again ensue, perhaps dangerous to your health, even though you are older.'

She had turned to stare out of the window, at the great golden shoulder of Ben Chinn. Now she turned again, and looked at me long and searchingly. I stared back at her, alarmed, puzzled, a little annoyed. I did not like my illness being discussed, with strangers, behind my back. I did not like it being discussed in front of my face, either.

'No doubt your stepmother is right,' said Lady Aberfeldy. She added, almost under her breath, 'But what a pity. What a crying shame.'

She left soon afterwards.

Well, she was right. It was a pity. It was a crying shame. I felt so particularly well. I thought I was good-looking. Though much might be wrong with me, I thought I was not a fool.

I was the victim of an accident, like someone run over by an omnibus in a city. It was Tom's fault, they said, for giving me such a shock.

I was puzzled by Lady Aberfeldy's interest. I was still more puzzled by another thing. Mamma had truly reported that I was dreadfully sick at a children's party. It was after that, I think, that she sent for the doctors. I had been, indeed, quite monumentally sick, and hideously ashamed about it. The reason was cream cake – simply that. I ate far too much cream cake, an impossible amount, enough to have made a boa-constrictor sick. Why should Mamma say that I was sick from nervous misery, when I was sick from cream cake?

Lord Killin was to return, to fish for salmon later in the spring. He was to be warmly welcome. Mamma was placidly delighted. She had known him well, long before, as Papa's friend and protégé. He had made her laugh then, and did so still. He was the same age as herself – much more a companion for her than Colonel Blair or Sir Malcolm Rattray.

I wondered if Lord Killin would fall in love with Mamma. It seemed unlikely that he would not – other gentlemen did, who came to the Castle, even if they came with their wives. He had no wife. I wondered if, perhaps, he had been in love with Mamma all these years, and stayed away from Ravenburn for that reason. Books were full of such things. I thought it very romantic.

He was to bring a friend, called Sir George Fraser. Sir George was another friend of Papa's and had been, like Lord Killin, a sporting pupil when he was a schoolboy. So he was another old friend of Mamma's. She did not seem as delighted at this reunion, as at her reunion with Killin.

'Mr Willis,' said Uncle Frank in the drawing room, with a letter in his hand, 'writes to say that he arrives on Wednesday.'

'Who is Mr Willis, Frank?' asked Mamma. 'Is he a friend of ours? Did I ask him here? Or did . . .?'

'The Reverend Walter Willis, Isabella. Jamie's tutor.'

'Ah! Poor Jamie. Back to lessons, my dearest, after your holiday.'

Jamie was sitting on the window-seat, looking at a book of pictures. He was astonishingly like Malvina – they were the most unmistakable of twins. His face and form were plump, his complexion pink, his eyes blue, his hair bright golden. Of course, at the time, he should have been away at school, at the Reverend John Gillespie's Academy at Crieff, preparing to enter Eton. But he had just been taken away, owing to the harshness of the Reverend John Gillespie, who did not appreciate the fineness and sensitivity of Jamie's character, and used his cane as it should not have been used upon a lord.

'He comes by the public coach to Lochgrannomhead. He asks in his letter how he shall proceed from there, by which he means that we must send a carriage. Jamie should go to Lochgrannomhead, to bring him back, I think?' Uncle Frank beamed at Jamie, and went on cheerfully, 'It would be a welcoming, friendly thing, Jamie. It would start you off on a good footing.'

'I am shooting all day on Wednesday,' said Jamie. 'I have told Murdo MacKenzie. It is all arranged.'

'All arranged,' sighed Mamma. 'His last free day, Frank dear.'

Uncle Frank nodded, as though there could be no argument with this. He pondered for a moment, tapping a pen against his teeth.

'Wednesday,' he remarked.

He glanced at Mamma, and then at me.

He said, 'I do think one of us should go, as a gesture of welcome. Mr Willis is a clergyman, a learned man – he merits that courtesy. It will be more interesting for him, if he has someone with him who can point things out on the way, objects of interest . . . Katharine, my dear, you know more than any of us about local history—'

'I?' I asked, greatly startled, and nearly dropping my teacup.

'Miss Anderson,' concurred Mamma, 'was always such a fund of . . .'

'It is years since you went so far afield as Lochgrannomhead,' said Uncle Frank, smiling at me with the greatest kindness.

'There is a new library, you know, which with your bookish interests you will like to see. And on the way back you shall bear Mr Willis company. Yes, upon my word, that is quite an ideal solution. An overdue adventure for you, my dear, and a wealth of local information for Mr Willis.'

I was much surprised. Yet, when one considered it, everything that Uncle Frank said was quite true. I looked forward to my unusual outing. But I was not sure that I wanted to inspect the new library. There were, in my life, more books already than I wanted.

I was driven to Lochgrannomhead on Wednesday.

From the public coach descended a pale young man in bands, an Episcopalian clergyman, with an old trunk, an older portmanteau, and a greatcoat quite shiny with age. There was no mistaking the Reverend Walter Willis.

'My brother Jamie could not come to meet you,' I said, having awkwardly introduced myself. 'He sends apologies. He – he had made an arrangement, before your letter came, and did not – did not feel that he could break it.'

'No! Of course not! A promise given – adherence to a promise given – mandatory on us all!'

I told him such stories as I could remember, on the way back, about the places we passed. He seemed interested. He seemed interested in me, also, and watched me as often as he watched the countryside. I thought perhaps he was more intelligent than he looked. I wondered if he had heard about me, and what he had heard.

'Sae ye missed his Grace,' Flora Morran said, with gloomy satisfaction, as she was turning down my bed.

'His Grace?'

'The Duke o' Cromarty. Ay, he ca'd the day, an' spent hoors wi' Mr Dundas. Yin o' the lassies wettin' tae the table tellit he waur speirin' for ye.'

That awesome grandee had been asking after me? What was his interest in me?

And why had I been sent away, the day that he came? Was it so that he should not meet me?

two

I was still deeply intrigued by the behaviour of the ravens, in their half ruined tower on the island. There *could not* be anything, in that wild and forbidden place, to alarm them.

A ghost? A man?

But the ghosts had been there always, as the ravens had been there always. The ghosts had never troubled the ravens before. The ravens were not superstitious, and did not drink illicit whisky.

I became more and more firmly convinced that a man had been on the island. But who? Why? How dared he? How could he?

My own wild plan seemed to form itself without any decision on my part.

Before anything else, I needed a boat. There was only one way to get one. I had to steal one.

Fifty yards east of the mouth of the Raven burn, there was a cove in which my grandfather had built a boathouse. It was a miniature of the Castle itself, and not so very miniature – it had battlements, and buttresses, and turrets; its windows were slits in the walls; its door had hinges six feet long, and was studded with iron spikes. It was in the charge of the head boathouse-man, assisted by two under boathouse-men: officers who were not, I think, normal in Scottish households.

The boathouse at this time was a scene of furious activity, for the boathouse-men were busy with paint and varnish, and canvas and cords, getting boats ready for the March salmon fishing, and for the picnics and expeditions of the summer. I strolled in there one afternoon, making myself inconspicuous, as I was well used to doing in the drawing room. All was a confusion of paint-pots and cushions and awnings; there was a pleasing smell of varnish and tarred rope. Most of the boats were too large for me to handle on my own, but there were some little ones.

I picked a small rowing boat, berthed at the watergate end of the boathouse. It was on a kind of trestle, from which I thought I could push it into the water. They had not started painting it yet – perhaps they would not, for it was a little urchin of a boat among the others. Rowlocks were in the boat. Oars were stacked nearby, gleaming in new varnish.

The massive door had a massive lock. But I thought it would not be difficult to climb round the outside of the boathouse, on the rough 'medieval' stone, using the 'medieval' knobs and ornaments. I could climb out over the water, and in at the water-gate. This was not locked, but barred; once inside I could slip the bars.

But if I rowed from the boathouse towards the island, I should be in full view of hundreds of windows of the Castle. They were the south windows, the largest, the ones in which people were most likely to be standing and looking out. Therefore, I must steal the boat by night, and row westwards by night. I would not actually approach the island by night: a lively curiosity was very well, but I was not insanely brave. I would hide the boat on the overgrown shore at the foot of the spur. Then I would come back, by daylight. Out of sight of anyone, I would row to the island. What I did when I got there, depended on what I saw when I got there, and how brave I felt when I got there . . .

It may be wondered why I went about my expedition in this stealthy way. Could I not have asked a gillie to row me to the island? If no gillie would do so, could I not have asked Uncle Frank to arrange it?

Well, I could not, and I would not. No gillie would have landed there, or permitted me to land there. They wanted to get safe home to their wives; they wanted to keep their wits. As to Uncle Frank, I did not suppose he was frightened of ghosts. But he would not ask the servants to outrage their beliefs. My girl-ish whim – my highly eccentric whim – would not have been argument enough.

It may also be wondered, why I was so very concerned about the alarm of the ravens. Something had frightened a pair of birds: was this such a very great matter? Did it truly call for the theft of a boat, a hazardous expedition in the dark, and con-fronting the ghouls of the island? Looking back, I find this harder to explain. I think the reason may lie in this – there were very many questions in my life to which I could find *no* answer: but here was a question to which, entirely on my own account, perhaps I _could_ find an answer. It might not be an earth-shaking matter, but it would be a satisfaction to me.

With March came not better weather, but much worse. Snow returned, blown by a bitter north wind into huge drifts. There was no question of taking a small boat on the loch.

To most of the people at Ravenburn, the snow made not the slightest difference. Mamma sat smiling in the drawing-room, with her friends about her. Lord Killin and Sir George Fraser were prevented from coming; Colonel Blair, Sir Malcolm Rattray, Mrs Seton, Lady Wood and Miss Serena Wood were prevented from leaving.

At last, after weeks, warm rain came and the snow went. Bright weather followed the rain. I no longer had any excuse to delay my expedition.

It had become, by now, a sort of challenge, like the 'dare' that a schoolboy makes. I should despise myself, if I did not go to the island, and investigate the puzzle of the startled ravens. In some ways, I was not at all grown up.

I sauntered near the castellated boathouse in the late afternoon, and saw the boathouse-men lock up the door and leave. I saw that the evening was fine and clear, the east wind gentle, and the loch smooth.

It was very late when I tiptoed down the back stairs, carrying a dark lantern I had borrowed from the stables. I heard the night watchmen by the kitchens; they were supposed to patrol separately, but alway patrolled together. Because they talked, they were easily avoided. I unbolted and unchained my usual postern door, and slipped out over the footbridge.

Though the evening had been clear, the night was cloudy. The wind had freshened, and gone round to the south. I felt a hint of rain in it. The night was impenetrably dark. This was, I told myself, exactly what I would have wished.

I went gingerly down beside the burn, longing to unmask the flame in my lantern, but not daring to, in case it was seen. Many of the bedrooms of the Castle faced down towards the lochside. Uncle Frank's was one. He sometimes had trouble sleeping, and paced to and fro in his bedroom, in front of a low fire, owing to the worries of a great estate. If he saw a furtive lantern-light, he would ring the alarum-gong, and a dozen men with cudgels and pistols would be after me.

And if I were caught?

Well, it would seem so very mad, what I was doing. I would seem in need of more than care and quiet. I had heard of institutions. Miss Maitland, looking at me, had whispered to Dr McPhail about a suitable institution. She did not know, perhaps, how loud her whisper was. It was very necessary not to be caught.

My eyes became used to the darkness, which was not as intense as it had seemed. (Indeed, darkness is never total out of doors, but only inside four walls.) I went more confidently along to the grim bulk of the boathouse.

There my confidence ebbed a little.

The climb along the wall had not looked formidable on a fine afternoon. I was well used to climbing rocks, and could go up them like a goat. But the greasy wetness of the boathouse stones made a difference. The awkward burden of the lantern made a difference. The darkness made a large difference. I almost dropped the lantern into the loch a dozen times; I almost dropped myself into the loch a dozen times; I took the skin off my knuckles; I was exhausted and panting violently by the time I got to the end. Then, clinging by the barest tips of my fingers, I rounded the corner, and so came safely to the watergate.

It was safe now to use the lantern. I uncovered the glass, and played the light over the gate, and saw that I could easily climb over it. I saw wrong. It was not easy, because of the wretched lantern. But I needed the light in the boathouse, and so contrived at last, with fearful squeezing and grunting, to get myself inside.

I played the light about the boathouse, and let out a helpless scream. For dozens of vicious yellow eyes were staring at me. There were rustles and scampers and flappings, and things brushed against my ankles.

I wanted to scream again, but took firm hold of myself. Of course the boathouse was a natural home for a colony of bats, and a natural winter refuge for a host of rats. I told myself that the rats would *not* bite me, or the bats get tangled in my hair. It is humiliating, when you know you are telling yourself the truth, that you still cannot quite believe it.

The little boat I had chosen was in the same place. I put down the lantern where its light most helped me; I pushed the boat off the trestles without difficulty, and off the platform into the water with enormous difficulty. When it was floating, I put in two oars, a boathook, and a coil of rope.

I had another desperate struggle with the bar of the water-gate, but at last it shot back in its staples, nearly pitching me into the water. I pushed the gate open against the pressure of the water. I darkened my lantern, put it in the boat, scrambled aboard, and poled myself out of the boathouse with the boat hook.

Of course I was well used to boats and oars, having lived all my life by a loch. Other young ladies might not have been – one could not imagine Malvina rowing – but I was.

I picked up the oars, fitted them in the rowlocks, and began to pull manfully towards the spur.

It seemed a very long way.

I could just see the line of the shore, to steer by. The water was choppy from the wind. My hands began to get sore, and my muscles to complain. Yet I was enjoying myself. I cannot imagine why – who but a lunatic would enjoy a long, solitary row, in pitch darkness, on choppy water, with sore hands and aching muscles?

The wind freshened, slopping more waves against the side of the boat and into it. There was more moisture in the wind which gusted against my cheek.

The wind grew wetter and wetter: and it began to rain. It was heavy, gusty rain, sheets of it, cold. First it soaked my face; then saturated my skirt, so that it clung like cold porridge to my legs; then trickled down inside my collar, so that I felt it between my shoulder-blades and between my breasts. The rain hissed into the loch, and made a puddle in the boat, which soaked through my boots. I rowed furiously, to get warm; but the oars were wet, so that they were hard to grip, and I several times nearly lost one.

I could admit to myself, without disgrace, that I was no longer enjoying myself.

Well, I got to the spur in the end, and rowed round it to the far side. By the time I nudged up to the shore, I was more completely wet than I had ever been before in my life.

I slid the oars and boathook under the thwart, so that they could not fall out, and scrambled ashore onto a fringe of gravel. I pulled the boat along the shore, slipping on the wet rocks. I fell more than once, partly into the water. It made me no wetter. At last I pulled the boat deep into a tangle of lochside hazels, where I thought it would be invisible. I tied my rope to a ring in the bow of the boat, and the other end to a hazel trunk.

It was done.

Now I longed, with the most desperate yearning, to crouch at once in front of a hot fire, in dry clothes or none at all. But what I had to do was walk home, through rain which felt every moment harder, in clothes so heavy with water that I could hardly lift myself along.

And then – as though to prove to myself that I was in truth demented – I found I was enjoying myself again. I laughed in triumph at the black and teeming sky. I went up to my knees in a peat-hag, and I laughed. I tripped on a heather-root, fell, and heard the lantern smash on a rock: and I laughed.

I reached the castle at last, and crossed the footbridge. I was bottomlessly exhausted, but I was back. In two minutes I should be safe in my bedroom, stripped of my saturated clothes, and rubbing myself with a rough towel. Then I tried the postern door, and my laughter died.

It had been bolted.

The night-watchmen disobeyed some rules, but they obeyed others.

I crept round the Castle in the pouring rain, trying door after door, the great doors, the lesser doors, the almost invisible doors, and the trapdoors for coal. I knew they would all be locked, and they all were.

I went to the outbuildings, which squatted at the foot of the Castle like a small town. There were sheds, game-larders, coal-houses. Some had doors I could open. But I did not want to spend the rest of the night squatting, in my soaking clothes, among garden tools, or the carcasses of red deer, or piles of sea-coal.

I could go to the stable-yard and coach-houses, a furlong away. The horses would be locked up, but I might find hay to nest in. But, however soft I lay, I did not think I could spend hours of a cold night soaking wet.

I could rouse up grooms, coachmen, gardeners, carpenters, masons, boatmen, keepers, gillies. I could get warmth, hot broth, dry clothes. And, first thing in the morning, Mamma and

Uncle Frank would know I had been out in the small hours, in pouring rain.

If I explained myself, what would they think? If I refused to explain myself, what would they think?

They would realize that I was more unbalanced than they had supposed. At worst, the result would be Miss Maitland's idea. At best, it would be more supervision, observation, care, new stringent rules for my safety, an intolerable, suffocating surveillance.

I could go a little further off still, to the steading of the home farm: I could huddle for warmth among cows in the byre, or folded sheep, or sows in the sty. This was the nearest I had had to a good idea; but it was not a very good idea. I did not want to spend hours, in wet clothes, clamped to the flank of a cow. I was not sure she would keep me so very warm, either. She would certainly not dry my boots.

In the midst of utter despair, I saw that, though it was still teeming with rain, the sky was beginning to grow pale. House-maids must be already stirring in the Castle, and hands on the farm. Soon bolts would be shot, and doors thrown open. Possibly, if I was clever, and lucky . . .

I was not clever, but I was very lucky.

I made a sort of dodging, snipe-like progress from my postern to the East Tower, ducking sometimes behind chairs and into doorways. I dripped everywhere, and left trails of mud. I did not see how I could be blamed, if no one knew I had been out. I hoped no one else would be blamed.

While I was out later in the day, I saw Murdo MacKenzie with some rabbits he had caught. He was a friendly man, one of the youngest of the Ravenburn keepers, and the one who most often had time to talk to me. He told me, as a great joke, that the boathouse-men were in a state of dismay and confusion, since a kelpie of the lochside had wriggled into the boathouse during the night, and unbarred the watergate. It did not seem that they had noticed the disappearance of one small shabby rowing boat. If they did, that would be blamed on the kelpie, too.

The next day the wind swung, and the weather cleared, and I resolved to put my boat to use. But, as I was making ready to go out, a carriage rattled over the drawbridge into the courtyard. A moment later, two gentlemen were in the great hall, while bags and fishing rods were unloaded from the carriage.

One of the newcomers was Lord Killin. I had only seen him, before, on the back of a pony. Now that he was on his feet, I saw what a splendid figure of a man he was – tall, with fine broad shoulders, powerfully built, yet graceful in his movements. His thatch of brown hair was untidy, but that suited him, because he was a man of outdoors and of vigorous pursuits. His eyes were grey, his nose short and straight, his chin square and deeply cleft by a dimple. His face had a high, healthy colour; best of all, it had what I best remembered about him – a look of amusement at everything, and enjoyment of everything.

He saw me, and in his strong cheery voice called out, 'Miss Irvine! Delightful to see you again, and delightful that you should be the first denizen we see. May I present Sir George Fraser, who was my fellow sporting pupil under your father?'

Sir George was a surprise, because he was so very different. He was thin, and looked frail. He had a long nose and pale eyes, and his face had a curious ill-tempered twist, as though there was constantly something under his nose that gave off a displeasing smell. His mouth turned down at the corners, and his lips were pinched and pursed, as though he had eaten a sour cherry. His hair was dark and lank, and although he was little more than thirty, it was already quite thin, and I thought he would soon be bald. It was hard to imagine him as a close friend of Lord Killin's, and hard to imagine him a sportsman.

Henderson the butler showed them to the drawing room, and announced them to Mamma. Mamma sat surrounded by her guests, as usual. I did not want to go in, but somehow, by a kind of magic or magnetism, Lork Killin drew me in.

Mamma had her most brilliant smile, and her warmest greeting, for Lord Killin.

To Sir George Fraser she said, with a cooler smile, 'It is a very long time, Sir George. I am so glad you honour us at last, while, of course . . .'

For once it was impossible to tell how the sentence would have ended, had not Mamma become exhausted by it.

Colonel Blair greeted Lord Killin as an old and intimate friend. They had met once before, for half an hour, weeks previously. Sir Malcolm Rattray took the knob of his stick out of his mouth, and glared at Lord Killin with tragic fury.

Mrs Seton said, in her most imperial voice, 'I understand that you are to inflict a severe reduction of numbers among the salmon, Lord Killin. My late husband, Admiral Seton, was devoted to fishing. He swore, you know, by the Tay. Ah, the Tay! Glorious sash, he used to call it, across the bosom of Scotland!'

Lord Killin made a polite reply, though looking a little startled.

Lady Wood said, 'Glorious sash across the . . . hm.'

She did not venture the word 'bosom' in mixed company.

The newcomers sat down, and there was general conversation about which Scottish river was the most beautiful. Some said one, some another. I did not think it was an exchange of ideas, but simply a series of noises intended to pass the time.

I thought Lord Killin was beginning to look as restless as I felt.

I made to slip away. Lord Killin noticed my going, and immediately jumped to his feet.

He said, 'I feel as if I had been sitting in that carriage for a month. My legs will be permanently contorted unless I stretch them. Will you excuse me, Isabella? May I scamper up and down the policies? Coming, Fraser?'

'I believe not,' said Sir George in his thin voice.

Lord Killin strode out of the room, and somehow once again pulled me along in his wake. I felt like a puppy on an invisible lead.

'You're dressed for walking, Miss Irvine,' he said.

'Yes. I was just going out, when you came.'

'What bad luck that you should be caught, and dragged into the drawing room.'

'Oh no!' I said, more earnestly than I intended.

We crossed the moat, and strolled towards the loch. It was the most perfect of spring days; but I knew that none of the people in the drawing room would leave it, except to go to the dining room. I thought they were mad.

'The drawing room,' said Lord Killin, 'is not precisely your natural or favourite habitat, Miss Irvine, I think?'

I was taken aback to have my thoughts read.

I said awkwardly, 'I prefer this.'

'This, and your lonely aerie. Lady Aberfeldy told me about your isolated chambers in a tower.'

37

'Yes. It is – it seems better if I am off by myself.'

'Why?' He turned and looked at me searchingly. 'Do not you like other people, company, society?'

'It is not that I do not like other people,' I said slowly, stumbling a little over the words. 'But that I *am* not like them.'

'I heard a little of this. Please do not think me impertinent. I am concerned because of my affection and gratitude to your father. I understand about the – doctors, and so forth. But I do find it strange. You were horribly normal as an infant.'

'Did you know me as an infant, sir?' I asked, most startled.

'Of course I did. So did Fraser. We stayed with your father, when we were schoolboys, at Kilcraig, when you were born. I stayed here later. You showed no instinct for solitude in those days – quite the reverse. In fact, you made me distressingly conspicuous. Your attentions to me were quite embarrassing. Nobody, upon my word, knew where to look. The shamelessness of your behaviour! You wanted, Miss Irvine, to spend all your time sitting upon my lap. It caused a great deal of comment, some, I regret to recall, of a deplorably ribald order. As a painfully self-conscious ten-year-old, I was appalled at the brazen way you singled me out, and the glare of attention to which I was consequently subjected.'

I laughed.

'You did have,' Lord Killin went on, 'the most remarkable pair of green eyes. You have them still. As well as . . .'

'As well as what?' I asked, in a funny little high voice. I was anxious for him to continue a remark, which sounded as though it would be unlike any remark I had ever had addressed to me.

'To be continued in our next,' said Lord Killin, 'as they say about the serialized novels in *Household Words*. However, since I bounced you in my lap a thousand times, I think I can call you Miss Katharine?'

I felt myself blushing. I nodded that he might.

He asked me about myself, my life, how I spent my days. I gave him short answers, because there were only short answers to give.

'You read books,' he said, 'and you look at birds and animals through a small telescope.'

'Yes.'

'No balls? Parties? Archery? No beaux? Pursuers? Intimate female friends? No friends of any kind?'

'Well, no, because . . .'

'Don't be distressed. I have heard the stated reason. One is obliged to accept . . .' He turned to look down towards the loch. He went on absently, half to himself, 'No – Lady Aberfeldy is wrong. I'm sure of it. I sniff a deliberate, consistent policy . . . But I wonder why. I do wonder why.'

'Policy of what?' I asked, making no sense of what he was saying.

'Diverting the Raven burn,' he answered at once, 'from the course which nature intended, into a spurious and tortuous course, with the object of serving some purpose of the Castle, and those inside it . . .'

As we crossed the drawbridge, I saw Uncle Frank looking at us from the window of one of the offices. Someone in the office, I thought, must be annoying him, for his face wore a black frown which was very seldom to be seen there. He turned away from the window, no doubt to argue with whoever was annoying him.

It was the kind of thing which gave him a sleepless night.

The next day was a day for loch and for island.

Lord Killin and Sir George Fraser were away before the rest of the company was stirring; I knew they were going to the far eastern end of the loch. My voyage was in the other direction. Neither they, nor anybody else, would see me.

The night had been free of frost. The morning was brilliant; a very light south east wind carried small clouds across a pale sky. I went first up on to the bluff, and along to the end, keeping in the cover of its untidy topknot of little trees. I looked for the ravens. She was in the nest, sitting tight, almost hidden by her untidy barricade of sticks. There was no one on the island to disturb her.

I inspected the rest of the island minutely through the spyglass. I had thought that, on such a bright and lovely day, it might have lost its mystery and menace. It had not. It wore an air of utter secrecy. The frowning cliffs, and the hostile tangles of the brambles, seemed to shout 'Keep off!' across the shining water. It was three acres of primeval chaos, as uninviting as a wild cat's nest.

Well, I had not been invited. I was inviting myself.

All in my boat was as I had left it – oars, boathook, rope. All that I was lacking was a baler, to get rid of the puddle in the bottom. I scooped as much water as I could over the side with my cupped hands; the rest stayed, to soak through my boots again.

It was no labour, under the perfect conditions, to row four hundred yards. Every so often I turned, trailing the oars, to look at my destination. It grew no more hospitable as I approached. There was nowhere I could possibly land, without wings.

I thought the bright sunlight on the south shore might help me find a place. I paddled gently to within a few feet of the shore; I could touch the rocks with an oar blade. Nowhere did landing seem possible even for a water-vole.

By and by, I began to have a strange sensation that I was being followed and watched. I felt eyes upon me. I stopped rowing, and looked all about me, alert, unreasonably frightened. Birds peeped and rustled on the island; birds floated on the sun-silvered loch. That was all. There was no other living thing to be seen.

Living things were not the only inhabitants of Eilean Fitheach. Thoughts of dead things watching me clutched at my heart like cold fingers. I rowed on slowly, feeling miserably nervous, feeling a sense of eyes upon me that sent prickles up my back. The menace of the island seemed to reach out to the boat, for all the sparkle of water and glory of sunshine. The Hargues were still defending their own.

And then I saw the eyes that were watching me. They were in the water, bright as jet buttons, each side of a whiskered nose. It was an otter. We stared at each other. The head disappeared. But the loch water, though golden coloured, was very clear, and I could see the otter plainly, not five yards from the boat. It spun, catapulted, cavorted in the water, like an amazing mechanical toy. It sped to the surface again, and its head popped out.

The otter is a very shy creature, and hunts at night, with great stealth. I expected this one to be gone like the memory of a shadow. Instead, to my amazement, it darted to the shore, ran out, and crouched on a grassy hummock. Water streamed from its thick coat. It looked at me with curiosity, but without fear.

I had heard of tame otters. They were not unusual. My father had had one at Kilcraig. This was, most evidently, another. What was a tame otter doing on an uninhabited island? Who and where was its master?

He dived in, and sped away under the water. I prepared to row slowly on. Then I saw what, but for the otter, I should never have noticed. Behind the grassy hummock rose a cliff some thirty feet high, crowned with a ragged crest of trees. The cliff came to an abrupt end, almost vertical. Up against this face was piled a monstrous tangle of brambles. But at the foot of the cliff, under the brambles, was an arch – a round masonry arch, made of seven blocks of granite. One side rested on a sort of natural corbel on the cliff-face; the other rested on a masonry column, just visible through brambles.

I could see the arch only from one spot. If I drifted onwards or backwards a foot, rock and brambles hid it. Nearly all day long it would be in deep shadow, but at this brief point of the sun's journey, it was lit up.

The otter had, by the most amazing chance, showed me the Hargues' back door.

I could step out of the boat, dry shod, on to the hummock the otter had used. I could tie the boat to an alder trunk. The place might have been designed for my convenience. I gulped at this thought. It had been designed, of course – for the Hargues' convenience.

I went ashore, and under the arch. There was a sort of miniature lawn, then tangled wilderness. I began exploring, going very stealthily. I was horribly aware of the Hargues. After all, the people who had surrounded me all my life never doubted their presence.

I scrambled towards the eastern end of the island: towards the fortress, Daingneach Fitheach, Castle Raven. I rounded a stone crag, badged with golden lichen, and paused by the starfish roots of a fallen pine tree. Suddenly a head, a Satanic head, was poked round the tree roots, and a pair of malevolent yellow eyes stared at me, full in the face, not a yard away. I gave a stifled scream.

It was a goat – a large, blackish nanny goat. After staring at me, she returned to browsing on the roots of the fallen tree.

I was stupefied. How came a goat on the island? Was she the last descendant of a flock the Hargues had kept? If so, she would be completely wild, as nervous as a field-mouse. But I did not alarm her in the least. I did not interest her. She was as tame as an old milch cow.

I went stealthily on to the tower. I found I could see only the fringe of the ravens' nest. I waited, hiding. Presently the cock bird flew ponderously towards the place, landed with surprising delicacy, and folded his wings. He flapped away again. He did not see me. I did not disturb them. No one was disturbing them, and no one must be allowed to do so.

This was a pressing reason for keeping quiet about the island – for giving nobody the notion of trespassing here. There were others. I would not be allowed to row out by myself to the island. That was certain. But I was determined that no one else should set foot on it. The thought of Jamie and his gun, among all the little wild birds . . .

When I got home, I found that another guest had come to stay, the Lady Victoria Arlington. She was not the least of the day's surprises. I had heard, from Miss Anderson, of emancipated ladies, who exerted themselves in politics, and made themselves notorious. I had imagined masculine creatures, with baritone voices and thick ankles. Lady Victoria had a voice like a box-wood flute; her ankles were no thicker than Mrs Seton's fingers. Yet they said she was a crusader, involved with the improvement of women's prisons, and the control of child labour: and there was a sort of indomitable strength in her little square chin. She was a young old maid – about twenty-eight years old, with the most perfect miniature figure, and a complexion like Malvina's.

Lady Victoria, to my surprise, turned out not to be a friend of Mamma's, nor of Uncle Frank's, but of Lord Killin's. She was asked at his suggestion. Mamma was quite agreeable to entertaining the daughter of a Duke.

In Lady Victoria's honour, Mamma said she would give a dinner party. There were two families within dining distance: General and Lady Angela Ramsay of Tulloch, and Sir Campbell and Lady Stewart of Crossmount. The trouble was, they could not be asked together. Tulloch and Crossmount were not on speaking terms. There had been a bitter quarrel between the gentlemen, some years before, when unforgivable things were said. Forty years earlier, they would have fought; in our civilized age, they merely glowered, and avoided each other. The quarrel had something to do with the eviction by one, or the other, of crofters and tenant farmers. General Ramsay violently disapproved of Sir Campbell's actions; or else it was the other way about.

There was discussion about which should be asked to dinner. To my surprise, Lord Killin begged that it should be the Stewarts of Crossmount.

'Do you know Crossmount, Killin?' asked Uncle Frank, looking as surprised as I felt.

'No,' said Killin, 'whereas I have known the Ramsays all my life. I like making new friends. That is why I hope you will indulge me by inviting the Stewarts.'

'Oh! Well, it is a good reason, I suppose . . .'

Uncle Frank glanced at Lord Killin, looking puzzled and a little uneasy. Lord Killin did not see the look, for he was exchanging a glance with Sir George Fraser. I could not imagine what all these glances were about.

'We shall invite Sir Campbell and Lady Stewart,' said Mamma placidly. 'They are always, in any case, more . . .'

'Hullo, Katie,' said Lady Victoria. 'May I come in?'

She came into my schoolroom. She had not been up there before. She had not called me 'Katie' before. She had hardly spoken to me before.

'Ah,' she said, looking round. 'My Aunt Mariota told me about this crow's nest of yours.'

'Your aunt—?'

'Lady Aberfeldy. She told me – a number of things. When Charles Killin sent her up to your room—'

'Lord Killin *sent* her?'

'Not precisely, of course. She is not a person you would *send*. He requested her to come here, in order to . . . But I should not be saying this, I daresay. I talk a great deal too much. Probably that is why I am not married. Men are repelled by domineering women, and I am a *very* domineering woman.'

'Well,' I said, 'Mamma does say . . .'

'What does Mamma say, supposing she can finish her remark?'

'Oh! Have you noticed that? It is fatigue, you see . . . Well, Mamma says gentlemen recoil from bookish females.'

'Yes, I had heard you were another one of those. George Fraser is greatly impressed. In fact, George Fraser . . . but I daresay that's another thing that I should not discuss. We'll talk of other things.'

She sat down, and began to talk on a million subjects, in the most friendly way. She put me so much at my ease, and made me laugh so much, that I quite forgot that this was the redoubtable political lady, the earnest prison reformer. I had not talked so much to anybody since Miss Anderson went away.

The Stewarts were pleased to be asked to dinner.

Sir Campbell was a big man, with a red beard and a booming voice. He made me think of a whiskered bull. He often sought advice from Uncle Frank about investments. Lady Stewart looked a little older than her husband; she had a quacking, honking voice, sometimes like a duck and sometimes like a grey-lag goose. They were both devoted to Mamma and to the twins. A dozen times, during the autumn, Sir Campbell had asked Jamie to Crossmount, to shoot the pheasant preserves. Once Jamie went. He came back with a sour face. He said the birds were no good at all – they flew too high and too fast. He liked birds to be close to his gun, and flying slowly. He said it should have been arranged so, and he would not go again.

The morning after the Stewarts came, Lady Victoria joined me in the park and told me about the evening. (I never dined downstairs when there was a party; it was just the sort of thing that would overexcite me, the doctors said. I might scream hysterically, as when the sharp-nosed lady had tortured me with questions about Tom; I might be sick, as when I ate too much cream cake.)

'Your Uncle Frank,' said Lady Victoria, 'told us a great deal about the extension of the Highland railway system.'

'How interesting,' I said dubiously. I had never been on a train or even seen one; there was no railway within forty miles of Loch Chinn. 'Is the Highland railway system to be extended?'

'Your Uncle is determined that it shall be. He is closely involved with starting a new company. Sir Malcolm Rattray is to join the Board of Directors, you know, and buy a great number of shares. That, at least, is your uncle's intention. I am not sure if Sir Malcolm quite shares his view.'

Of more interest was that, after dinner, Sir Campbell gave Lord Killin and Sir George an open invitation, to go fishing whenever they liked on the Crossmount water, which included the best pools of the Chinn.

Perhaps, I thought, that was what Killin wanted from the Stewarts.

We walked about in the park, and Lady Victoria made me talk as I had seldom talked before. She asked me questions quite as searching as those of the Edinburgh doctors: and some of them were the same questions.

Later, I saw her deep in conversation with Lord Killin. The two of them were joined by Sir George Fraser.

Uncle Frank glanced at them. Lady Wood was talking to him, but I do not think he heard what she was saying.

That night, about midnight, I took my candle and tiptoed down to the library. Something Lady Victoria and I had talked about awoke an irritating half memory. I could not sleep until I had looked it up. It was not at all important, but it kept me awake and fretful.

On the way to the library, I passed the door of Uncle Frank's bedroom. There was a crack of light under the door. To and fro across the room I could hear his footsteps pacing, turning, pacing.

three

'I am glad,' boomed Sir Campbell Stewart, 'that Killin and Fraser found time for a day on the Crossmount water. I am sorry they did not have better sport.'

'Sir George hardly wet his fly; did he, my love?' asked Lady Stewart.

'Hardly at all. He said he spent his time more profitably, talking to some of my keepers, and learning about our methods.'

'Did he so?' murmured Uncle Frank. The placid smile did not leave his face, but I thought it left his eyes.

'You said, did you not, my love,' Quacked Lady Stewart, 'that you never met a man so anxious for information?'

'In relation to improving some fishing of his own, I believe, in Inverness-shire,' explained Sir Campbell.

Lord Killin and Sir George were promised elsewhere. Lady Victoria had had to go south.

She said to me, before she left, 'I must pester the Home Secretary on a number of matters, because I have left him alone for weeks, and he will begin to feel unloved. Do you think Lady Ravenburn will allow me to come here again?'

'Of course she will!' I said.

Of course she would. Mamma knew many Dukes' daughters, no doubt, but somehow few came to Ravenburn.

Mamma pressed Lord Killin to come back. He said he would, in June or July.

'I do not suppose,' said Mamma to Sir George, 'that we dare hope that *your* engagements will permit . . .?'

'If you will allow me to return,' said Sir George, 'nothing will keep me away.'

Mamma kept her joy under disciplined control.

Lord Killin's farewell to me was hurried, and a good deal puzzling.

'I shall be back, Katie,' he said. 'We have unfinished business.'

'You and Sir George?' I asked stupidly.

'And Lady Victoria. And you.'

'Me?' This was not grammatical, but I was thrown off balance. I had no business of any kind, with anybody.

'The Crusaders who set out from Europe,' said Killin, 'sometimes got diverted on the way, by local feuds and fleshpots, and never got to the Holy Land at all.'

'Oh,' I said, baffled by the turn the conversation had taken. I added idiotically, 'What exactly is a fleshpot?'

Killin's face, which had been unwontedly serious, assumed its usual look of imminent laughter. 'I always imagine a beef stew,' he said. 'But I daresay, on the Crusaders' route, it was more likely goat. Anyway, you will not find us beguiled by either. Imagine Lady Victoria being diverted from any Crusade she embarked on! Even by stewed goat . . . Goodbye. Be of good courage. God knows how this will end, but I don't think it will be as it began.'

Sir George Fraser afterwards sidled up to me. I looked at him nervously, for he always filled me with a certain uneasiness. I did not like being aware of his eyes on me. I did not like his face, or his voice. I did not look forward to his return.

He said abruptly, 'In your reading among the Classics, Miss

Irvine, have you come across the legend of Pygmalion and Galatea?'

'He carved a girl out of marble,' I said awkwardly. 'She came to life.'

'Yes, because she was too beautiful to remain a lump of stone in the corner of his studio. She came to full life, a legendary beauty, remembered and celebrated still.'

He added something in Greek, twisted his face into a smile, and hurried out after Lord Killin.

I thought they had both been drinking brandy, to avert a chill on their journey.

My magic island welcomed me back. I even felt a greeting from the ghosts. I explored all the parts I had not looked at before.

When at last I rowed away, the tame otter swam with me. I was alarmed. I knew that otters were nomadic, moving freely from place to place, going wherever food was to be had. This one might find a new holt on the loch-side. He would be seen by a keeper. There was a pack of otterhounds at Lochgrannomhead; sometimes Sir Campbell Stewart asked them to Crossmount, or Uncle Frank to the loch.

I splashed my oars at the otter, and told him to go away. He was delighted at this game and caught my oar in his forepaws.

Then he cocked his head on one side, in the water, to listen. I could hear nothing except the crying of birds, and the lapping of water against the boat. He swam away, at high speed, towards the island.

I thought the ghosts must have called him back to sanctuary.

On my way home, I met Malvina's maid, the cheerful Wilson, with Murdo MacKenzie. She was bubbling with excitement, and flushed to the colour of a ripe wild strawberry. Murdo, too, wore a grin which he could not snuff out.

They told me they were engaged to be married. Murdo had been to make formal application to Wilson's father Angus, at the tiny farm he held from Ravenburn. Angus was delighted, it seemed, since Murdo had a fine future at Ravenburn, and people said he would one day be head keeper.

It was Wilson's afternoon off (she had few), and they were on their way to see the Free Kirk Minister, to arrange the date of the marriage.

I shook their hands, and promised to come to the ceremony. I was delighted, because I liked them. I thought Uncle Frank would be generous to Murdo, when they were wed, and Malvina to Wilson. I thought their children would be splendid.

'Where is Wilson?' said Malvina. 'I want her. I need her. Neither of you understands my hair.'

'Wilson is entitled to an afternoon off, Malvina,' said Miss Maitland, 'rightly or wrongly. Your lady Mamma is so indulgent.'

'You must get used to doing without Wilson,' I said.

'Why? I won't. I will not.'

'She is going to be married.'

'What? She can't. Who to?'

'Murdo MacKenzie.'

'Who is he? I don't know him. I don't like him.'

'You do know him, and you do like him! Everybody does!'

'You must not become excited, Katharine,' said Miss Maitland. 'You must be quite calm, and as sensible as possible.'

'But I am excited,' I said. 'They are very nice. They love each other. They are to be married. I think that is exciting.'

Malvina seemed to brood.

She would not play or sing to the company in the drawing-room; no amount of cajoling prevailed on her. She had something very particular to discuss with Mamma.

Next morning I saw Murdo MacKenzie go into Uncle Frank's office in the outer courtyard. His grin was as broad as the Castle wall. A few minutes later, I saw him come out. He looked like a man who had been hit by a falling wall.

At tea-time, Wilson was back helping Malvina to dress. Malvina was in holiday spirits, and less exacting than usual.

Wilson's eyes were red and her cheeks pale, and she said nothing.

Sometimes in May there is a bright, windless day, as hot as August. One should wear cotton clothes, and a big hat, and do nothing energetic. But, because it is May, one is still swathed in serge, with copious wool next to the skin (at least in the Highlands of Scotland), and one launches into strenuous activity, so that one becomes as hot as a cutlet on a griddle.

Most unsuitably clad in heavy wintry clothes, I was steaming with heat when I reached the granite spur. By the time I had rowed to the island, I had almost melted.

I saw the otter. He looked marvellously cool in the clear golden water. I envied him violently.

I went ashore with the otter at my heels. Water was pouring off his fur. My own woollen underthings were clinging to my skin in a most disagreeable fashion.

The otter slid back into the loch. The temptation to follow him was tremendous. The water looked infinitely inviting. I could climb in and out, at this thrice-blessed place, as easily as the otter.

Why not?

No one could possibly see me. No one would ever know. This was my island, and I made my own rules of behaviour.

I ducked under the stone arch, into the secret wilderness of the island. I took off my hat, and my boots. I looked slowly round: scrubby vegetation, a few big trees, tumbled rocks and fallen masonry, numberless birds. Well, I thought, I had no need to be bashful in front of birds – or ghosts.

I took off my bodice, and my ridiculously heavy skirt. I stood in my shift, hesitant again. This was such very amazing behaviour. Not so much as my knee had ever been bared under the sky. It might have been normal to the athletic virgins of Sparta, but it was very strange to a cloistered virgin in Scotland. I shrugged to myself, gulped, and took off the rest of my clothes.

As naked as the day I was born, I picked my way back to the grassy hummock. I sat down on the hummock, and put a toe in the water. It was freezing. The loch had been fed for weeks with the melting snow, and there had been no hot sun, until today, to warm it.

I nerved myself, and slipped down off the hummock into the water. I screamed. The shock of the cold was a sort of exquisite agony. I kicked about madly, but very few seconds were enough. I pulled myself out onto the hummock, the water pouring off my skin in sunlit dribbles. I felt marvellously refreshed, and tingling, and delighted with myself.

I sat, hugging my knees to my breasts, feeling the sun on my bare shoulders, feeling the dampness of my hair. I wondered how long it would take for me to get dry. I thought that, in my present position, it would be a long time, because the sun could only reach part of me. I realized that I must stretch out, supremely shameless, so that the sun could warm and dry as much of me as possible.

I crept back under the arch, and stretched myself out on my back beside my clothes, my head pillowed on a mossy log. Now the sun could reach all my front, and I felt it doing so. I closed my eyes, and stretched luxuriously with my arms above my head. I blessed the sun, and the secrecy.

I opened my eyes, shading them from the sun. Since my head was propped up, I was looking down the narrow white vista of my body – small firm breasts, flat stomach, slim hips and thighs and, between, the triangle of raven-black hair. It might not be what Mamma and her friends admired, but I thought my body was passable, and it suited my active life.

I spread my legs, so that the sun could dry the damp inside of my thighs. I flung out my arms. I closed my eyes, and lay like a starfish, feeling the heat soak into me.

Suddenly I knew I was being watched.

I sat up quickly, covering my breasts with my hands. I looked all round.

The nanny-goat was standing five yards away, staring at me, with a cynical expression. I sighed, and relaxed. My moment of panic evaporated, as the loch water had evaporated from my flanks.

As I dressed, I wondered again how the goat had got to the island.

'I have received a letter from my colliery manager in Lanark-shire,' said Sir Malcolm Rattray, at luncheon the next day.

'Bad news?' asked Colonel Blair hopefully.

'An accident. Some unfortunate men have been killed, I am sorry to say. My presence there, at such a time—'

'Quite right,' said Colonel Blair.

'Your manager is a competent fellow, I suppose?' said Uncle Frank.

'Oh yes. He knows the business as well as I do – better, I dare say.'

'He knows the families of the unfortunate men, for instance?'

'I imagine so, indeed.'

'Whereas you, I suppose, do not?'

'I? Ha-ardly. Colliers' families ... I can just see myself ... Irish, you know, many of them, in that locality.'

'I do not precisely see, then,' said Uncle Frank, smiling placidly, 'quite what good you can do, by going all that way.'

After tea, Mamma asked Sir Malcolm, most particularly, to sit beside her. She had found an album of water-colour sketches, done by an aunt of hers. Some were of Lanarkshire, or perhaps some other county, and so of special interest to Sir Malcolm.

They pored over the pictures, side by side. Mamma smiled, and talked more than usual, in a low voice. She was looking as beautiful as I had ever seen her look.

'I have searched my conscience,' said Sir Malcolm next day. 'I conclude that no useful purpose would be served by my going into Lanarkshire at this time.'

'Even the reverse,' suggested Uncle Frank.

'Added disturbance to the bereaved – added distraction to those engaged in repairs – exactly. The reverse – exactly so. I am better to stay away.'

Sir Malcolm spent the afternoon in Uncle Frank's office, and the evening sitting beside Mamma.

I found a knife, at the foot of a tree on the island: a clasp knife, with a bone handle. I looked at it blankly. It meant nothing to me. It was not an ancient relic of the Hargues, dropped in their final battle. There was not a speck of rust on the blade, which was very sharp. I dropped it in the pocket of my skirt. I was utterly puzzled.

I had explored the island minutely. There was not a yard of it I did not know. I had never seen the faintest trace of another visitor – not a footprint, no newly cut branch, no ashes of a fire. Had anyone else been on my island, I must infallibly have found a mark.

More – another invader must have disturbed the ravens. They were my absolute assurance that the island was still sacrosanct.

More still, and to clinch the matter, the country people would not set foot on the island. The wildest tinker boy would not dare. Rory Beg, a notorious and violent poacher, would not dare. That was quite certain.

I concluded that the male raven had behaved like a magpie. Hunting for food, he had seen the bright steel of the knife, caught by the sun. He had brought it home, like a magpie, to beautify the great untidy nest. His mate had rejected the gift, or one or other had accidentally dropped it. I had never heard of a raven collecting bright objects; I decided that I had made a discovery, with which I could have astonished the experts.

I was in Malvina's room, while she sat up in bed and ate an enormous breakfast. She said she wanted to wear her pink morning crinoline. I went into the little room adjoining her bedroom, which had once been a nurse's, but was now to all intents and purposes Malvina's wardrobe.

Mamma came in, wrapped in the blue gown that matched her eyes. She sat on the edge of Malvina's bed, with her back to me. She did not see me, through the half-open door.

'All alone, precious child?' said Mamma.

'No,' said Malvina with her mouth full. 'You're here.'

Mamma was in a mood to talk. But Malvina was eating a lamb chop in her fingers, and was not in a mood to talk.

Uncle Frank knocked, and called, and came in, as he often did. He said, 'I have finally heard from Loudon in Edinburgh, Isabella.'

'I have no notion, Frank dear, who Loudon in Edinburgh ..'

'A solicitor, a most trustworthy fellow. He gave me an account of Rattray's situation which Rattray himself has since confirmed.'

'If Sir Malcolm will tell you about his own situation ...'

'Why bother with Loudon? I need not have done, in that case. But nothing is lost by being careful. Since the facility exists, I use it. Well – today Loudon reports on Killin and on your friend Blair. Killin's reputation as a man of wealth rested, as far as I knew, on his own statement, his manner of life, and his choice of friends. Loudon has given me firmer information.'

'And ...?'

'Killin's statement is exact. He is very rich. How Loudon finds out as he does I don't know. Indeed, I am better not knowing. A man's investment portfolio is supposed to be a secret between himself and his bankers. But Loudon finds a way to peep at it.'

'Did you come up here just to tell me that Charles Killin is rich, dearest Frank? Because . . .'

'I thought you would be glad to be reassured on the point. I am, very. There's another point. Loudon has been looking into the Colonel's affairs, too – your gallant friend with the racing stable, the grouse moor in Yorkshire, the fortune in the funds. He has none of those things. He's a fraud, an adventurer. Loudon says he has hardly four hundred a year.'

'How painful for him. One feels quite . . .'

'He'd better be sent packing.'

'Oh no, dear, I like him. He has the most astonishing stories of life in India. He told me, only yesterday . . .'

'But he's only interested in your money, Isabella.'

'So are you, dearest, so it is quite safe from him. Poor Colonel Blair shall stay, until he begins to repeat his stories. Then you must do as you think best.'

'Loudon has a third piece of news. I asked him for the name of a doctor—'

'Another doctor, Frank?'

'A particular doctor. He has recommended a Dr Andrew McAndrew, of Stirling. What is particular about this gentleman is that, two years ago, his son got a maidservant into trouble, and the good doctor got the maidservant – out of trouble. The poor girl died. Loudon got to know of it . . . however the Loudons of this world do get to know of such things. He can denounce McAndrew at any moment. Or, to put it more relevantly, I can denounce McAndrew at any moment.'

'He did a dreadful thing – that poor, poor girl! – but why, dear, should you wish to denounce . . .?'

'I do not wish to. But it remains a possibiliity. It is another facility to be used if occasion demands. It puts us in a supremely comfortable position. If doubts are expressed, they can be resolved. If a written opinion is called for, McAndrew shall provide it. I thought you would be pleased at this, Isabella.'

'I am pleased,' said Mamma vaguely, 'if you are pleased, dearest . . .'

'What are you talking about?' asked Malvina, rather crossly.

'Your future,' said Uncle Frank, as he went out of the door.

Soon afterwards Mamma left, and I went into Malvina's room with the pink crinoline.

Malvina said, 'I think Mamma will marry Lord Killin.'

'Oh,' I said. 'Are you glad?'

'Yes. I like him. And then she will have all his money.'

'But she already has all Papa's money.'

'Oh no. I have often heard them talk about it. Stupid Katie, you don't know anything, do you, in spite of reading all those books and looking like a housemaid. Most of Papa's money is Jamie's, and some of it is mine, and some of it is spent. That's why I think Mamma will marry Lord Killin.'

I was amused about Colonel Blair. I was pleased about Lord Killin's wealth, and frankly incredulous about his marriage to Mamma. I did not understand about Dr McAndrew.

I was not, I think, so very stupid as this may make me appear. I was still in the way of trusting the people who had looked after me all my life.

It was another lovely day, but there was a light north-east wind, distinctly cool. I was not at all tempted to bathe.

I made my regular pilgrimage to Daingneach Fitheach, going delicately, as always, so as not to disturb the ravens. I went into the big cool chamber at the foot of the tower, which was so massively built that it had survived almost undamaged. It was floored with earth. Ivy had crept in, and little ferns clung palely to crannies in the masonry. There were no window-slits, but only the narrow doorway, which was almost blocked by an older clump.

I wanted to climb up to the ravens' nest. I was sure I could have done so outside, because of the bushes and ivy and broken masonry: but not without so disturbing the ravens that they might desert the nest for ever. Then the chicks would starve; and the island and the castle would lose the truth of their names. My hope, therefore, had been to climb up inside the tower; I thought I could peep at the nest without disturbing the birds. But I could not get up out of the bottom chamber to the next level. As far as I could see in the gloom, there was no opening or hatchway in the roof of the chamber – I supposed the Hargues had gone up by means of a ladder outside the tower.

More light in the chamber might have taught me more. But

the alders choking the doorway screened all but a glimmer of sunlight. I had been in my mind to bring a lantern. But I would be seen leaving Ravenburn, in the middle of a brilliant morning, for a walk on the hill, with a lantern in my hand. What would they all make of *that*?

For the twentieth time, I squeezed myself between the alder stems. It was a few moments before my eyes got used to the darkness, after the glare outside. Unsighted, I stepped cautiously forward. My foot struck something soft. I dropped to my knees, completely puzzled, for I knew the floor of the chamber was as bare as a shingle beach.

I had the most awful shock of my life. My fingers, groping in the gloom, felt a head – a face. It was a man. He was dead.

'Oh God,' I moaned aloud.

The body felt cold, and completely limp. It was unspeakably horrifying. Hysterical ideas raced through my head – about the Hargues, about re-embodied ghosts. A scream rose in my throat. I wanted to rush out of the dark chamber into the blessed sunlight, and abandon the horror to the ravens. I wanted anything except to touch the poor corpse, or be with it for another second.

I forced myself to be rational. It was not a ghost. It was the dead body of a man who had been alive – lately alive. Who? How came he here? What manner of man? Alone, or one of many?

Though my eyes were now used to the dark, I could see no more than that he was a man, bearded, in rough clothes. They were clothes of 1861. This was no Hargue, but a man of today.

I should know no more until I could see more. I could not bring light to him; I must bring him to light. Gritting my teeth, fighting down my horror, I began to drag him by the shoulders towards the doorway. His head lolled pathetically between my hands. His eyes were shut, for which I thanked God, but his mouth gaped open. He was completely flaccid. Fortunately, he was light, and almost as slim as I.

I struggled through the tangle of alders in the doorway, and pulled the poor corpse after me. I pulled him – it – at last clear into the sunlight. I laid the corpse out as I thought right – I put the feet together, and crossed the hands over the chest. The arms were like bundles of rags; the cold limp hands were the saddest things I ever touched.

I knelt by the body, fighting down once again the horror that threatened to stifle me. I said a prayer. I prayed for the departed soul of the man, and I prayed for courage for myself.

I opened my eyes, and made myself look at it.

It was a young man. I guessed his age at thirty, but the beard hid much of the face. The beard, short and neatly trimmed, was mousey-brown, like the hair. The face was unlined, but very sunburned and weatherbeaten. It was a thin face, wedge shaped, with a broad brow and pointed chin. The nose was high bridged; the mouth was gentle. The face was tranquil in death. Whatever horror had happened, none of it showed on those neat brown features.

The hands were narrow, with long strong fingers, brown like the face. They were dirty, but I noticed the fingernails were clean.

The clothes were of well worn tweed, in soft brown and green checks: a belted jacket, and knickerbockers. They were the clothes of a sportsman going out to shoot, who does not expect to be seen by a fashionable eye. He wore brown leather boots, laced up the ankle. They were good boots, with hobnails.

As I had found when dragging him, he was a light, slim man, perhaps two inches taller than myself, and of similar build. His ankles and wrists were narrow, and his neck slender.

I wondered, stupidly, what colour his eyes had been.

That was all I learned, by looking at him. It was nothing. A small, unremarkable man of about thirty, in the most ordinary country clothes.

I could not guess how he had died. There was no mark on his face, or on any part of him that I could see. I did not think he had perished by bullet, or knife, or cudgel. The thought of disease flickered through my mind – smallpox, cholera, plague – dreadful infections, that struck down suddenly. Would I, having touched him, die likewise? But I thought these diseases left marks, bloatings or blemishes. The dead face was as clear as a child's.

Were the Hargues still defending their own? Were the country people right? Would I be slain also, for my foolhardy trespass? But I thought I knew the ghosts of the Hargues, and I thought they were gentle spirits.

What was I to do? He could not lie here for the ravens. They were carrion eaters; no human remains could be left to be served so.

I could bury the corpse on the island. God knew, he would

join a large company. Even without a spade, I could lay him in a cleft between rocks, and cover him with earth to a decent depth. There were no dogs here, to dig and desecrate . . .

No – that was wrong. He might have a family, wife and children, friends. They must have the body, for proper burial. They must be told.

Told? By me? That I had found him dead on Eilean Fitheach? I should never again be allowed to visit my island, my secret kingdom. It could not matter to anybody *where* he had died, so he was dead, and had been found.

Plainly, I must contrive to load the corpse aboard my boat, and take it to the mainland. I must drag it out onto the lochside, and, having hidden my boat, 'discover' the body. He would be no worse; his family no worse; and my secret safe.

I hated every bit of this plan. But, the more I thought about it, the more inescapably right it seemed to be.

I was desperately sorry for the man. He was young, and had a nice face. I was frightened to think how he might have died. And I was consumed by curiosity.

Ghoulish as it may seem, I was seized with an overmastering wish to go through his pockets. Men carried, I thought, things which identified them – letters, engraved watches, notebooks, cards. In the fullness of time, after I had 'found' him on the lochside, it would become known who he was. But nobody but me would ever know he had been on Eilean Fitheach. The question of why he was there would never be answered, because it would never be asked. Yet it was a question I most earnestly wanted the answer to. Possibly his pockets would tell me. A snare, for example – birdlime, fish-hooks, a sketch-book and pencil.

I debated with myself. It seemed a dreadful thing to ransack the pockets of a corpse. I could not do it. I recoiled. Yet I found my fingers stealing towards the hip-pocket of his jacket.

A finger twitched – one of the limp dead fingers on his breast. I screamed.

His eyelids flickered, and he groaned.

I nearly fainted with shock: because I had been so sure he was dead.

His eyes opened. They were grey. They rolled about, as though he could not control them.

I should have said, 'Are you hurt? Can I help you?' But I said, 'How dare you come to my island?'

His eyes seemed to at last focus on my face. He said faintly, 'Oh, it's you. I hoped you had drowned.'

He groaned, and put a hand to the back of his head.

He muttered, 'A lump like a raven's egg. The wretched owl made me lose my footing.'

I said severely, 'You are delirious. I suppose you want a damp cloth for the back of your head.'

'No, not at all,' he said more firmly.

'Very well,' I replied, and went to soak my handkerchief in the loch.

If there was something I knew very well, it was that there were no owls on the island. I could not have failed to see or hear them. I supposed it was because there were no mice for them to eat. The stranger's babbling about owls was the result of his blow on the head. If the blow was hard enough, I guessed, he might never recover his wits.

After all, the Hargues were on guard: the country people were right.

When I got back to the tower, with a dripping scrap of cotton, he was sitting up. His hair stood on end, and his face was rueful.

'Lean forward,' I ordered him.

He demurred for a moment, but then did so. I put the wet handkerchief on the lump on his head. It was a large lump. There was a little smear of blood, which I dabbed at.

He gave a yelp of pain.

'Don't be a baby,' I said.

'I apologize,' he said stiffly. 'The bruise is slightly tender.'

'There,' I said, handing him the handkerchief. 'That is all I can do. If you want another cold compress, you know where the loch is.'

'I do not wish to deprive you of a valuable handkerchief, Miss . . .'

'I can spare one handkerchief, to an indigent criminal.'

'You call *me* a criminal?'

'Yes, of course. You are a trespasser.'

'Please be clear, once and for all,' he said, turning his head sharply towards me, but wincing as he did so, 'that while I am properly grateful for the tender solicitude of your nursing—'

'I shouldn't wonder,' I said, 'if that wasn't meant to be sarcastic.'

'You are perceptive. Allow me to finish. My gratitude is tempered by extreme resentment of your persistent and intolerable intrusion here. I have been put to great trouble avoiding you. I had hoped to continue to do so. I would have succeeded, but for the clumsiness of an owl—'

'There you go again,' I said. 'It is delirium. You should not talk at all, for a year.'

'I will not permit you to come here again.'

'*You* will not . . .' I choked with rage. 'You are impudent. I shall come here at my convenience. If you are here, it will be the worse for you.'

'You will tell people you saw me here?'

'Well,' I said 'no, not at once. For my own sake, not for yours.' I had an idea, and added, 'I will keep quiet about your having been here, on condition that I never see you here again. But if I do—'

'Let us rephrase matters,' he said. 'I will allow you to go in peace, on condition that you do not return.'

'Allow me to go in peace?' I repeated incredulously. 'What will you do else? Kill me?'

'I have done it before,' he said grimly. 'I daresay I can do it again.'

'Wait until your head is better,' I advised him. 'Meanwhile, you will be glad to know that you have ruined my day.'

I walked away briskly, and rowed back at prodigious speed, ire lending a new strength to my arms.

Then, as I slid into the undergrowth under the spur, I asked myself why I was so very incensed. Was it shock at finding a corpse? Shock that the corpse came to life? No doubt it was that double shock, in part: but the stranger's behaviour *had* been monstrous. He showed resentment, instead of gratitude, when I ministered to him. He had the effrontery to order me away from my own island. He had probably frightened away the ravens. He had threatened to murder me!

He spoke like a gentleman, but his manners were worse than a drunken tinker's. That made it worse, because he should have known better.

Worst of all, worst by far, was that my secret was discovered, and my private paradise invaded by somebody else.

I had not found out his name. I had no idea why he was on my island. I did not think I would see him again. I had ordered him away, on the threat of reporting his presence. He was a law-breaker, and he knew that I knew it. He was committing trespass, if no more.

I wondered where he hid his boat, and where he had stolen it from.

Next day I examined the ravens from the spur, using my spyglass. They were behaving quite normally. The stranger was not there.

But he was: standing on my grassy hummock, with a furious frown on his face, and a tawny owl on his shoulder.

He said, 'You had fair and sufficient warning—'

I said, 'There *was* an owl. I thought you had brain-fever, and were raving.'

'I shall be raving directly, if you do not turn that boat around and go away.'

'Does it eat mice?'

'It eats anything. Fish, and rabbit, and beefsteak . . . We are not discussing my owl!'

'Yes, we are,' I pointed out. 'I didn't know they liked fish . . . *You* had fair and sufficient warning. You are a law-breaker. Are you a poacher, or a fugitive?'

'I am an angry and impatient man.'

'Yes. Will you be kind enough to move, so that I can come ashore?'

He said, 'Certainly not,' but did so.

I landed, and tied up the boat. I said, 'Where do you hide your boat, and where did you steal it from?'

'The purpose of hiding it is that intruders will not know where it is. I did not steal it.'

'How long have you been here?'

'Off and on, since January.'

'*Living* here?'

'As I say, off and on.'

'It was you,' I said thoughtfully, 'who frightened the greylags, when I could see no reason for them being frightened. It was you who disturbed the ravens, when they were courting.'

'Once. Were you watching? What a savage mischance.'

'You must have been as careful as I, not to have disturbed them since.'

'Of course. They are my camouflage. Anyone, seeing the ravens nesting—'

'Is bound to think there is no one on the island,' I agreed. 'Did you bring the goat here?'

'Naturally. Do you think she flew? Isabella is my milch-goat—'

I looked at him in astonishment. 'Why do you call her Isabella?'

'After someone I heard of, a long time ago, who was said to have a placid but selfish character ... It was the same time as I heard about the loch, and this island.'

'Oh ... A milch-goat is a good idea, as she can feed herself. You tamed the otter. Is the owl tame, too? Is that why I have never heard him? What is he called?'

'She is completely tame. That is why you have never heard her. Her name is Violet, because she has a clinging and affectionate disposition.'

'Violets don't cling,' I objected. 'They droop.'

'One I knew did.'

'Oh. I understand. A lady.'

'Stretching a point, yes.'

I pondered this for a moment. All the implications were thoroughly distasteful.

I said, 'I cannot understand how it is that I never found the least trace of you.'

'Because of the infinite pains I took to leave none.'

'But footprints—'

'Rock shows none.'

'Cut branches, and stumps—'

'Of course, I cut many branches, for all sorts of purposes. Having done so, I induce the goat to chew anything that looks like a clean cut. She is always agreeable.'

'That,' I said reluctantly, 'is rather clever ... Who are you?'

'My name is Robert Scott. Who are you?'

I was ready for this. I said, 'My name is Miss Maitland. I am a governess.'

'That I might have guessed, from your manner yesterday. You are young for a governess, Miss Maitland.'

'Yes,' I said without expression. 'But I am extremely well read.'

'Who is your fortunate pupil?'

'She is called Malvina Irvine.'

'Ah? Of the Ravenburn family? You live there?'

'I am employed there.'

'I appreciate the difference. I prefer my castle.'

'Do you live *there*?'

'Obviously, as it is the only habitable building on the island.'

'But how do you get up? You can't go outside, or you would frighten the ravens, and you can't go inside.'

'I am beginning to revise, cautiously revise, my opinion of you, Miss Maitland. But I am not yet disposed to trust you entirely. I shall not tell you how I get up.'

'At least, you sometimes fall down.'

'When the owl flaps her miserable wings, blinds me, forces me to stagger—'

'How is your head?'

'Sore. But thank you.'

'You should keep out of the hot sun.'

'I dare say I should, but I don't think I will . . . What is your intention, Miss Maitland?'

'About what?'

'About me. Do you propose to lay an information before the authorities?'

'Well,' I said, 'I will postpone that.'

'Thank you. I can stop being quite so careful. The trouble I have been at, to leave nothing lying about—'

'You left this lying about,' I said, and handed him the clasp-knife.

He smiled. It was the first full smile he had given me. It was a smile of great sweetness. I thought there was sadness in the grey eyes. Perhaps he regretted Violet, the clinging not-quite-lady.

'Why do you come here?' he asked. 'And how is it that you can?'

'I can because my pupil is, er, pampered and delicate, and feels that books and lessons are quite unnecessary to her, which is true. So that I am often completely free to do as I like. Lady Ravenburn is – indulgent. So you see, I am very lucky.'

'And you do come because . . .?'

'I came first because of the ravens. The time they were alarmed. I did not think the Hargues had alarmed them. But, as far as I knew, no man could have done it. I was curious.'

'You came in a spirit of purest scientific inquiry?'

'Well,' I said, 'it was a dare, too. A sort of internal dare. But I don't expect you know what I mean.'

'I know very well what you mean. When I was a boy, internal dares made me do a great number of very ill-advised things – some with consequences that are by no means worked out, even now ... Why did you continue coming, when you saw that there was no one here?'

'I fell in love with the island.'

'I understand that, too. I regret it, Miss Maitland, but I don't regret it as keenly as I did.'

He was just the height I had guessed – two inches taller than myself. He was wiry and active. His shoulders were broader than I had realized, but his waist very slim. He was hatless. His mousey-coloured hair blew about in the soft breeze. There was still a lump on his head.

'We had better make a pact,' he said, 'to respect one another's confidence.'

'Oh yes. It would be disaster, if anybody knew I came here.'

'I imagined it would not be convenient for you. Ungovernesslike behaviour, in the last degree. It would be disaster for me, likewise. Shall we shake hands?'

We shook hands, with perfect solemnity, sealing our bond of silence. His hand felt warm, quite dry, and unexpectedly strong. It was almost unbelievably different from the cold limp hand of yesterday.

'Why are *you* here, Mr Scott?' I said

'Oh – the story is long and tedious, but the reason is overwhelming. I don't say I shall not tell you, but I shall not tell you yet.'

'You are a gentleman.'

'No.'

'But yes!'

'Well, thank you, but the fact is, I simply masquerade as one. My parentage – well, the little that is guessed is better not menttioned. I was adopted by a gentleman, and brought up as a gentleman, but I did not behave quite like a gentleman. I suppose I reverted, like a briar rose. Trouble led to trouble, and at last brought me here.'

'For ever?'

'Oh no.'

'You *are* a fugitive?'

'In a sense, yes. But it is not as simple as that. Don't press me now, Miss Maitland, for I won't be pressed.'

'But you can at least tell me—'

He smiled again, very broadly and sweetly. He said, 'If I decide not to speak, you can be sure I shall not speak. I am quite proof against female cajolements, even by governesses.'

'I wish you would forget I am a governess.'

'I wish you would forget I am – whatever you imagine me to be.'

'I imagined you to be a poacher,' I admitted.

'Oh yes,' he said cheerfully, 'I am indeed that.'

I looked at him in astonishment 'You admit, to me—'

'Why not? We have made a pact. We have shaken hands.'

'Oh,' I said, 'so we have . . . How did you call the otter back, when he was swimming with my boat?'

'I whistled.'

'But I must have heard.'

'No. He comes to a dog-whistle, which is too high for us to hear.'

'Oh. That does explain it. I thought . . '

'That the ghosts had called him?'

'Well,' I admitted, 'yes.'

'I would have thought so, too.'

'You believe in ghosts, then?' I asked dubiously.

All this time, the owl sat tight on his shoulder. Sometimes her eyes were open – bright dark brown, staring intently from the grey disc of her face. Much of the time, they were shut. She may have been clinging and affectionate, but she seemed to me an aloof personality.

'You believe in ghosts?' I repeated.

He did not answer, but smiled at me a third time. I felt myself smiling back, and I felt the breadth of my own smile.

four

'Good morning, Miss Maitland.'

'Good morning, Mr Scott.'

'Will you please to come ashore?'

'Thank you, sir.'

As he tied up my boat, he said, 'I looked for you yesterday, and the day before.'

'I tried to come,' I said. 'But – but I am not my own mistress, you know. I mean, I am only a sort of servant. I was lucky to get away today.'

A sort of servant. Why did I maintain this fiction? Well, I had not decided whether to maintain it. I was beginning to like Robert Scott, at least some things about him, such as the warm dry pressure of his hand on mine, and his gentle mouth, and his grey eyes, and his slimness, and his mousey-brown hair. But I knew almost nothing about him, and to keep my secret was the most important thing.

'Your little pupil,' he said, 'decided against lessons today?'

'She – she has a nervous headache ... You were *looking* for me, Mr Scott? A few days ago you wanted to kill me.'

'It is a sign of great stupidity, not to be prepared to change one's mind.'

'Well,' I admitted, 'I have changed mine, too. Where is the owl?'

'Asleep in my bedroom.'

'She is not always clinging and affectionate, then.'

'Yes, always, but sometimes sleep overcomes her.'

'Did that happen with the – the lady you named her after?'

'Of course. It sometimes happens to all ladies. At least, it has to all the ladies I have ever known.'

'Oh.' I digested this. 'Have you known a prodigious number?'

'Well, I have travelled a great deal. When one is in a distant and savage country, under a blazing sun, or a blazing moon ... One must do something, you know, to while away the time during those interminable tropical nights.'

He was laughing at me. But I thought his bantering tone concealed the truth. I thought he must have bewitched any lady who caught his fancy.

'The conversation is becoming distasteful,' I said. 'Where do you hide your boat?'

He showed me; it was very well hidden in the undergrowth only a few yards from mine. I could have searched for a year and never found it. It was bigger than mine, though equally shabby. There was a stumpy mast in the bottom, with a small rusty-red sail wrapped round it.

'I can step the mast in the bows,' explained Robert Scott. 'I try never to travel except when there's a sailing wind. I hate rowing.'

'But why has nobody seen you?'

'Because I only sail at night.'

'Oh, I see . . . I did that once, and hated it . . . But of course, I had to steal my boat from the Ravenburn boathouse.'

'So did I,' he agreed cheerfully.

'But – you promised me the boat was *not* stolen.'

'Nor is it.'

'I don't understand.'

'Nor will you.'

'It is your boat?'

'I am entitled to the use of it.'

'Oh . . .'

Mad ideas – wild crazy theories – began to rush into my mind. *His* boat? He had named a goat after Mamma. He knew about the island, and the Hargues . . .

'Who are you?' I asked sharply.

'Robbie Scott, once masquerading as a gentleman, more lately an indentured servant in Australia, now returned to the land of his fathers, whoever they may have been. I have sometimes wondered. I emerged, or was pulled, from some unspeakable wynd in Glasgow. You see, I am not at all a suitable companion for a strictly brought-up young lady. I don't know who found me, but I was installed in the Foundlings' Hospital. Mr Archibald Scott of Danvie, childless but desiring a son, adopted me into his household. This, of course, is hearsay. My earliest memory is being taught to poach salmon by my fosterfather's water keeper.'

'Taught to *poach,* by a *keeper*?'

'Yes. Keepers are always the most effective poachers. They are experts, you know, and unlikely to be suspected.'

'But that is a great betrayal of trust.'

'Yes, it is. Life is full of great betrayals of trust. I committed a number, myself ... Do you remember we talked of internal dares, the other day? Nerving yourself to do something, or convicting yourself of cowardice? They were my undoing. The exterior was a – not precisely a polished gentleman, but at least an adequate masquerader. Inside, I suppose, beat the heart of the Gorbals. Scrape succeeded scrape, and the excellent Mr Archibald Scott despaired.'

'You showed yourself very ungrateful. Oh dear, that sounded like a governess.'

'Horribly like a governess. Oddly enough, I was not ungrateful. But it was – confusing to a boy, you know, to be two things at once, two such conflicting things ... Anyway, I ran away at last from the various lairds and gamekeepers who were chasing me, and begged and stole my way back to Glasgow, and signed on as a steward in a ship taking ironware to Australia.'

'Oh,' I said. 'Things are beginning to come clear to me.'

'Are they? Many things are still most obscure to me ... I was hungry, when I left the ship in Sydney. I wanted regular food, and a roof over my head. So I allowed myself to be indentured, as a servant to a mining engineer. It was a grave error, as it posponed my departure for a dozen years. Though, of course, I was fed. There was that about it.'

'You were not fed very much,' I said. 'You're hardly bigger than I am.'

'I have always,' he said gravely, 'esteemed quality over quantity. You are, for example, exactly right. To add to you would be to detract from you. Whatever your diet is, cling to it ... The best thing that happened to me in Australia was the friendship of a lad called Tom Irvine. The worst was his death.'

'Robert Scott,' I said: and suddenly the name was an echo from the distant past. 'I read ... I heard ... it was you who wrote ...'

'It was I who identified the poor crushed body, far underground in the Yellow Springs silver mine. I had to make a statement, and swear to it, because of inheritances. Poor Tom. His lot was far worse than mine, because he started so much higher. I would never have become his friend, but for his misfortune. Running away is a great leveller ... Well, I am back, in his country, and he is buried on the other side of the world. But this is all miserable ancient history – how do you come to know about Tom Irvine?'

'Oh, I have heard them talk, of course—'

'Who?'

'Mr Dundas, and Lady Ravenburn, and some of the servants.'

'What do they say?'

'Everyone was very shocked at the time of the – the accident on the river bank. At least, I think they must have been. I was not here, of course. I don't really know what happened.'

'Nor did Tom.'

'He told you, before he died—'

'He told me an enormous number of things. We used to talk for hours. He told me about Isabella, and the island, and the ghosts of the robbers. He said that if ever I came here, I could be his perpetual tenant on Eilean Fitheach. The island was his, he said, and he gave it to me.'

'Oh. Then you were in your rights, to order me off. I did not realize.'

'Certainly I was. Tom said that all the boats in the boathouse were mine, too, if I needed them. He gave me free use of them. But he said other people might not agree. I think you mentioned a Mr Dundas? I remember that name. Tom said Mr Dundas might not agree, to any of these arrangements. Accordingly, he told me how to climb round the outside of the boathouse, and over the watergate, and unbolt the watergate from inside, and then bolt the watergate again, after getting a boat out, and climb out into the boat. The point of the last manoeuvre being of course, that nobody would know a boat had been borrowed.'

'I didn't think of that,' I said. 'The boathouse-men thought a kelpie had undone the watergate.'

'*You* took your boat the same way?'

'Yes, of course. How else could I take one?'

He stared at me. An astonished grin spread over his face. He said, 'What a very exceptional governess you are.'

'Yes,' I agreed, 'very. You know, when you talked about *your* boat, and so forth, the notion came into my head . . .'

'That I was Tom Irvine? Lord Ravenburn?' He laughed. 'Well, I suppose you could call me his representative. I know what he intended to do, if he ever came home. I may be able to do it for him. I owe him that much.'

'What did he intend to do, Mr Scott?'

'Since you know my Christian name, do you think you could bring yourself to use it?'

'Good gracious,' I said primly, 'that would be very unconventional, after so very brief a fr— an acquaintance.'

He smiled the broad, sweet smile that I was not yet getting used to. He said, 'You might finish saying "friendship", since you started to. It is a much nicer word.'

'So brief a friendship,' I said.

'Brief, yes – but this is altogether unconventional, don't you think? My presence here? Yours? Besides, who are we, to be ruled by the conventions of the gentry? A Glasgow foundling and a little governess. A governess, I should say, of exactly the right size. Can we not make our own rules, on our own island?'

Since I had had exactly the same thought, I nodded.

'What is your name?' he asked.

'Katharine,' I answered, without thinking.

'Do they call you Katie?'

'Yes. Some people do. My family, and old schoolfriends.'

'That is odd. Tom told me there was a Katie—'

'Oh yes. Poor Miss Irvine.'

'Poor?'

'She is odd, you know. She does not mix in society. If she tries to, she is sick from – from nerves, and so forth. At least, they say she would be. She is under the care of doctors. Nobody sees her very much.'

'I am sorry to hear that. Tom spoke very well of her.'

'I expect she has changed since then. Perhaps she had a shock. She reads books.'

'That is not so very strange. I read books myself. Is it not confusing, having two Katies in one castle?'

'No, because I am called Miss Maitland. In any case, very few people ever speak to me ... Do you read books *here*?'

'Certainly.'

'May I see your house?'

'Yes, but first tell me about yourself.'

I was strongly tempted to do so. He was himself so open, that I hated to deceive him. I was sure now that I could trust him. Everything I told him would be safe with him.

But I wanted to be his friend and companion. I wanted to share the island with him, in a friendly and unembarrassed way.

For that, it seemed to me, we were better as equals. He was so aware of the difference between Tom and himself, that he would be equally aware of the difference between me and himself. To a conventional eye, it was certainly daunting. I was a Lord's daughter, and the young lady of the colossal ugly Castle on the mainland; he was a foundling from the slums. I had to be Katie Maitland, the little governess; then there need be no constraint between us.

So I borrowed what I knew of the history of the real Miss Maitland.

'It is a very dull story,' I said, 'compared to yours. No tropical moons, and so forth. My father was a Minister in – in Stirling. I was sent to school in Edinburgh. I secured the position here, on the recommendation of a friend of my father, a – an Elder of the Kirk in Stirling, who knew Mr Dundas, and so . . .'

'And so we steered two wildly different courses, and yet we collided on Eilean Fitheach. After all my travels, I became a hermit on this haunted island . . . But, of course, I have stopped being a hermit.'

'Have you?' I asked, appalled. 'You're going away?'

'Certainly not. This island was always delightful; now it's blessed. The impact of a little governess – a governess of correct size – has improved what I had thought perfection. A hermit who had you for a friend, Katie, would forget all his vows in a twinkling.'

'Oh,' I said, extremely pleased.

'Of course, at Ravenburn Castle you are surrounded by rank and fashion.'

'Yes, but I am not much in contact with Lady Ravenburn's friends. Indeed, they terrify me.'

'I expect they're toad-eating bores.'

'Oh no! They are full of accomplishments, and frighteningly elegant, and have the capacity to talk for hours without saying anything.'

We came to the tower, and he led the way into the bottom chamber. I shuddered, remembering the limp bundle on which I had stumbled. I was unsighted, as always, going from the glare into the gloom. But he, with the certainty of long practice, went straight to a cranny I could not see, took out a candle, and lit it.

The chamber looked very ghastly and gothic in the candlelight, all dark rude stone, with sinister flickering shadows. Even the little ferns in the crevices cast dreadful shadows, like clutching fingers.

Robbie went to the far wall. He reached up, and brushed his hand to and fro, feeling for something.

'Ah,' he said.

I saw in the candlelight that he had found a nail, driven into the wall between two blocks of stone. To the nail was tied a cord. Robbie untied the cord, and gently paid it out, taking the weight of something I could not see. There was a squeaking from above, like a tiny cartwheel.

Then, down from the dark ceiling, slowly descended a rough ladder.

'I slung a block at the top,' said Robbie. 'What you probably call a pulley, but we old seafaring men have our own names for things. Very ridiculous most of them are, too. I got used to saying "port and starboard", but I never quite saw the advantage. Why not "left and right"? But it would have been unwise to put that view to my shipmates. The ladder is hinged at the top, you see. When I go out I haul it up.'

'But – there is no hole in the ceiling.'

'Yes there is.'

He held up the candle. At the top of the ladder there was a hole, a yard wide by a foot and a half. It was completely invisible without the candle, and hard to see even with it.

'Not all Lady Ravenburn's friends,' said Robbie gravely, 'or even Lady Ravenburn herself, would get through that orifice in comfort. One is reminded of the rich man, and the camel and the eye of the needle. But a correct-sized governess will have no trouble, I think.'

'Did you make the ladder?' I asked, although a prolonged discussion of the correctness of my size would have been agreeable to me.

'Yes.'

'And left no trace?'

'None that the goat was not glad to help me hide.'

'To make a ladder—'

'Is not so very difficult. Australia is a young country, you know. There are no shops selling ladders. If a man wants a ladder, he cuts down a tree and makes one.'

'Is – is there anything you can't do, Robbie?' I asked him.

'Yes,' he said immediately. 'I can't get over the delightful shock of having you drop from heaven into – if you'll forgive the metaphor – my lap. Nor the delightful sensation of hearing my name in your voice. Now – will you permit me to show you the way?'

'Please do,' I said faintly.

He went up the ladder quickly and lightly. I followed, more cautiously, when he called to me to do so. The hole in the ceiling was amply big enough for me.

My head rose above the level of the next floor. I squeaked, and nearly fell off the ladder with astonishment.

'Hush,' he said with a grin. 'We must be fairly quiet, because of the ravens. Or were you imitating a mouse, to lure them in here?'

'This is . . .' I said, at a loss for words, 'this is . . .'

'Do come all the way up. You look like a victim of the French Revolution, decapitated by the guillotine.'

He took my hand, and drew me up into the room; I took a deep breath, and gazed round.

It was the same shape and size as the chamber below, but there the similarity ended. Where that was dark, clammy and dirty, this was bright, dry and clean. Where that had an airless and tomblike feeling, this was airy and cheerful. Where that was forbidding and even frightening, this was most friendly and welcoming.

Loopholes in the walls were the only ventilation intended by the builders, but Nature had repaired their omission. The southern wall of the tower had suffered most of all from the centuries, I suppose because it faced the wettest winds. Above, the tower was all a tumbled ruin; below, it was intact; at this level, there was a gaping hole in a wall otherwise complete, of irregular shape. but the size of a fair window. Since this hole faced due south, the chamber was flooded with cheerful sunlight.

The room was simply but adequately furnished. There was a bed of a kind I had never seen before – simply a piece of canvas, stretched on a light wooden frame. In it, very neat, were blankets and a pillow, with a bright tartan rug over all. There was a chair, of similar construction, before a small folding table. Part of the floor was covered with rush matting, of the kind you see in farmhouses; but by the bed there was an Indian rug with a gay pattern. A chintz curtain hung from ceiling to floor, from a square wooden frame, forming a wardrobe. Other curtains, of heavy stuff, hung on rings from a wooden rod over the window hole; they were drawn wide now, but when closed would be warm, and conceal any gleam of light.

'I would like glass in the window,' said Robbie, 'but I make do with wooden shutters when the wind blows very keen.'

He pointed to the shutters, neatly stacked in a corner. He had made shutters not only for the window, but also for each loop-hole.

'I took up residence here in January,' he said. 'I needed the shutters then. I only use them now when the rain comes in.'

There was a long shelf of books; the shelf was a single rough plank laid across stones. On the tallest book, her eyes fast shut, perched Violet the tawny owl.

In the corner near the window, there had been another small collapse of masonry. The effect of this was to leave a hole in the ceiling. Immediately underneath there was a fireplace – a pile of white ash, and a metal grill resting on stones.

'A chimney,' said Robbie, 'was beyond me. The crofters do very well with a hole in the roof.'

On one side of the fireplace there was another rough shelf laid across stones, with cooking-pots and plates, all very clean. On the other side was a stack of firewood.

'I choose my wood very carefully,' said Robbie. 'Anything wet or rotten or too green makes telltale smoke.'

'You did burn some wet wood, I think.'

'Yes, before I was expert.'

'There was smoke. People saw it.'

'And thought the Hargues were cooking a ghostly haunch.'

'And foretold disaster . . .'

On the folding table there were piles of papers, held down by bright-coloured pebbles. There were pens, and an ink pot, and an air of business.

'There are some tangled matters to be sorted out,' said Robbie, following my eye. 'Not my affairs – I have none – but poor Tom Irvine's. I told you I was, in a sense, his executor.'

'You told me you were trying to do – what he would have done, if he had come back.'

'Yes.'

'What would Tom have done? I mean, Mr Irvine? I mean, Lord Ravenburn?'

'First he would have found out what had to be done. That is what I have been engaged on, since January . . . I apologize for the absence of a chandelier, and of fine French furniture.'

'I think your furniture is very nice,' I said, 'but very odd.'

'Its merit is portability. It all had to come here in my boat, you know. It is the sort of thing army officers take on punitive expeditions to the North West Frontier – they can furnish a tent from a couple of pack-saddles. Until I can launch a steam-yacht on the loch, this will have to serve.'

'French furniture would look silly here. Besides, it would be spoiled.'

'How practical you are.'

'No,' I assured him. 'I know nothing about anything useful at all. Only things from books, and a little about birds and animals. I have had no chance to learn anything.'

'How did you learn to row a boat?'

'Oh well – to live beside a loch, with a boathouse full of boats—'

'But you can only have been here a short while? You can only have left school a short time ago?'

'I am older than I look. You think I am a child—'

'No,' he said. 'Not a child.'

'Oh, good . . . At any rate, as soon as I came to Ravenburn, and saw the boats, I had the ambition .. And then a keeper called – Murdo MacKenzie was very kind, and taught me how to row.'

'How did Lady Ravenburn react to that?'

'I am not *sure* she was quite aware of it.'

'Deceitful, Miss Maitland.'

'Yes.' I hung my head.

'Did Murdo MacKenzie teach you also to climb into the boathouse and steal a boat?'

'No, I taught myself that.'

'You're a marvellous girl, Katie.'

'Am I?' I asked, speaking with difficulty.

'Unique among governesses. Will you join me for luncheon?'

'Yes, of course. I brought some bread—'

'I was going to suggest cold salmon, with a bottle of Rhine wine.'

I goggled at him, like the frogs the otter ate.

Robbie pulled an iron box from under the shelf of kitchen

things. Lifting the lid, he revealed most of a salmon, gloriously pink, wrapped in a damp cloth.

I continued to goggle.

'Twelve pounds,' said Robbie cheerfully. 'I speared him the night before last. I baked him yesterday on the fire here—'

'Where did you spear him? In the loch?'

'Oh no. The Horseshoe Pool, on the Chinn.'

'But – that is part of the Crossmount water!'

'Oh yes. I believe Sir Campbell makes a great deal of money out of his salmon fishing. He can spare a mouthful, to those less fortunate.'

'How did you know about Crossmount, and the Stewarts?'

'I have lived here, or hereabouts, for four months. I've had what they call a crack with a number of well-informed people. Have you heard of a man called Rory Beg?'

'Oh yes! A violent and desperate felon.'

'Not often violent. Still more rarely desperate. A mine of information. And, of course, Tom had told me—'

'The Horseshoe Pool was where he – he—'

'Yes, I know. The wine is cooling below. Excuse me.'

He went down the ladder like a cat, and reappeared in an instant with a tall narrow bottle in his hand.

'An ancient castle,' he said, 'could be described as one large wine-cooler. Now, let us set the table.'

He took the papers off the table, and laid them carefully on top of the books on the shelf. He brought the table to the window, and put the chair and a stool beside it. Plates, knives, forks and glasses were spread upon it as neatly as by a Ravenburn tablemaid. He drew the cork of the bottle, and filled both glasses. Then he sat down, and helped me to a noble quantity of cold salmon.

Though grown up, I was not in the ordinary way allowed more than a thimbleful of wine. This was, no doubt, on the instructions of the Edinburgh doctors. Of course they knew best. But just as Ravenburn rules of behaviour and decorum were left behind when I came to Eilean Fitheach, so Ravenburn rules for my health seemed here unnecessary. The island was enchanted: the tower was enchanted: no harm could come to me. I drank my wine, with unbecoming speed, and enjoyed it very much.

'Where,' I asked, 'did you get this delicious wine?'

'A little more? It comes from – I am not *quite* sure how you will take this – from Ravenburn.'

'You *stole* it?'

'I am Tom's guest.'

'As well as Sir Campbell Stewart's. It is all *very* immoral, you know.'

'Yes, I know it is. Do you mind?'

'No,' I said, 'not a bit. I am so happy to . . .'

But I did not tell him how very happy I was, to be eating luncheon with him in his home. To be friendly is very well, but to be forward is unattractive.

'I am happy, too,' said Robbie. 'I drink to our happiness.'

I drank with him, to our happiness, as it would have been discourteous not to have raised my glass.

While we ate, he asked me about Ravenburn, and the people there. I told him as much as Miss Maitland might have been expected to know. He asked what guests had recently come. I told him about Lord Killin, and Sir George Fraser, and Lady Victoria Arlington.

'I have never heard of the lady,' he said, 'but Killin and Fraser – those are names Tom mentioned. Friends of his father, I think? Tell me about them.'

I was about to launch into an account of Lord Killin's kindness, and drollery, and infinite good humour and to say that he was quite as rich as everyone supposed and to mention Malvina's idiotic theory that Mamma had decided to marry him. I was going to tell also of Sir George's oddness, and twisted mouth, and thin voice. But I checked myself; Miss Maitland the governess would have had little contact with these resplendent strangers.

'I think they went fishing,' I said. 'They did not come to my school-room.'

He nodded, and asked about Uncle Frank.

'Mr Dundas has always been quite kind to me,' I said.

'It was he who engaged you?'

'Yes. I think he – he takes charge of all arrangements like that. Lady Ravenburn is – easily fatigued.'

Robbie nodded again. He looked at me speculatively, his grey eyes very cool and direct in his thin brown face. I felt myself blushing under that steady inspection.

'You were an odd choice, Katie,' he said at last.

'Not at all!' I said stoutly. 'I am *very* well read.'

'You burgle boathouses and steal boats. You have a tête-à-tête luncheon, unchaperoned, in a gentleman's bedroom—'

'*Oh.*'

He laughed, and filled my glass a third time.

At last I said, 'Would you like me to wash the plates?'

'Well, I have a method for cleaning things. You may not quite approve of it. It is not like the methods of the Manse in Stirling, or those of Ravenburn Castle.'

He put the things we had used in a rush basket, and went down the ladder. I followed. We went out into the sun, and he called the goat. He put the plates down in front of her, and she licked them clean.

'That,' I said, revolted, 'is much worse than poaching.'

'I was afraid you would disapprove. To me it seems so very sensible. We can wash them in the loch, if you insist.'

I did insist. While we washed them, I said, '*How* did you steal the wine from Ravenburn? The cellars are like dungeons. And *have* you been up the tower, to look at the ravens' nest?'

'What an ill-assorted brace of questions.'

'Yes, but they both suddenly occurred to me.'

'And you brought them out with commendable frankness. The wine? That was a lucky chance. A carrier's cart, bound for Ravenburn, broke an axle about four miles away. The carrier went off to get help. I was passing.'

'Would your friend Tom have liked you to . . .?'

'On reflection, I think he would.'

On reflection, I thought so too.

'As to the ravens,' he went on, 'I thought I should leave them undisturbed until the young birds are flying. Then I can steal a look.'

'I want to look, too.'

'Of course. I might have known you would want to look. We had better go up together, roped like climbers in the Alps.'

All too soon, it was time for me to leave – to rejoin the cushioned treadmill of my home, which seemed more tedious and purposeless than ever, in contrast to Eilean Fitheach.

As we went to my boat, Robbie said, 'That salmon will not last another day. We need another.'

'Can you get another?'

'Oh yes. The Crossmount water is full of fresh-run fish, beautiful fish. Ewan McNair the head keeper will be away, the night after next.'

'Where?'

'Visiting his ailing mother in Lochgrannomhead. She will be calling for him pitifully.'

I knitted my brows. 'The night's night, this old lady will be taken sick?'

'Yes, quite suddenly. Her health has been good, but, you know, with elderly people . . .'

'How *can* you know this?'

'Because I shall send a message to Ewan McNair, to that effect. In the later afternoon, so that he will have time to go to Lochgrannomhead, but no time to get back before morning. He is very attached to his mother. She has a stockingful of silver laid by, and he wants to show himself her most devoted child.'

'How can you know *that*?'

'Oh, I am full of information about the Crossmount keepers.'

'Did you have to go to all this trouble, to get the salmon we have just eaten?'

'No, but I was alone on the water. I was not using a flare. It was a much simpler method, but I was lucky to get that fish. I cannot rely on such luck again. I want to try something else, and I want more fish than one. We must have Ewan McNair out of the way.'

'There are other keepers at Crossmount.'

'Not very conscientious ones, when Ewan McNair is not by.'

'Oh. That is treacherous of them.'

'Yes, it is reprehensible, but I hear that Sir Campbell does not command very passionate loyalty among his servants.'

'But he is – such a jolly, booming sort of man.'

'Popular at Ravenburn?'

'Yes, very. That is to say, as far as *I* can tell. I believe they are quite often asked to dinner.'

'When he booms at everyone. How endearing. Well, perhaps his water keepers judge by different standards. At any rate, with Ewan McNair away by his mother's sickbed—'

'What is so different about this – this visit to Crossmount? Why do you need such precautions?'

'A flare is one difference,' he said. 'A great flaming torch, to attract and dazzle the fish.'

'Yes, I see that.'

'So will the keepers, if they are there. Now, I cannot hold the flare and use the spear. I need a companion.'

'Oh,' I said, a little dolefully. I had imagined him quite friendless, except for me, and perhaps Rory Beg. I did not precisely *wish* him friendless: but I did not quite like the idea of boon companions sharing his midnight adventures.

'You'll come, won't you?' he said. 'Please come, Katie! I beg you!'

'Are you demented?' I asked him, deeply shocked that he should phrase his invitation in such a way. 'How dare you *beg* such a thing? Of course I will come.'

I was standing now on the grassy hummock, with the gunwale of the boat nudging the hem of my skirt. I held the painter in my hand, ready to climb aboard and go.

Robbie smiled. He said, 'Remember we make our own rules here. The laws and customs of Eilean Fitheach are not the laws and customs of Scotland. You agree?'

'Yes,' I said, wondering what he was leading up to.

'Yes,' he repeated. Then he took my face between the palms of his hands, and kissed me on the forehead.

I was so astonished that I fell back into my boat. I think my legs waved in the air – heaven knows what a ludicrous and unseemly sight I was. I scrambled up from the bottom of the boat, sat on the thwart, seized the oars, and began to row with great energy away from the island.

Robbie stood, with his broadest and sweetest smile, waving to me from the hummock.

I dropped the oars and waved back. I could feel the breadth of my own involuntary smile, almost splitting the skin of my cheeks.

five

I was back in time to change my clothes, and make myself tidy, and assist at the ritual of dressing Malvina.

In the drawing room, there was a curious sense of excitement.

Mamma's cheeks were unusually flushed, and her eyes wide. Lady Wood whispered furiously to her daughter. Colonel Blair and Sir Campbell Stewart, in a corner, were having an argument in low voices. Lady Stewart was quacking at them, but they were too preoccupied to hear her. Sir Malcolm Rattray was pacing up and down, chewing the knob of his stick. Jamie, on a window seat, was looking at a book; but for once he was gobbling it avidly, rustling through the pages, and silently mouthing lines that caught his attention.

Only Mrs Seton seemed detached from all this excitement. She was looking from face to face with a frown; disapproval creaked from her.

They were all so busy, that none of them noticed us come in. This was distasteful to Malvina. She went forward hesitantly, the hoops of her silk dress swinging as she walked.

'Whatever are they all doing?' she asked me. 'Whatever is bothering them all?'

Mrs Seton heard her, and turned. 'Ah,' she cried, 'one innocent amongst us who will not, I trust, be involved in this questionable frolic.'

'There you are at last, my precious,' said Mamma. 'Of course you shall be involved. She will be,' Mamma assured Mrs Seton, 'a very sweet Lucy.'

'Lucy?' cried Mrs Seton, 'Is that not the part of the pert maidservant? You would allow this pure child . . .?'

'She will be kissed by Sir Malcolm Rattray. At least, so the author directs. Will you object to that, my sweet? We can always, I suppose, make changes . . .'

'No. She will be kissed by me,' said Jamie, looking up sharply from his book. 'I am going to be Sir Lucius O'Trigger.'

'Oh – my love–' said Mamma. 'I thought you wanted to be Mr Acres, or Captain Absolute.'

'Well,' said Jamie, 'yes, I do. I haven't decided.'

So here we all were again, I thought with exhaustion. There was to be another glittering presentation by the Ravenburn Theatricals – Mamma as the delightful young heroine, Uncle Frank as a comic servant, and all the others desperate with jealousy about the importance of their parts.

I thought *The Rivals* a very good choice to be done by the people then at Ravenburn. I wondered if, in suggesting it, Uncle Frank had intended a joke.

'Colonel Blair is to play Sir Anthony Absolute,' said Mamma to Malvina. 'Or perhaps it is to be Sir Campbell—'

'I submit it is ridiculous,' boomed Sir Campbell, 'to have a younger man, like myself, play the father of a considerably older man, such as Colonel Blair—'

'Captain Absolute, the son,' proclaimed Colonel Blair in a parade ground voice, 'is represented as a soldier. A serving officer, sir. He must be played by a military man. A mere civilian can never capture, that is to say, the bearing of an officer is ... In short, a few years of age make a less significant difference ...'

'Mrs Malaprop,' said Uncle Frank, 'lies at present between Lady Stewart and Lady Wood. Julia, the sighing, romantical young lady, is of course Miss Serena Wood.'

'I think I might be Acres,' called Jamie from the window seat, 'if we take out all the parts where he says he's frightened.'

'As to Captain Absolute,' said Colonel Blair, 'I take it we are agreed—'

'Do you so?' asked Sir Campbell Stewart.

'I wonder,' said Mamma thoughtfully, 'if Charles Killin will return in time?'

'The perfect choice, of course,' said Uncle Frank.

'But a civilian!' said Colonel Blair. 'The best of fellows, and a great friend of mine, but a civilian!'

'Perhaps,' said Mamma, 'if I wrote, or rather, if *you* wrote, Frank dear ...'

Colonel Blair and Sir Campbell Stewart were silenced. They glared at each other.

Of course, though the matter had not been mentioned, the bewitching seventeen-year-old Lydia Anguish would be Mamma.

And of course, though the matter had not been mentioned, I should have no part. It was, of all things, what the doctors would most have forbidden.

For once, I was thankful to suffer from disordered nerves. My heart sank, all the same, in contemplation of the project. I foresaw weary hours of helping Malvina with her lines, and Mamma with her costumes. I foresaw copying out all the parts, and then copying them out again, when Jamie had improved on Sheridan. I foresaw being tied to Ravenburn, when I wanted to be on Eilean Fitheach.

I wished them all joy of it, and escaped from the drawing room.

'So they will all be here all summer,' said Malvina, sitting up in bed as she ate her breakfast. She had a copy of *The Rivals* open on the pillow beside her.

'So they will,' I said, startled, because my mind had been somewhere quite different.

So they would. Sir Malcolm Rattray had looked intoxicated – though deliciously terrified at the same time – by the thought of playing the part of Sir Lucius O'Trigger. Nothing would prise him away from Ravenburn now -- not a hundred accidents in his mines, or a thousand colliers killed. Uncle Frank could do business with him to his heart's content.

'I hope Lord Killin comes back in time,' said Malvina.

I hoped so too. I hoped so very much. Yet, when I tried to picture his cheerful and friendly face, my mind's eye could not focus on it, because another face intruded.

Malvina said, 'Mamma, I have been looking at *The Rivals*. Lydia Languish is only seventeen. I must be Lydia, not you, because I am only four years too young, but you are sixteen years too old.'

'Nonsense, Malvina,' said Mamma, with an asperity I had seldom heard her use.

The discussion, after tea, was of the immense party that should be invited to witness the performance. There had not been a really big party, filling the rooms of the Castle, for over a year. Mamma was enchanted at the prospect. She sat engrossed with lists and leather-bound address book. She murmured names, wonderful catalogues of names. I had forgotten that she knew intimately so very many Dukes and Marquesses. It was odd how few came to Ravenburn.

'After all, I will be Captain Absolute,' said Jamie. 'Listen to this – "You puppy! Ha – you blockhead!" He is shouting at his servant, you know. I like that.'

'Do you, precious?' said Mamma. 'How nice. But if Charles Killin can come . . .'

Uncle Frank came into Malvina's bedroom, while Malvina was holding her levée, carrying a letter.

'I wrote to Killin yesterday,' he said to Mamma, 'but our letters have crossed. Here he is, asking if he may come in the first week of June.'

'Good,' said Mamma. 'But how strange that he did not write to me.'

'He did,' said Uncle Frank, and handed her the letter.

I thought this very odd. But Mamma did not seem to think so. She read the letter, her head on one side. She held it close to her face, because in spite of the startling beauty of her eyes, they did not see handwriting well at a distance greater than six inches.

'George Fraser is to follow,' she said.

'Yes.'

'He has gone to . . . What is this strange word? Oh – a place in the Hebrides. I wonder why? There is nothing there, no company . . . But that is why he cannot write. He sends apologies, by Charles . . .'

'He will not be here in time to take part in *The Rivals*, I think,' said Uncle Frank.

'No. In any case, I don't think . . . George Fraser's voice is so . . . I suppose he could do Sir Lucius O'Trigger. Do you think so?'

'No,' said Uncle Frank. 'Rattray must play any part he chooses, and he chooses Sir Lucius.'

'Is that final? Because, you know, my dearest Jamie . . .'

'Jamie must settle for another rôle. Good heavens, he has the whole play to choose from.'

'Yes, but . . . It is just the kind of thing . . . He is apt to be determined, just because . . .'

'Well, you must tell him.'

'Oh, *you* must tell him, dearest Frank. I quail, you know, from . . .'

'Mamma,' said Malvina, shifting impatiently in her bed. 'I still think—'

But she was silenced by the look in Mamma's eye.

I was in no mood to pay attention to the squabbles and politics of the Castle. To some extent, they were thrust upon me. I saw Lady Wood clutching Colonel Blair's arm, and whispering to him. He was nodding, and whispering back. It was a treaty. She, I surmised, would support his claim to be Captain Absolute, if he would back hers to be Mrs Malaprop.

The thought of either, in those roles, filled me with a sort of fascinated revulsion.

But only for a moment, for into my mind kept flooding a wave of expectation, of suffocating suspense, which drove out all other thoughts. I longed for nightfall, yet I dreaded the going down of the sun. I had done a few ill-advised things, but none so criminal and desperate . . .

Nothing would keep me in my bed that night, except a torrential downpour or a gale of wind. Either would keep Robbie in his bed, too (that odd but charming little piece of canvas, stretched on its wooden frame) – for he said we needed a clear and calm night for the torchlight spearing. We had agreed that, if the night was foul, we would postpone all. I prayed for bright stars and the gentlest of breezes. I prayed, in moments of recurring terror, for cloudbursts and tempests.

Robbie was to come to the landing stage by the boathouse at eleven o'clock. He would already have everything he needed, he said, except me. He promised to get me home before dawn.

The thing that I had to arrange, entirely on my own account, was a way of getting back into the Castle before daylight. I could not expect to do again as I had done – creep in and up to bed, after the maids were up, unseen by anyone. I had to find a door that locked from the inside and the outside, and had no bolts or chain. But I had to find it without being seen looking for it.

This was my preoccupation all day. I prowled about the cellars like a rat, dodging away from stillroom-maids, and inspecting a hundred doors.

I found the door I wanted, at last. It went from one of the outside game-larders, direct into an empty vaulted cellar. The purpose of the door was so that a kitchen-porter could get a carcass from the game-larder, without going out into the open. It was probably the solitary example, in the whole of my grandfather's design, of an arrangement being made for a servant's convenience. I supposed it was done by mistake.

The door was kept locked, at this time of the year, because the game-larders were empty. With August would come grouse and early stags, but there was nothing in May to hang in those cold tombs. The key, unused for weeks, was very stiff: but it turned. I decided I would not take it with me, for fear of losing it in the loch, but I would hide it just outside the door. I found a place for it, in the game-larder. That all seemed well. The one risk was that the night-watchmen, inspecting the door, would see that the key was missing. But the door would be locked; they would not worry unduly; they might report it in the morning, but they would hardly rouse the Castle.

That settled, there was no more I could do about the night's expedition, except feel my heart bump when I thought of it.

Tension was still evident in the drawing-room after tea. Mrs Seton, alone, was outside it. She stared round at the excited groups, so stiff that I wondered her head could turn on her neck.

I looked round at them too, but I hardly saw them. Other things filled my internal eye.

Sir Campbell Stewart's voice boomed across the room, 'I assure you, Dundas. After all, I know the fellow's face as well as I know my own. He spent a day on my water, you know. Talk, talk, talk, hardly wet his fly. I'm not likely to forget that in a hurry.'

'He is in the Hebrides,' said Mamma.

'No, ma'am, he's not. This morning he was in Lochgrannomhead.'

There was a choking noise; it was Uncle Frank, in a fit of coughing. There were cries of concern, and Sir Campbell slapped him on the back.

Uncle Frank stopped coughing, forced a smile, and said hoarsely, 'I beg your pardon. A coughing-fit is more disagreeable for others, I believe, even than for oneself.'

He said he was quite recovered, and his smile became placid again.

But I had seen his face, in the split-second between the choke and the coughing-fit. It had a look of death and desperation.

The Castle was later abed than usual, which was a nuisance. I supposed there was continual excitement about the play.

The hands of the clock crawled round. Part of me wanted them to race, part to stop dead. I was committed to a supreme folly. But it was not an internal 'dare'. I was going because I wanted to go. I was going because Robbie Scott had asked me.

I leaned out of my window and sniffed the night. There was a light breeze, not cold, and a scattering of stars between small clouds. My heart rose like a lark, and dived like a peregrine.

85

We were not going to be cheated of our adventure; or, to put it another way, I had no excuse to draw back.

At long, long last I was able to creep downstairs, avoiding only the chattering night-watchmen, and plumb the depths of the cellars. I took no candle or lantern, for fear of being seen, but groped my way. I knew it well enough. I found my little door into the game-larder, and was soon out and on the bank of the Raven burn.

I was in good time.

I stopped and looked back at the immense bulk of the Castle, black against the sky. In all the dark south front, two tall upstairs windows were lit – the windows of one bedroom. The curtains of one window were shut, but of the other, open. A figure passed and repassed the uncurtained window, silhouetted against the lamplight behind.

Uncle Frank was pacing, pacing, wearing a track in the Turkey carpet of his room.

I wondered very hard about this – but only for as long as it took me to descend to the mouth of the burn.

I heard a boat crunching gently on the shingle, and in a moment saw it.

'Katie?' called a voice softly.

'Who did you expect?' I said. 'Lady Ravenburn?'

'I didn't know whether to expect you. I was almost sure you wouldn't come.'

'What?' I said, greatly incensed. 'That is almost ruder than—'

I heard the ghost of a laugh. 'Shall I help you aboard?'

'Certainly not. I will not accept help from somebody who does not trust me.'

But I regretted my hauteur, because I slipped on a wet rock, and nearly fell into the water, and got my legs very wet before I was in the boat.

The stumpy mast was set, with the scrap of sail flapping from it. Robbie pulled on a rope; the sail filled; the boat heeled, and whispered away from the shore. The sail took us gently down the loch towards the mouth of the River Chinn. We went as silent as a swan. It was much better than rowing.

We talked softly, because voices carry far over water.

'I should never have asked you,' said Robbie.

'Why not?'

'I was mad and wrong to ask you, and you were mad and wrong to accept.'

'Mad, of course. But why wrong?'

'This is no ploy for a girl. Any girl. Least of all a demure young lady, the daughter of a Manse—'

'A governess.'

'Yes. That makes it worse. If you get caught – your position—'

'A governess,' I said, misquoting something or other, 'can be a man.'

'That, thank God, you're not,' he said.

I could not see his face, but I heard a smile in his voice.

He thanked God I was a girl – a woman. For the first time in my life, perhaps, I found myself doing so too.

I had lived always a boy's or a tomboy's life – both indoors, with books, and outdoors, with rambles and scrambles. I lived so still. Of course, my body had changed as I grew up. I became self-conscious about it, sometimes ashamed and sometimes secretly proud. Yet, though I was physically a woman, I might as well not have been one, for all the difference a bosom made to me. My life was still books and scrambles. I had little other, because the doctors said I must not be subjected to the nervous strain of a grown-up life.

But Robbie thanked God I was a woman, and so did I. I felt a sense of my woman's body, and a tingle of my woman's skin. I felt myself blush.

My thoughts were a jumble. I did not know who or what I was. I thought of Uncle Frank, pacing up and down in his bedroom, and of his stricken face in the drawing room, because he heard that Sir George Fraser was in the neighbourhood. I thought of Robbie Scott, the dark figure a yard away, who thanked God I was a woman. My puzzled doubts fled before such a wave of happy excitement that I almost burst out singing. I controlled myself. The banshee noise of my voice would have frightened every salmon out of the Chinn.

'Last time I came,' said Robbie, breaking a long silence, 'when I came alone, I had only a throwing leister. I brought it tonight, but I don't think we'll use it.'

'What is it?'

'A cross between a javelin and a table-fork. Well, it has a heavy metal head with five barbed prongs, and a curved wooden shaft. A rope of goat's hair, twelve yards long, is tied to the head. The rope is called the lyams, but I don't know why. The idea is to throw the harpoon, and impale a fish, and pull the fish in by the lyams.'

'That,' I said, 'sounds *very* difficult.'

'Yes, it is. Especially as things under the water are not where you think they are. You have to adjust your aim, as though you were shooting an arrow in a strong cross-wind. I did spear a fish—'

'A *very* good fish.'

'But I cannot imagine how. It was the purest luck. So tonight we will use a surer method.'

'Tell me.'

'We must go up the river to the Horseshoe Pool. We can't go higher, because of the falls. We can't sail against the current—'

'Rowing will be hard work.'

'Yes, too hard. We go ashore, and pull the boat upstream by a rope. It's surprisingly easy. The river's not high, and the current's moderate. When we get to the pool we tie the boat, by a long line, to a particular tree. The current swings us out into the middle. Then we can cover quite a lot of the pool, simply by pulling on the line or paying it out. The fish hang in the pool, quite still. Fast asleep, I suppose.'

'Deep?'

'Yes, deep. But the leister has a fourteen-foot shaft.'

'It is not very sporting,' I said, 'to spear a sleeping fish.'

'Good heavens, Katie, we're not here for *sport*. We're filling our larder.'

But it was sport – great sport.

With oars as well as sail, we struggled a short distance up into the broad estuary of the river, then ran ashore on a shelving beach. Robbie wrapped the flapping sail round the mast, and tied it up. We began pulling the boat upstream, like bargehorses on a towpath. The river gradually narrowed. There was broken water, which creamed over rocks. The boat bumped among the rocks, and once or twice got stuck; but a heave cleared it, and we went on. Then we were on the smooth, straight length of the bottom pool of the Crossmount water.

'The Baillie's Pool,' said Robbie. 'No good to us.'

'Why?'

'Too narrow, fast and deep. Experts might get fish here – indeed, I know they do – but I don't think we would. It's a great thing to know one's limitations. Besides, we'd need a man at the oars, to keep the boat steady in midstream. I *might* have found a man – but I'm glad I didn't.'

'So am I,' I said.

More broken water took us up into the Horseshoe Pool, another long smooth stretch where the salmon lay, pausing on their way upstream to their spawning-beds. The left bank was steep rock, with a few clumps of small trees and whins, just visible in the starlight. The right bank, where we stood with the boat at our feet, shelved gently to rocks and shingle. The seventy yards of the pool were curved like an archer's bow.

'Why they call it a Horseshoe,' murmured Robbie, 'I can't imagine.'

'A laird's horse once lost a shoe, fording the shallows at the top,' I told him. 'In the reign of James V.'

'How on earth do you come to know that?'

I knew it because it was the sort of thing Miss Anderson, that devoted antiquarian, loved to teach me. I said to Robbie, 'I think Sir Campbell Stewart must have told me. Or rather, told someone else, when I was by.'

'I wish my memory was as good as yours.'

'When anybody sees the horseshoe in the water,' I went on, 'something happens.'

'What happens?'

'Oh . . .' I had forgotten whether it was a good omen or a bad, but I knew it was very strong magic. 'Something very nice or very dreadful.'

'That's too equivocal for me. I hope we only see a salmon. Now – we'll pull the boat into this slack water. Can you hold it here?'

'Yes, easily.'

'I'll take the rope up and tie it to the tree. Then we'll pole off with the shaft of the spear, and swing out into midstream. That's the advantage of a curving pool.'

'I hope you know how to tie a knot,' I said.

He laughed, and disappeared upstream into the darkness.

I crouched on a flat rock, holding fast to the gunwale of the boat. It needed only a finger, but I used both hands. I was determined to do nothing wrong. It seemed very important that

Robbie should get a salmon, and still more important that I should not let him down.

He thanked God I was a woman; but the governess had to be a man.

The river slid by, smooth and powerful, the surface sheened in the starlight. There were no rocks at all in midstream here, to punctuate its smooth eternal progress; but it whispered and gurgled among the rocks of the bank. There were a few sleepy chirrups from birds on the ground or in the trees; from some way off I heard the low, insistent whirring of a nightjar, like a spinning-wheel in a croft. There was no other sound.

I waited in the darkness, taut as a fiddle-string.

Nightjar and river were infinitely comforting, infinitely soothing. But I did not need comforting, and I was far too strung-up to be soothed. This was a wild and dangerous game Robbie and I were playing. I could not think why I was so stupid as to be dragged into it. If we were caught, I faced God knew what disgrace, what closeted and joyless future; Robbie faced years in prison. Well, we had better not be caught. I strained my ears for a voice, the scrape of a hobnail on a rock, any sight or sound of a keeper. Robbie's strategy was very well, but he could not *know* Ewan McNair would be all night in Lochgrannomhead, or that the others would shirk their duty the moment his eye was removed. There might be, even now, creeping up on me . . .

I heard a *chink* in the darkness behind me. It might have been a bird; it might have been a nailed bootsole on a stone. I spun round, and strained my eyes to pierce the darkness. There were more clouds, fewer stars. I could see nothing except the tumbled bank, and guess at the heather and bracken and rickles of stones. *Clink*. Was it a bird? What bird made that sound? It was nearer. I was holding the boat. In the boat were the utterly damning spears and the flare, the tools of the poacher's trade.

Here or hereabouts, a dozen years before, my brother Tom had lurked thus, with net or spear or rake-hooks. The keepers had jumped him, and evading arrest he had . . .

Did the ghost of the murdered keeper haunt this bank? Almost certainly the country people thought so. It was horribly easy to think so. *Clink*. Was it a ghostly hobnail?

My heart thudded in my throat, almost suffocating me. I

clung to the gunwale of the boat, as though for reassurance, until my hands hurt. All about me there were little furtive noises, rustles, whispers, squeaks. Things seemed to lurch towards me in the darkness. I dared not move, for fear of making a noise, the tiniest noise. I was certain that men, hostile men, surrounded me. They were within yards or feet of me. I tried to hold my breath, but it rasped in my throat. I thought the thudding of my heart must boom out over the river like a drum. The keepers would strike first, with cudgel or pistol, and ask questions afterwards – especially as one of their number had been murdered here, by a poacher. There was a movement! And there! And a rustle behind me, and a chink of bootnails beyond!—

There was an undoubted movement just behind my back. A dark figure loomed over me as I crouched. I spun round, a scream forming in my throat. A hand was clapped over my mouth, and another seized my arm. I struggled like a maniac, but I was gripped by hands like steel.

A voice murmured in my ear, 'It's all right, Katie. It's me.'

He let go of my face, and grabbed the gunwale of the boat, which was just about to swing out into the river.

'*Oh*,' I whispered furiously. '*Oh*.'

'Did I hurt you?'

'Of course not. Yes! But that is nothing. You nearly tore my nose out by the roots, and my arm, but that is nothing. You frightened me almost to death.'

'I'm very sorry. But I could see you were nervous—'

'I was not nervous!'

'No?' I heard the smile in his voice.

'I was – edgy,' I admitted.

'If I had popped up at you out of the darkness, you might have—'

'Screamed?' I asked indignantly, 'Me?'

He was holding the boat with one hand; with the other, he still had hold of my arm. He let go, and took my hand instead. He lifted it to his lips, and kissed it.

'A governess in a million,' he murmured. 'Let's go and catch tomorrow's dinner. Will you hold the boat?'

I did so, and he took from the bottom two long poles. At the end of one I could just see a metallic gleam – the vicious five-pronged head of the leister. Robbie screwed the two poles together, by what he said were good bronze threads; this made a single pole, of awkward length, which he laid in the bows like an elongated bowsprit.

'The flare?' I asked.

'When we're out there. Flares on the bank are tempting Providence.'

I nodded (which was a ridiculous thing to do in the dark), and he helped me into the boat. He did not need to pole us out from the bank – the current took us, and we swung out into the midst of the inky river. After fifteen yards, the boat was held by the current and by the rope at the bows. The river gurgled under the stern. We had come as silent as a bird, and we were almost as silent now as we hung like a salmon in the current.

'An old-fashioned flint-and-steel,' murmured Robbie, 'and some home-made tinder. It's laborious, but it works in the end.'

He conjured a series of sparks from the flint-and-steel. At last his tinder caught. He ignited the torch. It was like a mop with a swollen head – a great bundle of ropes'-ends, soaked in some kind of oil. It spluttered, and immediately blazed. It looked to me as bright as a lighthouse (though I had never seen a lighthouse). I thought it must be visible at the far end of Loch Chinn, and glare into the bedroom windows of Ravenburn Castle.

I gulped, and said, 'Are you *sure* the keepers—?'

'No,' he said cheerfully. 'Not *quite* sure. Will you take the flare, Katie? Thank you. Hold it so, over the water, and I'll see what I can see.'

The flare shed a ghastly light, of horrifying brilliance, over us and the boat and the water. Anyone standing on the bank must have seen every hair of Robbie's beard, every lash on my eyelids. I felt we were appallingly vulnerable – one bright-lit island in an ocean of darkness. Men would come like moths to the light, armed with guns and warrants. And, dazzled as we were, an army could have mustered on the bank without our seeing it.

'One does feel conspicuous,' said Robbie, as though reading my thoughts. 'Like Hamlet alone on the stage.'

'Or Lydia Languish . . . Does the flare last long?'

'Hours, I hope. If not, I paid too much for the oil.'

He crouched in the bows, the leister in his hand, and stared down into the depths. Presently he shook his head, took hold of the rope, and pulled the boat upstream two yards. He took a turn with the rope, to hold the boat in its new position, and stared down into the water again. He did this twice more; then gave a grunt of satisfaction.

'Don't move,' he whispered urgently. 'Hold the torch just so.'

He lowered the leister into the water, slowly, keeping it vertical against the pull of the current, going deep and deep. Then he held it still, braced himself, and plunged it downwards. Immediately the shaft began to jerk and kick in his hands. He pulled it up, as quick as he could, hand over hand, and in a few seconds a great silver fish lay flapping in the bows of the boat. Three of the prongs had skewered it, full in the back, just behind the head.

Robbie knocked it on the head quickly, with a small club, from his pocket, of the kind they call a 'priest'.

'Well done!' I crowed, the torch shaking in my hands.

'Not a monster. Tomorrow's dinner. Now we need the next day's luncheon.'

'You do have a lot of mouths to feed.'

'Including yours, I hope?'

'I hope so, too.'

He smiled (his teeth were brilliant in the glare of the torch), and peered down into the water again.

By slow degrees we worked up the rope towards the head of the Horseshoe Pool. Robbie missed two salmon (very nearly falling overboard as he lunged at the second) but caught two more. They were beautiful fish – not long, Robbie said, up from the distant sea; he guessed the largest was thirteen pounds, the smallest eight.

They would have given good sport to the rich Englishmen who paid Sir Campbell so much to fish the water. I felt an extraordinary indifference to their loss. I was almost giggling with excitement and with the thrill of sporting triumph.

'One more?' said Robbie.

'A hundred!'

'That would be greedy. I'll sell one of these as it is, but I'd like to sell a brace. I don't need much money, you know, but I need a little.'

I nodded. Buying or selling poached game was a criminal offence, as much as poaching it, and carried a prison sentence.

But it seemed most proper to me that Robbie should sell the fish he had speared at Crossmount. I was a little surprised to find that I had a criminal mentality.

Robbie pulled us another two yards up the pool. The current swung us in a curious way here, and pulled us much closer to the far bank. There was a little spinney of trees, barely visible against the sky, above a tumble of rocks.

A voice called softly from the trees. It called a phrase I did not understand – two or three words of Gaelic.

I almost jumped out of my boots with the shock. My instinct was to plunge the torch in the water. I looked tensely at Robbie for orders.

Robbie smiled, and waved at the darkness.

He called softly to the bank, 'Ye'll hae a guid word, mon?'

'Ay,' called a hoarse voice, just loud enough to hear across the water. 'I foond yer fellie. He bides in a wee croftie ahint a hull, intil a wee glen ye ne'er haird o'.'

'Is't sae?' answered Robbie. 'Whaur s'all I seek?'

There followed another and longer Gaelic phrase from the hoarse voice in the spinney. I could make nothing of it at all, for I knew few words of the Gaelic. But Robbie nodded, satisfied.

'I'm obleeged,' he called. 'Wull ye tak' a saumon?'

'Na, na!' called the hoarse voice. 'I'll hae mair fush tae masel' than yin. I'll tak' a bit siller, whan siller bides in the richt haands.'

'I'm obleeged,' said Robbie again. 'But . . .'

He shrugged, and murmured to me, 'He's gone.'

'You were expecting him,' I said, suddenly realizing.

'Yes. We had a rendezvous. That is one reason we fished with a flare tonight. It is also a reason I took so much trouble about Ewan McNair.'

'Who is your friend?'

'Rory Beg.'

'Oh! I never expected . . . He saw me! In the torchlight, he saw my face as clear as—'

'He saw you were a friend of mine, Katie. He may wonder who you are, but he won't share that speculation with a soul. We call it honour among thieves, you know.'

'But – he has been in prison.'

'I've been lucky to escape it.'

'When? Where?'

'The outback of Australia is a violent place, sometimes. Don't worry. There never were gyves actually upon my wrists.'

'What did he call you? I couldn't make that out.'

'He called me Seabhac Seilge. It's my – nom de guerre, with Rory Beg and his ilk. Its literal meaning is "wandering hunter". It's the name for a peregrine falcon.'

'Oh,' I digested this. 'The Gaelic for osprey would suit you better, catching fish with a spear . . . What was that other Gaelic he spoke?'

'The name of a place. Of a burn, to be exact. Allt a' Choire Odhain Bhig.'

'Where a man lives in a croft?'

'Where a man lives, and I pray goes on living.'

'Where is Allt a' . . . what you said?'

'I'll take you there, I think. Your help will be very useful, for soothing the terrors of a – of something, I suppose, like an old hoodie-crow feeding on scraps dropped by a wolf.'

'I don't understand a word you're saying.'

'No. But if all goes well, all will come clear. So much depends on so many things, Katie! And I have been away so long. There is still so much to do. Though I have friends, better friends than I deserve, quietly helping me—'

'Do they come to the island?' I asked, with a pang of jealousy I despised myself for feeling.

'Good heavens, no! They have no idea I am there. Nobody has, except you.'

'Why not tell them, if they are your friends?'

'For my sake, and theirs. Suppose one of them got drunk – which one of them sometimes does – and blurted something out? And suppose they were asked by an Inspector of Police, or by a Procurator Fiscal, on oath, if they knew where I was? On *oath*? Men of standing, of honour? Do they perjure themselves?'

'Of course they do, if they're truly friends.'

'Yes, I daresay they do. But I can't ask them to. Just because they're true friends. You understand that?'

'Yes,' I admitted. 'But suppose a judge asks me, on oath, am I to perjure myself?'

'Would you?'

'Of course I would. What a stupid question. Do you really want another salmon?'

'No. I think you should get home. Dawn is not so very far off. Are you cold?'

'No.'

'Wet?'

'Not now.'

'Good. Let's drown the torch and we'll be away.'

By pulling on the rope, Robbie worked us up and across to our original bank. He scrambled ashore, and helped me out. He hurried up the bank the short distance to where his rope was tied.

It was more difficult to hold the boat in this place, because of the pull of the current sweeping under the bank. I lost it at one moment. I reached out, and managed to grab the gunwale again. But in doing so, I almost fell forward into the river. I saved myself by putting out my other hand, which splashed into three inches of water close under the bank.

Something moved under my hand — something curved and metallic. I picked it up. It was heavy, a loop of iron.

When Robbie came back with the rope, I said, as steadily as I could, 'I've found the laird's horseshoe.'

six

'Let me see,' said Robbie. 'Or rather, feel.'

I handed it to him. After a moment, he said, 'This is new. Heavy, not much worn, with sharp edges. This has not been here since the reign of James V.'

'Yes it has,' I said.

He laughed softly. 'Is it a good omen or a bad? I wish you could remember, Katie.'

'So do I.'

I tried to remember what Miss Anderson had told me. It was as I was trying that disaster struck.

From the top of the long slope of the bank above us there was a *chink*, which might have been bird or hobnail. Then a stone rolled. I could hear it clearly, in the quiet night, knocking against other stones, bouncing, and finally coming to rest a few yards from us. There was a hoarse oath from the top of the bank.

'Ye fule,' came a voice, sharply.

'Och, I spy them, doon 'til the water!'

There was another call, and another. There were four men, at least.

And then, at the top of the bank, the bright eye of a lantern was uncovered.

'Doon we gang, boys! Dinna shute ma backside wi' yon pistol, Geordie—'

There was a great noise of scrambling, as the keepers came down the bank in a line, and more stones tumbled. I thought there were more than four. In the midst was the lantern, casting a beam that looked as bright as our torch. They had pistols, one or more.

Dimly, my sight sharpened by terror, I saw Robbie stand at the waterside, erect, absolutely still. I wanted to flee. I thought he was mad. He had the horseshoe in his right hand. He swung his right arm across his breast, then flung the horseshoe, back-landed, hard, up the bank. There was a crash of breaking glass, and the lantern went out.

Robbie shouted, 'Intil the boat, Angus ! Donald! Dougal! Ye'll hae the guns on the cock, lads! Ay – shute when I gi' the wurd.' He whispered to me, without any urgency, 'Time to go, Katie.'

We scrambled into the boat. He poled it off, and we were caught by the current. The boat swung out into midstream, and went fast down the Horseshoe Pool.

They saw us in the starlight. There were shouts. There was a flash of light, and a split-second later an explosion.

'They won't hit a moving target, at this range, in the dark,' said Robbie conversationally. 'At least, I don't *think* they will.'

We could hear shouts and crashes from the bank. Though we were now drifting rapidly downstream towards the loch, they were keeping up with us.

'They'll – they'll run down, and cut us off at the falls,' I wailed.

'They'll try.'

Robbie seized the oars, and began pulling mightily. With oars and current our speed became frightening. I could hear the broken water ahead. I clung to the thwart, and struggled not to scream.

We rushed towards the rocks and angry water at the tail of the pool.

'This is the interesting part,' said Robbie, still cheerfully conversational.

'We'll have to land,' I sobbed.

'I hope not. Our friends are coming up.'

'The other bank!'

'No, my love.'

He was right. The river ran under a cliff on the far bank.

The boat went faster, rolling and pitching in the broken water. Rocks loomed. The bows bumped and the bottom scraped. We splashed and jolted down through the long run towards the next pool. Then, with a great jar under the keel of the boat, we stuck. The boat tipped almost over. Water splashed in over the side.

Without a word, Robbie jumped out of the boat. He heaved, and pulled the boat clear. He was up to his chest in the fast water. Waves splashed over his head. He nearly tipped the boat over again, and I clung and shrieked. The whole world was a black turmoil of rocks and angry water. The boat bumped wildly down through more rocks. It tipped dangerously again as Robbie climbed in and seized the oars.

We sped down the long fast straight of the Baillie's Pool. This time we left the pursuit behind. Robbie had to jump into the water again, to get us through the rocks and racing shallows at the tail of the pool. But, as he cheerfully said, he could not be wetter than he was already.

It seemed to me that I had crouched for a long lifetime on the thwart of the boat, clinging and almost screaming, with rocks and boiling rapids below, and angry keepers with pistols beside. We drifted down the gentler current of the estuary, and so out into the loch.

'I am very sorry, Katie,' Robbie said. 'Somehow my plans miscarried.'

'That's all right,' I said, shamed into keeping my voice as steady as his. 'I enjoyed it. It makes a change, you know, from – from teaching Malvina to spell.'

'A governess in a million,' said Robbie, a very broad smile in his voice.

He unwrapped the sail from round the mast, and we started our gentle voyage the length of the loch.

He had called me his love. 'My love,' he said. He had thanked God I was not a man, and then called me his love. But he had blurted out those words at a moment of extreme tension, among pistols and whirlpools. It would not do to hold him to them. It would not do to build upon them. It would not do to think about them.

I thought about them, off and on, all the way back to Ravenburn.

'It had every appearance,' said Robbie thoughtfully, after a long silence, 'of an ambush. As though they were waiting for us.'

'Yes.'

'If so, they knew where to wait and when. Which suggests that somebody betrayed me.'

'Rory Beg.'

'No. I would hate to think so, and I don't think so. I think the keepers were waiting for him, not us. Someone betrayed him.'

'Who would know he was going to be at Crossmount tonight?'

'I don't know. Very few. Those few not of the – the highest moral type. Perhaps one had a price, which someone was willing to pay. Another possibility is that someone has been following Rory Beg. Not an easy thing to do, unless . . . I pray that he wasn't followed to Allt a' Choire Odhain Bhig. I doubt that he was, but *if* he was, my cake is dough . . . At least, the keepers ought to think we were ordinary poachers.'

'We were.'

'You, Katie? You're the most extraordinary poacher in the history of crime. But I don't think they saw you.'

'They heard me,' I admitted. 'I screamed. It was very spiritless and foolish of me.'

'I very nearly screamed, myself,' said Robbie. 'If they heard you, they must have thought you were a boy. Who but Tom o' Bedlam would bring a woman poaching?'

'It was clever of you to call out those men's names.'

'I thought that would deter them more than it did. I shouted about guns, too. But still they came on, trying to cut us off at the falls.'

'It's *not* what you led me to expect,' I said, 'with Ewan McNair away to his mother.'

'No, it's not what I was led to expect. They were out, they were armed, they were even brave. I think ... I think there must have been some very special incentive. Someone has been keeping an eye on Rory Beg, and badly wants him caught or ... I shall have to be careful now. Ten times more careful than before. What a nuisance.'

'However did you hit the lantern with the horseshoe?'

'That was a good shot, wasn't it? My teacher would have been proud of me. He was an American sailor I knew in Sydney. They have a game in America, pitching horseshoes at a peg in the ground. He taught me, and we used to play in the yard behind a tavern. We formed a regular club after a time – the Muldoon's Hotel Horseshoe Pitching Society, honorary secretary Mr Robert Scott.'

I sighed. 'What a lot of amusing things you have done,' I said. 'And I have never done anything in my life at all.'

'We are doing our best to put that right,' said Robbie.

We talked about ourselves and about each other, with long companionable silences in the intervals of talk. I heard about Robbie's childhood in the household of Mr Archibald Scott, and his years at Eton – for Mr Scott had been determined to make Robbie a gentleman, and to my mind had completely succeeded. He told me more stories about Australia, too. He would not tell me about Violet, the clinging and affectionate female, or about any other females. But I remained sure that he had bewitched large numbers of them. How could he have failed to do so? I told him more about my life among books and birds, keeping as close to the truth as I could, for I hated to lie to him. (Since he had called me 'his love', it was more than ever necessary to lie to him ... even though the words had been forced out of him by excitement, and carried no meaning at all.) It seemed that he knew all the books I knew, and thousands more besides.

'For,' he said, 'time often hung heavy on my hands in Australia, and my second master was a *very* learned man.'

'Your second master? Were you indentured twice?'

'It was after the pit-props broke at Yellow Springs – after poor Tom's death. My master thought I was a Jonah. My indentures were transferred, and I found myself the servant of an unfrocked clergyman.'

'Oh! ... Unfrocked?'

'It is a metaphorical term. You are not to imagine him going about in indecorous small-clothes, to the scandal of the people. He had been a fashionable London vicar, but developed a ruinous passion for gambling. One thing led to another, I believe, rather as in my own case. He shed his Holy Orders, or had them snipped off him, and took ship to the Antipodes. He became a teacher, a maker and seller of patent medicines, and a leading tipster on the race-course. I suppose he was the worst moral influence a nice young man could have had.'

I burst out laughing. 'Were you a nice young man?'

'No, of course not. So he could do me no harm.'

It was oddly dreamlike, gliding in a soft wind, over calm water, in not-quite-perfect darkness, talking quietly to Robbie, or listening to his gentle, pleasant voice, and trying not to think all the time about what he had called me . . .

The eastern sky began to pale. A milky sheen overspread the huge face of the loch. The high hills to the north stood out against the dawn, and below them the grotesque bulk of Ravenburn Castle. We whispered along in a freshening dawn breeze. I could see Robbie's thin brown face, and his mouse-brown beard, and his clear grey eyes.

Of course, he could see me too, in the cruel dawn light. I shuddered to think how I must look – my hair wild, my face dirty, my clothes draggled and disgraceful, my boots heavy and wet.

Too soon – but only just soon enough – the bows of our boat nuzzled the jetty by the boathouse. Robbie jumped ashore and handed me out. I sighed deeply as I set foot on dry land. Because of his having helped me ashore, I found myself standing close to Robbie on the jetty, face to face, inches away. His face was a little above mine. I glanced up at him.

I felt his hands on my shoulders. I felt him draw me towards him. His face swam down towards mine. I felt his lips on mine, briefly, gently.

He let me go, and smiled down at me. I almost collapsed on the jetty.

He said softly, 'A governess in a million.'

I watched, as numb as a statue, while he jumped into his boat, pushed off, and sailed away briskly. I managed to raise an arm to return his wave of farewell. I felt the breadth of the idiotic smile on my face.

As I hurried up the burn towards the Castle, I thought: the laird's horseshoe was a *very* good omen.

Days passed. Miss Maitland and I, at different times, began to try to teach Malvina her lines. I could not get away to Eilean Fitheach.

A formidable Frenchwoman arrived from some distant city, with a carriage full of silks, and two little seamstresses. They were to make Mamma's costumes.

A date was fixed for the performance, the Friday before Perth race-week. This would find everybody available, in the right area, but with nothing to do.

All this time, I hugged my memories to my breast, as a young child hugs her doll. The brief phrase, spoken in the dark turmoil of the river. The brief and gentle pressure of his lips on mine. I told myself a thousand times that the words meant nothing. But they were spoken to me. They were mine. Nobody could ever take them away from me. The kiss meant nothing. But it was my lips Robbie had kissed. It was my kiss. Nobody could take that away from me, either, though my lips never felt another kiss as long as I lived.

Mamma said, in the drawing room, 'What has come over the girl? There is a sort of silly, dreamy smile on her face. She looks like a housemaid who . . . It is almost as though . . . One could bring oneself to believe . . . But of course . . .'

'We have all of us a great deal to smile about,' said Uncle Frank, 'with the excitement ahead of us.'

'You've stayed away for so long,' said Robbie, 'I couldn't keep any of our salmon for you.'

'I have been teaching my pupil to act a lady's-maid. No salmon at all?'

'It was going bad. There have been some hot days, though none as hot as this.'

'There was a very hot day at the beginning of May,' I said.

I blushed to remember how I had cooled myself, and how I had felt the nanny-goat's yellow eye on me, as I lay naked, sprawled and shameless, in the sun.

The nanny-goat's eye?

An appalling, a mortifying suspicion jumped into my head. I

cringed at the thought. I said, choking, 'That hot day at the beginning of May . . .'

'I remember it well,' said Robbie softly.

'Were you – on the island?'

I waited, aghast, for his answer.

'Oh yes,' he said.

'In – in the castle? In your room in the tower?'

'You took me by surprise, that day,' said Robbie. 'I had to climb a tree.'

'Which tree?' I asked, hardly able to speak, utterly unable to look at him.

'That one,' said Robbie.

It was one of the fir trees near the low stone arch. Its trunk stood not six yards from the sward where I had stretched out on my back.

Suffocated, I said, '*You were up there?*'

'Yes.'

'Then . . . But, of course, you did not look.'

'Not look? *Not look*?'

'A gentleman would have—'

'A gentleman would have done what I did. Stared and stared, transfixed, bewitched, enchanted, unable to believe what he saw.'

'You,' I muttered miserably, 'you horrible peeping Tom.'

I remembered my luxurious abandon. I remembered stretching my arms above my head. I remembered splaying my legs wide, to dry between them. I remembered gazing down at my own white naked body, with the swell of breasts, and the nipples awakened by the cold water, and the secret triangle of raven-black hair . . .

I cringed in one enveloping, agonizing blush.

'You are unforgivable,' I muttered.

'Oh Katie,' he said gently, 'I should have looked away, but I could not. Your body is the most beautiful thing I have ever seen. If I am blinded now, I shall still be far luckier than any other man, because I have seen you lying in the sun. Look at me, Katie!'

I would not. I could not. I writhed to think how I had behaved under his appraising eye. I wanted the rocks to split. I wanted to fall into a deep pit, and be hidden from his eyes and from all eyes under a million tons of earth.

I had lain. He had looked.

Suddenly, into my embarrassment and misery, a new feeling crept. I could not tell, for a moment, what it was that I felt.

Then I identified the feeling, and I almost fainted with shock at myself.

I felt a sort of glee. I felt proud. I felt excited.

I had *never* expected to entertain such a thought.

I stood tense, rigid, staring into nothing, my back to him, violently aware that he was only two paces away. I felt a hand, very gently, touch my head. I jerked and recoiled, as though I had been stung by a hornet. My feelings were in such turmoil that I could not have spoken, or taken a step, to save my neck from an axe. I felt as though all the fury of the river were rushing through my head and my stomach; I felt that I was drowning.

There was only one person who could save me. So I turned and threw my arms round his neck. I felt his arms go about my body, and hold me until I was near crushed and breathless against him. I clung to him as though for salvation. And I was safe.

Safe, but almost swooning, as his cheek was pressed to mine, and as he began to kiss my brow and eyes, and the tip of my nose, and my chin, and at last my lips; and somehow my mouth was open under his, and our tongues met.

And somehow, without my knowing how it happened, we were no longer standing on the sward, but sitting, and then lying, passionately embracing. I stroked his head and he mine; he kissed every part of my face, and I every part of his. I felt him gently caressing my body, my hips and my breasts, and I trembled at the touch through my cotton clothes.

And then, through the swirling mists of my self-forgetting passion, I heard the last sound that I ever expected to hear from him: a sob. I opened my eyes, and looked at him in wonder: and there were tears in his eyes. And then I lay above him, and held his face in my hands, and kissed his tears away.

'Oh Katie, my very darling,' he murmured at last into my hair. 'I love you. Oh God, how much I love you.'

'I love you,' I said.

The words, in a voice I did not recognize, were like a flood-gate suddenly raised, to release a new torrent of passion. We kissed and murmured in each other's arms, and it was I who sobbed, and it was my eyes which spilled tears onto his dear cheeks.

We became a little more sensible at last, but not very much more. We still lay where we had happened to lie, on the sweet turf, in each other's arms, but we could talk in connected sentences.

Robbie said, stroking my cheek with one hand, while my head rested on his other arm, 'I won't talk about your body any more, my dearest love, because I shall go mad if I let myself think about it.'

'I might go mad, too,' I admitted.

'I have not forgotten everything that Mr Archibald Scott tried to teach me.'

'Must you be a gentleman?' I asked, not at all ashamed at my shamelessness; for this was Eilean Fitheach, where the rules and customs of the world did not apply.

'Not for ever, my very darling. But now I want to talk about your face. You have – are you listening closely? – a startling, astonishing, unique, incredible face, unlike any other in the world, which is – which is insanely beautiful.'

'Beautiful women,' I said dubiously, 'look like Lady Ravenburn. Everybody says so, everybody who comes to the Castle.'

'Stately, flaxen-haired, with prominent blue eyes, cupid's-bow lips, pink cheeks, capacious bosom?'

'Well, yes, and—'

'And fat hands and arms, and fat legs and knees?'

'Well, rounded, and—'

'That is prettiness. It is ordinary, and insipid. Your beauty is as far above that as the treetops above the floor of the loch, as far as the peregrine's highest gyre above the home of the mole. Your eyes, Katie!'

'Green,' I said despondently.

'A most magical clear bright green, fantastic windows to the spirit behind them.'

'The spirit? Oh, that is a very poor—'

'I'll return to that later. I want to tell you first about your eyebrows.'

He stroked them with a fingertip – first one, and then the other. I kissed his hand as it passed my lips.

He talked about my nose, my cheekbones, my ears, my hair, my lips, my chin, the setting of my head on my neck, my neck

105

itself; and then about my hands and fingers and wrists.

'Am I boring you?' he said, after a long time.

'No,' I said.

He laughed. His chest was pressed close to my breast, and I felt his laugh all through my body.

'If you had nothing but your face and your figure,' he said, 'I should be wild with love for you. But, in every other way . . .'

I hoped he would go on. He did. He spoke about my being quick, and amusing, and making him laugh, and being always the liveliest and most entertaining of companions; he spoke with great approval of my spirit, which made me do such foolhardy things.

I sighed, lying in his arms in the sunshine. I thought about all the things he had said. I thought about all the things the doctors had said. I was, perhaps, a different person on Eilean Fitheach. I was a different person with Robbie. I was cured.

'I think,' I said faintly at last, lying with my arms tight round his neck, 'that it is time I talked about you.'

'No no, I—'

'I have listened very politely to you for about two hours. It is my turn to talk. I do not wish for any interruptions.'

'My darling governess. Great heaven, what a governess!'

'This is rather unprofessional,' I admitted. 'But I asked you not to interrupt. I like your eyes best, except for your nose, and cheeks, and so forth, which I like equally. You are an excellent height, because you can kiss me without bending down too much. You are an excellent weight, because I can drag you into the fresh air when you fall down ladders. You are an excellent salmon poacher, and you tell excellent stories about Australia, although you omit the details that would interest me most. Let me think. There must be more I can say.'

I could not see his face, because my cheek lay on his, but I felt it crease with his smile.

I stayed with him on Eilean Fitheach for another two hours – I dared not stay longer, as things were at Ravenburn. It seemed that, all that time, we could not keep our hands from each other – we must be always touching hands, or putting out a finger to a cheek, or kissing. If our kisses that day could be counted, the stars would fall out of the heavens, in very shame at being so greatly outnumbered.

He could have done with me anything that he chose, and well

106

he knew it. I was fathoms deep in love with him, and well he knew it. But, though he kissed me passionately, and caressed my body outside my clothes, he did no more.

I was speechless with relief, and wild with disappointment.

'Oh Katie, my precious girl,' he said, 'I have never loved like this before. I have never known anyone like you before. I have never felt a millionth part of what I feel now.'

'That is not very loyal to the memory of Violet,' I said, 'But I will pretend to believe you, because it is nice to hear.'

'I want to walk a yard behind you, wherever you go, for the rest of your life, to stop the rain falling on you, or the wind blustering at you.'

'But I like the rain and wind,' I said. 'Won't you walk beside me, instead of behind me?'

He said that he would, and I tore myself away.

I undressed, and washed myself, and brushed my hair.

I was conscious, as never before, of my face and body. I was me. 'I am Katie. I am Katie. I am myself. I am not quite like anybody else.' I stared at myself in the glass, as intently as ever Malvina did. When I took off my grubby island clothes, I stared at myself as intently as Robbie had stared at me. I felt a strange, uneasy, trembling sensation. It was the same flesh and bones as in the morning, enveloped in the same pale skin. I was the same person, with the same face and body, as in the morning. I saw the green eyes, the heavy straight eyebrows, the aquiline look of nose and cheekbones. I was the same, no better than before, no different.

I had thought myself handsome, though eclipsed at Ravenburn by the flaxen beauty, the delicious curves, of Malvina and Mamma. Now I knew that I was beautiful. I saw that I was beautiful. I was loved by an adorable and fascinating man, who had been to far places and known a thousand women.

What was I? Who was I?

'I am Katie. I am Katie.' I was a little governess, of most obscure background, head over heels in love with a foundling from a Glasgow slum. That was real. They said I was the Honourable Katharine Irvine of Ravenburn. That was a bad joke.

Who was I? What did I truly look like?

Item, two eyes, indifferent green. Nose, and eyebrows, and so forth. Breasts, and hips, and legs, and so forth. Robbie had gazed at them. Robbie said . . .

My hands trembled as I dressed. When I glanced in the cloudy glass, as I left my bedroom, I saw the smile on my face.

I followed Malvina into the drawing room, and stood by the door as usual, so that I could leave without causing disturbance. I did not see who was in the room. I could not be bothered to look. There was the usual quack of voices. They were all phantoms, half alive. This was a false place. My reality was far elsewhere, and far otherwise.

'Miss Katharine,' said a pleasant voice at my shoulder. 'How well you look.'

I turned, knowing the voice, delighted to hear it.

Lord Killin looked well, too – browner than before from the sun. He looked cheerful, smiling with great warmth, as though ready any second to burst into laughter.

We shook hands. He said that he had come before his expected time, because some other arrangements had broken down. He told me about the sport he had been having on various rivers, making it appear that he had been the most ludicrous fumbler. He told me also about trouble he had been put to, on one of his own estates, making it appear that he was a helpless ninny, at the mercy of any rogue. He made me laugh very much.

I caught Mamma's eyes upon me as I laughed. Her eyebrows were raised, and her face pained. Perhaps my laugh *was* unmusical. I fought to control my mirth, and faced Lord Killin with maidenly solemnity.

'And for yourself?' he said.

'Oh – my life goes on as it has always gone on. Which is what I want, you know. It is what is best.'

'Extensive reading?'

'N-no. It is hard to be indoors, just now.'

'So I find. And abroad? Still wedded to the spyglass?'

'It is better,' I said, 'than no marriage at all.'

He laughed, but glanced at me keenly. '*Something* has happened to you, Miss Katie.'

'I found a lucky horseshoe.'

'I believe in magic,' he said, half seriously. 'I was brought up in the Highlands. My nurse came from the Western Isles. Of course I believe in magic. Was the horseshoe made of fairy gold?'

'Yes,' I said, 'I think it was.'

'That would help, no doubt. But I do not think it is all you have found. I watched you, some weeks ago, entering this room, as you have just done, in the wake of your little sister.'

'You watched me, when Malvina was coming into the room?'

'I have never had a taste for the obvious. I watched you, and saw—'

'A funny little bookworm.'

'You exaggerate. I saw a lovely young lady, but one whose shoulders drooped. Whose back sagged. I am not at all certain that your toes did not point together.'

'Oh no!'

'I am very much afraid they did. Frankness, between friends! Not too much, though – I don't want any frank remarks about myself. That would be quite a different thing. We are discussing your appearance, in this room, on my previous visit. You looked – how can I put it? – like a yearling filly, well bred but ill broken, awkward, unhappy, ill at ease. And your face was closed. It looked like a shuttered house. You looked like *this*.'

He sagged as he stood, drooped his shoulders, pointed his toes inwards, and put on an expression of bored stupidity.

I laughed, but ruefully. What he said was what Mamma had been saying, ever since I could remember.

'But when you came in just now,' said Lord Killin, 'I had difficulty in recognizing you. You came in like a queen, your head high, your eye bright, your chin arrogantly tilted—'

'Arrogantly?' I asked, unnerved by this formidable word.

'The arrogance of the angle of your chin,' Lord Killin assured me, 'would have been absurd, even insufferable, in a young lady less startlingly beautiful. But it suits you to admiration. *Never* allow your chin to sag again! *Never* allow your shoulders to droop! When you stand as you stood just now – don't sag, Katie! – one could appreciate not only the masterful personality, radiating well-justified confidence—'

'But I – I—'

'But also the classic perfection of face and figure. I hope I am not disagreeably personal?'

'No,' I said.

'I used to think of you as a lovely lost opportunity. I thought

109

so when I first saw you, with Lady Aberfeldy, among the peat-hags. I revise that view. You are now, I imagine, a serious menace to the established order. If I were a wife, I would blindfold my husband. If I were a husband, I would blindfold my wife, before she perished of jealous mortification. If I could only give you an idea of how you looked, standing by the door!'

'You could try,' I suggested anxiously.

'I saw a queen. An empress! Superbly confident. sublimely aware of beauty, desirability. Standing gloriously tall, but without stiffness – I hate stiff ladies, you know—'

'You like ladies to be malleable, my Lord?'

'Let us say, flexible . . . I don't think you would have said a thing like that, a month ago.'

'Oh. It was not so very pert, was it? Or such a very strange word? I was only interested in the answer.'

'I was interested in the question – in the fact that you asked it, showing an adult social confidence which, a few weeks ago . . . I will tell you an extraordinary thing, Miss Katharine Irvine.'

'If you think you should, Lord Killin.'

'I top you by inches. Yet, when you survey me through those astonishing green lakes of light, I get the overwhelming impression that you are looking down at me. I think I should add that your smile, which seems to appear more frequently than heretofore, is the most attractive I have ever seen. I would have supposed that your face in repose was incapable of improvement. But, seeing your smile, I would have been proved wrong. Pedantry does not allow the concept of perfection being improved. Pedantry is thrown into baffled dismay by your smile, my dear Miss Katie, because—'

'Charles!' called Mamma from the other end of the room. 'You are to be Mr Acres in *The Rivals.*'

'I hate to be disobliging,' he murmured to me, 'but sometimes one must do things one hates. I will not be Mr Acres in *The Rivals.*'

'Good,' I said, for I did not like to think of him part of anything so stupid.

He left me, to join the crowd round Mamma.

I left the room, with much to think about.

'Lord Killin is to be Mr What's-his-name,' said Malvina, sitting up in bed with her breakfast. 'I am glad. We do not have a scene together, so I will ask Uncle Frank to write one in. He can kiss me, instead of Sir Malcolm Rattray.'

'Lord Killin is ... Are you sure, Malvina?'

Malvina did not answer me, as her mouth was full of egg.

'Not shocked, exactly,' I said that afternoon in the drawing room, 'but surprised.'

'No more so than I,' said Lord Killin. 'But I allowed myself to be persuaded.'

'By Mamma?'

'Hers was one of the voices to which I heeded.'

'Yes. She hopes ...'

'I can guess some of the things that she hopes. What in particular?'

'That – that a lot of Dukes and Marquesses will come to the play ... Since you are to be here, I wonder if you can help?'

'Help you? Need you ask?'

'Oh, I need no help,' I assured him. 'I am already ... It is another problem.' I told him about Wilson, and Murdo MacKenzie, and Malvina.

He looked solemn, though not very solemn. 'Defying Isabella has proved difficult. Defying Malvina would be impossible.'

'Perhaps if you consented to kiss her, in the play?'

'I don't *want* to kiss her.'

'Oh. She thinks you do.'

'My kisses are carefully hoarded. They are not prodigally strewn abroad. The recipients are few in number and exceptional in quality. Malvina does not qualify.'

'Everyone says she is angelically beautiful.'

'Her mother's friends say so, for obvious reasons. Malvina will be fat in a few years. She eats too much, and never takes a step of exercise. I like—' he glanced at me – 'active, lithe, unencumbered women. I like wood-nymphs, not lolling goddesses. I prefer dark hair, too.'

Mamma interrupted him, calling him over to her. He sighed comically to me, as he went; but he went.

It was decided, at length, who should do what in *The Rivals*, and Uncle Frank began to call rehearsals. The routine of the Castle was entirely subordinated to them. It was all very exciting for everybody; Sir Malcolm Rattray was in ecstasies. The grim Frenchwoman and her seamstresses set about the huge task of Mamma's costumes.

Mrs Seton continued implacably hostile, on moral grounds. But she did not leave Ravenburn.

I was called upon to help Sir Malcolm with his lines, and Miss Serena Wood, and Colonel Blair, as well as Malvina. I was called upon to help Mme Duplage with Mamma's amazing dresses. I could not get away from the Castle.

I could not get away to my island. I was ill with yearning to go there.

'I know you still think it deplorable,' said Lord Killin, 'that I consented to take part in this charade.'

'Well,' I said, 'many people like ... Sir Malcolm, for example, is ...'

'Had I refused,' he said, 'I could have stayed here at Ravenburn for ten days, perhaps. A fishing invitation can hardly extend beyond that. As it is, I can go away for a day or two if need be, but I can be here, unquestioned, expected, welcome, for weeks and months.'

'Yes, you can,' I said, 'but why ever do you want to be here?'

'My beautiful goose, can't you see?'

'No.'

'Because,' said Lord Killin, smiling, but with a new sort of nervousness that made him seem much younger, 'because I want to be where you are. I want to be with you. I want you. That's why I'm staying – the only thing that could make me. That's why I'm joining in the play. It gives me an excuse I could hardly have dreamed of, to be here, to see you as much as possible. I love you, Katie. I loved you before, without altogether realizing it. I loved you among the peat-hags, with mud all over your face. Then, when I saw you come into the drawing-room, with an aloof smile and the bearing of an empress, my heart gave such a lurch that I nearly dropped my teacup. I *did* drop a piece of Dundee cake. That will show you the state of my heart, because I am very fond of Dundee cake. I love you Katie.'

seven

It was funny, sad, amazing, deeply gratifying, ridiculous, exciting and ironic.

My smile aloof, was it? And my chin at an arrogant angle? I radiated confidence? I stood like a . . .? Well, Lord Killin said an empress.

Of course I did! Robbie had kissed me, and said he loved me. I looked different, because I was different. Oh, I was the same – all the same flesh and bones, inside the same pale envelope of skin – but I was different. Robbie had changed me. I was the same, but after his kisses I would never be the same again.

Lord Killin admired me, simply because of what Robbie had done to me. That was the funny part. He would never have admired me so much, but for what Robbie had done. That was the sad part. That such a great man should want me, even after what Robbie had done, was the amazing part. It was also the deeply gratifying, ridiculous and exciting part. And the irony was this: if I had never known Robbie, I would have thought Lord Killin the most wonderful man in the world. But, if I had never known Robbie, Killin would scarcely have taken a second glance at me. I would still have been – what was it he said? – a lost opportunity. I would still have been a creature with sagging shoulders, and shuttered eyes. My toes, I suppose, would still have pointed inwards.

'I have written to Lady Victoria,' said Lord Killin. 'She is writing to Lady Ravenburn. She will come here when she can.'

'Oh good!' I said. 'When?'

'I don't know. When other Crusades permit. I think she will *not* take a part in *The Rivals.* George Fraser is also highly anxious to return.'

'Oh,' I said, without enthusiasm.

'He is shy, poor fellow, as I am sure you realize. But don't underestimate his goodwill.'

'Uncle Frank does.'

'Yes, I'm afraid your Uncle Frank does. They are not altogether in sympathy. *Le coeur ne choit pas son goût.*'

'That is quite true . . . Who said that?'

'Well, it might have been Pascal, but I think it was myself. A *pensèe* sounds better in French, don't you think? Especially if you call it a *pensèe*. It acquires wisdom. It has more weight. Latin, of course, would be weightier still. *Cor gustatum non eliget,* which might be Juvenal, or even Cicero, but I don't think it is. As to Greek—'

'Spare me the Greek,' I said. 'Anyone hearing us would think I was a bookworm.'

'I will spare you the Greek,' he said, 'because I have forgotten it. We need George Fraser. Or your brother's reverend tutor, with whom, as it happens, I must have a serious conversation . . .'

I drew my head back a short way from Robbie's, and said, 'I don't wish to question my good luck—'

'Then don't,' he relied promptly.

'But the better I know you, the more surprised I am that you're here.'

'Are you, my sweet?'

'Well, of course I am! You must see yourself how odd it is. You, so clever, and witty, and handsome, and travelled, and learned, and so forth – why do you hide in a ruined castle, living with a nanny-goat and a clinging owl?'

'I could not bring myself,' he said solemnly, 'to leave my goat.'

'You could take her with you.'

'To Edinburgh parlours?'

'Well, that is where you should be.'

'Of course you're right, in a way. I should be making up for the follies of my youth, by pursuing a useful career. Well, I might have gone long since, in spite of Rory Beg and his news. But now, *nothing* would prise me away. I have stayed, I stay now, I shall stay, because of you.'

'Oh,' I said, deeply pleased. 'That is lucky. If you went, I should have to follow, and I have no money for travelling . . .'

Robbie never tired of telling me how beautiful I was. I never tired of listening to him. He was fascinating on all topics, but that was my favourite.

'You ought to stop,' I said. 'I hope you won't, but you ought to. You are making me insufferably conceited.'

'I want you insufferably conceited,' said Robbie. 'I want you to go into a crowded room, and say to yourself, "I am the most beautiful woman here. These people are lucky to be looking at me." '

I laughed. I believed him. I was appallingly conceited.

Robbie's word was my law, so I obeyed him. I went into the drawing room, after tea, behind Malvina. I said to myself, 'I am the most beautiful woman here. These people are lucky to be looking at me.'

Lord Killin, who was listening to Mamma, turned to stare at me. By his face, I thought he was no longer listening.

Colonel Blair darted forward, tugging at his whiskers. He was heavily gallant. His breath smelled of cigars, but his compliments were amusing to listen to.

I was avid for praise. I lapped it up, like a kitten at a cream bowl. It was childish of me, very undiscriminating, really very vulgar. My excuse is, that it was new to me. I was like a child being given chocolates for the first time.

My chin, I am sure, was at a most arrogant angle.

I came on Lord Killin in the library, talking to Jamie's tutor the Reverent Walter Willis. Their voices were low and their expressions solemn.

'I am sorry,' I said, beginning to leave. 'I am interrupting you.'

'No indeed!' cried Mr Willis. 'Not the least in the world! In your own library! . . .'

'We did have something to discuss, Mr Willis and I,' said Lord Killin, 'but we have sufficiently discussed it. He has confirmed, from expert knowledge, some ideas of my own. We can turn to lighter topics.'

We did, and the three of us chatted for a time. Lord Killin was very friendly to the pale and embarrassed tutor.

At length Lord Killin said, 'Willis, where is that Bible you spoke of?'

'On the shelf on the left of the fireplace, down at the bottom where the largest volumes are.'

'Oh yes.'

Lord Killin crossed the room briskly, knelt down, and pulled out a huge leather-bound book. He blew the dust away, and opened the book on the floor.

'I do possess a Bible of my own,' he said. 'Please don't think that I am obliged to consult this one because there is no other available. Nor that my eyes are incapable, like Lady Ravenburn's, of reading small print. But this is a family Bible – the Irvine family Bible. It may contain a record ... Many people, you know, enter family dates in their Bibles. Births, baptisms, confirmations, marriages, deaths. I wonder if the late Lord Ravenburn did so?'

'My papa?' I asked. 'That was actually his Bible?'

'Yes, of course, in this library ... Ah!'

'Are you trying to find out how old I am?' I said. 'Because that is ungallant. Anyway, it is no secret.'

'Yes, Katie. I am sorry if it is ungallant, but that is one of the things I am trying to find out.'

He frowned at the fly-leaf of the Bible. It seemed a curious way to spend a fine afternoon.

After a time he shrugged, and put the Bible back in the shelf.

'No help,' he said. 'My late and very dear old friend was *not* an orderly man. When things needed to be written down, he left it to someone else to write them. But the entries in his Bible were a task he forgot to delegate. What a pity. I am called to a rehearsal in half an hour's time, Katie – will you walk with me until then?'

'Yes,' I said.

'The Reverend Walter Willis,' said Lord Killin, ten minutes later in the park, 'has a misfortune in his family, which he has been telling me about.'

'I am sorry.'

'I also. He is a gentle and learned creature, who should have an appointment far more congenial than this one ... This misfortune is a sister whose nerves are ... who is obliged, on medical instruction, to lead a very quiet life.'

'Oh yes,' I said drably. 'Many families have a misfortune of that kind.'

'Forgive me if I wound you. That is the last thing in the world I wish to do.'

'Then talk of something else, for the love of Heaven!'

'I am very sorry, Katie. You are angry with me, for my tactlessness and clumsiness. Forgive me. What shall we talk about?'

But I left him, and went indoors. I had almost forgotten, in

116

Robbie's arms and in Killin's admiration, that I was the misfortune of Ravenburn.

I still lied to Robbie, but it was no longer a lie. In his arms, I was Katie Maitland, the little governess, bookish, interested in natural history, with a certain wild tomboy streak that sent me poaching at midnight, loving him completely with all my soul and body. That was the truth, when his arms were about me.

I never thought of the future, but lived in the delirious present. In the present – on those occasional stolen sun-drenched days on the island – I was Robbie's love, and that was all I was.

But walking with Lord Killin by the Raven burn, I was the Honourable Katharine Irvine of Ravenburn Castle, eldest surviving child of one very rich lord, courted with laughter and gentleness by another. This aristocratic person was, as it happened, bookish, and interested in natural history; and she had a certain wild tomboy streak. She did not quite love anybody, but she viewed Lord Killin with gratitude and respect and affection (when he did not talk about family misfortunes); she found him endlessly rewarding company; she basked in his admiration; she laughed loud and long at his jokes.

This proper young lady, walking by the burnside, did sometimes think about the future. Lord Killin constantly invited her to do so, and painted it in highly attractive colours. His home was beautiful, his fortune large, his friends the most delightful people in three kingdoms. He was kind, droll, and sufficiently handsome. And he was in love. Banteringly, self-mockingly, often with absurd loquacity: but he said, and I believed him, that he was truly and deeply in love.

To the Honourable Katharine Irvine, waking up from her island dreams, Lord Killin was the best of all conceivable futures. And it was very flattering to be loved by him.

It seems strange, in retrospect, that I was able to live two lives and keep my sanity. The Edinburgh doctors could hardly have approved of the stress to my mind and to my nerves. The reason was, I think, that I *was* two people, who might chance to have much in common, but scarcely overlapped. The abandoned little governess on Eilean Fitheach would never have addressed a word to Lord Killin. The young lady in the Castle would have fled, in well-bred dismay, from the Glasgow foundling.

*

Lord Killin was in hot pursuit of me. He said he was, and it was most evidently true. I sometimes stood back amazed at this fact, but fact it was.

But he was very discreet about it. He said he regretted the necessity: but he never took my hand, or praised my beauty, when anyone else was by. In public, he treated me with casual friendliness – an older man, a family friend, kind to the unfortunate daughter of the house.

He flirted with Mamma, and sometimes even with Miss Serena Wood. He said he regretted the necessity of that, too.

My miniature was stolen – the miniature of my mother, on the mantelpiece of my bedroom. I was distraught. I screamed at Flora Morran. Her big red face crumpled with outrage. She was not a thief. I knew it. I begged her pardon for shouting at her, but she was not pacified.

I told Uncle Frank. He said he would have the bedrooms of the servants searched. The sense of outrage, of unjustified suspicion, spread outwards and downwards from Flora Morran, and into every cranny of the Castle. There was a very disagreeable atmosphere. Some of the maids and footmen looked at me as though it were my fault. Mamma thought it *was* my fault. She hated clamour, and this was a loud clamour.

There was no trace of the miniature. No servant, except Flora Morran, had been seen going up into the East Tower. No one admitted to having been there. Jamie thought it all a great fuss over nothing, because the miniature had little value, except to me.

Uncle Frank said he could think of no more he could do. No servants were dismissed, because none could be suspected. But it was horrid to think that there was a thief among them.

'When will you take me poaching again?' I asked Robbie.

'I won't.'

'But you must!'

'Do you realize what those keepers did? Things were so confused at the time that I didn't think about it properly. But since then I have woken up in the night and trembled. My darling child, they *fired* at you! They fired at *you!*'

'You said yourself,' I said hopefully, 'that with a pistol, in the dark, at long range, with a moving target—'

118

'Lucky shots in the dark have killed or wounded before now. I will *not* take you poaching again. It is war, you see.'

'A poaching war? Like in the old days, in my grandfather's time?'

'No, not at all. It is worse than that. It is a man-hunt.'

'For you?'

'Nobody knows I exist. I am an executor, an agent, a nameless nothing. I am not worth hunting. At least, if I am, nobody knows where to hunt.'

'Who, then?'

'Rory Beg.'

'Rory Beg,' I repeated blankly.

'He was a friend of Tom's. I imagine you didn't know that, but there are those who know it well. Therefore, he is a friend of any friend of Tom's. They know that, too. Tom's friend, Tom's agent, needs the help of Rory Beg, and that help is freely given because of the love which Rory Beg bore Tom. All this they know, so they're hunting him. If they catch him, he can help us no more—'

'Us?'

'If he is killed,' said Robbie, ignoring my interruption, 'it will be by a keeper in self-defence. Rory Beg has a bad reputation. I'm bound to say, he's done a good deal to earn it. No jury would convict a keeper who shot him. I doubt if charges would be brought. I am worried for him. I don't think he knows the danger he runs.'

'I don't understand. What is he doing? For whom? Who is "us"? Why is Rory Beg in danger for doing – whatever he is doing?'

'I can't tell you, Katie. It's better you don't know. It's not my secret only.'

'You aren't staying here because of me,' I said. 'You're staying because of ... because of a conspiracy, I think, to rob the bank in Lochgrannomhead. Or put a Pretender on the throne of an independent Scotland. Or avenge the Hargues.'

'I would like to do that. They have been so very hospitable.'

'They have taken you to their hearts.'

'No, you.'

'No, you.'

We had a bitter and prolonged argument about which of us was the more beloved of the Hargues, and Robbie made me laugh until my ribs ached. Then he kissed me until I felt ill with love for him.

I forgot about his secret conspiracies, and the pistol in the dark, and the danger to Rory Beg.

Lord Killin was frowning, which was as unusual with him as it was with Uncle Frank.

'I have had a letter from George Fraser,' he said quietly to me.

'From the Hebrides? Or from Lochgrannomhead?'

'From – it does not matter whence. He dictated the letter, to an obliging dominie.'

'Why? I would have thought he wrote—'

'Because his arm is broken.'

'Oh. I am sorry.'

'His horse came down. He says he could see no reason for it to do so. That is all he says, on that score, because of the dominie taking his dictation. But I think I can read between the lines. I think the worm is turning. This settles it.' Killin tapped the letter thoughtfully against his thumb. 'I must go away for a few days.'

'What about your rehearsals?'

'Dundas calls an entirely unnecessary number of rehearsals.'

'Not unnecessary for Malvina, or Serena Wood, or Colonel Blair.'

'No.' He laughed shortly. 'But I will not go until my place here is taken.'

I looked at him stupidly.

'Lady Victoria Arlington is on her way,' said Killin. 'When she arrives, I will leave.'

'Well,' I said, 'of course I am glad you are staying here until she comes. But I do not see why you *must* stay until she comes.'

'This accident to George Fraser makes me feel careful and frightened.'

'Frightened, Charles? I can't believe you are ever frightened.'

'Oh yes I am,' he said. 'I am frightened for myself. I am frightened for you.'

Lady Victoria came ten days later, neat and active and lively and lovely, flute-voiced, very friendly to me. I was very glad to see her again.

She walked, with Lord Killin and me, by the burn and down to the lochside.

'So you are strutting and fretting your hour upon the stage, Charles,' she said.

'Yes. It is highly convenient.'

She nodded. I wondered if she knew why Lord Killin was staying so long at Ravenburn. Since they were such old friends, he might have told her what he felt about me. Since they were such old friends, she might have guessed. I did not think she was a person it would be easy to keep things from.

I would have to keep the island from her. She would not approve of my love for a Glasgow foundling. She would not tell anybody, perhaps. But she would do her best, because she liked me, to stop me committing such destructive and suicidal folly. Her best would be all too good. I vowed to be very, very careful with Lady Victoria.

'This is a curious business,' she was saying to Killin, 'about poor George.'

'Yes. It's why I must leave. But it's why I wouldn't leave until you came.'

'I think that was right. This chase has turned out more dangerous than foxhunting.'

'Than flying raspers with the Cottesmore, as old Blair so often boasts he does – yes. And the innocent will suffer.'

'The innocent,' said Lady Victoria, glancing in my direction, 'have suffered too much already. Lord! The Elizabeth Fry streak has dominated me, until now, in this affair. But I feel a twinge of Boadicea coming on.'

'Strap the scythes to your chariot-wheels, Victoria,' said Killin. 'We shall need them . . . I'm sorry, Katie. This is double-Dutch to you. You'll know all about it one day, but we daren't tell you yet. Not only for your own sake, but also because it is not our secret.'

'People keep saying that to me,' I said. 'I am sure it is well meant, but like most well-meant things it is maddening.'

'*Who* says that to you?'

'I think it was . . . Miss Maitland.'

'Shall you see George?' Lady Victoria asked Killin.

'Yes, of course. That is the reason I am going away. I want to know what happened.'

'It is obvious what happened.'

'I want to know what they were trying to do.'

'That is equally obvious.'

'Yes. I never expected to get involved in anything so – primitive. We are like characters in *Macbeth*, with the first and second and third murderers behind every bush. I wish we could call in the law, and have done—'

'With only wild suspicions of respectable people?'

'I know. We should make gigantic fools of ourselves, and lay ourselves open to gigantic damages for slander—'

'And fail.'

'And fail,' said Killin. 'Meanwhile, George probably knows by now more than he's had a chance to tell us. If so, I must hear it from him. I think there must be more wrong with him than a broken arm – that wouldn't keep him bedridden.'

'Where does Dundas think you're going?'

Killin glanced at me before saying, 'I have no secrets from Dundas. He and his sister are my very good friends.'

Lady Victoria nodded, looking out over the loch.

If the angle of my chin was arrogant, the angle of hers made her look like a small avenging fury.

'Goodbye, my very dear Katie,' said Killin. 'One day everything will come right. One day you will know everything. Trust Victoria.'

'I do.'

'Trust me.'

'I do, Charles.'

He bent and kissed me on the forehead, taking me utterly by surprise; then he turned away and hurried towards his carriage.

Would I have shrunk from his kiss, or prevented it, if he had given me the chance? Would the Honourable Katharine Irvine of Ravenburn have forbidden the advances of Lord Killin, because little Katie Maitland the governess was used to kissing her Glasgow foundling?

The question was academic, because I had not expected his kiss. But it filled my confused brain, and troubled my confused heart.

It was only later that the thought struck me: Lord Killin's first kiss had landed on exactly the same target, on my forehead, as Robbie's first kiss.

It was as though they were in league.

'Your little sister,' said Lady Victoria, 'is a freak.'

She was sitting in the cane armchair in my bleak little school-room (where Miss Anderson had always sat). She looked like a rare flower transplanted into the shabby back-garden of a cottage.

'Malvina a freak?' I said. 'A freak angel?'

'At her age,' said Lady Victoria, 'I was an almost absurdly normal child. It was a grief to my Mamma, who thought that a Duke's daughter should be visibly different. But, try as I might, I was *no* different from other thirteen-year-old girls. I have become in some ways unusual since that time – which is another source of grief to my Mamma – but I was not in the least unusual then. This is not fancy. I knew dozens, scores, of girls of my own age. They clustered round me, the British social order being what it is – or rather, their mothers clustered round mine. Knowing them. I knew I was one of them. As I say, almost offensively normal. You sometimes read, in political utterances of "the average man". I have never met this person, and I sometimes doubt if he exists. But the average thirteen-year-old girl – oh, she exists. She is horribly numerous, and quite dreadful.'

I laughed, and asked about her.

'Her principal quality is shyness,' said Lady Victoria. 'It goes with uncertainty, lack of confidence. These things make her gauche and often *farouche*. She is abrupt. She answers questions in monosyllables, avoiding the eye of the questioner. Because, you see, even if she is inclined to like other people, she is dreadfully uncertain of her effect on them. This makes her unwilling to – what is that awful masculine phrase – unwilling to stick her neck out, to chance her social arm. It makes her silent, and anxious to avoid notice. She is apt to be nearly sure, nearly all the time, that people are laughing at her cruelly. That, or pitying her, which is worse. She is nearly sure they *ought* to be laughing at her, or pitying her.'

'Perhaps she's right?' I suggested.

'No, not at all. Now – she's aware of growing up, often in painful and embarrassing ways, but she feels an infinite distance from being grown up. She is caught between child and adult – often for years. Part of her longs to bolt back into the safety of the nursery – so, as a matter of fact, she often *does* bolt back into the safety of the nursery. She is convinced she is ugly. She is convinced she is boring. Her body seems to consist of knees and elbows, which knock into small tables on which valuable china ornaments are resting. If she is physically precocious, she is miserably aware of her bosom. If she is not, she is miserably aware of its absence. Large assemblages of grown-up people are a nightmare to her. She would far rather be left alone with a book, in the sanctuary of the schoolroom, or out of doors, or with her pets, or with servants who make no demands on her.'

'Th— this is,' I stammered, 'a *normal* girl you are talking about?'

'Yes, certainly. I will tell you some more things about her. She feels she is not understood, least of all by her immediate family. She feels she is isolated, among enemies, or at least people of doubtful neutrality. She feels she is betrayed. She sometimes feels so different from the creatures round her, that she wonders if she is some kind of pathetic monster, some sport of nature—'

'Th— this is *still* a normal girl?'

'I am describing myself at Malvina's age, Katie. Faithfully and exactly describing myself. And the majority of the girls of the same age that I knew. Not all, of course. There *were* Malvinas, as I suppose there always will be – precocious little madames, with social graces and infinite confidence. Freaks, the lot of them. It's *unnatural,* at the age of thirteen, to sail into a drawing room, distributing smiles, certain of being admired.'

I stared at Lady Victoria. I have an uncomfortable feeling that my mouth dropped open, out of sheer amazement.

What she was saying exploded bombs inside my head. Yet she spoke with the authority which swayed Committees, and sent Home Secretaries back to their desks with new convictions.

She went on calmly, in that cool flute-voice, 'In some ways, of course, it is nice to know one is exceptional. I am, on account of my taste for politics and meddling. You are, on account of being so beautiful. But it is also nice to know that one is normal. Which you also are, and always have been.'

'B-but ... people have said ...'

'I am very angry when I think of what they have said. To you, and not only to you. Do you remember my Aunt Mariota?'

'Lady Aberfeldy?' I shuddered at the terrifying memory. 'She was very shocked at my clothes.'

'She will be a lot more shocked at some other things, which I am going to tell her in a letter this evening ... Oh, by the bye, you can do someone a favour, Katie.'

'Can I?' I said dubiously. I could think of few favours anyone would want from me.

'Madame Duplage wants your measurements.'

'Who? Oh – the grim lady who is making Mamma's gowns for the play. She wants *what*?'

'She wants to make a new dummy, a lay-figure, you know, for dresses for a *jeune ingénue*. She saw you walking with Charles Killin, and said you were the right size. You don't mind, do you? It will not take long, and it will be a favour to her.'

'Of course I don't mind.'

'I will send her up, then.'

'But Mamma's gowns ... Is not Madame Duplage fully occupied?'

'She is entitled,' said Lady Victoria, 'to a change. To a shorter walk round hips and bosom.'

I was amused at the thought of being a model for a dressmaker's dummy. But I was surprised that Mme Duplage had many customers of my unfashionable shape.

She came and measured me with great brusqueness, chanting numbers to one of her little seamstresses.

When she left my schoolroom, she turned in the door to stare at me. There was something so coldly appraising in her look, that I stared back defiantly. I daresay my chin was at a *very* arrogant angle. Suddenly she nodded about thirty times, very quickly, so that the flesh of her cheeks jumped up and down. That was the nearest she came to thanking me.

'Would *you* say I was normal?' I asked earnestly.

'*You*?' Robbie burst out laughing. He was still laughing when he kissed me. 'You mean, usual? Ordinary? Run-of-the-mill? Humdrum? Everyday? Average? Unexceptional? Unremarkable? Dull?'

'Well,' I said, 'you have proved you know a lot of adjectives, but you have not answered my question.'

'Why do you ask me such a demented question?'

'A – a lady who is staying at the Castle told me yesterday that I was normal. I was *extremely* relieved to hear it, because I had got in the way of thinking myself odd. A sort of freak. On account of reading books, you know, and inspecting birds, and so forth. I have told you all about that.'

I had not told him about the doctors. I knew I should do so. But I could not bear him to think ill of me – or to think me ill – and he would scarcely believe in a governess under the care of doctors.

He looked at me thoughtfully, with those very clear and cool grey eyes. 'You got in the way of thinking yourself odd, because you read books and looked at birds?'

'Not exactly that, but because when I was younger I did not like large assemblies of grown-up people, all chattering and mocking, and frightening me into fits. But she said yesterday that it was normal, when one was young, to be very shy in a company of people.'

'Of course it's normal. It's true of boys, as well as girls. Who is this intelligent friend of yours?'

'Not a friend. She is called Lady Victoria Arlington.'

'Oh – you mentioned her before, I think. You do hobnob with the great in the Castle, then?'

'Oh no, not at all! But – hum – I think Lady Victoria is *so* great, that she does not mind being seen talking to a governess.'

'I understand perfectly. What I don't understand is why she stays in such a place, with such tawdry people.'

'*Tawdry* – that is a truly awful word. I don't think you should use it, when you haven't even seen them.'

'I have, through your eyes. You've told me quite enough about them. Lady Victoria sounds quite different. She seems to talk sense. You got in the way of thinking yourself odd. I wonder if you were encouraged to do so?'

'Well,' I said, 'I am beginning to wonder that, too. And I am beginning to wonder why . . .'

'I am tempted,' said Lady Victoria, 'to eavesdrop on a rehearsal, but I think I shall be strong willed, and wait for the performance. I shall get the full beauty then.'

'You will be here for the performance?' I said, much surprised. 'That is courting punishment.'

'I shall be here, and my Aunt Mariota will be here.'

'Good gracious,' I said. 'Mamma *will* be pleased.'

'I wonder,' said Lady Victoria.

I thought a good deal about what Lady Victoria had said, and about what Robbie had said. I did not see all the implications all at once; but I saw more and more of them.

I had always believed I was a nervous 'case', because I had beeen brought up to believe so. If I felt perfectly well, in mind as in body, it was because I obeyed the doctors, and lived my quiet life, avoiding all excitement. So I had always believed. Who would not?

But now I felt myself being tugged between old and new ideas. The habits of a lifetime cannot be shaken off overnight: but I found myself forced to look with new eyes at the people I had always trusted.

Sometimes anger is a form of self-defence, sometimes a childish indulgence, sometimes a right. I began to wonder if I had not the right to be very, very angry.

And yet – and yet – there remained the opinion of the doctors.

So occupied was I in egotistical thoughts about myself, that it was a day or two before I started pondering about another matter.

Yet it merited pondering.

There were two conspiracies. They were close together – at Ravenburn, and on Eilean Fitheach. I was not to know the details of either, for my own sake. The conspirators would tell me nothing, because in both cases the secret was not theirs alone. In both cases, people had been hurt, or might be. In both things were turning out more dangerous than the conspirators had expected.

It was all too much of a coincidence.

I could not ask Lady Victoria about it, without giving Robbie away. I could not ask Robbie about it directly, without revealing that I was on far closer terms with Lady Victoria, and with Killin, than was possible for Katie Maitland the little governess.

I longed again to be frank with Robbie, and tell him all the truth about myself. But, when he kissed me in greeting, I dared not. He would not ignore the future, as I was deliberately doing.

He would not make love to the Honourable Katharine Irvine of Ravenburn. I would lose him.

I was the abandoned little governess, when I said to him carefully, 'Your friends you told me of, or rather, didn't tell me of, who are helping you, but don't know where you are—'

'Yes?'

'Since you are acting as Tom Irvine's – executor, I think you said—'

'Not in a legal capacity. I am self appointed. The poor fellow did not make a will.'

'Well, since it is on his account that you are here, it seems likely to me that your mysterious friends would go to Ravenburn.'

He looked at me, smiling, surprised. 'I'm sure they would, if they could,' he said, 'but can you imagine Rory Beg in Lady Ravenburn's drawing room?'

'Rory Beg is not your only friend.'

'In a number of important ways he is typical of my friends.'

'Oh . . .' Still more carefully I said, 'Of course, I am not in a position to see, or hear, but there does seem to me to be . . . an atmosphere of . . . well, conspiracy.'

'At Ravenburn?'

'Yes.'

'Among whom?'

'People I have told you of. Lord Killin, and Lady Victoria, and Sir George Fraser.'

'Perhaps Lord Killin is having a passionate affair with Lady Victoria.'

'Oh no!'

'How are you so certain? Do you spy on them?'

'Well, of course, I am *not* certain – and I do *not* spy on them. It is intuition. My intuition is *always* correct. It tells me that Lady Ravenburn is after Lord Killin, only she is too easily exhausted to run after him very fast. Nobody is after Sir George Fraser, because he is not very nice.'

'These are very grand, rich, brilliantly-connected people?'

'Oh yes. Far more so than most of the – what did you call them – tawdry people at Ravenburn. That is to say, as far as *I* am able to judge . . .'

'Do you picture these glorious persons in league with a Glasgow foundling and a notorious poacher?'

'Well – no. All the same, it did strike me as a coincidence.'

'Heaven knows,' said Robbie, 'what people like that would conspire about. Something far outside our sphere, I imagine. I would guess it is either a love-affair, or politics.'

Robbie was speaking absently. He was not interested in the mysterious doings at Ravenburn. They did not affect him; and he was deeply preoccupied with his own concerns, whatever they might be.

But when he kissed me, he did not let his preoccupation come between us.

eight

Lord Killin came back, after an absence of eleven days. He was greeted by Mamma with something approaching energy, by Colonel Blair as his oldest friend, by Sir Malcolm Rattray with jealous despair, by Malvina with her prettiest curtsey, by Miss Serena Wood with a furious blush and a dangerous swaying, by Mrs Seton with a sniff, and by Lady Victoria with an intent, quizzical look.

I expected Killin to have at once a long, confidential conversation with Lady Victoria. I expected him to have one with me, too. But he had one with Uncle Frank.

Uncle Frank did not appear in the drawing-room at tea time, though he rarely missed this cheerful reunion.

Lady Victoria, no doubt, had her conversation with Killin. I had mine, too.

'The angle of your chin, Katie, is beyond praise,' he said.

'Sufficiently arrogant?'

'Just right. You don't want to *over*do it, you know. You are Helen of Troy, not the Empress Catherine of Russia, whose name is usually spelled differently from yours. My little Katie, I have missed you excruciatingly. I have thought about you constantly. I have pictured you all the time. I thought I knew what to expect, when I saw you again, but I am dumbfounded.'

'I am ugly after all?'

'Even more beautiful than I remembered. You have a new look, a new air. What is it? When I left, you had confidence, a growing and glorious awareness of your own loveliness. An awareness, I suppose, of being worshipped, by myself and God knows how many others. Incidentally, has Colonel Blair been making advances to you?'

'Yes.'

'At least he has taste, though, as far as I can see, nothing else whatever to recommend him . . . Never mind about Blair. What is new with you, Katie? What is it that I see? There's a flash in your eyes. A sort of tigrish or pantherine gleam. It suits you *very* well. Is it greed? Shall I give you chocolates? Is it drink? Have you been at the whisky?'

'I think,' I said, 'it is probably anger.'

'Ah. That is *good*. You have been listening to Victoria. I hoped you would. You're learning about yourself, and about other people. That is very good. You're truly growing up. That is the best possible news to me, for I want you completely grown up as soon as possible.'

'Good gracious,' I said. 'Why?'

'So that I can marry you. At this moment, as a conventional preliminary, I would think it apt to kiss you. As a matter of fact, I very deeply want to do so. But I see Mrs Seton observing us – the Admiral of the Home Fleet, or the First Sea Lady, or whatever her rank is. I expect she'd capsize at the sight – start her seams, break up, plunge to the bottom. We must leave it to another time. Meanwhile, be angry, Katie.'

'Have I . . . Things are still very confused in my mind . . . Are things as Victoria hints? And as . . . as I am obliged to guess? Have I the right to be angry?'

'The right? Listen, Katie – you remember how I hurt and annoyed you, by mentioning the Reverend Walter Willis's unfortunate sister, who has all her life been under medical care for a nervous complaint? Well, the point of my examining Willis about it, was that he has had a lifetime of observing a – nervous case. He knows precisely what such unhappy people are like, how they talk, and look, and act. Of course, symptoms may vary widely – what shows in one case may be quite different in another. But he is not a fool, that little man. He has keen observation and keen sympathy. After watching and talking to his sister for all those years, he has watched and talked to you. You understand what I am telling you? Have you the *right* to be angry? Good God, girl, you have the duty.'

Two days later, I was astonished to see Murdo MacKenzie, coming out of Uncle Frank's office in the courtyard. His face was as cheerful as, the last time I saw him, it had been miserable.

I called to him, and he strode across the courtyard to me.

'Ay, Miss Katie,' he said, 'I waur summonit hame frae Glendraco, an' Mr Dundas hae reinstattit me in ma auld poseeshun. Blithe I am tae be back.'

'And Ellen Wilson?'

'Ellen's the blithe lassie, tu! Ye ken, Ellen's sire, auld Angus Wilson, waur threatenit wi' notice o' eveecshun frae the croft, if Ellin didna renoonce oor betrothal. But a's weel the noo! Mr Dundas hae telt me, a whilie syne, that Angus waur safe in yon croft, an' Ellen sud wed me when we wull.'

Wilson's face was transformed. Malvina was inconsolable.

'Charles?' I said. 'Was this your doing?'

'I helped, I think,' he said cheerfully.

'But *how*?'

'Never discount the power of an appeal to a man's better nature.'

'I think that is an evasive answer.'

'But a highly moral one.'

'But—'

'My life offers me few opportunities to moralize, Katie. Don't seek to deprive me of one of them. I am a parson *manqué*, you know. I should like to preach interminable sermons to vast, frightened congregations.'

He would not be serious. He would not tell me what he had said, to change Uncle Frank's mind.

Malvina rushed to Mamma, and whispered long and urgently.

Mamma looked grieved, and called in an exhausted voice to Uncle Frank.

Uncle Frank said sharply, 'You are being selfish and thoughtless, Malvina. Do you expect me to destroy the happiness of two decent people, so that you can have your hair brushed? Let us have no more of this childish whining.'

Malvina was reduced to flabbergasted silence. Her great blue eyes opened so wide that I thought the eyeballs would fall out. Tears fell, instead.

On a thousand previous occasions, Uncle Frank had been reduced by those tears to instant indulgence of Malvina – instant compliance with her wishes. It was a law of nature that he should be – a divine, eternal, immutable law. Now the law was broken. Malvina must have felt like Louis XVI of France, when the Revolutionaries ignored his Divine Right, and chopped off his head.

'But, Frank dear . . .' said Mamma piteously, trying to comfort a sobbing Malvina.

'MacKenzie has my permission to marry Ellen Wilson,' said Uncle Frank. 'And Angus is confirmed in his tenancy. I have given my word, in both regards. I intend to keep it. There is no more to be said.'

'I have not properly thanked you,' I said to Killin. 'It was *extremely* kind of you, to bother yourself about servants you don't know at all. I've never seen two such happy faces. Will you come to the wedding? They would be so pleased. It was *extremely* kind of you.'

'You are pleased with me, Katie?'

I was so pleased with him, and so very grateful to him, that, by way of friendship and thanks, I kissed him impulsively on the cheek.

I felt his arms round me. I felt myself crushed against his body. He was a big, powerful man, much taller than I. I felt like a kitten in the clasp of a bear. Kisses came thundering down on my hair and brow.

I felt him trembling violently. He was saying delightful things in a voice so hoarse and shaky that I could hardly understand him.

I felt great warmth for him. Everything about him had a kind of excellence. His arms were no bad place to be.

Whatever little Katie Maitland might have felt, the Honourable Katharine Irvine of Ravenburn was a very, very lucky young lady.

*

'Why and how?' murmured Lady Victoria to me. 'The reason, I suppose, is good heart. Perhaps it is unjust and impertinent to look further. I wonder why one is so inclined to look for a secret motive behind a generous act? Especially with a man like Charles. Expunge the question "why?" Consider it unasked. But how?'

'He had a long talk with Uncle Frank.'

'So I hear. I wonder what he said.'

'Have you asked him, Victoria?'

'Yes, of course. He said he appealed to Dundas's better nature. He says he doesn't know anything I don't know. Do you know what I am driven to conclude? I think he *did* appeal to your Uncle Frank's better nature. People are always more complicated than one thinks . . .'

Lady Victoria went away. She said she felt able to do so, because Killin had come back.

Time passed. Killin was sometimes away, for two or three days at a time. Always, after two or three days, he came back. He said I was the reason, though he still hid his feelings from the world, in order that Mamma should still make him welcome. I knew there were other reasons. *The Rivals*, of course, was still the excuse.

From the little I heard, and the less I saw, the play seemed to be going as well as could have been expected. Uncle Frank's patience was getting its reward, even with Miss Serena Wood.

But the effort told on Uncle Frank – the effort, or something else. In company, he was his bland and placid self; but, when he thought himself unobserved, a sick look came into his eyes. The conspirators had put it there – Killin, George Fraser, Victoria, and others I did not know. They were sure they were doing right. I did not know what they were doing.

Uncle Frank had apparently completed his business with Sir Malcolm Rattray. Instead Sir Campbell Stewart, coming over from Crossmount for rehearsals, spent a number of hours in Uncle Frank's office.

A new maid was found for Malvina. She did not look as happy as Ellen Wilson.

In the blazing midsummer, Eilean Fitheach called me with an insistent siren voice. I slipped away there as often as I could, but it was not often.

I longed, often and often, to strip off my clothes again and swim. I loved Robbie so completely (Katie Maitland the governess did) that I thought I would feel no shame. Why should a little governess obey the rules of grand ladies in Castles? But, though we kissed and caressed as happily passionate as ever, that was all we did.

I still felt a consuming mixture of relief and disappointment.

To my very great surprise, there came a message from Lady Angela Ramsay of Tulloch, asking me to tea.

I never received invitations to go anywhere on my own. I had not for many years received one to go anywhere even with other people. The doctors said I must stay quietly at home. The Ramsays perfectly well knew this, which made the invitation such a surprise.

Mamma, hearing of Lady Angela's note, put on a face of astonished concern. 'I do not think that Katharine will really want . . .' she said. 'The nervous effects . . . Much better to . . Lady Angela should know . . .'

'Write Lady Angela a note, Katie,' said Uncle Frank with his kindest smile, 'saying that you regret—'

'Why?' asked Lord Killin. 'Of course it is no business of mine, but a cup of tea with Lady Angela Ramsay is hardly likely to produce nervous prostration.'

He glanced at Uncle Frank, who seemed to shrink a little in his chair.

Colonel Blair said that General Ramsay was the best of good fellows, and an old friend of his own. Though superbly irrelevant, as well as palpably untrue, this testimonial seemed to convince Uncle Frank. Though Mamma frowned and fretted about my health, I was to be allowed to go to Tulloch.

I wanted to ride there on a pony, or drive myself in a phaeton. But I had never been allowed to ride or drive (in case I became dangerously overexcited); so I was taken by Calum Macnab in the victoria.

Killin saw me off.

'I do wish,' I said, 'I had some proper clothes.'

'Never mind about your clothes,' said Killin. 'Just remember the angle of your chin.'

He was a great comfort to me.

*

Tulloch was a big, low, white house, with extensive out-buildings. Some of the walls, they told me, were a dozen feet thick. Though a large house, and very old, it had none of the awesome magnificence of Ravenburn. In the hall, there was a distinct and pleasant smell of dog, coming from a great heap of deer-hounds and Labrador retrievers, which thumped their tails on the floor.

I was shown into the drawing room, and went in with my chin at the angle which Lord Killin approved.

I had three shocks.

The first was that Lady Angela Ramsay, standing like a weathered wooden figurehead by a window, turned and stared and said, 'I don't believe my eyes. You *can* make a silk purse out of a sow's ear, even without the silk.'

The second was that Lady Victoria was there, small and beautiful and radiating energy. She kissed me, then pointed to a little middle-aged lady on a sofa, sitting very neat and prim, with the sunlight twinkling on the gold wire of her spectacles, and her hands clasped in her lap.

This was the third shock; it was my old governess, my dear Miss Anderson.

We had a joyous reunion. She was as affectionate as ever. She told me all about her life since she left Ravenburn; I told her a little about mine.

At last she said, rather reproachfully, 'Why did you never answer my letters, Katie? I was quite hurt that you neglected me so.'

'But – but why did you never write to me?' I said. 'Of course, if you had written, I would have answered. I would have written on my own account, but I did not know your new address, and Uncle Frank said you were not to be found at your old one. But you never wrote! I was dreadfully hurt that *you* neglected *me* so.'

'I wrote a dozen times, dear! A score of times! And I begged for a reply, because I was worried and concerned about you.'

'You did address those letters correctly, Miss Anderson?' asked Lady Victoria.

'I lived at Ravenburn for six years, ma'am,' said Miss Anderson, with a touch of asperity. 'I would scarcely mistake the direction.'

'Someone,' said Lady Angela, 'has committed the unforgivable, not once but repeatedly, not by accident but by design.'

Miss Anderson glanced at her sharply. Her little pale eyes were bright with intelligence behind the gold-rimmed spectacles.

She said, 'It is a dreadful thing to have to accept. But it would be dishonest, I think, not to accept it. It must be so.'

'What did your letters say, Miss Anderson?' asked Lady Victoria.

'Oh! It is such a long time ago. After sending several, you know, and getting no reply, I grew disheartened, and stopped ... Well now, you must understand that Mr Dundas encouraged Katie to live a – a very retired life in the schoolroom, with myself as virtually her only companion. He had what seemed the *most* compelling reasons. There was an Edinburgh physician, and some other eminent physician from still further away, who came from time to time to examine Katie. Of course, I was not present at those examinations, nor was it my place to discuss the matter with the doctors. But their opinion was quoted to me by Mr Dundas. The gist was, that a *very* quiet life was necessary to Katie's mental and nervous state. At first, the whole arrangement accorded so well with my own temperament, that I rather welcomed it than the reverse . . .'

'Which is why you were there, and not some other,' said Victoria.

'Yes. That is one of the thoughts that began to strike me, especially as Katie grew older. It was rather a – an *unnatural* life, you know, just the two of us up there in that gloomy tower – natural enough for me, but *not* for an active, intelligent child. I put this view, with all respect, to Mr Dundas. He was most patient with me, most considerate, but adamant that the views of those eminent medical men should prevail.'

'Did you see those views, on paper, Miss Anderson?' asked Lady Angela.

'Oh no! Mr Dundas summarized them for me. It did not occur to me, at the time, to doubt a word that he said.'

'So you allowed yourself to be persuaded.'

'For a time, yes indeed. One does not disbelieve famous doctors. But I felt an ever-growing doubt. Then a woman arrived, to take charge of Katie's little half-sister. I saw that the child was going to be permitted, encouraged, to blossom forth, and be taken notice of, while my dear Katie was to be treated always as a sort of invalid. I thought this very wrong!'

'And said so?' asked Victoria.

'Certainly! But always most respectfully. I said that, having been Katie's intimate companion for six years, I felt competent to give an opinion about her, and – the upshot was – Mr Dundas and I were obliged to agree to differ.'

'You were dismissed?'

'Mr Dundas said that – he was sure I could not – that my conscience would not permit me to accept instructions contrary to my own convictions, nor to act contrary to the instructions of an employer.'

'As I said,' said Victoria with a smile, 'you were dismissed.'

'Ah,' I said. 'That was how it was. I wondered what had happened.'

'That was how it was, dear,' said Miss Anderson. 'And my very first letter to you explained the whole. In part, I was anxious to justify myself to you. I did not want you to think that I had, as it were, in some way betrayed you by leaving. But, more important, I did want you to do, what I would have endeavoured to help you to do, if I had stayed. I wanted you – I urged you, in that letter and in many subsequent letters – I urged you to emerge from the – the virtual purdah into which you had been committed by the doctors.'

'Into which,' said Victoria, 'Dundas said Katie had been committed by the doctors. I wonder what they really said.'

'Miss Anderson's message,' said Lady Angela, 'was hardly one which Dundas would wish Katie to receive.'

'Are things coming clear to you, Katie?' asked Victoria.

'Yes. No,' I said. 'Why did Uncle Frank want me in purdah? Why was I made into a sow's ear?'

'That was an overstatement,' said Lady Angela apologetically, 'forced out of me by astonishment at the grace and confidence of your entry just now.'

'It was no overstatement at all,' I said. 'You can make a sow's ear out of a silk purse, much easier than the other way about . . . But I can't understand *why*.'

There was a silence.

Miss Anderson said, deferentially, 'Mr Dundas is extraordinarily devoted to his sister. I remember being struck, again and again, by his quite unusual concern for her.'

'Unnatural concern?' suggested Lady Victoria.

'Unusual,' repeated Miss Anderson, in a slightly shocked voice. 'Anything that he has done of a – of an inexplicable nature, is more than likely to be explained by that concern. Katharine was a strikingly beautiful child, although I don't think you ever realized it, dear—'

'Was she?' asked Lady Angela. 'She's strikingly beautiful now—'

'Am I?' I asked: because I was anxious to get confirmation of a proposition to which I was still not quite accustomed.

'You never saw her, ma'am,' said Miss Anderson to Lady Angela.

'Hm. I daresay you're right. How selfish and thoughtless that makes me feel. Near neighbours, yet one lets a thing like this go on under one's nose. I could have helped you, Katie, in one way or another, but I didn't. Too busy rushing about. I'll make up for it now, though, if you'll permit me.'

'Thank you, ma'am,' I said; but I did not see how Lady Angela could help me in any way.

Lady Victoria said to Miss Anderson, 'Katie was a beautiful child, and then a beautiful young woman, hard as she herself tried to hide the fact. Is that all that has bothered those people? Are you suggesting that Frank Dundas kept her in the background, kept her browbeaten and obscure, purely so that she would not eclipse Isabella Ravenburn? Among those tenth-rate hangers-on they call their friends? Would any sane man go to such lengths, with such a puerile object?'

'So devoted as he is to his sister,' said Miss Anderson uncertainly, 'so concerned that she should shine pre-eminently—'

'There must be more to it,' murmured Lady Victoria. 'There *must* be more to it.'

As we had tea, Lady Angela and Miss Anderson had a great meeting of minds about the eviction of crofters and tenant farmers by modern lairds. Lady Angela expressed herself with remarkable force on the subject of Sir Campbell Stewart of Crossmount. It was funny to see the two of them, in the most earnest agreement – Lady Angela looking as though about to leap on the back of a pony and gallop up a vertical cliff; Miss Anderson looking as though about to disappear, squeaking, into a mouse-hole.

'I think,' said Lady Victoria when I left, 'there is no need to say anything about meeting either Miss Anderson or myself, when you get home.'

I had already made this decision, which showed how far my mind was working in new directions.

'But,' I said, 'I can tell Killin?'

'Oh yes. I suppose so. As long as you are certain nobody is listening. I wish I knew what he said to your uncle.'

'He appealed to Uncle Frank's good nature. He knows no more than you do.'

'Yes, I know . . . I wish I could completely believe him.'

'But – *don't* you completely believe him?'

She smiled. 'Never completely trust a man you are in love with, Katie. Your judgement is likely to be unsound.'

'A man you are in . . .' I said, blinking, horrified.

'It can happen even to Crusaders, you know . . . And this is a *much* greater secret than any we have been discussing.'

'And is he . . .? Is Lord Killin . . .?'

'He doesn't know it yet. But he'll face the reality of his heart. You have brought us together, Katie. He and I were friends before, but by making us colleagues you have brought us close. I am very grateful to you. He will be, too.'

In an unhappy daze I took farewell of Miss Anderson. We agreed to correspond, at once and always, using Tulloch as an accommodation address and General Ramsay as postmaster.

'Since dear Lady Victoria has contrived to bring us together, dear,' said Miss Anderson, 'we must never lose touch again.'

Kissing Victoria goodbye, I felt like Judas.

'What did Lady Angela . . .?' murmured Mamma. 'And who . . .?'

'We discussed, hum, education,' I said, 'and tenure on Scottish estates, and the postal system . . .'

The noise of hammering penetrated every nook of the Castle; it climbed unimaginable heights, and reverberated round the meaningless battlements and turrets; it plumbed the profoundest dripping depths; it seemed to go on for weeks.

For a single night's performance, such a stage was being built in the great hall that any grand opera could have been performed on it, complete with chorus, cavalry soldiers, and troops of elephants.

139

The hall was suddenly a forest of ladders. A gigantic curtain was hung across the stage, and hundreds of oil-lights were fixed to glare down on it.

A flight of broad, shallow steps was built, facing the stage, so that every member of the audience would be able to see Mamma without difficulty. On the steps, hundreds of small gilt chairs were placed, brought out of the storehouse where they had lain since the last giant party at Ravenburn. Every one was repainted. The brightness of the effect was overwhelming.

Costumes began to appear, sent for from a supplier in Edinburgh. Sir Malcolm Rattray looked extremely absurd in his wig. Killin looked fine in his, which fitted better. No one was allowed to see Mamma's costumes.

I foresaw that, with the changes of scenery and Mamma's changes of clothes, the performance would last ten hours. But I had not given credit to Uncle Frank's ingenuity. He had shortened the original text so severely, that there was hardly any of it left: except the scenes involving Lydia Languish, Lucy her maid (Malvina), and Sir Lucius O'Trigger (because Uncle Frank was intent on keeping Sir Malcolm Rattray's goodwill).

On top of the preparations for the play, there were preparations for entertaining half Scotland.

Mamma confined herself to gazing, with a weary but gratified eye, at the list of ladies and gentlemen who had accepted her invitation. (She held the list close to her eyes.) Something quite strange had happened, in regard to the acceptances. The very grandest people, whose attendance Mamma most wanted, had nearly all refused – and then many had written, saying their previous engagements had been altered, and begging to be allowed to attend after all.

It was as though someone had gone all over Scotland, bribing the highest aristocracy to come to watch Ravenburn making a fool of itself.

General and Lady Angela Ramsay accepted, even though Sir Campbell Stewart was taking part in the play. This was even more surprising than the acceptance of the old Duchess of Bodmin, or the terrifying Marchioness of Aberfeldy.

Mamma crooned over her list of audience and guests. Others concerned themselves with the immense supper which was to follow the performance, with the musicians, the wagonloads of champagne, the cartloads of ice, the further hundreds of gilt chairs, the throwing open of vast unused rooms, the thousands of candles, the extra servants, the direction of coachmen and disposition of horses; and with the prodigious number of bedrooms to be got ready for the scores of guests who would have come so far that they were staying.

Oh how I yearned, in that confused and hysterical period, for the peace and the passion of Eilean Fitheach. But I could very seldom get away there. Robbie laughed very much when I told him about the play. Our kisses acquired a desperate quality, because they were so brief.

'This is like Heaven,' I said, in Robbie's arms, on the sweet turf near the low arch.

'Not quite.'

I knew exactly what he meant, and blushed. 'No,' I said, 'not quite.'

'I am so wild with love for you, my darling girl, that I cannot do you harm. That is the irony. If I loved you less . . .'

'You cannot do me harm,' I repeated his words to him, but with a new meaning.

'Oh yes,' he said, 'I can. I have lived in different places, with different people, and in all of them I have seen young lives blasted by the thoughtlessness of a man, and by the generous love of the girl herself. Good men, sometimes, not rakes. Moral girls, not strumpets. I can do you great harm, Katie, and I have an unceasing struggle not to.'

'Will . . . Will we ever . . .?'

'I hope so,' he said softly into my cheek. 'I think so. There is still a long road ahead of us.'

'Why is there? What road? Leading where?'

'To justice.'

'Justice is only an idea. I do not care about justice. What I care about is . . .'

'Me?'

'Yes.'

He kissed me with a sort of gentle ferocity which left me unable to stand.

All this time, my mind was trying to grapple with the things I had learned at Tulloch. I could see no end to the troubles ahead. The whole fabric of life at Ravenburn was threatened, it seemed; my friends, with fused bombs under their cloaks, were preparing to blow it into Loch Chinn.

Was that what I wanted?

I knew now what my family had done to me. But why had they done it? Was it simply to protect Mamma from the competition of a handsome step-daughter? Would a sane man go to such cruel lengths, with such a puny object?

My friends were fighting on my behalf, so much was clear. But I did not think they were concerned with me only. The war had a larger cause. They had frightened and distressed Uncle Frank, so much was clear. But they had not won. The worm had turned and would turn again. Meanwhile, I was not allowed to know what the battleground was, or the spoils of war.

At some time, Killin's pursuit of me must come out in the open. He wanted to marry me, and had said so a hundred times. What of Mamma then, if she wanted Killin herself? What of my friend Victoria?

Mamma would not fight her own battles. She was used to having them fought for her, and by a consummate general. I was frightened of what might happen if Killin announced his intentions.

But Victoria would fight. Her weapons would be fair, but they would be long, sharp and heavy. I could not win a contest against her. I did not want to fight one. I did not want Killin.

What did I want? What future would I choose, if I had any power of choice?

The best I could foresee, was a second best. And it would be set about with bitterness, with lost love and lost friendship.

I peeped out, past the edge of the huge plum-coloured curtain.

The audience was massed on the tiers of seats – a dense alternation of the black-and-white clothes of the men, with here and there full Highland evening dress, and the white shoulders and brilliant silks of the women. Innumerable jewels sparkled from throats, ears and brows. They were sitting quiet, attentive. I recognized a few faces. I saw Sir George Fraser, with his twisted mouth, between Victoria Arlington and Lady Aberfeldy; Sir George had his arm in a sling. I saw General and Lady Angela Ramsay, looking, for all their resplendent evening clothes, as though they had just come in from stalking a stag on the hill. I saw Lady Stewart of Crossmount, and Doctor McPhail, and Mrs Seton (who had overcome her scruples). All the rest that I could see were complete strangers.

Mamma and Malvina were on the bright-lit stage, in the second scene of the play. Mamma was sitting on the sofa, in the first of her gowns, looking superb, in a very low-cut bodice, and powdered hair. Malvina, as her maid, stood before her in a sky-blue cloak that matched her eyes.

The estate workmen had been a very long time moving away the scenery of the first scene (a street; the scene, as Uncle Frank had edited it, lasted barely two minutes), and putting up the second. The audience had grown audibly restive, especially as they had been sitting for half an hour on their little gilt chairs, before the curtain first went up, while Mamma changed her mind about her costume.

They were quiet now.

The situation in the play was, that Lucy the maid had just come back from all the circulating libraries in Bath, with or without various books that her mistress wanted. I supposed they were the titles of real books, which meant something to Sheridan's audiences. I did not think they meant much to the Ravenburn audience. I thought it a dull scene, and likely to be a failure, but Mamma had not consented to a word being cut out.

'Heigh ho!' cried Mamma, with great annoyance (you could see she was annoyed, because she frowned, and shook her fist at Malvina). 'Did you enquire for *The Delicate Distress*?'

'Or,' shouted out Malvina, '*The Memoirs of . . .*'

She stopped. Malvina had forgotten her lines.

'The Memoirs of . . .' she repeated helplessly.

'Lady Woodford,' I whispered, from the wings.

'What?' said Malvina.

'Lady Woodford!' I said more loudly.

'Lady Woodford,' said Malvina. 'Yes, indeed, ma'am . . .'

She stopped again. She had forgotten the next line, too.

Malvina's speeches thereafter took a long time to deliver, because I had to deliver them, phrase by phrase, before she did. A few persons in the audience thought it funny, that everything Malvina said was anticipated by an echo, as it were, from the wings.

The scenes changed. Mamma's costumes changed. The Reverend Walter Willis and Miss Serena Wood came on for a few seconds at a time, and said the few words Mamma and Uncle Frank had left them. It did not matter what had been done to Miss Serena Wood's lines, for not a word she said could be heard.

Colonel Blair was surprisingly good as Sir Anthony Absolute. Sir Campbell Stewart was bad at his dashing son. Lord Killin was good as Mr Acres, the cowardly squire, although there was little of his part left in the Ravenburn version. Sir Malcolm Rattray was bad as Sir Lucius O'Trigger, the Irish adventurer. Uncle Frank was good as one comic servant, putting on a broad accent which he did very well. Jamie had refused to be another servant, at the last moment, so his part was removed from the play, which created a certain confusion.

The scene changes grew slower, instead of faster, as the work-men became exhausted. Mamma's changes of costume were time-consuming also. I have heard of ancient Japanese dramas which last all day and night; the Ravenburn production of *The Rivals*, truncated as it was, seemed full as long.

Towards the end, there were noticeable gaps in the audience. But, at the end, the applause seemed to satisfy Mamma.

'Not quite bad enough to be funny,' said Lady Aberfeldy. 'It was heroic of Charles Killin to sacrifice himself. Is he after the Delectable Mountain?'

'No,' said Victoria sharply. 'Come on, Katie.'

'Where?' I asked.

'Upstairs. To your room.'

'Oh,' I said. 'Very well, if you say I must. But I had hoped to get some champagne.'

'What a good idea. We will take some with us. Are you coming, Aunt Mariota?'

'To make the interminable ascent? Oh yes, I shall come.'

Before I could protest, or ask any questions, the two form-idable ladies started sweeping me upstairs – far up to my little bleak room in the East Tower.

I was completely puzzled. Did they want to drink champagne in my schoolroom, rather than in the great rooms of the Castle?

There was a knock on the door. Madame Duplage, the grim French dressmaker, came in and curtseyed. She was followed by her two little seamstresses, who carried between them a wickerwork hamper, as though we were all about to sit down and eat a prodigious picnic.

'Off with your clothes, Katie,' said Victoria. 'All of them. Those underthings, dear, and those stockings – they will not do tonight.'

'But – but—'

I began to undress obediently. I was embarrasesd to do so in front of strangers; and embarrassed to reveal how very dowdy all my clothes were. I was still utterly baffled.

Madame Duplage began, reverently, to lift clothes from the hamper, and lay them over the backs of chairs.

'That,' said Lady Aberfeldy, pointing at a grass-green silk gown, 'needs a cage, surely?'

'Ah, oui, Madame la Marquise,' said Madame Duplage. She nodded to one of her acolytes, who brought in, from the passage outside, the largest cage I had ever seen. The top was tiny, and meant for some very tightlaced lady; but the bottom was a good three yards across. It was made of very fine springy metal, which looked like steel. The girl bent it all out of shape, to get it through the door, but it sprang back into shape as soon as she released.

'Watch-spring,' said Lady Victoria. 'A new invention.'

'Good gracious me,' said Lady Aberfeldy. 'I have graduated, myself, from whalebone to wire, but I never heard of watch-springs. Does the child require to be wound up, before she is launched?'

I looked from Victoria to Lady Aberfeldy, from her to Madame Duplage; I imagine my mouth was hanging open with bewilderment.

'Nous avons ici des corselets,' said Madame Duplage. 'Mais il n'y a aucun besoin.'

'Vous avez raison, madame,' said Lady Aberfeldy. 'It is agonizing for me to have to admit it, but that child's figure is so perfect it needs no lacing at all. The agony does not derive wholly from jealousy, you understand, but in part from my own corsets.'

They began to dress me, in such silk stockings and underclothes as I had never even seen before.

When I was half dressed, they sat me down. Another Frenchwoman arrived in my room; she was Amélie, Lady Aberfeldy's own maid. She did my hair. I wondered dumbly if she would do something astonishing; but she did it very simply, drawing it, satin-smooth and raven-black, to a great smooth knot low on the back of my neck.

'Un tel visage, d'une telle beauté,' said Amélie, 'mérite le complément d'un très simple encadrement.'

Mme Duplage grunted agreement.

'What,' I asked nervously, 'does "encadrement" mean?'

'A frame,' said Victoria. 'Like a picture frame.'

'Oh. Thank you. Somehow it suggested a coffin . . .'

They put me in the enormous watch-spring cage, the first cage or crinoline I had ever worn. The top, which looked too small for an ankle, fitted snugly round my waist. The bottom filled half my schoolroom. It was very light.

The women spread a vast silk petticoat over the cage, and at last buttoned me (with dozens of tiny buttons up the back) into the grass-green dress.

I glanced down at myself, and gulped. The dress, as was fashionable, was cut straight across at the top: but it seemed to me the top was a long way down. My shoulders were bare, my upper arms, my neck, and much more of my bosom than anyone had ever seen before.

(Except Robbie, I thought, for a trembling moment.)

'Now,' said Victoria, 'as you have been quite a good and obedient girl, you shall have a glass of champagne, and you shall have a look at yourself.'

There was no full length glass in the schoolroom, or in my bedroom. But there was one in Miss Anderson's deserted little bedroom. The seamstresses brought in lamps. I stared at myself, without recognition. I saw a pale young lady of the highest fashion, in a superb gown which matched her eyes. Most evening dresses of the time were more or less complicated in design, with panels, and frills, and tassels, and rows of flounces over the crinoline skirt. The pale young lady's green dress was completely simple – smooth, grass-green silk, skin-tight to the waist, and then ballooning outwards, like a giant blossom upside down, to the floor. The pale young lady in the looking-glass had a slight, cool smile on her lips. Her chin was arrogantly tilted. She held a glass of champagne.

'It's more than I can bear,' said Victoria. 'Nobody will look at anybody else.'

'Then let us get downstairs before all the men are drunk,' said Lady Aberfeldy.

I tried to thank Mme Duplage.

'Ah, bah!' she said. 'On n'a pas tous les jours la chance de vêtir une déesse.'

' "Déesse",' said Victoria helpfully, 'means "goddess".'

I never knew whether what happened next, happened partly by accident or wholly by design.

When we crossed the great hall, we went not to the drawing room, but to the picture gallery. This was a room so large that it could not be called a room at all – it was a Parliament house, or a railway station, or a cathedral. It was hardly ever entered. The pictures collected by eighteenth-century Irvines on their Grand Tours, and nineteenth-century Irvines from London dealers, were not interesting or valuable. But, like everything else of my grandfather's, they were extremely large. The ceiling of the gallery was very high, as it had been designed to house battle scenes the size of bowling-greens; from it hung a dozen of what I had heard said were the largest chandeliers in Scotland.

Beyond the picture gallery was the ballroom, which was almost its twin. Normally, great oak doors divided the two, into which a small door had been let, as I have seen cottage doors with a miniature door for a cat. The ballroom was as seldom entered as the gallery. Reels were often danced in the servants' hall, and sometimes in the great hall; but there had not been a full dress ball at Ravenburn for many years. Mamma found the very thought exhausting. The ballroom had what I had heard called the second largest chandeliers in Scotland.

The two rooms, or adjacent railway stations, had been thrown together by the opening of the huge doors between them. Coming in at one end of the gallery, we saw a vista that looked a mile long. It was moderately full of people, and very full of noise, animation and colour.

Down each side of the picture gallery, somewhat away from the walls, long tables had been placed, covered with supper and wine and other comforts. It was, perhaps, this circumstance which had drawn nearly all the people to one side of the gallery or the other, leaving a sort of avenue between, which stretched to the great doors of the ballroom.

'Go on, Katie,' murmured Victoria. 'We are just behind you.

We want to go to the ballroom. The champagne is colder there.'

I stood in the doorway, contemplating the huge gauntlet that Victoria was telling me to run.

Then came an event which I did not see. It was an appalling sudden noise, a crash, as though ten footmen had dropped ten brass trays on the marble floor, each tray carrying a hundred brass pots full of nails. The crash was just behind me, outside the door, in the hall.

Every head in the picture gallery swivelled. Every face turned towards the door: towards me.

I gulped, and said to myself: I am the most beautiful woman in the Castle tonight. These people are *very* lucky to be looking at me.

Then I started slowly forward. I felt the smile on my face, and I felt the angle of my chin.

There was a curious buzzing noise. It was something between a swarm of wild bees in April, a murmuration of starlings in November, and a school full of children whose dominie has left early.

It was a noise I had never heard before, but I knew what it meant. I felt my smile broaden a little, and my cheeks colour a little.

I knew the truth. I *was* the most beautiful woman in the Castle.

When we reached the portals of the ballroom, I knew it all over again. There was no need of dropped trays. Somehow, the message had travelled from the gallery to the ballroom, that a strange young lady in a huge green crinoline was to be stared at.

I enjoyed it very much indeed.

Of the rest of that magic night, I can remember only glimpses. But they are nice, clear glimpses.

I was presented, by Lady Aberfeldy, to a number of great ladies. A number of great gentlemen were presented to me. Wherever I went, a crowd followed; so that it seemed simplest, and more considerate, to remain in one place.

There was a rattle of cheerful talk in the crowd about me, and many very gratifying compliments. People laughed at things I said. I do not remember the things, so it may have been Mamma's champagne, rather than my wit, that made them laugh.

'Do you feel sick with excitement, child?' murmured Lady Aberfeldy. 'Are your nerves about to snap from the strain?'

'No, ma'am,' I said. 'Did you trip up a footman with a tray?'

'Certainly not. How dare you make such a suggestion? I would not dream of doing such a thing. I took a tray from a footman's hands, and dropped it.'

'*One* tray, ma'am? It sounded like a dozen.'

'I dropped it, as it were, with a certain downward violence.'

I burst out laughing.

The effect of this inelegance was two offers of marriage during the next ten minutes. One was from Lord Killin. He whispered his latest proposal. I refused it.

'Why, my darling Katie?'

The reason was a Glasgow foundling, remote by a million miles from this new-conquered world of mine.

'I find it so strange and so interesting,' Mrs Seton was saying to General Ramsay, 'that nobody has been discussing the play at all! It is all Katharine, Katharine, Katharine. Curious, is not it? One would have thought someone would have a word to spare for dear Isabella and her performance!'

'You spare some, Mrs Seton.'

'I? Oh no. I entirely disapprove.'

A blurred time later, Sir George Fraser came up to me, with his twisted smile and thin voice. He said polite things about my appearance, and assured me that his arm was mending.

'Your horse came down?' I asked.

'Yes. Slipped, or stumbled. My fault, I daresay. What has happened to you, Miss Katharine?'

'I have a new dress,' I explained.

'You have more than that. You have a new heart, soul, spirit. It blazes out of your eyes. You came into this room like a queen.'

'I hoped it was like an empress,' I said. 'It was *meant* to be like an empress.'

'It was like a child,' he said, twisting his face into a smile, 'given a box of chocolates for the first time.'

I stared at him, startled at this echo of a thought I had had about myself.

'It is,' he went on in his thin voice, 'the sight to make one happiest in the world – the sight of a poor child, a hard-treated child, with a box of chocolates for the very first time.'

'I hope the child will not be sick,' I said dubiously.

'I hope so too.'

Mamma said, with exhausted disapproval, 'What a drearily plain skirt to your dress, Katharine. A few flounces, in a different colour ... Jewels, but of course you have none ... But, we cannot expect ...'

The skin of Mamma's face was tired, but her eyes were bright with hatred.

nine

The next week made up for a lifetime of not getting letters. Sackfuls came for me. If Uncle Frank steamed them all open, and read them, the management of the Ravenburn estates must have suffered.

Most were from ladies, and most of those were invitations.

Some were from gentlemen, and some of those were proposals.

The Duchess of Bodmin and the Marchioness of Aberfeldy, who were staying on at Ravenburn for a few days, both offered to present me at Court, since such a thing was too fatiguing for Mamma. I was also asked to join various great parties, in various great houses, under the wings of various great ladies, for all the Highland balls and meetings and races. I was asked to Edinburgh, and Inverness, and Perth, and Fort William, and Aberdeen.

My instinct was to accept every single invitation. But that would mean exile from Eilean Fitheach. I felt torn in half.

They were calling me Katie Queen of Scots. This was because of the grass-green dress Mme Duplage had given me; and the anger Lady Victoria and Miss Anderson had given me; and the angle of chin Lord Killin had given me; and the things Robbie had given me.

I liked being Katie Queen of Scots. I liked being a lovesick little governess.

Most of the birds of passage, who had settled on Ravenburn for *The Rivals,* flew off after only a night, or two nights, to assemble in other rookeries. Many stayed longer. Of these, most were bound to Mamma by ancient ties of loyalty, or affection, or something. They were a funny lot: widows who bent and echoed, like Lady Wood; single young ladies, who had been presented ten years earlier, but were still single young ladies; Colonels and Majors with noses veined like the marble plinths of the drawing-room candlesticks, or eyes rimmed as redly as a bantam-cock's; a Viscount who was said to be bankrupt, and the lawyer who was said to have bankrupted him.

'Isabella's friends from the old days,' said Lady Angela Ramsay, 'who have managed to go on clinging to her skirts.'

Some of those who stayed were of a completely different kind. They knew Mamma, of course, or they would scarcely have been asked to Ravenburn. They did not seem to know her well, or to mingle with her closest cronies, or to coo over Malvina's gowns and curtseys, or to make bluff advances to Jamie. They did not seem at ease, in the adoring ritual of the drawing-room after tea.

Yet they wanted tea.

I had an audacious idea. On a particularly fine afternoon, I asked Henderson the butler to have an awning stretched out over part of the west terrace, and tea brought there. As I expected, he made difficulties that would have been untold, except that he told all of them.

Mamma, in an exhausted voice, supported Henderson. To have tea on the terrace, in the open air, was the wildest folly. Killin gently said it was a pity she took so negative a view, as he himself would relish cucumber sandwiches and Dundee cake on the terrace. Uncle Frank, contriving to be bland, said that many of their guests might feel as Lord Killin did.

With a face of shocked dismay, Henderson arranged matters. It was very nice, eating cucumber sandwiches and Dundee cake on the terrace.

Thereafter, there were two parties in the afternoon. There were two parties of people staying at Ravenburn. One set orbited round Mamma. The other seemed to go where I was.

'In one sense,' said Lady Angela Ramsay, 'Isabella is lucky. People she has always wanted at Ravenburn are here. Mariota Aberfeldy, Violet Bodmin, Alicia Odiham, the Dracos.'

'They came to see *The Rivals*,' said General Ramsay.

'They came because our dear Victoria persuaded them to come. The irony is, that they are here in spite of Isabella, not because of her.'

'They are the loving subjects,' said Sir George Fraser, 'of Katie Queen of Scots.'

'They are sending for a doctor,' Malvina said to me. 'I heard Uncle Frank talking to Mamma about it. I wonder why? Do you know? I wonder why they don't get Dr McPhail as usual?'

I wondered also, but not very hard, because my head was a whirl of conceited thoughts.

'He is called Dr McAndrew,' Malvina went on, 'and he is coming all the way from Stirling.'

'Oh yes,' I said, hardly listening. The name meant nothing to me. I had better things to think about than unknown doctors.

I took off my royal crown. (It was a saucy little round hat, with a single feather, almost a yard long, sticking straight upwards. Sir George Fraser wrote a poem to it in Greek: but he would not tell me what it meant.) I took off my royal robes. (They were a glorious peach-coloured silk afternoon dress. which Mme Duplage had made for me.) Like Haroun al Raschid, I put on humble clothes, and went among the rabble.

I jumped ashore into Robbie's arms. We kissed as though after a parting of years.

He was preoccupied. He did not listen to all I said, or laugh loudly enough at my jokes.

'I will go and talk to your owl,' I said. 'She may be jealous, but at least she sits still and looks at me, when I talk to her.'

Robbie laughed, but he was constrained. 'I am so sorry, my darling,' he said. 'But there are things even you cannot drive out of my mind at the moment. Matters are coming to a crisis. I know much more than I did, thanks to my very good friends, and the more I know the more solemn I become ... You remember those keepers, who fired on us? I thought they were after Rory Beg. Now I am sure of it, and I know why.'

'Why?'

'They were paid, of course. Paid a lot of money, by a man with a secret to keep.'

'He would kill to keep it?'

'He has killed to keep it, and will again. Rory Beg, thank God, has kept away, far away, clear out of harm's way – but quite useless to me. He's coming back, to a meeting place he sent me word of. It is high time, because there's something urgent he must do for me.'

'That is good.'

'But I'm frightened for him.'

'Need you be? He must be cleverer than a parcel of water-keepers.'

'Oh yes. But not as clever as the man who's paying them. The devil of it is, I have got to be away, a long way away, when he comes. There is a man I must see, a lawyer. There is advice I must have. An appointment has been made for me to see – someone very important, in great secrecy. He is doing me a tremendous favour, consenting to it. I must keep that appointment. I shall never have another such chance.'

'This is – Tom's business? I mean, Mr Irvine, or Lord Raven-burn, or whatever he should be called?'

'Tom's and my own. They have become a little intermingled.'

'I thought you had no business of your own?'

'I had not. I have now. You are my business.'

'Oh,' I said. 'I don't like being business. I would rather be pleasure. But if I am your business, then, of course, I am your messenger to Rory Beg.'

'No.'

'But yes, my dear love.'

'No, Katie. It might be very dangerous.'

'I can run fast. I can climb any rock, or any tree. I can dress as a boy, if you think that would be wise. Shall I wear knickers, or breeches, or trousers?'

'I think the best would be . . . *No,* Katie.'

So we had another of our arguments. Robbie passionately insisted that I could not carry his message to Rory Beg, urgent and vital as it was. He had only mentioned the whole matter, because he wanted me to understand that he had reason to be preoccupied.

I said at last, 'You need a messenger you can trust. How many people can you trust?'

'Three,' he said. 'One is Rory Beg.'

'One is me, I hope.'

'I was not counting you. The other two . . . You *could*, perhaps, get a message to one of the other two.'

'I *could*,' I said reluctantly. 'But it adds another complication.'

'It has more drawbacks than that. It has advantages, but dare I arrange it so? You would have to know who my friends are—'

'But you trust me.'

'I tell you again and again, Katie, that your safety lies in complete ignorance. At the moment, nothing links you to my friends, because you do not know who they are. Therefore, nothing links you to me. But, if a link is formed, and it is visible to certain eyes . . . Then again, they would know you were my friend. I don't want even my allies to know that, yet.'

'Why? Are you ashamed of me?'

He smiled, as though the question were not worth answering, and went on, 'Another point is, they would know I was close by here, very close, to give you the message. They might guess, or get from you, where I am.'

'Never,' I said.

'Tongues wag. Things slip out.'

'My tongue *never* wags,' I said indignantly.

'On the contrary, darling Katie, it wags incessantly, that is why you are so restful – one only has to sit and listen, without the effort of thought . . .'

He evaded the blows I aimed at his chest, and then smothered them by embracing me.

He went on, 'Even if we forget all those hazards, a much greater one remains. If one of my friends delivers the message for me, that one will have to go, at a strange hour, to a strange place. My enemy suspects them already. He more than suspects them. How difficult it is. There's a Jewish proverb which says, "My enemy's enemy is my friend". By the same token, my enemy's friend is my enemy—'

'You are leaving me a long way behind,' I said, 'when you gallop off among proverbs. *My* friend's friend is my friend, so I will go and meet Rory Beg.'

'*No*, Katie. But let me think this out. My friends are under my enemy's eye, directly or indirectly. He has had them followed before, and harm done to them. He has them watched now, that I know for certain. If one slinks out, from wherever he is, at a strange hour, to a strange place, he will be followed. That is pretty certain, too. They are not people who, like Rory Beg, can baffle bloodhounds, or disappear up trees—'

'I can.'

'*No*, Katie. Whichever one of them goes, he will very likely lead the followers to Rory Beg. That will tell my enemy far more than I dare let him know. It will also put Rory Beg, and my other friend, at the most frightful risk.'

'Well,' I said, 'of course you must *not* imperil Rory Beg, or this other mysterious friend who cannot climb trees. But no one knows I am anything to do with you. I am nobody's friend, except yours, and so I am nobody's enemy. I am nobody at all, in fact. No one is going to watch me, or pay any attention to my comings and goings.'

'But—'

'It is so *obvious*,' I said impatiently. 'I can go safely to Rory Beg, and give any message you wish. If I go for a walk at midnight, no one will think twice about it. If I am seen talking to Rory Beg, they will think I am asking the way. I am a little governess, from a Manse in Stirling.'

'A governess in a million. But you will not go.'

In the end, he had to agree that I was the only person who could go.

He told me the message he wanted given to Rory Beg. He told me exactly where to go, and when, and what noise to make to identify myself to the old poacher. He thanked me again and again.

'You talk too much,' I said dreamily.

He laughed, and used his lips in a more acceptable fashion.

But his face was tense with worry when I left him.

My face was tense with worry, too, three nights later, a little before midnight.

Once again, a sort of mad defiance had led me to take on something which frightened me half out of my wits. Of course, it was not entirely an internal 'dare', like the theft of the boat, or the first expedition to the island. It was helping Robbie, too, in something that was important to him. But he had resisted being helped, violently, and for a long time: and it was obstinacy which made me batter down his arguments.

With all my heart, as the clock rushed towards midnight, I wished I had not got this perverse streak.

I had slipped into Jamie's room, the day before, and borrowed some clothes – a tweed knickerbocker shooting-suit, a flannel shirt, and a big tweed cap. Now I climbed out of one of my new evening dresses, and into my clothes for the night. The contrast was most peculiar – the scratchy tweed and wool after the luxurious silks, and the unfamiliar, swaggering freedom of separately-covered legs. Jamie was shorter and much fatter than I, but I thought the breeches would stay up, if I tied them tight round the waist with a sash. For my trousers to fall about my ankles, in the midst of my midnight expedition, would be more than humiliating. Suppose I had to run in earnest! Gentlemen, I knew, dangled their trousers from straps over their shoulders, but I had forgotten to borrow any such things, and it was too late now.

I twisted my hair into an untidy knot on the top of my head, and jammed the tweed cap upon it. The effect was as ludicrous as the Reverend Walter Willis's wig, when he acted in *The Rivals*. But I was in no mood for laughter.

I had explored again my secret way out, by the cellars and game-larders. It still served. Some of the game-larders were filling up with grouse and early stags, but my way was not blocked by carcasses, and the key was easier to turn for being in regular use. Minutes after leaving the East Tower, I was on the bank of the Raven burn and hurrying down towards the loch.

I stopped, and glanced back at the Castle. The sky was dark. The old moon would rise later. There were no lights in the Castle. I half expected to see a light in Uncle Frank's window, and a shadow interminably passing and repassing. But he had not appeared at dinner, sending apologies, and pleading urgent estate business. Perhaps his business still held him in his office in the courtyard.

I had, myself, been admitted to dinner since the night of *The Rivals*. There was no further mention of the crisis of nerves or stomach to which such excitement might give rise. That demon was laid; I wondered if it was laid for ever. Others showed signs of rising. When I came into the drawing room before dinner, in my new dress, laughing at something ridiculous the Duchess of Bodmin said, I caught Mamma's eye.

I wondered if she guessed about Killin. I would not have wished to meet her, on a dark night, in a lonely place.

I turned west for a short way, and then north-west, and found the bank of the Tarruinchon burn. This came down a deep fold in the hill behind, Meall na Cuigealach. It was all low ground where the burn ran gently to the loch, until far back into the hill. Then the ground rose in a startling green cliff, with the burn leaping in a series of spectacular falls down the face. The steep ground and the high ground were bare grass and heather, of course, but the deep Tarruinchon glen was heavily wooded. The wood varied in width from a few yards to a hundred, according to the tortured shapes of the walls of the glen; it was not quite a mile long, going from the lochside to its abrupt end on the shoulder of Meall na Cuigealach.

I was in the midst of the wood by two o'clock, going stealthily upstream beside the gently chuckling burn, waiting for the moon to rise, stopping and listening often, straining my eyes in the darkness. I went carefully over the broken ground in the dark. I did not want to sprain my ankle, or to make any noise. I was glad of boy's clothes.

It was frightening, in the dark tangled wood on the burnside at two o'clock in the morning. My nerves jumped and jangled. I was free of girlish trailing skirts, but I was not free of girlish terrors. The eldritch wail of a wavering owl, sudden and savage, nearly brought a scream to my throat. I started a deer, almost at my feet, which crashed in panic away through the undergrowth. Thorns caught at my cap, and brambles at my legs; hazel-twigs whipped into my face, and boggy patches sucked at my feet. I had the sense that a million malevolent eyes were following my every step: that ears were cocked, nostrils quivering, hackles raised.

Bitterly and violently I wished myself anywhere in the world except this lonely, crowded, tangled, terrifying wood in the Tarruinchon glen. I was frightened of Rory Beg. I was frightened of whatever he might be doing. I was frightened of whoever might be following him, and I was frightened of whoever might be following me.

I seemed to hear footfalls all around me, just audible over the gurgle of the burn – snapped twigs, branches brushed aside, heavy breathing, whispers. I seemed to see eyes all around me.

A few hours before, I had been Katie Queen of Scots, in my new evening dress of cream-coloured silk, very low cut; I had been sitting in the music room at Ravenburn, with new friends

157

and old friends about me. I had been beautiful, admired, praised, petted, and safe.

Now I was struggling through a thick scrubby wood, in pitch darkness, over broken ground, guided only by the sound of unseen running water, caught and savaged by branches and brambles, lonely and scared.

I thought I must be very mad.

The wood seemed endless. It was exhausting to push through it in the dark. I was terribly anxious to make no sound. Though my boy's clothes were practical, they were prickly and uncomfortable. By day, the midges in such a wood, at that time of year, would have been intolerable. At night they were hardly tolerable. I seemed to disturb unseen clouds of them, each time I brushed against a leaf; they gathered round my head like an umbrella; I felt them sticking to my damp brow and cheek.

I came at last to the obstacle Robbie had told me to look out for – a grassy bluff which sprang from the wall of the glen, and jutted almost to the burn-side. At the foot of the bluff, there was a thin fringe of little trees, thorns and hazels, between the steep rise of ground and the rocks of the burn. On the other side of the burn, the ground was almost level for a long way, before it rose steeply, and so the wood there was broad and dense.

The place had many merits from Rory Beg's point of view, and Robbie's, and mine. First, I could not mistake it. There was no other such high grassy bluff jutting to the burn-side. If that was where I was to go, I could be sure to get there. Second, the dense and deep wood opposite would shelter the fugitive poacher, impenetrably, from any treachery or pursuit. Third, there *could* be land-rails in the grass of the bluff.

The sky opened above me. I could just make out the bare ground rising steeply before me and to my right. The burn gurgled invisibly ten feet away from me, ten feet below, a little summer trickle among its rocks. I crouched down at the edge of the wood, using the utmost caution. I put my head close to the ground, into the whiskers of grass below the trees.

I raised my voice softly: '*Creck-creck.*' A pause. '*Creck-creck, creck-creck . . . Creck!*'

I did not suppose I sounded exactly like a land-rail, the little, furtive, harsh-voiced brown bird of the grassy spaces. I was not at all sure that a land-rail would call, in the small hours of the morning, at the end of August, on the close turf of the bluff. But it was the signal I was to make.

I listened, tense and motionless, for a long time. There were sleepy night-sounds, insects, an owl far away, a sedge-warbler chattering discordantly on the burn-side, in spite of the lateness of the hour and of the season, and the rustling gurgle of the burn itself.

I rehearsed in my mind the identifying rhythm which Robbie had taught me, and nervously raised my voice again in hopeful imitation of a land-rail: 'Creck-creck.' A pause. 'Creck-creck, creck-creck ... Creck!'

Then there came, from the depths of the wood on the other side of the burn, a sound which was possible in nature – but only just possible, at that season of the year. It was the soft whirr of a night-jar, sounding like a spinning-wheel in a croft.

I let the night-jar sing while I counted twenty. Then, obedient to my orders, I called: 'Creck ... Creck-creck-creck.'

I was trembling with excitement. I guessed that my imitation land-rail was harsher and louder than before, and even less like the real bird. It should not matter. Contact was made. All was going well. I was winning my insane 'dare'.

I edged myself cautiously through the belt of trees to the bank of the burn. There was nothing but blackness before, below and about me. I could hear nothing but the gurgle of the burn. I waited, my heart bumping painfully in my throat.

Then the old moon peeped over the dense-packed trees of the wood. Rough ground and rougher undergrowth were badged with splashes of silver; the shadows were blacker than the previous blackness. The deep gash of the burn yawned below me – sharp ugly rocks, and a curl of water suddenly illumined, as though by a drowning glow-worm. The moonlight fell on me also. I crouched down, and backed further into the skinny belt of trees on my side of the burn. I stared at the dense black wood, which came almost to the edge of the steep, treacherous bank opposite to me.

From the deepest shadow, a soft voice said, 'Ye cam' frae Seabhac Seilge.'

It was the Gaelic for 'wandering hunter' – for the peregrine falcon. It was Robbie Scott's name, among Rory Beg and his like.

'Yes,' I said. 'You are Clamhan.'

Clamhan means buzzard – perhaps hawks of other kinds. It was the name used for Rory Beg.

'Ay,' he said. 'I spied ye lang syne intil the river, wi' Seabhac Seilge. Ye waur a lassie, yon tide. Ye're a braw laddie the nicht. Unco ploys, hey, cailin ro mhaiseach?'

That Gaelic phrase I did know, for Robbie had used it of me. It means 'very beautiful girl'.

He asked me if I were alone – if I were certain, truly certain, that I had not been followed. I was certain, and told him so.

He believed me, and came forward out of the deep shadow of the trees. He came to the very lip of the burn's steep rocky bank. The moonlight struck him, and I saw him for the first time. I saw him clearly in the bright moonlight – every line of his face, every patch on his ancient clothes.

I was startled by his appearance. He was tiny – not a mis-shapen dwarf, but a perfect miniature of a man. He was not five feet tall. He looked thin and frail: but I noticed that he held himself as erect as a strong youth, and moved with grace and assurance. He was very old. His face was deeply lined, with a sparse white beard below the chin, and a little white hair, very long, on his old skull. His face was as gentle as Miss Anderson's, and as intelligent as Lady Victoria's. He looked supremely unlike a notorious violent poacher.

He wore a rough coat made of some animal's skin, with stuff breeches and leather leggings. The coat was full of stitched three-cornered tears, and the breeches of odd-shaped patches. I imagined they were of all colours, like Joseph's coat: but one cannot distinguish colour by moonlight. He carried his cap in one hand, and a thorn stick in the other.

It was extraordinary that this gentle-faced, ragged old man lived a life of furtive and perilous theft, with every man's hand against him. He looked like a little old dominie, dressed up as a tattiebogle to amuse young children at a Hogmanay party.

He said, 'Seabhac Seilge hae gangit til Embro, lassie?'

'Yes. He sent me with a message. He said it is urgent and vital.'

'Ay, I speirit near an' far, an' there's ill ploys afut.'

'He wants you to go to – the place you told him of, where the man bides in the croft.'

'I ken the yin.'

'He wants you to bring that man away, and fetch him to this place, three nights from now.'

'Yin, twa, three nichts frae the nicht. Ay. Wull Seabhac Seilge be hame, yon tide?'

'Yes. He says he will be back.'

'The auld yin, in yon lane croft – he'll no' wush tae cam.'

'He will be killed if he does not come.'

'Stands ut sae? Ay, nae doot.'

The old man did not seem in the least surprised or shocked at words which had horrified me. Robbie had been clear that the man hidden in the remote croft was in deadly danger if he stayed there. Rory Beg accepted this, as though it were just what he had himself expected.

There were ill ploys afoot, indeed.

'Ay,' he said, 'tis airgent, as ye say. Wi'oot yon meeserable cateran, Seabhac Seilge hae flingit a' tae naethin'. Bide blithe, lassie. Three nichts, the sam hoor. Goad keep ye, cailin ro mhaiseach.'

Even as he called me a beautiful girl again – even as he raised the hand that held his cap, in a very gracious, antique gesture of farewell – there was a crash in the wood close behind him. He turned, and dropped to a crouch, alert as a badger.

A voice rang out hoarsely, 'Ye're cowerit wi' sax shotguns, Rory Beg! Gi' yersel up, mannie! Ye'd tak' oor troots an' oor wee phaisants, hey?'

Rory Beg began to slip like a vole, into the deep shadows of the wood. But more voices called, from all about. Men were on my bank of the burn, as well as his. I shrank back, crouching, in deepest shadow. But, as I watched, two men thrust out of the wood on the far bank, above and below Rory Beg. He might yet have slipped away into the wood, going between them, but I could hear the whimper of hounds. He was trapped.

One of the men I could see carried a shotgun, which he raised to cover Rory Beg. The other was armed with an immense club. They closed on Rory Beg, and stood each side of him. He was dwarfed between them. I could see them clearly. I did not know them. They were not local people.

The man with the gun ordered Rory Beg to turn to face him. The old man did as he was bid. The moonlight fell full on his gentle old face. It was tense. It did not cringe, nor look defiant.

It was thoughtful. I was sure he was even now thinking of some subtle trick which should get him out of this toil.

I prayed desperately for the safe escape of Rory Beg, who was my friend's friend.

They stood so – Rory Beg, with the moonlight on his face, two yards from a much bigger man with a levelled shotgun to his shoulder: and, a yard behind him, a still bigger man with a heavy club.

'Resestin' arrest,' said a voice from the depth of the wood. 'Ye ken fine wha' tae du, Wattie.'

The man with the club said nothing. But he raised the club, and brought it down with all his strength on Rory Beg's old head. The noise of its striking was the most dreadful I had ever heard. I watched in sick despair. Rory Beg slumped to the ground on the lip of the steep bank. His face and skull were suddenly marked in black. By daylight, the mask would have been red. The man with the gun stepped forward, and with his foot tipped Rory Beg head-first into the burn.

This contemptuous, callous treatment of an injured or dead man was somehow more shocking even than the treacherous blow from behind.

The bed of the burn was almost empty, after the long hot summer. Ugly, pointed rocks studded the banks and bed. Rory Beg crashed onto them, striking his head again. He lay like a little bundle of rags in the gurgling water of the burn.

I longed to jump to my feet and run, run away from the place of butchery and nightmare. But they would hear, if they had not seen. They were big men, and many, and they had hounds. Some might already be behind me, to cut off my escape if I showed myself, or made a noise.

Sick, trembling, near fainting, I crouched in the darkness.

Another man came out of the wood on to the bank. He carried a dark lantern, which he uncovered to look down at the little motionless bundle in the burn. Because of the glare of the lantern in front of him, I could not see him.

He raised the lantern, and shone it at my bank. He swung the beam along the bank, and found me. I was impaled on the beam of the lantern.

'The laddie we haird,' said the murderer with the club. 'Gi' us yer gun, Sandy.'

He took the shotgun from his friend, dropping his club, and

raised it to his shoulder. He aimed it full at my face, a bare five yards away.

'No,' said the main with the lantern sharply.

'Och, ye're fou,' exploded the murderer. 'Yon bairn spied me hut the auld yin.'

'Ye'll no' shute!'

'Ye're fou, mon! I'll no' hae a wutness gang tae the Fiscal!'

He raised the gun again. Dizzily, in a state of numbness beyond terror, I thought: he is right. Of course, he is right. I would do the same. A man hangs no higher for two murders than for one. He is right. He must shoot. I waited for death, trying to remember the words of any prayer. With a shotgun, at this close range, my death would be instant. He could neither miss nor maim.

I thought, idiotically: I have been Queen of Scots for such a short time. It is a pity, I thought, I could not have reigned a little longer.

As I heard the click of the gun's catch, I thought of Robbie Scott.

There was a loud report from the other bank. But I felt no searing, hot wound. I was alive, untouched. I opened my eyes, incredulous.

The man with the lantern stood over the body of Rory Beg's murderer. In his hand was a pistol.

The other, whom they called Sandy, dropped to his knees by the body.

'Daid,' he said unemotionally. 'The hairt.'

'I'll no be disobeyed,' said the man with the pistol.

His voice was harsh with anger and authority. There was something strange about it. It was as though he was speaking a language he had learned. I wondered numbly if he could be a foreigner, an enemy of Robbie's from some far place . . .

'Wull we ketch the laddie?' asked Sandy.

'No. 'Tis naethin' but a bairnie seekin' eggs. We'll no waste the time or the toil. Come awa', ye men!'

He tossed his pistol down into the bed of the burn. It landed with a crash on the rocks beside Rory Beg's body.

I understood, dizzy as my mind was. It was to seem Rory Beg's pistol. It was to seem that Rory Beg had shot the man with the club, who killed him in the second before he himself died.

Three men crossed the burn, from my side to the other, some way away from where I crouched. I heard the voices, and the noises of movement through the wood, growing fainter, as they all went down the burn towards the loch. I heard the whimper of the hounds, which must have been muzzled until Rory Beg was found . . .

I was left alone, cowering, trembling, at the edge of the little strip of wood between the bluff and the burn, alone with Rory Beg's body, and the body of his murderer, who had wanted to save his neck by killing me . . .

Why not? Why had the man with the lantern gone to such ghastly lengths to save the life of a birds'-nesting boy? Not from humane scruples. He had shot his companion down, in cold blood, to save my life. Why?

The thing was too difficult for me. And I was in no state to think. I was in no state to do anything about Rory Beg's body: to do more than stammer a prayer over the little crumpled heap.

I was not in good state to walk back to Ravenburn. I felt bottomlessly tired, ill with horror at what I had seen, numb at the thought of my own hairbreadth escape from death, desperately sorry for the gentle-faced old man – my friend's good friend – that I had known for so short a time, that had called me cailin ro mhaiseach, very beautiful damsel.

I forced foot in front of dragging foot, and came miserably to Ravenburn as the sky began to pale.

I lay at last in my bed, waiting for Flora Morran to call me. I stared at the brightening sky, because, if I had closed my eyes, I would have seen what I had seen in the night.

I desperately wanted to see Robbie, but he was not due back until next day. There was no one else to whom I could turn. I dared not confide in anybody – not Killin, not Victoria – until I had talked to Robbie.

I tried to play at being a fashionable young lady, all that long beautiful summer's day, at ease among my friends. It was amazing to me that the events of the night had not left some clear, visible brand on my face. How could I look the same, seem the same, after what I had seen? There must, I think, have been signs of abstraction, fatigue, misery in my face; but no one mentioned them.

Perhaps they thought a grown-up life *was* too much for me.

All day, my mind circled round and round the events of the night, trying to find answers to huge questions.

At first, I assumed that Rory Beg had been followed, by the muzzled bloodhounds and the men. Then I decided that this was impossible. He was far too alert, far too skilful, to have been hunted across the dark countryside by such a large party. He would have heard them, infallibly. He would have led them astray, and given them the slip.

Therefore, the followers were in the Tarruinchon wood before ever Rory Beg arrived. He had walked into an ambush. How had those enemies known where and when to come? Because Rory Beg had been betrayed.

This must be the way of it. It must have been the way of it, when Rory Beg met us by the Horseshoe Pool on the Chinn. The keepers, if they were keepers, were waiting for him. They fired a pistol at what they thought was him. Rory Beg was betrayed that night, which was why he then went far away to a safe place.

Rory Beg himself had made the appointment with Robbie. It was he who had named the time and place. Somehow, he had sent a message to Robbie. One messenger only, probably – for if there was more than one, there was the greater chance of the message being garbled as it went from mouth to mouth. One messenger only, and that messenger was the traitor. I supposed it was another poacher or thief, bought by pieces of silver.

The leader of the murderous party had called out that I was only a boy collecting birds' eggs. Could he have thought so? Would any young lad go birds'-nesting in a remote wood in the small hours of the morning? Would anybody at all look for eggs in late August? He cannot have thought that was what I was about. He must have realized I was there to meet Rory Beg. That I was, at least, a friend of Rory Beg's friend. Yet he shot down one of his companions, in order to save my life.

An explanation struck me which, the more I thought of it, became the more convincing. The leader kept me alive because I was of use to him alive: more use even than his own hired assassin. I was of use because I was a messenger between Rory Beg and Seabhac Seilge. I would lead the enemy to Seabhac Seilge, in his secret place.

Yes, if they followed me. But who was I? A young boy in knickerbockers?

I had not been followed back from Tarruinchon to Ravenburn. I was completely sure of that. Even if I was wrong, and they were cleverer than I thought, and cleverer than I was – even if I had been followed, and seen creeping into the Castle at dawn – they would be looking for a lad in knickerbockers.

Would they set a watch on Jamie, and wait until he led them to Seabhac Seilge?

Rory Beg had seen me once, across yards of water, by the light of a salmon-leistering flare. He had seen me again, briefly, by moonlight, dressed as a boy, with all my long hair under a boy's cap. He had known me at once.

Was it so with the leader of the murderers, too? Had he seen me in the boat with Robbie, that night on the Horseshoe Pool – and known me again, by the Tarruinchon burn? Who would he take me to be, what manner of wild strange tinker-girl? If I was followed to the castle, who then would he take me to be? An adventurous scullery-maid?

Whoever and whatever they guessed I was, they could have spyglasses trained on the Castle and its policies. I might be seen and followed. I might lead the enemy to Eilean Fitheach and to Robbie.

Safety, for him and for me, lay in my staying completely clear of him. But disaster lay there, too. Robbie was expecting the man in the hidden croft to be brought to him, by the Tarruinchon burn, in two nights' time. If he were not brought, he would be killed, and Robbie's cake was dough. I could not guess why, but so Robbie had said, and so Rory Beg had said. Besides, there might all too likely be another ambush in that bloody place, and Robbie struck treacherously down from behind by a club or knife.

I must go to the island next day, when Robbie would be back. I must go without fail. I must get there without being seen or followed . . .

My plan was not very good. The best I could think of, was to slip out of a side door, huddled up in a plaid, and limping with a stick, so that I would be taken for an old country-woman who had come to the Castle to sell something, or to visit a daughter who was a maidservant. Other disguises suggested themselves, but that one seemed to me the most complete.

I was making my preparations – finding a plaid and a stick – when a footman came to me with a letter on a salver. This was an event to which I had now grown quite used. I was also used to finding that the glue on the envelope was not very strong, as though it had been steamed open, and insecurely fixed.

The message was the best possible – an invitation from Lady Angela Ramsay to luncheon that day at Tulloch. Lady Angela apologized for the short notice, but said she had something that would interest me.

I thought it was a letter from Miss Anderson. I wondered what Uncle Frank thought it was.

I dressed up very smart, as a compliment to Lady Angela and her extreme kindness, in a new red silk day dress with the most absurd, enormous 'pagoda sleeves', which were tight at the shoulder, and expanded and expanded until, at the wrist, they were a yard across. It was a ridiculous dress. It was the height of fashion. I adored it! Mme Duplage's milliner had made me a matching hat, of the same red silk, with a plume like a Gascon bravo's.

I was driven to Tulloch by Calum Macnab, in the victoria. I carried a white parasol. Fifty people, perhaps, knew where I was going when I set off. It was the most public of all possible departures.

As we went, I tried to place myself in Robbie's enemy's shoes, and think what I would do if I were he. Obviously, there was no need to dog the victoria every inch of the way from Ravenburn to Tulloch. What was important was to know who was at Tulloch to meet me, and where I went from Tulloch if I did not return home direct.

Lady Angela laughed when she saw me. There was nothing derisive in her laugh. I laughed, too.

'Dear me,' she said, 'the butterfly has emerged from the chrysalis with a vengeance. Can you *eat* in those sleeves, Katie? Won't they trail in the gravy? Are you going to sweep all our wine-glasses off the table?'

'I expect so,' I admitted. 'I haven't tried yet.'

The General was as heavily gallant as Colonel Blair at his worst. But there was a great difference. There was a twinkle in the General's eye, and I burst out laughing again at his stately compliments.

Two of the Ramsays' grandchildren were at Tulloch, staying for a week, little girls of ten and eight. They stared saucer-eyed at my extravagant sleeves. The younger giggled. The elder was shocked at this impertinence.

There was a letter from Miss Anderson. It was very long and loving; one could almost hear the squeak of her voice in the tiny, meticulous handwriting, and the elegantly correct sentences. She modelled her style, I think, on Lord Macaulay.

I was sure, completely sure, that I could confide in the Ramsays. The General was a man of the most perfect honour, who would keep to the death any secret entrusted to him. Lady Angela was determined, as she said, to make up by active friendship for the thoughtless neglect of the old days. But I could tell them nothing they did not know already, until I had spoken to Robbie.

But I could ask them to help me, even though the request seemed utterly strange.

After luncheon, the children were taken away to rest, and we three strolled on a terrace among topiary yews and little geometric box hedges.

From Miss Anderson and Lady Victoria, as well as from myself, the Ramsays knew enough to be aware that I had been, for unknown reasons, the victim of a sort of conspiracy. The excessive surveillance of me was active still – this was proved, to the Ramsays as to me, by Lady Angela's note having been steamed open. Lady Angela was very angry about it, even though she might have expected it. I hoped this would make it easier for me to make a weird request to them.

'Here I am, away from Ravenburn on my own,' I said. 'What is the – the equivalent of opening my letters and reading them?'

'Having you watched,' said the General at once.

'Yes. It is humiliating, and it makes me cross.'

'They can watch you walking up and down here until their eyes drop out,' said Lady Angela crudely. 'Much good it may do them.'

'Yes, but I might,' I said carefully, 'without wishing to appear ungrateful for your kindness and hospitality, ma'am—'

'Don't get too elaborately fashionable, Katie,' said Lady Angela. 'Just say it, whatever it is.'

'I might want to, hum, slip away for an hour or two . . .'

'Oho,' said the General. 'Oho. Who is it?'

He meant, what admirer did I want to meet in secret. It was odd that he should have guessed so right, while guessing so wrong. It was sufficiently right to make me blush. They noticed, laughed, thought they were correct, and were the more anxious to help me however they could.

My plan was now fully formed in my mind: but it involved such strange behaviour on Lady Angela's part that I still hesitated before suggesting it.

Lady Angela herself suggested it.

'You and I are about of a size, Katie,' she said. 'Not quite the same shape, but not far off. With you it's slimness, and with me it's stinginess, but the practical effect is much the same. Not all those funny little buttons up your back will do up over my back, but I can cover up the gap with a shawl. And then, you came in a most distinctive hat, and twirling a most distinctive parasol . . .'

'Your faces are . . .' began the General: then cleared his throat.

'Of different shades of colour,' said his wife. 'That is, alas, all too true. The crab-apple, beside the magnolia. Is there anything a bag of flour won't put right?'

I nearly fell on my knees with gratitude.

'Where would you like your coachmen to take me, Katie?' asked Lady Angela. 'Shall I go shopping in Lochgrannomhead?'

The General gave a burst of laughter. 'Will you go to the circulating library? The pharmacist? The butcher?'

'Call on Lady Stewart at Crossmount, ma'am,' I suggested.

'Not,' said Lady Angela firmly, 'with the back of my dress unbuttoned . . . You know, dear, we can't keep this from your coachman. I don't suppose he'll keep it from Frank Dundas.'

'No,' I agreed, 'but by then . . .'

'You will have kept your tryst. And another time, we'll concoct another device.'

So, a little before three o'clock, an astonishing red silk dress, with astonishing pagoda sleeves, crowned with an astonishing hat, and protected from the sun by a parasol, stepped up into the Ravenburn victoria, and rolled away eastwards from Tulloch. The lady in the carriage had a ghastly white mask, like a clown in a nightmare; nevertheless, her shoulders shook as she turned to wave goodbye to her host.

Calum Macnab, a dour character, sat stolid on his box, while a Tulloch groom held the horse's head, and a footman helped the passenger aboard. He did not turn round. The groom told him where to go. It might be miles before he knew whom he carried.

Peeping from an upstairs window, I had sudden and dreadful qualms. Lady Angela thought she was being followed, if she were followed at all, by a Ravenburn servant, carrying out the orders of an officious step-uncle – a respectable, God-fearing, law-abiding person, who would do no more than report where the lady in the red dress had been. She would in fact be followed, if she were followed, by a violent criminal, acting on the orders of a murderer.

What orders? My life had been saved, on the bank of the Tarruinchon burn, because I was more use to Robbie's enemy alive than dead. No harm would come to Lady Angela. Surely, no harm could come to her . . .

If it did, I would never be able to live with my conscience.

The General came indoors and upstairs, looked at me speculatively, and said, 'You look like a groom to me, Katie.'

I was swathed in a morning-gown of Lady Angela's, with my hair down my back, while we discussed my own disguise. I cannot imagine that anyone ever looked less like a groom.

The General said, 'Have you ever clung to the back of a wagonette?'

Of course, I never had. Grooms did, if a wagonette was full of passengers or baggage.

I hoped I might be dressed up like a Ravenburn groom on a state occasion, in white breeches, boots with coloured tops, a frock coat, and a tall hat with a cockade. But I was to be a country groom on a working afternoon. I wore drab knickerbockers, and canvas gaiters, and a serge coat, and a billycock hat with my hair in a knot underneath. General Ramsay laughed consumedly when he saw me; his younger granddaughter shrieked and fled.

The General himself drove the wagonette, behind a single fat cob. As it was empty, I did not have to cling on behind to the 'spoon', but sat on a wooden seat and bounced up and down. Since I was facing backwards, it was easy and natural to search intently for any sign of a pursuer. I was sure that there would be none; I was sure that there was none.

General Ramsay stopped the wagonette in the midst of a coppice of trees, which the small back road bisected.

'I'll pick you up here in three hours' time,' he said. 'I'd like to see the look on your friend's face, when you meet him.'

I laughed, pink with excitement at the thought of seeing Robbie. But behind my laughter there was furious urgency to tell him my story; and there was the dreadful fear that he might not be on the island.

He was not there.

His boat was. I found it at once, and my heart leaped. I went inland, towards the half-ruined tower of the ravens. I searched Eilean Fitheach, from end to end. I called softly. I went up into Robbie's chamber in the tower.

There was no sign of Robbie. His boat was there; he must have come back. But there was no trace of him. I could only imagine utter disaster. I could not imagine what disaster.

I collapsed on the sweet springy turf near the low arch, where we had so often embraced. I buried my face in my hands, and wept in despair.

ten

'Good gracious,' said Robbie, 'Like Niobe, all tears. Is that how governesses dress nowadays?'

'Oh,' I wailed, 'oh oh.'

Blinded by my tears, I struggled to my knees, groped towards him, and buried myself in his arms.

With a shock, I realized that his back and chest were bare, and very wet. I found that my cheek was resting on his wet bare shoulder, and my hands felt his ribs and his spine and the hard muscles of his back. I did not think anything could feel so comforting, so friendly, so exciting as that warm bare skin.

He was wearing breeches, but he had not yet pulled on his stockings and boots.

'I swam,' he explained, answering the astonishment in my face. 'I keep a bundle of clothes in a portmanteau in a rabbit-hole on the shore. They are just respectable enough to take me to – a place where I keep slightly better clothes, in a civilized wardrobe. And so we go on, getting smarter by stages, all the way to – wherever I'm going.'

'Edinburgh.'

'Yes, sometimes. If I'm going away for more than a day or two, I keep the boat here.'

'Why?'

'I don't like leaving it on the lochside, for days on end, while I'm far away. It would be a great nuisance to borrow another from that absurd boathouse. I'm sorry I had only got this far in dressing, when I came on you.'

'I'm glad,' I said: but blushed to hear what I was saying.

Stripped to the waist, he looked almost delicate, though his shoulders were broad. The deep sunburn on his neck and forearms contrasted with a skin as milky as my own.

'I'm not quite as beautiful as you,' he murmured, smiling.

'Yes, you are,' I sobbed (I don't know why I sobbed) and we embraced passionately. My hands went all over his bare back, and I kissed his shoulder and neck.

'I must put on a shirt,' he muttered, 'before I go mad ... Now, Katie, for God's sake tell me what has been happening. Did you meet Rory Beg?'

All elation and excitement, joy and passion, ebbed out of me, as though a bung-hole had been knocked in the bottom of a beer-keg. Heavily, I told him everything.

He listened intently, interrupting with anxious questions so that he was sure of understanding exactly what took place.

At the end he said, 'Poor Clamhan, poor Rory Beg. He died going about my affairs, not his own. I am very sorry. He was loyal and brave. One day I would like to set up a monument to him—'

'Just carve those words on the stone – that he was loyal and brave.'

'Yes. I think that is quite right.'

'Why was he loyal to you? I mean, how did you ever come to meet such a man?'

'He was loyal to Tom Irvine's memory. They were friends, as you know. Tom once saved Rory Beg from being caught. I was – the representative of Tom.'

I nodded. That was exactly how the old-fashioned Highlanders felt. Robbie was Rory Beg's friend's friend, and that was enough.

'I'm sure you're right,' Robbie went on, 'that they were waiting for him in the wood, the hounds ready, the men placed. You must have gone through the middle of them.'

'But they never touched me.'

'No . . . What can I have been thinking of, to consider for an instant allowing you to take such risks as that?'

'You had no choice. There was no one else who could go.'

'Your memorial, my darling, will have the same words graven as Rory Beg's . . . They were waiting for him, as they had been at the Horseshoe Pool.'

'Who could know he was to be there, those two times?'

'Some friend of his, bought by more money than mine. Or – oh God, some friend of mine, bought by I don't know what . . .'

'Why did they not kill me?' I asked.

'You were dressed as a boy . . .'

'Yes. I was wearing Jamie's clothes. That is, Lord Ravenburn's. He is fat, but his clothes were better than my own, for that sort of thing.'

'Yes, of course . They said you were a boy. Did they think so? Did they spare you, because they saw you were a girl? They said you were birds'-nesting. Could they have thought so? A townsman might be so ignorant of when birds lay eggs, but those men moving and hiding silently in a wood at night must have been countrymen, surely . . . You saw Rory Beg's death. You saw his murderer. You saw the other man, called Sandy, with a gun. Would you know him again?'

'Yes. I am sure I would. It was bright moonlight.'

'And the man who seemed to be the leader, with the pistol and lantern? You saw him?'

'Hardly, because he was behind the lantern.'

'Can you describe him at all?'

I thought hard. 'No,' I said at last. 'He seemed – well, of normal size, you know, and with a normal voice . . . But there was something odd about his voice. He spoke with a Scottish tongue, a local tongue, yet . . .'

'What?'

'As though it was not *quite* natural to him. Did you make any enemies in foreign countries, Robbie?'

'Yes. But none that would hide in a wood at midnight to kill Rory Beg, I think . . .'

'What about the man hidden in the croft in – the place with an impossible name?'

'I must fetch him from there at once, tonight.'

'Yes, I thought you must. That is why I have come here today, in these clothes.'

'In those clothes, in case you were followed?'

'Yes. It seemed safer.'

'It was safer. If you were followed, they did not know who they were following. It was very wise and clever of you, my darling. Those words must also be carved on your memorial slab – ah, heavens, what ghoulish thoughts. You must rejoin your farmer friend and his cart, and turn back into a governess again . . . How did you persuade him to help you in this hare-brained adventure? What did you tell him?'

I frowned for a moment. For the thousandth time, I ached to tell Robbie all the truth about myself. But I dared not. I was the sister of his dead, aristocratic friend. I was Katie Queen of Scots. I was to be presented at Court by the Duchess of Bodmin. I was . . .

Present and future, the possible and the desirable, swayed and grappled in my mind. I would have given up anything for Robbie – I knew that now, beyond doubt of hesitation. Perhaps feeling his naked back with my hands, and laying my cheek on his naked shoulder, created this new and total certainty. Castles and kingdoms were nothing, in the balance against him and my love for him. But I was only eighteen. Mamma's permission was necessary to me. Scottish law was more tolerant than English. A runaway marriage was possible, and would be legal. But, at eighteen, I could be cut off, and would be. I could do so much more for my foundling, if I held something of what I was sure my father must have intended for me. A sudden, clandestine marriage would leave me a disgraced pauper, wife of a Glasgow slum-urchin whom no one would ever thereafter befriend.

And would he ever take me, knowing who I was? I asked this question in a new way, now knowing him better. I thought it blankly impossible. Because he loved me, he would not drag me down. The more he loved me, the less he would assent to ruining me. We were caught in impossible toils. I could only pray that, one day, some miraculous knife would cut all the cords away. I could only go on deceiving Robbie about myself, though it turned a spade in my heart.

'How,' I repeated his question stupidly, 'did I persuade . . .? Oh, well, by telling them a part of the truth. I said – well, I let them believe – I was anxious to meet a – a beau, an admirer, a man – of whom Lady Ravenburn would not approve, whom she would never allow me to meet—'

'So the romantic hearts of the farmer and his wife were melted?'

'Yes, and they will say nothing to anybody. And if they do, no harm is done.'

From his chamber in the tower, Robbie brought down a horseshoe – new, shining, heavily scratched but not much worn down.

'From the river,' I said suddenly.

'Yes, I took it from you, if you remember.'

'Of course I remember. We wondered if it was a good omen. You threw it at the lantern.'

'Two days later I went back to the place, and found it. No doubt the men would have picked it up, but in the dark they didn't see it. They probably thought I threw a stone.'

'You went back and collected it? You took that risk? Why?'

Robbie smiled. 'It was the first thing you had given me,' he said, 'and the moment you gave it to me, I threw it away. *Not* the way to treat a gift from one's lady love. Of course I went back to get it. Look at it, Katie. New. Cast not long after being put on. The horse that wore this had hardly taken a stride on a paved road. Who cast a new shoe in that pool at Crossmount?'

'Does it matter who?'

'I thought it didn't. But after what you have told me, after what happened to Rory Beg—'

'Oh,' I said, 'I see. The man who betrayed Rory Beg, both there by the river, and by the Tarruinchon burn—'

'May have left us his name. This iron visiting-card.'

'But can you tell where a shoe comes from, just by looking at it?' I asked dubiously.

'I can't. But I think the farrier who made it will know his own work.'

'Will you take it about, to every farrier in Scotland?'

'I want you, Katie, to take it to one particular farrier. Can you do that innocently? Say that you found it, by a roadside. That it seemed so new it could go back on a horse's foot, that it seemed a shame to waste it.'

'Yes, of course I can do that. I will. What farrier am I to take it to?'

'The one at Ravenburn. I devoutly hope and pray he says he did not make this shoe, and has never seen it before. But I have a dreadful growing suspicion, after the affair of Rory Beg, which I cannot help facing. All logic points in one direction. It's a direction I hate, but I can't ignore the logic ... Ask the Ravenburn farrier if he made this shoe. If he made it about the beginning of June, for a horse at the Castle.'

'A horse belonging to the Castle?'

'Yes, or a horse at the Castle, a visiting horse. It must belong to a saddle horse. A carriage horse goes on roads, and how would a carriage be by the bank of the river? A farm horse could be there, but this shoe would be bigger. The farrier may remember that he made this shoe for a saddle horse, and he may even remember—'

'Which horse he made it for,' I said, 'which needed another new shoe immediately after.'

'Yes. That second new shoe, replacing one so recently put on – that he will surely remember. Oh God, but I hope he doesn't.'

I took the heavy, shiny horseshoe, and said, 'You told me I should come with you, when you went to – that place with a long name.'

'Allt a' Choire Odhain Bhig. I may have said that, but—'

'You said the old man would be difficult. Rory Beg told me the same thing. He said, "The old man will not want to go." You said that I could help you—'

'*No,* Katie.'

'I believe that is your favourite phrase. We can argue and argue, and I shall win in the end, but there is no time, because I must get back – to – to the farmer and his cart. So you must simply say where and when I am to meet you, and we will go to the place together.'

'*No,* Katie.'

'Very well. It is not so friendly, but I shall go there on my own. I shall meet you there.'

'You'll never find it. You won't remember the name.'

'Allt a' Choire Odhain Bhig. Somebody will tell me where it is. The Ravenburn shepherds will know.'

'But – but you can't go about asking all the Ravenburn shepherds—'

'Why can I not?'

'Because they'll know – somebody will hear – somebody will go there—'

'There is that risk,' I agreed sweetly. 'So wouldn't it be better if I came with you?'

He pretended to be angry. But, when he kissed me goodbye, he said some things I repeated to myself all the time I rowed, and all the time I walked to my rendezvous with General Ramsay.

'And what did your gallant say, when he saw you?' asked General Ramsay.

'He compared me,' I said, 'to Rosalind. In *As You Like It,* you know.'

'Oh yes,' said the General bluffly, pretending he knew what I meant.

Lady Angela was certain she had been followed. But nobody came close, or bothered her.

Calum Macnab had nearly fallen off his box, when at last he turned for instructions, and saw whom he was driving. Lady Angela said it was a joke, to surprise her grandchildren.

I put on my own glorious red silk dress again, and the groom's clothes went back to the Tulloch stables.

Lady Angela kissed me goodbye, and I kissed the children goodbye, and there were many arch looks and roguish references to my secret meeting with my adorer. I think they guessed I was meeting Killin, secretly because of Mamma.

Calum Macnab was glummer than usual when he drove me back to Ravenburn. Though a man of very few words, he was bound to use *some*, among the grooms and strappers. He was bound to talk about Lady Angela's drive, on the little hill roads, in my dress: and about her clown's white floury face.

Word was bound to get to Uncle Frank, who knew everything that went on in and about Ravenburn. Well, if he asked me about it, I would say it was an innocent joke. I would say, with almost complete truth, that it was all Lady Angela's idea. The Ramsays would say the same. They would say nothing about my being watched. They would say nothing about letters being opened. Presumably Uncle Frank, like the Ramsays, would suspect a secret assignation. He, like them, might suspect Killin.

Yet Killin had done nothing to arouse suspicion. He was still at Ravenburn, putting off and putting off his departure. We had little time alone together, he and I, owing to the other people there. He did contrive to find me alone, for a little, once a day or more often: and then he was funny, and adoring, and very comforting. He did not press me. He was gentle. His words were ardent, but his manners controlled his actions. I could not doubt the strength of sincerity of his feelings. I could not forget my gratitude, or hide my esteem and affection. I did not wish to give him false hope, but I could not treat him with a coldness I did not feel. But for Robbie, I would have loved him. But for Robbie, all my problems would have been solved.

It was hard to say if Mamma still had plans about Killin. She sat about, as always, surrounded by her intimates. It seemed to be what she wanted to spend all her time doing. Her life revolved between the drawing room, the dining room, and her boudoir. She was never out of doors, and Killin seldom indoors, so they can hardly have clapped eyes on each other, except at meals and in the evening. Mrs Seton sometimes talked as though an eventual match were inevitable. But that might have been simply to annoy Lady Wood.

Suppose Uncle Frank thought the masquerade at Tulloch *was* to enable me to meet Charles Killin in secret? Suppose Mamma thought so? Suppose Lady Victoria thought so? Would they tax Killin with it? Would they believe his denial?

My mind struggled in a thicket of ifs and buts and suppositions, which almost distracted me from thoughts of the night ahead.

Why was I going on another demented escapade, when Robbie had once again tried to forbid me? Because I thought he would be better for my help. Because I wanted to look after him, and see that he came to no harm. Because, by helping him, I thought I could make him love me even better than he did. Because I wanted to be with him.

Added together, they were not really adequate reasons. But they were good enough for me.

I put on Jamie's shooting clothes again, and crept out by my usual route. I walked fast, for I was a little late. I walked directly up the hill behind the Castle, until the ground dipped again. I struck a burn, and followed it, going always up. I fell often, catching a foot in the long tendrils of the old heather in the dark. I was soon panting and perspiring, in Jamie's stuffy prickly clothes. I came at last to a little ruined steading, long ago deserted, called Moinglas. I approached the ruin cautiously, crouched down in the heather near it, and made land-rail noises.

A night-jar answered. Two seconds later I was in Robbie's arms, embarrassed at the unladylike dampness of my face, which he must have felt even through his beard.

Robbie gave me a minute's rest, then we set off into a steep glen. The night was very dark. I could not tell where we were going. We changed course often, because of the severe ground; soon I had no idea in which direction we were heading. Robbie seemed to know the way perfectly – either to see in the dark, or to be guided by sure instinct. My legs began to ache with climbing; my heart pounded and my lungs laboured.

Robbie let me rest again. I took off my cap and collapsed full length on the heather. Robbie stroked my dampened hair.

I said, when I had got my breath back enough to speak, 'I am sorry. I am slowing you down. I am a liability.'

He laughed softly, and said, 'No man I know would cross rough country so well in the dark. How does a governess learn such things?'

'From books.'

'Of course. Did you ask the Ravenburn farrier about our horseshoe?'

'No. I got back too late from – from the farm. The farrier would have been off to his supper. I will go in the morning, if I can.'

'It depends on your pupil, of course. Will you be in a state to teach her tomorrow?'

'It depends what lessons we have. I'll suggest the adventures of Montrose as a fugitive, or Bonny Prince Charlie . . .'

We went on, God knows where, over ground that seemed wilder and wilder.

We came to a place where nature had constructed a strange

179

formation. I could just make out, in the dark, that there was a narrow notch between towering cliffs, which was the apex of a triangle of level grass. The sides of the triangle were the cliffs, and its base the ridge topping the steep slope we had just climbed. Beyond the notch, the ground fell away precipitously into the blackness of a deep glen.

'Almost there,' said Robbie. 'We'll rest a minute. Be very careful from now on. Take my hand, Katie, when we start off. There's an enormous scree in front of us. We must go down it. It's all broken stone, little pebbles and big rocks, all ready to slither down in a rush.'

'We could start a land-slide.'

'Easily.'

'Do we come back this way?'

'Yes, but it is much safer going up a scree than going down one. I would go another way if I could, but it puts five miles on the journey.'

'What is this place?'

'Choire Odhain Bhig. The scree fans out as we go down the corrie. It's treacherous. The cliffs keep crumbling, with every frost, and pieces fall and make this slippery rickle of stones.'

'And down there is the burn? Allt a' Choire Odhain Bhig?'

'Yes, and close beside it a croft you can hardly see even by daylight. You'll understand why when we get there. I would never have found it, but for Rory Beg.'

'A man lives hidden there.'

'And has, for many years.'

'Lives how? I mean, on what?'

'The ravens feed him. Well, a predatory bird feeds him. He is brought whisky and meat and oatmeal, on a pack pony, by night.'

'This way?'

'Another and much longer way.'

'Does no one come here? Herds, after strayed sheep? Or people stalking the deer?'

'No. The only sheep here are a few old ewes which have gone wild. As to the deer-stalking, I don't think this corrie is a place for deer. Also, the burn is the march of two forests. No one stalks a deer right to a march, in case they find themselves killing it on a neighbour's ground.'

'What forests, Robbie? Where are we?'

180

'This is still Ravenburn ground. Beyond it's Crossmount.'

I nodded, though not much the wiser. The march between the two estates was many miles long, and went by some very punishing country. There were parts even I had never explored. This was one of them. No one came here. The reason stags were not stalked here, I thought, was not because of the nearness of the march, but the severity of the country. Mamma's guests, and Sir Campbell Stewart's tenants, took their sport gently.

'Are you rested, my darling?' said Robbie. 'Shall we go on? Very gently, now – douce, douce – don't set any stones rolling. By day, if we dared, we could go down in a great rush. I think we'd break a leg or a back. Now we must walk down on eggshells, slippery eggshells, with cannonballs waiting to roll . . .'

I held Robbie's hand. Very gingerly we crept down that enormous scree in the heart of the great corrie, which was scooped out of the side of the hill as though by a spoon. Our feet crunched in the shingly stones of the scree. It was steep. I did not understand how millions of small loose stones could cling to so precipitous a slope: nor the much bigger ones which were poised among them. It was treacherous. If one of us had stumbled and fallen, the faller must have slid helplessly down the scree, perhaps all the way down to the bottom, pulling the scree down after, pulling small stones from under bigger stones, so that tons of rock might thunder down the hill.

My heart jumped when a pebble rolled. I concentrated, as hard as I knew how, on keeping my balance, and putting my feet down securely on the shifting shingle of scree. I relied heavily on Robbie's hand, to keep me steady and to guide me. It must have been twice as difficult for him, supporting me as well as himself, and worrying about me as well as himself.

The descent seemed endless.

At last the gradient of the scree flattened. We picked our way through tumbles of big rocks which had crashed down days or centuries earlier. There were deep drifts of shingle which had slithered down, perhaps with rain or melting snow. We were no longer in danger of starting an avalanche, but it would have been very easy to sprain an ankle.

And then we were on heather, clear of the horror of the scree. I looked back. The moon had not risen, but I could just see the great pale ramp of the scree against the black sides of the corrie.

It looked too steep to climb. But Robbie said it was easier to go up.

We heard the whisper of a burn, and Robbie marched confidently towards it. There was no longer any need for me to hold his hand: but I still held it.

The burn was no more than a trickle. We could step over it easily from rock to rock. We climbed a gentle slope for a few yards, then met much steeper ground. Instead of climbing on, Robbie skirted the steeper ground, and going parallel to the burn, came to a rocky outcrop which stuck out of the hillside like a buttress on the side of a church. On the far side of the outcrop there was a great pile of broken rocks, as though the top of a mountain had fallen off and broken into pieces. Up against this pile of rock, nestling against it and into it, was something resembling a wall.

It was a wall, so rough and crude that it felt to my exploring fingers little different from the natural jumble of rocks.

'Some kind of anchorite once lived here,' said Robbie softly.

'Was he brought oatmeal and whisky on a pack-pony?'

'Yes, I expect so, by the faithful. Can you feel a doorway?'

I groped on in the dark. I said dubiously, 'I can feel a sort of gap between the stones.'

'That's the doorway. I'd better go in first, in case—'

'In case what? What might have happened?'

'In case someone got here before us. That's the thought that has given me nightmares, every minute since you told me about Rory Beg. Wait here.'

'I'll come in with you.'

'No, Katie. Wait here until I say all's well. If I say anything else, run and hide. Promise me.'

'All right.'

I did not mind his giving me orders. I did not mind not going into the croft until he said all was well. But I did not like being left alone in that weird place in the dark.

Robbie disappeared into the blacker blackness of the gap between the stones. He stood just inside, I think, listening and waiting. I listened intently, too.

I heard an inarguable snore.

I heard Robbie's chuckle of relief. I heard flint and steel, and the hiss of his tinder, and then saw a dim glow of light from the gap in the rocks.

'All's well,' said Robbie in a normal voice. 'At least, it could be much worse. Come in. Welcome to the anchorite's cave. But duck your head, or you will push it through the roof.'

I went in, bending double to clear the top of the gap. It was like a cave, dimly illuminated by a candle Robbie had lit. One wall and part of another were living rock. The rest of the walls were piled up, rather than built up. The roof was supported by two solid beams of wood, on which rested a dozen hurdles.

'Ancient thatch above that, I imagine,' said Robbie. 'Probably heather. And live heather and grass grows on the top now.'

'So it doesn't simply look like part of the landscape, it is part of the landscape.'

Robbie nodded, and raised the candle. There was a fireplace in a corner – a ring of stones on the ground, with a gap in the roof above. Beside it lay a pair of big wicker baskets, that a pack pony might have carried. One was nearly full of oatmeal; in the other was part of the carcass of a sheep. Sticking out from the oatmeal were the necks of half a dozen black bottles. Other bottles lay empty on the ground nearby.

There was a single rough wooden bed, the only furniture in the hovel. A bundle of filthy rags lay on the bed, from which there came a snore.

The place reeked of whisky and cheap tobacco.

'I suppose,' said Robbie cheerfully, 'if the essentials are looked after, the details are unimportant. The food is all right. The whisky's all right. The tobacco smells terrible, but I daresay it's what he likes. A happy man, Katie. There's a moral there.'

'What moral?' I asked.

'One man's meat is another man's poison,' he said, wrinkling his nose in distaste at the smell. 'Anyway, the important thing is, we're here in time. Now we must wake this sleeping beauty up from his dreams of paradise—'

'And get him up the scree?'

'And into another refuge. Donald McWiddie! Wake up, my friend!'

At one end of the bundle of rags on the bed, I made out a face in the candlelight. It was an unpleasant sight – bloated, very dirty, with a matted beard full of scraps of food. The head was bald, but fringed with straggling hair, which lay, like seaweed, on a greasy plaid. I made out the rest of the man. He was fat. The rags which covered him were the remnants of breeches and a flannel shirt. There were boots on the feet – good boots, not old – but no stockings on the blackened and bulging calves.

'Boots come by pack pony, too,' I said.

'So they do, indeed. Those are not relics of his active years. He hardly needs them, I think. He doesn't look as though he has taken any exercise since he came here. No need, of course, with locusts and wild honey arriving fortnightly in panniers.'

'Who is this horrible man?' I said. 'Why is he hidden here and brought these things? Why does he matter to you? Why will he be killed if he stays here?'

'He is Donald McWiddie,' said Robbie. 'He is hidden here because he knows a secret. That secret matters to me. That is why he will be killed if he stays.'

'You have answered all my questions,' I said crossly, 'without answering any of them.'

'Yes,' he agreed cheerfully. 'But what I can't understand is why he wasn't killed years ago. That is very strange. All those years, on this fat pension of food and tobacco, whisky and boots ... And apart from the trouble and expense of keeping him alive, why take the risk? Why not be safe, kill him, bury the secret once and for all? Very strange. There must be a reason. Perhaps he knows it. Perhaps he'll tell us, if we ever get him into a state to speak.'

All this time, Robbie had been slapping at Donald McWiddie's bloated cheek, and pinching the lobe of his ear. The fat snores changed key, trumpeted, rolled round the hovel like thunder. There was a last violent grunt, and eyelids flickered over little pale pig eyes.

The eyes stared at Robbie, without recognition or understanding.

'You must come along with us, Donald McWiddie,' said Robbie gently.

Very slowly the fat man came back towards consciousness. It was as though he was wading there, reluctantly, from his oblivion, through deep mud.

He said nothing, but it seemed he understood at last that Robbie was telling him he must come away.

His look of swinish apathy changed immediately into one of terror. Still speechless, he clung to the rude side of his bed as though to stop us lifting him off it bodily and carrying him away.

Robbie talked to him slowly, soothingly, saying that he would be safe and comfortable where he was going.

Terror was succeeded, as suddenly, by rage. Donald McWiddie shook his fist in Robbie's face. His own face was contorted. His mouth dribbled.

Then apathy returned. He lay back, his arms limp, his mouth open, his eyes glazed, breathing noisily, forgetting us.

'He's still drunk,' I said.

'Yes. He may be like this for hours. We have not got hours. Nor, I think, has he, although that message has not reached him yet. It's time for desperate remedies. First I'll pull him off his bed on to the floor. Will you see that he doesn't hit his head?'

'Yes,' I said reluctantly. I did not want to touch him.

Robbie stuck his candle in a cranny between rocks, then took hold of Donald McWiddie's boots. He began to pull him feet first off the bed. Donald McWiddie made a little high moaning sound, like a child with a nightmare. He clutched at the sides of the bed. Robbie pulled harder. He pulled the man clear off the bed on to the ground. I prevented his head from striking the ground, by holding under it the plaid he had used as a pillow.

'Bring one of those full bottles, Katie,' said Robbie. 'Then blow out the candle and follow me.'

I did as he said. While I pulled a whisky bottle from the oatmeal in the basket, Robbie hauled Donald McWiddie feet first out through the gap into the open air.

'A bath is what this sinner needs,' said Robbie. 'Baptism by total immersion.'

'He'll catch cold,' I said.

'Better than catching a bullet. I'm tempted to drag him all the way, but I think I'd better carry.'

'But he's so fat! He's too heavy!'

'But he's precious to me.'

Donald McWiddie was whimpering like a puppy, lying helpless on his back on the rough ground. Robbie put one of the brute's arms round his own shoulder, and hoisted him clear of the ground. He staggered under the dead weight, but kept his footing, and started slowly down towards the burn.

'Just put his head in,' I suggested, 'not the whole of him.'

Robbie grunted, too heavily burdened to speak.

He lowered Donald McWiddie to the ground beside the tiny burn, then dragged him by the shoulders so that his head lay inches from the water. Robbie filled his cupped hand with water, and dashed it repeatedly into Donald McWiddie's face.

The whimpering changed into a screech like a spring vixen's. Donald McWiddie struggled, trying to twist his head away from the incessant douches of cold burn-water.

'Na na,' he moaned, 'na na. Whaur's ma whusky?'

'You shall have a dram,' said Robbie soothingly, 'as soon as you are up on your feet.'

'A canna stan'! A canna stan'!'

'Try,' said Robbie encouragingly, dashing another half-pint into his face.

Howling like a baby, the fat drunken man struggled into a sitting position, and begged in a torrent of words for his whisky.

'When you're standing on your own two feet,' said Robbie inexorably.

It seemed an hour before Donald McWiddie was shakily standing, begging with outstretched hands for the promised dram.

I handed Robbie the bottle. He uncorked it, and handed it to Donald McWiddie. The latter seized it and raised it. The neck of the bottle rattled against his teeth. After two seconds, Robbie took hold of it. They had a struggle. Donald McWiddie was like to fall over with a crash into the burn. He was like to spill all his whisky, too.

In a moment, Robbie had the bottle in his hand and safely corked. Donald McWiddie was on his knees, scrabbling at Robbie's legs, whining and begging for more whisky.

'It's degrading,' said Robbie to me quietly, 'but it may make him easy to manage. Stick and carrot, you know. Will you get another carrot from that basket of oatmeal, please? Can you find it in the dark?'

'Of course,' I said. I fetched another bottle of whisky.

Donald McWiddie tried to crawl back to his croft, where he knew there was enough whisky to buy him oblivion for a week.

Robbie said sharply, 'No! You will come with me. If not, I shall break all those bottles. And this one, over the stone here. There will be no more whisky for you. You hear that, Donald McWiddie? There will be no more whisky for you!'

This was the stick. Donald McWiddie cringed and blubbered at the threat.

'Come along with us, like a sensible man, and you shall have a dram every half-mile.'

This was the carrot. Donald McWiddie mouthed and swallowed and licked his lips.

It *was* degrading – horribly degrading. I had never before, in my over-sheltered life, seen a man the abject and drooling slave of liquor in a black bottle. But it seemed it did make him easier to manage.

Stick and carrot took us uncertainly towards the foot of the great scree. Donald McWiddie stumbled and moaned. Robbie had hold of one of his arms, with the bottle of whisky in his other hand, where Donald could glimpse it in the dark. I had hold of his other arm. I held the second bottle safe under my coat. When Donald McWiddie turned to face me, the whisky reek of his breath nearly knocked me over.

Robbie murmured, as we stumbled along, 'It's lucky they didn't come last night. It's lucky they didn't come before us tonight.'

'Perhaps they're coming after us tonight,' I suggested. 'Perhaps they're on their way now.'

'That's exactly what I've been thinking, for the last three hours. It seems likely to the point of certainty. It's something I would have guarded against, but there was no way of guarding against it. It will not be a big party, I think. Not a troop, like the one they called up to catch Rory Beg.'

'One man,' I said, 'would be enough for . . .'

'For our friend here. Yes. But I think more would come. One man alone might twist an ankle, or get lost. If I were in his shoes—'

'Whose?'

'My enemy. My friend's enemy. Tom Irvine's enemy. If I were in his shoes, I'd come myself, with two others. How would I come? Well, without a pack-pony or any burden, I'd come our route.'

'If that is right, they will come down the scree. Shall we wait for them to go by?'

'If we were sure they were coming, and just three, and by that route, yes. But we might wait uselessly until daylight, Katie.'

'I can't do that.'

'Nor I, with this travelling companion here.'

'We rested at the top of the scree,' I said. 'We were tired. At least, I was. We needed to be fresh, for coming down. Will they know the place well enough to do the same?'

'Yes, of course. One will, at least. If they rest—'

'If they are there and resting now—'

'They must have heard us. Donald McWiddie's fine new boots make a noise like a company of drunken guardsmen.'

Hearing his name, the shambling figure between us began to blubber for whisky. Robbie let him drink for two seconds, before pulling the bottle away from him again.

'Not only his boots make a noise,' I said.

I could just see Robbie's nod in the dark. He said, 'Nothing is more likely than their coming tonight. If they come tonight, nothing is more likely than that they're hereabouts by now. They'll want to finish their business, and be safely away to their beds long before dawn.'

'If they're waiting at the top of the scree, in the cleft,' I said, 'and if they've heard Donald McWiddie—'

Again the drunken man reacted with moans and cries to the sound of his name.

'They'll wait for us to climb,' said Robbie.

'Well then, we'll go round the other way, even if it's longer.'

'No. They'll hear us, and follow. We can't keep this fellow quiet. We'd be no match for three of them. I can't risk any sort of fight, with him here, and you here. Thank God the moon won't be up for a while yet.'

'But,' I gulped, 'we can't climb the scree, if we think they're waiting at the top.'

'We can seem to,' said Robbie. 'There's a coil of thin rope round my waist. I brought it in case we needed it for getting Donald McWiddie home. I think we shall need it for that, but it's useful now, too. I'm going to tie one end to a stone near the bottom of the scree. Then I'm going to climb up the face beside the scree, as far as the rope will let me.'

'But you can't, in the dark!'

'Oh yes. Higher up it's impossible, but for some way it's not bad. Once I'm up, I'll pull the stone up after me, so that it bumps and rattles—'

'And sounds like people climbing.'

'I hope so.'

'Then what?'

'Then we'll see what they do, if they're there. You stay behind, in the shelter of this rock here, Katie. Look after Donald

McWiddie. Give him a dram in five minutes, but only a dram, and not before five minutes.'

'Yes,' I said unhappily. I did not want Robbie to leave me. But I thought his plan such a good one that I could not object.

Robbie uncoiled the rope from his waist, then coiled it again, and looped the coil over one arm. He kissed me behind Donald McWiddie's back, then slipped away into the darkness.

'Gie us the whusky, laddie,' said Donald McWiddie.

'No. You heard what he said—'

'Och, ye'll du as ye're bid, ye ill bairn!'

He reached for the bottle which I was holding. I struggled to keep it from him. But in spite of his grossness and the whisky he had drunk, he was far stronger than I. He hurt my arm, and hurt my back by knocking me against the rock, and grabbed the bottle. The neck rattled against his teeth as he raised it and drank.

He would be insensible. We would never get him away.

'Robbie!' I called desperately.

Robbie loomed up through the darkness. He pulled the bottle roughly away from Donald McWiddie, who wailed and beseeched.

'I'll take the liquor with me,' said Robbie. 'Any more trouble, and I'll break it.'

'Na, na! A'll kull the laddie!'

The desperation in his voice was too acute to ignore. Though his life was being saved, he threatened to kill one of his rescuers, in order to be sure of his whisky.

'Oh God,' said Robbie. 'This is impossible.'

'Not at all,' I said, surprised that the solution had not come to him. 'I am not strong enough to control Donald McWiddie, and you are. But I am very good at climbing.'

We argued, briefly and passionately, while Donald McWiddie begged for whisky.

'I'll tie him up,' said Robbie.

'Nonsense. I need the rope.'

'I'll knock him unconscious.'

'And then get him up the scree, and all the way back?'

'It's far too dangerous for you to climb in the dark.'

'You said it was easy for the lower part.'

I took the coil of rope from Robbie, and went to the foot of the scree.

Just where the shingly scree became really steep, I found a stone the size of a man's head, but so shaped that I could knot the end of the rope securely round it. Then I went to my left, paying out the rope as I went. I found the foot of the broken rock-face, which was the wall of the corrie beside the scree. Obeying Robbie's reluctant directions, I began to climb. I moved with the utmost caution, so as not to make any noise, and so as not to break my neck. It was not a difficult climb, though higher up, Robbie said, there was a formidable over-hang, impossible to ascend even by day.

I came to the end of the rope. I had no idea how long it was – how far I had climbed, how far below me lay the rock at the other end. I was a few yards from the edge of the scree, on a ledge, under an overhanging rock.

I was panting heavily, and streaming with perspiration. My hands were sore, and I thought bleeding, from the sharp edges of rocks. But I felt exultant. I was necessary to Robbie. He could not have accomplished tonight's ploy without me.

I began to pull on the rope. The stone at the end was heavy, and the rope snagged on rocks below me. I tugged and heaved, and then heard a crunching far down the scree, as my stone was dragged across the shingle. I gave a series of short tugs at the rope, unevenly timed, hoping that this would give the im-pression of feet climbing and stumbling up the scree.

All the time, the thought was horribly present in my mind that I might be play-acting to a non-existent audience.

The thought was banished, when I heard a movement and a voice above me, in the cleft at the top of the scree. I did not recognize the voice. It spoke one word, softly, which I could not make out.

I tugged at my stone. The rope snagged on something I could not see, or my stone was jammed against another. I let it slide down a little, hoping to free it. There was a convincing crunch of shingle, and I heard a few pebbles roll and bounce away down the slope. My stone was by now well up into the steepest and most treacherous part of the scree. It came free from what-ever had obstructed it. I tugged again. It was heavy work, pull-ing that big stone up the steep slope.

I paused to get my breath, and because the rope was hurting my hands. It seemed to me realistic that a climber might pause.

There was another movement above. I thought someone had

come a small way down from the cleft. I hoped devoutly that the moon was not due to rise for a long time.

I tugged my rope again; the crunching recommenced.

Then there was a sort of groaning from above, as of two heavy objects rubbing together. Pebbles bounced and slithered, There was a noise like the end of the world, as a big rock plunged down the scree ten yards from my face. As it bounced thunderously down, it started a great roaring slithering descent of the gravelly scree, with other bit rocks displaced and rolling and bouncing too, and crashing like thunderbolts, and rolling on. Small stones, and some not so small, were somehow thrown out of the stream of the avalanche, Like handfuls of spray from a waterfall; and some were hurled not far from the ledge where I clung.

The greatest thunder lasted only for a few seconds. It battered at the senses; my mind reeled, it was so shocking and unexpected. I thought numbly of the fate of anybody who had been climbing the scree. They must have been pounded to a bloody pulp by those great bouncing rocks, and then buried deep in drifts of shingle.

Robbie's friend's enemy went to all lengths.

A few last pebbles scuttled and pattered down the scree. Utter silence fell.

I listened intently. There was a laugh from above, than a sharp word of command which cut off the laughter abruptly. I heard the noise of a very careful and circumspect descent. I saw the beam of a lantern.

Robbie was right. There were three of them. I could not see them clearly. I could not see at all the one who carried the lantern. They spoke softly. I heard no words.

After a long time, the beam of the lantern began to play amongst the wild jumble of new-fallen rocks at the bottom of the scree. They were looking for traces of us.

I climbed down, carefully and silently, and crept back to Robbie. He had gagged Donald McWiddie with a handkerchief.

Robbie took my hand, and whispered hoarsely, 'Thank God. Thank you, Katie. Thank God for you, Katie.'

'There was no difficulty at all,' I whispered. 'Making the plan was the only difficult part.'

We watched the lantern of the assassins. They gave up their

search after a few minutes, and the lantern wavered towards the secret croft.

'They'll think Donald McWiddie is dead and buried,' said Robbie. 'They must think so. And us with him.'

'Us? Who do they think we are?'

'Ah. How they must be wondering, and I am wondering still – *why* was not our friend here dead and buried years ago? I simply can't make that out.'

'It's lucky for you.'

'Yes. Inexplicable, but very lucky indeed. Come. They won't hear us now. At the top of this gentle little slope, Donald Mc-Widdie, you shall have almost all the whisky you want.'

The rest of the journey was infinitely wearisome, but not really difficult.

Robbie had rescued much of his rope, cutting it off with his knife (the one I had returned to him) where the end was buried deep in the rubble. It helped in getting Donald McWiddie up the scree, and down some of the steepest parts of our way. Stick and carrot got the man along somehow. To goad him, Robbie threatened to break a whisky bottle; to bribe him, he promised a dram at the end of a hundred yards. So we came at last, exhausted, to the shore of Loch Chinn.

'Don't mention the name of the island,' Robbie whispered to me, 'or anything about it.'

'Why not?'

'He's a local man. He knows the stories. He'd die of fright.'

'That *would* be a waste, after all our trouble.'

Robbie laughed, and set about trying to get Donald Mc-Widdie into his boat. But the man was in a state approaching delirium. He screamed and fought. He would be dangerous in the boat, and very likely to upset it.

'I am sorry to do this,' said Robbie, 'but I really see no alternative.'

He hit Donald McWiddie, not very hard, on the back of the head with a half full whisky bottle.

I was sickeningly reminded of Rory Beg's death. But the unconscious man's pulse was vigorous, and he was breathing like the bellows in the great kitchen ranges at Ravenburn. We pulled him into the boat, and he lay like an animal in the bottom.

I might, now, have gone straight back to Ravenburn. It

would have been the wise and sensible, the obvious and logical thing to do. It never occurred to me to do it. I climbed into the boat, and Robbie rowed to Eilean Fitheach.

The moon had risen some time before, but lay behind a bank of cloud. She silvered the upper edge of the cloud, which cast a diffused dim glow over the loch. It was absolutely windless. The water was like a sheet of steel. We did not speak. I felt dirty and exhausted and happy.

Donald McWiddie groaned in the bottom of the boat, returning to consciousness as reluctantly as from his drunken stupor.

'No harm done to him,' murmured Robbie, 'that a dram won't cure.'

We nosed into our landing place. We manhandled Donald McWiddie ashore, with a gigantic effort; though he was conscious, he was completely flaccid, a gross dead weight.

I sat down, panting and sighing.

'I'll put him to bed with a bottle beside him,' said Robbie. 'I fixed up a sort of lean-to hut for him this evening, before I set out, with a couple of blankets and a heather bed and a canvas roof. It's well away from the tower.'

'Why? Shouldn't you keep an eye on him?'

'He won't need an eye kept on him. Whisky will keep him docile. He can't go anywhere. I'm certain he can't swim – who ever heard of a Highlander who can? And I don't want him as a bedfellow, or even as a near neighbour.'

I agreed. I was not getting fonder of the reek of whisky, or the acrid odour of Donald McWiddie himself.

'I'll help you get him there,' I said.

'No. There's no need. You've done enough. More than enough. Far more than I can ever thank you or repay you for. Far more than any other companion I can imagine, man or woman. Rest now.'

Robbie dragged the mumbling, incoherent Donald McWiddie through the low stone arch. Then he hoisted the fat man on to his shoulder, and walked a little unsteadily off into the darkness.

Suddenly, urgently, I wanted to bathe again. I was hot and dirty and tired. I yearned to peel off Jamie's prickly and sticky clothes, and feel the clean cool water all over my skin.

Why not, in the dark? Why ever not?

I struggled out of the stiff, unfamiliar clothes. I stood naked, in the near darkness, suddenly sure the water would be icy, and freeze me half to death. I gulped, sat down on the hummock, and trailed my legs in the water. It *was* cold. I slipped in. I splashed and kicked. It was cold, but it was glorious! I felt instantly refreshed and clean; fatigue dropped away from me as easily as Jamie's breeches; I could have run up and down a hundred screes.

I stood waist deep by Robbie's boat, looking out over the loch. There was a quiet splash in the water behind me. I turned, startled.

Robbie was in the water, a yard from me. Only his head emerged from it. He straightened, and like me was standing waist-deep.

At that moment, the rim of the moon peeped over the bank of cloud. The milky light strengthened as it rose clear, clear, and flooded the loch with silver.

eleven

Robbie stretched out his arms to me, and I went into them. I flung my own arms around his precious neck. I felt all his naked body pressed against mine.

He climbed out of the water, and drew me out. We stood, dripping, facing each other, in the brilliant moonlight. We stared at each other. Our hands wandered lightly and lovingly over each other's bodies. His fingers were on my cheek, and my shoulder, and my breasts. His eyes were wide, wondering. I felt that he was trembling. I was trembling, too, with excitement, anticipation, desire, fright.

He took my hand, and led me through the low stone arch to the sweet turf beyond. Moonlight washed over the sward like a silver silken sheet. We were lying down, now passionately embracing with our bodies pressed so tight together that I thought my heart must enter his breast: now a little apart, looking at each other in solemn amazement. His hand, trembling, stroked my breasts. I pressed his hand over my breast, and my breast into his hand. I felt his fingers, like beautiful moths, all over me. I welcomed them to my most secret places. He took my hand, and guided it. We explored each other's bodies with loving wonder.

And then he was upon me in the moonlight, slim as a girl, muscled as a snake. There was a sharp brief pain. I cried out, and pulled him on to me and into me with all my strength. I sobbed for joy. Wonder filled me. Nothing in my life had prepared me for this intensity of happiness . . .

Oh, I had read, in romances of which Miss Anderson disapproved, of people being swept up in a tempest of passion. I thought this a fustian phrase, fanciful, novelettish. How wrong I was. A tempest, a hurricane of passion picked me up and flung me, crying with joy, through ringing skies.

'I am so happy I could die,' I said. 'Will you marry me?'
'Yes,' said Robbie.

We hardly spoke as he rowed me back to the shore. There were a million words to be said, but they could wait. I hurried to the Castle, slipped in by the game larders in the nick of time, and crept up to my bed.

I felt lonely in bed, for the first time in my life.

The miracle did not end. In the morning, when I should have felt heavy from lack of sleep, I felt like running and singing. When I should have been pale with fatigue, I was pink with remembered excitement.

When I should have been guilty, I was proud.

People looked at me, startled, as I went about the Castle. I saw several surprised smiles. I did not understand, until I saw my own face in a looking glass in a passage.

I was the cat that had got at the cream.

I heard Uncle Frank say to Mamma, 'He has had the grippe, or some such thing. He is still weak, but improving. He says he will come as soon as he can. It is highly annoying that he cannot come at once — that he could not have come days ago. This dangerous folly must be stopped, and by him. I begin to wonder if he is not prolonging his convalescence, in order to avoid coming here. Well, I know how to deal with that. He will come, however reluctant. He must come.'

'Who, dearest Frank?' asked Mamma.

'Dr McAndrew.'

A memory stirred. Malvina had spoken of Dr McAndrew, and the name had been dimly familiar when she mentioned it. He was coming from some Lowland place. Well, if he was coming to examine me, he was wasting his time and mine. I knew myself to be in the most perfect, abundant health, of mind and body. I felt better than ever before. If I was mad, it was only with love and happiness.

For all I cared, all the doctors in Scotland could come and peer at me: as long as they were not too long about it, for my days were very full.

I went to see Jaikie McBurnie the farrier, with the horseshoe from the river.

Jakie thought he had made the shoe. He could not say when, or for what horse. He thought it odd of me to want to know. It was not a big shoe; the animal that had worn it was either a pony, or a small-footed thoroughbred kind of horse. Jakie did not remember replacing an almost-new shoe lost by such a horse.

'When did ye find it, Miss Katie?' he asked.

'About the end of May,' I said, without thinking.

'An' ye've helt it syne?'

'I forgot about it. I found it again today, in – in my room. It seemed a waste of a new shoe, not to put it to use.'

'Ay, richt eneuch. We're no' ower fond o' waste here. Mr Dundas is terrible doon on waste.'

A groom came by the forge, leading a neat bay Galloway – between a small horse and a tall pony – in a leather halter.

'This yin hae lostit the off heend shue, Jaikie,' he said.

'Och, aye, the peeg.'

'He's a gran' wee horse.'

'I mind I mad' a fu'set for this yin – in May, wast'?'

'Hae ye a shue by ye wull fit the fut? The gentleman's awa the morn.'

'Nay, nay! Cam' the morn's morn. I canna mak' a guid shue in an hoor.'

'Wha' aboot the yin ye hauld in yer han'?'

Jaikie McBurnie coughed crossly. The shoe I had brought him looked about right for the neat foot of the Galloway. Jaikie bent down, made the horse bend its leg, laid its foot on his leather apron, and tried the shoe on the unshod foot. It fitted.

'Micht hae been mad' for the mannie,' said the groom triumphantly.

'I'm thunkin' 'twaur mad' for the mannie,' grumbled Jaikie.

'In May?' I asked.

'Ay, likely.'

'It was lost soon after. But you didn't make another?'

'The gentleman waur awa',' explained the groom.

'Ay,' said Jaikie, examing the Galloway's foot. 'An' fund a butcher 'staid o' a skulled farrier. I'm no' surpreesed he's lostit anither shue. A butcher, ay! He didna feel doon the hufe, sae 'tis meeserable crackit, an' the nails canna hauld . . .'

Getting his file to pare down the hoof, Jaikie went into a grumbling monologue about the iniquities of all farriers except himself.

I said to the groom, 'Whose horse is it?'

'Sir George Fraser's.'

I walked away slowly, thinking hard, trying to remember exactly how it had been.

The dates fitted.

Sir George had left the Castle, with Killin, in the second week of May. Soon afterwards, Killin wrote to Uncle Frank that Sir George was in the Hebrides. Then Sir Campbell Stewart reported seeing him in Lochgrannomhead. That very night, we found the shoe in the Horseshoe Pool of the Chinn. That very night, a trap was set for Rory Beg, and a pistol fired in the dark . . .

By the time I could get this vital news to Robbie, Sir George would be gone. Gone where? On past form, not to where he might say he was going. To somewhere nearby, where he could commit more treachery . . .

I had to see Robbie, with my news about the horseshoe as well as for more poetic reasons. But I decided to go by night.

There were two reasons.

For one thing, it was becoming more and more difficult for

me to get to Eilean Fitheach by day. If I were followed, it was more and more dangerous, too, especially as Robbie now had that precious prisoner on the island. (Why he should want that bloated, disgusting man, I still could not begin to guess; and he had steadfastly refused to tell me. His secretiveness did something to make me feel easier about how I was deceiving him.) We could not do again the trick with Lady Angela and my red dress. Other disguises might be pierced. To go by night was altogether safer and wiser.

It was less embarrassing, too. I knew – and trembled exultantly at the knowledge – what would happen when I saw and touched Robbie again. I knew his passion matched mine. There had been tears on his cheek, like pearls in the moonlight, and they were not all my tears. I knew what would happen, and my whole soul and body yearned for it to happen. I was altogether shameless and abandoned, lost to all decency and morality. But I was not lost to all shyness. Ridiculous as it may seem, I felt happier at the thought of making love to Robbie in the dark – even though the moon lit up our love like a leistering-flare . . .

By night or day, I had to go to the island as soon as possible, with my news on my lips as well as my heart on my sleeve. My news sickened me. My mood of exultation was not destroyed. I was sure nothing could destroy it. Though it was shot with a dark, unhappy suspicion – more than suspicion, far more – it induced in me a feeling of such benevolence that I did what I should have done before: I wrote a long letter to Miss Anderson.

I did *not* reveal any of the things uppermost in my thoughts. Miss Anderson's eyes would have fallen out with shock. I did describe *The Rivals,* and other matters of the most puny importance, such as my being nicknamed the Queen of Scots. It was good that Miss Anderson should hear about my emergence from the chrysalis, as Lady Angela called it, as she had been so concerned about my being locked in the chrysalis. But it was *not* good that Uncle Frank should read what I wrote on the subject. It must be our clandestine post-office again.

I ordered the victoria to take me to Tulloch in the afternoon. I could do that sort of thing, now. Nobody questioned my right. If I were followed, let it be so. I was Miss Katharine Irvine of Ravenburn, paying an afternoon call. I would not be followed at night.

I put on an afternoon dress of such pale green silk that you would hardly know it was green, except that green flowers and ribbons had a sort of whispered echo in the colour. Calum Macnab drove me. His face was full of the glummest foreboding, as though he expected more godless pranks at Tulloch. I had my letter to Miss Anderson hidden and safe.

We went along a piece of road, half way to Tulloch, bordered by low ground, where bracken grew densely and as high as a stag's antlers. It was turning to rich gold in the autumn, a brave colour. At the roadside, facing towards Ravenburn, stood a dog-cart with one man, alone, by the horse's head. He was making some adjustment to the blinkers. It was Killin.

He looked up when he heard the victoria, and waved cheerfully. Calum Macnab pulled up beside the dog-cart, and asked dourly if his lordship needed assistance.

'No, thank you,' said Killin. 'I am simply learning that it's a mistake to economize on harness, even for a dog-cart. Good heavens, Katie, you look like a snowdrop – green and white, and cool and beautiful.'

'Thank you, Charles,' I said. 'Where have you been?'

'To Tulloch, with a message to the General from George Fraser. Poor George is obliged to leave today, as you know, but he'd promised to kill a Tulloch stag. I drove over with his apologies. Are you going there?'

I explained about my letter to Miss Anderson.

He laughed approvingly. 'The Ramsays are friends worth having,' he said.

So was he, I thought. I suddenly decided to tell him about Sir George Fraser's horseshoe, at least indirectly – to warn him not to confide in Sir George. I owed him that much.

I stood up in the victoria, and Killin put out a hand and helped me to the road.

'Will you drive on for thirty yards, Calum,' I said. 'I have something particular to say to Lord Killin. It will not take two minutes.'

Calum grunted, touched the brim of his hat with his whip, and rolled away down the road.

'What is it, Katie?' asked Killin. 'It's a change for you to have something particular to say to me. Usually it's I who have something particular to say to you.'

'Well,' I said, 'it's about George Fraser.'

'Devoted as I am to George, he is the last topic I would choose for an unexpected, accidental heaven-sent tête-à-tête with you.'

There was a movement in the bracken, a yard from the side of the dog-cart. Killin looked sharply in the direction of the movement. Following his eyes, I was utterly amazed to see Robbie's head rise out of the bracken.

The astonishment I felt was as nothing to the astonishment in his face. He looked at me with a sort of numb and horrified incredulity, as though I had a single eye in the middle of my forehead.

I thought: He saw me being driven by a coachman in a victoria. He heard Killin call me 'Katie'; and I called Killin 'Charles'. He sees me dressed up, in pale green silk, in the height of the most expensive fashion. Me, Katie Maitland, the little abandoned governess.

'For heaven's sake,' said Killin, frowning, to Robbie.

'*Who are you*?' said Robbie to me.

Killin shrugged, and said, 'Since you are face to face, may I present two of my dearest friends to each other? Katie, I present Mr Robert Scott, late of Danvie, and Australia, and so forth – Robbie, I make you known to Miss Katharine Irvine of Ravenburn.'

'We have – met,' I said awkwardly, miserable to see the horror in Robbie's face. To Robbie I said, 'I was going to tell you. I was. I didn't tell you at once, because of – gaps, you know . . .'

Robbie's face was like a stone mask. He turned from me to Killin, and said with difficulty, 'I asked you . . . You told me . . . A governess . . .'

Killin raised his eyebrows. 'You asked me, some four months ago, to confirm that there was a governess employed at Ravenburn, with green eyes, handsome, called Miss Maitland. I so confirmed. There was such a governess. There still is.'

'Oh my God,' said Robbie.

He turned to stare at me blankly, then disappeared into the tall bracken.

'What on earth has got into the man?' murmured Killin, looking entirely baffled. 'Why did he show himself? And why that thunderstruck look? He knew you, Katie?'

'Yes. We met, as I said . . .'

'But where? How?'

'It was when I was – looking at birds. I came on him. He had hurt himself. We became – friends. I told him I was Malvina's governess, so as not to – to make a barrier—'

'I understand – a barrier of rank and wealth, between yourself and an adopted foundling. I understand, Katie.'

There was such a harrowed and harrowing look in his face, that I saw he did understand. He understood not merely why I had lied to Robbie, but how I felt about him.

'Now,' he said, 'I suppose he's upset because there *is* a barrier.'

'I suppose so,' I agreed drearily. 'And because I lied to him . . . You and he are in league, after all? You are the friend who has been helping him?'

'Helping little enough. But yes, certainly, we are in league. He came back from Australia with names that Tom had long ago given him – poor Tom Irvine, your brother.'

'Your name, because you were my father's friend.'

'Yes, mine and George Fraser's. As Tom's friend, he had a claim on us both we could not refuse – and did not want to refuse. He got in touch with us, very secretly, nearly a year ago.'

'Why? To do what?'

'To put right certain wrongs. For various reasons, he has lain completely hidden, ever since he came back to Scotland. Even we, George and I, had no idea where he was hiding. We still have no idea. That was sometimes inconvenient, but it was a necessary precaution. It still is.'

'That is what I have never understood. Why was it necessary, why is it, if he trusts you?'

'Because George Fraser occasionally gets drunk.'

'Oh . . .'

'Robbie got messages to us in various ways—'

'How?'

'Usually the simplest of all. The penny post.'

'To Ravenburn?'

'Ah, no. Sealed private letters are not sacred at Ravenburn. Notes are, if only the right people know they exist. This morning a note was left where my manservant couldn't fail to find it, and he brought it to me. It asked me to meet Robbie here. An unusual arrangement for him to make, an unusual risk for him to run, but he had important news, and an important message for me to pass on. He has – achieved a major *coup,* a significant tactical victory in our campaign, and it has implications in lawyers' offices in Edinburgh.'

'You're just as secretive as he is,' I said.

'Yes of course, dear Katie. The less you know the better, until suddenly you know everything. I have sworn to say nothing, and I will say nothing, even to you, until the right time. Now I think you must continue your journey, Katie, even though I make the suggestion against my own interest. The back of your coachman's head is developing an impatient look.'

I nodded. It was true that the back of Calum Macnab's head was eloquent with outrage. I took leave of Killin, and walked up the road towards the victoria.

Foremost in my mind was the memory of Robbie's blank, incredulous horror when he looked at me, and realized who I was. The gap between us had disappeared, for me, but for him it must have yawned as wide as Glen Chinn. And I had lied to him.

I was sure I could put that right. I could explain. My kisses would surely convince him that love bridged all gaps, and that it was love which had made me lie to him as I did.

I was sure I could put it right. I rehearsed words, as I walked towards the victoria; and I imagined actions to accompany the words; and my heart began to pound and my breath to come fast and shallow.

Meanwhile, I was agog to think that my friends at the Castle had after all been the mysterious friends Robbie talked of. Yet one was treacherous. The horseshoe could be no coincidence.

As I climbed into the victoria, I realized I had not warned Killin about Sir George Fraser.

I went up to bed early. I told them all I had slept badly the night before, which was beautifully true.

I slept for two hours, knowing I would wake up – that my need and desire to go to Eilean Fitheach would ring carillons of bells in my brain.

Just before midnight I was standing on the grassy hummock. A gentle drizzle was drifting down out of the black sky, and had been doing so ever since I crept out of the game larders. My hair was glued to my cheeks, and my clothes clung stickily to my body. Robbie stood on the bank, his face invisible in the dark, his silence strange and disconcerting.

I had a long and cool and logical speech prepared, but it came out garbled and distorted. I said, 'I'm sorry I lied to you. I thought it was best. There is no gap, but I thought you might think there was one. There is no gap! You said last night you'd marry me. Will you? I shouldn't have asked you. You should have asked me. Anyway, you promised. I shall be just as poor as if I were a governess. So you see, my lies will come true. I was going to tell you. Truly I was. I would have told you last night, only . . . Is Donald McWiddie all right? Have you enough whisky for him? Does he smell as horrible as ever? Have you given him a bath in the loch? I didn't mean to talk about him. I don't know what your interest in him is, and I don't care. Killin says the news about him will be important in a lawyer's office. Is that right? Can it be right? Is Sir George Fraser taking the news to Edinburgh? I hope not, because that horseshoe was his. Well, I'm nearly sure it was. Do you understand? Can't you reply? It was a new shoe he had made just before he left Ravenburn. He was seen in Lochgrannomhead, when he was supposed to be in the Hebrides. I don't want to talk about him, either, but I thought you should know about the horseshoe. Robbie, I'm sorry I lied to you! I'm sorry I'm Katharine Irvine, if it displeases you! Can't you say anything? Am I to stand here for ever, pouring with tears, talking and talking, while you stand like a statue in the dark? Can't you say anything? Can't you say anything?'

'No,' said Robbie, in the most wretched voice I have ever heard. 'No, I can't.'

Katie Queen of Scots was trying to enjoy herself at the Rannoch Ball.

I was staying with the Marchioness of Aberfeldy, at Inverbrake. Uncle Frank had not wished me to come; he could not prevent it without breaking one of my legs. The party at Inverbrake was as near my idea of perfection as any could be which did not include Robbie. There were General and Lady Angela Ramsay, as red-brown as little russet apples; Charles Killin, always on the verge of laughter; Victoria Arlington, with the voice of a boxwood flute and the energy of a steam locomotive;

the Marchioness of Odiham, whose glacial manner concealed a most kindly and amusing personality; her great friend the Duchess of Bodmin, who looked and laughed like a jolly cook; the Earl and Countess of Draco, he tall and dark and solemn but with an enchanting smile, she a beautiful witch with glorious dark red hair, only a year or two older than myself; half a dozen other older people, and a dozen young. They were all as gay and friendly as could be. My particular friends were a particular comfort; the strangers all became particular friends.

Lady Aberfeldy had asked Mamma and Uncle Frank, too. But Uncle Frank said he was too involved with the affairs of the Ravenburn estates, and Mamma said she did not feel able to desert her friends. Her friends did not seem able to desert Mamma, either.

The Ball itself was a sight so magnificent that it almost hurt the eyes. The dresses of the women, mostly huge crinolines, formed a forest of the most vivid exotic flowers; over white shoulders hung tartan sashes of colours more startling still; jewels blazed back the glare of the enormous chandeliers (almost as huge as those of Ravenburn), and eyes were as bright as diamonds. But of course the men outshone the women, the splendour of Highland evening dress turning even the drabbest into gorgeous savages.

The pipes skirled for the reels; the fiddles scraped for the country dances and swooned for the waltzes; there were shouts, cries of excitement and laughter, and a hubbub of cheerful talk; champagne hissed into glasses; forks clattered on plates.

I was swept up into the ball. My programme was full before ever I arrived. I was never alone, and often surrounded. I whirled and swung and swayed to the music, with a succession of delightful laughing faces before my own . . .

'What's the matter, Katie?' murmured Kirstie Draco. 'Don't you like being the Queen of Scots?'

'There's only one place I want to be queen of,' I said, 'and I'm not welcome there any more.'

'Something is going on. My husband says my imagination has been heated by your success, but that is nonsense. It is only your eyebrows I envy. I don't think one's imagination would get heated, do you, simply from envying someone's eyebrows?'

I laughed in spite of the puzzled misery that lay in my mind like a sandbag.

'Something *is* going on,' Kirstie continued. 'Charles Killin is almost as bad as you are. I danced with him just now, and he was all the time looking at the door. The door! With me a few inches away! I asked him if he wanted to dance with the door, but I don't think he's quite as unnatural as that ... Oh, Katie, do look. Who has just come in? Do you know him? He bowed to you.'

'I don't know him,' I said. Nor did I, at once.

It was a slight figure, with mouse-coloured hair and a sun-burned forehead. He was slim, and quite small, but with broad shoulders. He was clean shaven; except for his brow and cheeks his face was pale, as though something had kept the sun off his jaw. He was superbly dressed in kilt and green velvet doublet, with a badger sporran, and a jewelled hilt to the skean dhu in his stocking.

'Katie! You do know him! You've gone as red as my tartan!'

I nodded, speechless, as Robbie, without his beard and dressed as a gentleman, stood talking to Charles Killin. Some others went up to him. He exchanged warm greetings with the Ramsays, and with Neil Draco, Kirstie's husband.

'Now what is happening?' said Kirstie. 'Look! This is better than your stepmother's play.'

Three more newcomers came through the door into the ballroom, following a liveried footman. The footman pointed to Robbie. The newcomers stepped purposefully towards him. One was in a long frock coat. He carried a tall hat. He had grey mutton-chop whiskers, and looked like a sternly moral innkeeper dressed for the Sabbath. The other two had serge suits and billycock hats.

'Policemen,' said Kirstie Draco in an astonished voice.

They approached Robbie, who looked at them composedly, as though he had expected them, and was rather glad than otherwise to see them.

Killin signalled to the leader of the fiddlers. A country dance petered to a standstill. There was a buzz of surprise, with some annoyance, and some amusement.

The man with the tall hat said, rather apologetically, to Killin, 'There's nae ca' tae interrupt the festeevities, my lord. We can be preevit an' discreet.'

'Oh no, Inspector,' said Robbie mildly. 'We did not ask you here to be private and discreet.'

The man he called the Inspector shrugged and frowned. He laid a large hand on Robbie's velvet-clad sleeve.

He said loudly, 'Thomas Irvine, Lord Ravenburn, I hae a warrant for yer arrest on a chairge o' murder.'

Robbie nodded, and held out his wrists for the handcuffs.

The chandeliers swung in a great arc above my head; the brilliant tapestry of the ballroom spun round me; the excited hum of voices rose to a roar like an angry sea; I fainted.

My brother. He was my brother. The gentle, exciting, adorable man, whom I loved to desperation, was my brother. I had given myself joyfully, in the moonlight, to my brother.

And he was arrested for the murder of a water-keeper by the Horseshoe Pool of the Chinn.

They took me back to Inverbrake, trying to comfort me. Charles Killin held my hand tight in the carriage. It was all the comfort there could be – the best comfort there could be.

'You knew?' I said.

'Of course I knew.'

'But why . . .? Who was . . .? My mind is going round—'

'Don't think about it now, Katie.'

'I must think about it now. I must understand, or I shall go mad.'

'Tell her, Charles,' said Lady Aberfeldy. 'Tell us, too, or we shall all go mad.'

'I cannot tell her or you everything,' said Killin. 'I am still bound by certain important confidences, and – everything has not happened yet.'

'A trial for murder has not yet happened,' I said drearily.

'That, and the return of a man to be master in his own house,' said Killin. 'Well, then. There was an – episode, an accident, on the banks of a river. A man died. Tom was there. He was seen, recognized. He knew this, and fled.'

'We have known all this for a dozen years,' said Lady Aberfeldy. 'Little as one wished to believe it, his running away had the look of guilt.'

'Yes, ma'am, it did. So I thought. So the whole of Britain thought, and all the newspapers, and the police. Running away was virtually a confession of guilt, and was so seen by the legal authorities. Well, he ran away. In some disguise or other, he got himself to Glasgow and on board a ship. It might have been going anywhere in the world, so it got him out of Scotland and the shadow of the scaffold. It took him in the event to Australia. He had a variety of adventures, and after two years was working, as we all know, in the Yellow Springs silver mine. He there befriended another Scottish lad, also some kind of scapegrace.'

'Robert Scott,' I said.

'Yes. He was an indentured servant, who had just transferred from one master to another. The new master had scarcely seen him.'

'That is strange,' said Lady Aberfeldy.

'So I thought, ma'am, but Tom explained to me that indentured servants are passed from hand to hand there, as need arises, like coach-horses. Robert Scott's new master was not buying a person, but a capacity to write a clear hand and total up a column of figures. Well, Robert Scott was buried in a collapse of the workings of the mine. Tom Ravenburn borrowed his identity.'

'Why?' said Lady Aberfeldy.

'Because in his own identity, he was a fugitive from a charge of murder. He was safe in remote parts of Australia, under any name he cared to use. But in Sydney or Melbourne men read newspapers. And remember how very many Scotsmen have gone out to make new lives in Australia. Thousands of people would have known about the Irvines of Ravenburn, and the sensational flight, after the violent death of a water-keeper, of the young Lord Ravenburn. If Tom was to go among people, he had to have a new identity. And, above all, if he was to come home.'

'Robert Scott,' I said, 'could come home.'

'Oh yes. He was a scapegrace, but not a criminal.'

'But,' I said dizzily, 'why did he wait so long before coming home?'

'Robert Scott was an indentured servant. Tom did not at first realize the full implications of this, until he did try to come home, years ago. He was treated like a runaway slave. To all intents and purposes, he *was* a runaway slave. What could he do? He could not say, "There is an absurd mistake – I am not the man you suppose, I have been lying to you for two years, I am in truth a fugitive from the Scottish police, who want me on a charge of murder." No – once he came up out of the mine saying, "I am Robert Scott", Robert Scott he had to remain. And he had to stay and work out his time, until Robert Scott was a free man.'

'And he grew a beard, to disguise himself,' I said.

'Yes of course, against his return. Well, he came to me one early morning, last autumn, having walked to my house from Glasgow. He asked if I owed any debt to the late Lord Ravenburn, William, my godfather and benefactor and dearest friend. Indeed I owed such a debt, an enormous and unrepayable debt. I acknowledged this debt, to a young man with a beard from Australia. I have been trying ever since to pay back some part of it, by helping my old friend's son.'

'Helping him how?' asked Lady Aberfeldy.

'By finding out what really happened on the river bank a dozen years ago. By finding out why it happened. By finding out what Francis Dundas and his sister have been doing to the estate, and to the family—'

'And to me,' I said.

'Yes, Katie. It was soon evident that Tom was not the only victim of the whole conspiracy. You were a victim, too.'

'What did you find out?' asked Lady Aberfeldy. 'What did happen on the river bank?'

'That,' said Charles Killin, 'we shall hear in court, God willing.'

'You should have told me who he was,' I said wretchedly. 'My brother. My father's son.'

'I could not, Katie. I could not have told my own mother, my own sister, if I had one. I could not tell his sister. Even when I got to know you well, and trust you completely, I still could not tell you that your brother was in Scotland. Besides, I had no idea that *you* had any idea that Robert Scott existed. It is curious you should have met him. He tried very hard to meet nobody. Even I never knew where he lived.'

'It is not curious at all,' said Lady Aberfeldy. 'Katie was prowling about, spying at birds, as when I first saw you, dear.'

'And I,' said Killin.

'And you, Charles. Tom Ravenburn was prowling about, spying at his own castle, I suppose. Nothing could be more natural than that, in their prowlings, they should meet. I imagine you meeting face to face in a ditch, Katie.'

'No,' I said, with a jab of lovely and hateful memory. 'He had hurt himself. I fell over him.'

'But Tom must have known you, Katie?' said Lady Aberfeldy.

'No,' I said drably. 'I was a little girl when he left. He didn't know me. I said I was a governess.'

'But why?'

'Because he told me he was a Glasgow foundling, adopted and brought up as a gentleman – but still a Glasgow foundling. It was a matter of gulfs, you see, and barriers . . .'

'I see,' said Lady Aberfeldy. 'Yes, that is natural too. If I made a friend, under those same circumstances, I think I should have done just the same. Especially if I had few friends of my own.'

'I had no friends of my own,' I said.

'We have put that right,' said Killin.

'No, Charles,' said Lady Aberfeldy. 'Katie herself has put that right.'

Presently Killin said, 'Half a dozen people in all Scotland knew of Robert Scott, and his interest in a crime, and a Castle, and a fortune. Of the half-dozen, most knew him by a Gaelic nickname—'

'Seabhac Seilge,' I said.

'The wandering hunter, the peregrine falcon, yes. Three people only, in the world, knew that Seabhac Seilge was Thomas Lord Ravenburn. George Fraser, myself, and an old poacher called Rory Beg, who himself owed Tom a debt of ancient gratitude. Everything depended, all our efforts depended, on the secret being kept until the right moment. If Tom had been identified, he would have been arrested at once. He was still a fugitive from a warrant for his arrest on a charge of murder. Such things do not lapse, you know. The case was closed, because Tom had himself reported himself dead. If the police had had the smallest reason to suppose that he was alive, and in Scotland, the whole country would have been combed with sleuth-hounds. He *had* to keep his beard and his false personality.'

'I understand that,' said Lady Aberfeldy. 'But since he *had* a beard and a false name, why did he have to lie so hid?'

'I knew him within seconds of seeing him,' said Killin. 'Hundreds of others would have recognized him, beard or no, though he called himself the Sultan of Muscat. Servants, crofters, farmers, keepers, herds, neighbours – all the people about here would have known him. He had to stay hidden, as well as disguised, to avoid arrest. If he had been arrested before we were ready, you know, he would have been tried and hanged.'

'He will be tried now,' I said.

'But not hanged, I think.'

'Why then,' said Lady Aberfeldy suddenly, 'are we so glum? This is joyful news! Should you not be singing and dancing, Katie, at recovering a long lost brother?'

'Yes,' I said, and burst into tears of unutterable despair.

Charles Killin's comfort to me now was more welcome that it had ever been – more welcome, more necessary.

By the most horrible mischance, the most savage jest of fate, Tom – Robbie – and I had committed a disgusting sin. The more joyful and beautiful it had been, the more loathsome it now seemed. Some fumbling and uncouth experiment, remembered with distaste or boredom, would have loomed less gross, because it would have been less important. But the miraculous surrender in the moonlight loomed gigantic, and made me recoil from any thought of Tom – of Robbie – with sick revulsion.

Charles Killin's arms were a heaven-sent refuge. In his kisses I could almost make myself forget. It was a return to sanity, to decency, to the laws of God and man, from the unspeakable accident in the moonlight.

I knew that I would marry Charles Killin. That I would be a great lady. That he would be always kind, and make me laugh.

Once it had been a very good second best. Now it was the Godsent best, the very best.

But we must still be secret about it. No announcement must be made, no consent sought, no formal betrothal declared. More – no loving glances must be intercepted, no clasped fingers observed.

'For,' said Charles, 'we're not home until Tom walks out of the court a free man, and comes to Ravenburn as its lord.'

The public sensation was tremendous – greater even, people said, than that when young Lord Ravenburn had fled, after killing a neighbour's water keeper. A Peer of the Realm had not stood trial for murder since Lord Ferrers killed his steward, and was convicted by his peers in the House of Lords. That solemn procedure was abandoned nowadays. Tom Ravenburn would stand his trial, before judge and a jury of ordinary men, like any other murderer.

The newspapers talked of nothing else. There were artists' impressions of the Horseshoe Pool, the dead keeper (though he had been buried a dozen years before), the big stone which had killed him, the struggle in the dark, and Tom. Ballads were composed, and sung by wandering clowns in the streets of cities, to collect pennies in their tambourines from the crowds.

Sightseers arrived in char-à-bancs, to inspect, like awed ghouls, the banks of the Horseshoe Pool. The Crossmount keepers charged them a shilling a head; and, according to Lady Angela Ramsay, Sir Campbell Stewart took half. Sightseers were forbidden on the Ravenburn estate, but scores crept in just the same.

A legend was invented that the heather on which the keeper's blood had spilled, had bloomed bright red ever since, instead of purple. Sprigs of red-flowered heather were sold in barrowloads by tinkers, each sprig guaranteed to come from the plant where the blood had fallen. As Charles Killin said, with slightly morbid humour, the poor man must have run about for hours, like a cockerel with its head cut off, and dripped his blood over the whole hillside.

Stones were sold also, as macabre souvenirs, guaranteed to come from the Horseshoe Pool. There were enough to build a new Hadrian's wall.

The whole of Britain smacked its lips.

There were changes at Ravenburn, but not many.

Miss Serena Wood went away, to stay with a schoolfriend in Perth. Lady Wood was still there, waving and echoing, and Mrs Seton, on whom Mamma seemed greatly to depend.

Jamie was still referred to as Lord Ravenburn, and called 'my Lord' by the servants.

'After all,' said Mrs Seton, 'it is what he will be again, in a few weeks; there is no point in us all getting used to calling him by a different name, just for that little time.'

Sir Malcolm Rattray was still there. His mines could do without him, but he could not do without Mamma. Colonel Blair was still there, tugging at his whiskers. I thought he could not do without four square meals a day.

Lord Killin came back with me from Inverbrake to Ravenburn, as an old and close friend of the family, who had known Tom longer than anyone else.

'I am coming to hold your hand,' he said to me privately.

'Good,' I said. 'I want my hand held.'

Uncle Frank occupied himself with engaging lawyers. He was surprised to find that Tom already had all the solicitors and advocates he needed, and those the most eminent in Edinburgh. It was one of them, I guessed, that he had gone to see, the night I took the message to Rory Beg. There was nothing that Uncle Frank could do for Tom. He could be excused for having a haunted look behind the blandness of his smile, and for pacing sleeplessly in his bedroom.

Mamma seemed unaffected by the sensational events of the previous week.

'Dear Isabella,' said Mrs Seton, 'will not, must not, allow her mind to dwell on distressing things. Her fair-weather friends have deserted her, but her true friends are with her still. We shall sustain her. The trial can have but one end. Nothing is to be gained by permitting her to suffer.'

'Nothing,' echoed Lady Wood, swaying from the waist and waving her arms. 'Suffer . . .'

There was no sign of Dr McAndrew.

I could not bring myself to go to Eilean Fitheach. I knew my heart would be rent by memories, and a sense of guilt would sicken me.

Part of me wanted to go there very badly. But landing meant standing on the grassy hummock from which I had taken my miserable farewell of Robbie – of Tom. It meant crossing the sweet grass sward where he and I had cried out in the moonlight. I could not go.

I wondered if I had a duty to see that Donald McWiddie was supplied with oatmeal and whisky. But I reflected that Robbie – Tom – would have made all necessary arrangements before he went to Rannoch, since he went there deliberately to be arrested in the most public possible manner.

I could not go to my island, or even look at the ravens from the spur.

'It is the Solemn Procedure,' Charles Killin explained to me.

'The Summary Procedure is only for little things that can be dealt with by the Sheriff. Twelve years ago, the Procurator Fiscal from Lochgrannomhead conducted an investigation, as he is bound to do with any sudden or suspicious death. He got the Precognition of the witness – the one witness – the other keeper who was there. The Precognition, you know, is the evidence the witness will later give in court. That was all written down, and sent to the Lord Advocate in Edinburgh. The Lord Advocate issued the Indictment. Part of the Indictment is called the Libel. That includes the time and place of the – alleged crime, and the relevant facts establishing a presumption of guilt.'

'I think long ago I read that,' I said. 'The facts *did* establish . . .'

'A presumption, to put it mildly. Yes. Tom went poaching for fun, for adventure. He was the associate of known poachers and criminals. He was on the river-bank, by night. After the man was dead he ran away. Yes, all horribly convincing, virtually conclusive. Well, the indictment is supposed to be served on the accused, who is supposed to be brought from a cell to the Sheriff Court. His lawyers then see the Indictment. They get the date of the two Diets, the hearings. The first is the Pleading Diet, in the Sheriff Court, and then the Trial Diet, the trial itself, in the High Court of Justiciary. But of course, that did not happen twelve years ago, because the bird had flown.'

'But now the Indictment—'

'Has at last been served, in the Lochgrannomhead Sheriff Court, by the Sheriff Officer, on Tom and his lawyers. Now there is the Pleading Diet, and Tom is to give notice of his special defence.'

'Can he? Has he one? What can he say? He killed the man.'

'I don't know exactly how they'll go about it. Will you come?'

I opened my mouth to say 'No', but I said 'Yes'.

The Sheriff Court in Lochgrannomhead was in a raw new building of tremendous pretentiousness. If Ravenburn Castle was a gigantic Manchester cotton mill intended to withstand siege, this building was a small railway station intended to withstand earthquake.

The Sheriff presided – a small, fussy man with a pedantic

213

voice. Below him sat his Sheriff-Clerk, who was much more important, Killin said, and knew all about the procedures; he was a man with a face of deep misery, as though he had seen into the depths of human depravity, and expected to do so again. The Bar Officer, attending the Sheriff like a terrier, called us to rise, and to sit, and to be silent.

Robbie – Tom – was composed. He saw Killin, and gave a faint smile. He saw me, and looked away quickly.

The Procurator Fiscal, who was a Lochgrannomhead solicitor, acted as prosecutor in the Sheriff Court. What he had to do was only a formality. He read out part of the Indictment, I think, in a voice like a hoodie crow's. Perhaps other lawyers could understand it; I could not.

The Sheriff-Clerk whispered something to the Sheriff.

The Sheriff said, 'I understand that the Libel contains the Precognition of the single witness to the commission of the crime itself, as well as much other matter relating to the life and reputation of the accused, and that the evidence of this crucial witness will not be available to the High Court. Is the Prosecution relying for the heart of its case on hearsay evidence?'

This time I could understand the Procurator Fiscal, because he was speaking instead of reading. He said, 'I can personally swear to the statement herein being a verbatim rendering of what the witness deposed to me during my investigation, taken down by my hand at his dictation. The disappearance and presumed death of the witness, now under investigation by me, renders hearsay evidence admissible, under these special conditions.'

The Sheriff seemed surprised. The Sheriff-Clerk whispered to him: reassuring him, I supposed, that the Procurator Fiscal knew the law.

Presently a tall man, with a soothing manner, rose in a different part of the Courtroom.

'Fergus Hay,' Killin whispered to me. 'Tom's Junior Counsel.'

Fergus Hay gave notice – although it took a great many words to do it – that the accused would plead self-defence.

There was a stir in the Sheriff Court. The Procurator Fiscal frowned incredulously.

'Alternatively,' Fergus Hay said, but in many more words

than these, 'we shall plead homicide *Chaud Melle,* or In Rixa.'

'Killing in hot blood, without premeditation,' whispered Killin to me.

This caused less visible general surprise.

'I am to say,' said Fergus Hay soothingly, 'that we are applying to the High Court of Justiciary for bail.'

This time it was the Sheriff-Clerk's face that was overspread by a look of incredulity.

The proceedings were quite brief. After them, Robbie – Tom – was led away.

There had been a dense and unruly crowd outside, when we went into the Court. Uniformed men of the newly-formed County Police had to clear a way for us from our carriage to the door of the building. Some of the people knew who we were, and called our names to the rest. There were a few hostile rumbles, but there was a general murmur of sympathy and goodwill. All the crowd wanted to get into the Courtroom, but none succeeded. The *éclat* of the affair was such that the public gallery of the Sheriff Court was as difficult to enter as the Privy Council Chamber.

When we came out, the crowd was larger and much noisier. It had changed character. There were rougher faces and voices. People had joined the crowd from the taverns and whisky-shops. If there was still a murmur of sympathy, it was drowned by insulting shouts.

'The *Jacquerie*,' said Killin wryly, 'the leaders of revolution.'

There was a disturbance near the door of the building, a screaming woman, whom some men were trying to restrain, and others were egging on with shouts and laughter. She burst out of the front of the crowd and rushed at us, waving a heavy stick. She was a big, ragged, heavy-featured woman with coarse grey hair flying about her head, and bare legs below kilted petticoats ending in a man's ancient boots. She was very drunk. She was screaming abuse, with obscenities and blasphemies that would have made me blush had I not been angry and rather frightened.

It took half a dozen of the police to seize her and drag her away. She drummed her heels on the pavement, still screaming insults and filth.

'Oh dear,' said the tall, soothing Fergus Hay, who had come out of the building behind us. 'Unfortunately, that virago commands a good deal of public sympathy.'

'Who is she?' I asked.

'Her name is Phemie McVie. Widow of Jock McVie. A subscription was raised for her, and she has been drinking it ever since.'

'But,' I said, 'who was Jock McVie?'

'The man Tom Ravenburn killed,' said Fergus Hay.

'I've been talking to the lawyers, over the weeks,' said Killin, 'and there are all sorts of complications. They're rubbing their hands over the legal technicalities as though Tom's fate was the least important aspect. There's this question of hearsay evidence being admitted. Some lawyers don't like it, but as the law stands, if a witness is dead, and his Precognition is undoubtedly faithfully reported to the Court, then it's as though he was there. The complication is, that this witness is only presumed dead. His body hasn't been found.'

'Even if his story isn't admitted,' I said, 'there's Tom's reputation, and friends, and so forth. And his running away.'

'Yes. I'm afraid there's all that.

'The other side seemed surprised by self-defence.'

'Yes. It's very difficult, that one. It is a full answer to a charge of murder, apparently. But you've got to establish that you could *only* save your own life by killing the other man. If you could have run away . . .'

'And Tom could?'

'I don't quite see why not, in the dark.'

'Then perhaps they're right to have a second line of defence, the hot-blooded one.'

'*Chaud Melle*. It's a different crime from murder, and a lesser one. Asylum always used to be available if you killed a man *chaud melle*. The penalty's less than murder, and sometimes there's no penalty at all. The point, of course, is that there's no ill-will, no intention of deliberate murder.'

'It does sound more likely, that one.'

'Yes, but Tom *was* poaching.'

'Only for fun.'

'As a result of his fun, Jock McVie died and his widow's what you saw.'

216

'Yes . . . Will they get bail? Will they let Tom out?'

'I gather not. The High Court of Justiciary can grant it, even in a capital case. But Tom did run away once, and the police only found him a dozen years later. I think the learned Judges of the High Court might be influenced by that.'

'Don't worry, dearest child,' said Killin when we got back to Ravenburn. 'It would be no help to Tom. I shall go on holding your hand.'

'Oh, do,' I said, 'as much as possible.'

He kissed me quickly but passionately, before the coachman opened the door of the brougham. There was a kind of desperate hunger in his kiss. I realized suddenly that, if I needed him, he needed me, too. It is a wonderful feeling, to be needed. To be desired, to be adored, that is good; but to be needed adds obligation, and responsibility; it is an adult feeling; it is good for the soul, and for the self-esteem.

I let myself be swept by the great waves of Charles Killin's desire and need for me; and, as I felt his need and my own, I felt a new desire for him, too. I encouraged it in myself, because it was my future and my chance of happiness. I felt desire strengthen, and burgeon. I felt a surge of affection for him, my very dear friend, and I forgot – I almost forgot – other kisses than his.

Brief as this interval of happy madness was, I think we were both a little pink and dishevelled when we climbed down from the brougham. I saw a face at a window – a woman's face, a maidservant's. I did not know her. She had come with a visitor, perhaps. The woman looked intensely interested. I felt a little stab of uneasiness.

I would have expected all the talk in the evening to be about the hearing in the Sheriff Court, and about Tom's chances. But the subject was scarcely mentioned. It would have distressed Mamma.

Jamie made no secret of his own hopes for the trial.

In the morning, I had a curious series of encounters.

I went to Malvina's room, as I still sometimes did. Malvina gave a scream when she saw me – not one of her little affected screams, but a loud and terrified scream – and buried her face in her pillows. Miss Maitland looked at me with horrified disgust. Her bosom heaved. She turned away, and stared at the wall, and would not answer when I asked her what afflicted Malvina.

I saw Mrs Johnstone, the Housekeeper. She saw me, at the same moment, near the end of an upstairs passage. She looked aghast, turned, and scuttled away.

I began to think I had a disgusting disease, which had disfigured my face.

I went into the drawing room. Mrs Seton and Lady Wood were there. I smiled, and said, 'Good morning'. I was on my way out at once – I did not want to spend a minute with either of them – but they were quicker than I. Mrs Seton sniffed violently, and fairly raced out of the room. Lady Wood sniffed more faintly, in rheumy echo, and followed her at equal speed.

I came on Sir Malcolm Rattray on the terrace. He gave me a terrified false grin, and bolted away among the parterres.

I came on Colonel Blair in the courtyard. He winked and leered, in a grotesque assumption of complicity. It might have been funny, but I did not find it funny.

'Lord Killin was seen leaving your bedroom at two o'clock this morning,' said Uncle Frank to me, with a stricken face, in his study.

'Nonsense,' I said.

'I have Malvina's word for it,' said Mamma, who was also looking very distressed. 'She was wakeful, and went to you for comfort . . .'

'The comfort you gave her,' said Uncle Frank bitterly, 'was to reveal yourself to her as a whore. I have sent a message to Killin, ordering him to leave Ravenburn forthwith. You will be confined to your room until further notice. You will have no further use for the fine new clothes your friends have given you; I have already had them packed up and taken away. Since you are not fit to consort with decent people, you shall not do so. That is all.'

twelve

In all her life, Malvina had never come to me for comfort. Miss Maitland was next door to her, and Mamma three doors away. Malvina had scarcely ever climbed up into the East Tower even by day: she was not fond of steep stairs.

Mamma and Uncle Frank must have known all this as well as I. It was supremely obvious. They must have known Malvina's story was wild.

They both looked at me with pain and anger and disgust.

Mamma said, 'Frank dear, Malvina is . . .'

'Deeply upset,' supplied Uncle Frank.

'Oh yes! But I meant . . . I was going to say . . . She is so very young, so very impressionable, that . . .'

'She has been most strictly and correctly brought up,' said Uncle Frank. 'She has been subjected, we have hoped, only to the purest influences.'

'Oh, yes! That is just the point that I . . . I do not feel that I can, in conscience, allow her to associate with . . .'

'You may well say so, Isabella,' said Uncle Frank, looking at me with bitter contempt. 'We have seen the abject effects of undesirable influences, well-meant, no doubt, but horribly misguided. After years of meticulous care, in which we were guided not only by conscience but also by the best medical opinion, we have seen the effects of flattery and bad example. We have seen a head turned by admiration, or its kind imitation. We have seen the shamelessness, the flaunting. We have seen the miserable result.'

'Yes, Frank dear,' said Mamma earnestly. 'We cannot wish . . . Malvina at such an impressionable age . . .'

Brother and sister exchanged a long look.

Uncle Frank said, 'It may well be our duty to send this unhappy young woman away, to somewhere where she can neither get into trouble, nor lead others into it. The world will understand. Our friends will understand. Malvina must be protected. You, Isabella, should not be subjected to the necessity of living under the same roof as . . .'

'Bad blood, I suppose.'

'On the mother's side. Yes, one supposes so. An obscure West

Highland family. At any rate, for the moment, strict confinement to her room will remove the contagion from our servants and guests, from Malvina, and from yourself.'

I was conducted to my bedroom. They closed the door on me. I heard the key turn in the lock.

My wardrobes yawned empty. Uncle Frank had, indeed, had all my new clothes packed up and taken away. I wondered numbly what he intended to do with them. They would not fit Malvina.

I wondered where they would send me – to what institution for the vicious, the unbalanced, the untrustworthy, the devil-possessed.

I sat on the edge of my bed, feeling as though someone had hit me on the head as Robbie – Tom – had hit Donald McWiddie. I was incapable of movement, or action, or any connected thought.

I almost laughed, in my despair, at the savage irony of it. The unspeakable sin I had unwittingly committed would go unknown, unpunished. I was suffering for something I had not done. The fabricated story of a vicious child would destroy my life.

The punishment fitted the crime, perhaps, though it was the wrong crime. Miss Anderson might call it poetic justice. I had different words for it, learned from the drunken virago Phemie McVie, who had screamed at me in the streets of Lochgrannomhead.

Killin was disgraced also, when all the time he had behaved with the strictest morality, with unfailing consideration and propriety. He had kissed me when I wanted to be kissed – when I needed the comfort of his kiss. Now he was to be painted, by Malvina's lies, as the most cynical and ungrateful of seducers, repaying hospitality with dishonesty. Did such a thing damage a gentleman? I had a feeling that his reputation would comfortably survive the scandal, except among certain women of rigid views. The Colonel Blairs of the world, of all ages and types and rank, would simply snigger and envy, and Killin would be higher in their estimation, rather than lower, for seducing the stepdaughter of his hostess.

Mamma and Uncle Frank had sustained extremely well their masks of disgusted horror. I wondered why they bothered to act to me. Their performances were very convincing. Perhaps they thought to make me believe, at last, in my own guilt.

Perhaps she was disgusted with me, and did not want to come.

Early in the evening, the key turned in my door, and the broad red face of Flora Morran appeared.

'Oh,' I said, taken aback; for dusting and such had not been prominent in my thoughts during the long day. 'Thank you, Flora.'

'I'm tae lock ye in,' she said, 'but I'll no' du it.'

'What?'

'I'll no du it. The sairvants are crackin wi' awfu' things—'

'They're all talking about it? They all know?'

'Ay, 'tis the clash o' the cassel. An' 'tis a' lees an' fulishness. *I* ken fine. *I* ken ye're a guid lassie, maist roads. I'll no' lock ye in.'

'But – Flora – you're very kind, but when Mr Dundas knows—'

'Och, Mr Dundas maun du wha' he wull. I'll no' lock ye in. Gang or bide, Miss Katie, 'tis a' yin tae me.'

Flora took the key out of the lock on the outside of the door, and put it into the lock on the inside. Then she gave me her usual despondent scowl, and disappeared.

Go or stay – which? Go, of course. Where? The Ramsays of Tulloch were home from Inverbrake and the Rannoch doings. I would go there. I could not order carriage and coachman to take me – that convenient phase had died after a very brief life – but I could walk. It would take hours. I had hours. I had all night.

I put on old clothes, and good country boots, and went furtively downstairs long after dark: long after the Castle was abed except for the obtrusive night watchmen.

It was a very long walk. My legs grew very weary. Through my brain circled and snapped the puppy-dog emotions of the day. But, as I was free and physically active, anger and defiance were the strongest.

But when I reflected, every few minutes, that I had lost Charles Killin, having lost Robbie (who was Tom) – then misery and despair took me over, until anger thrust them out again.

I reached Tulloch before dawn. I waited, resting and watching, until the house was astir. The Ramsays, I knew, were early

I sat like a lump of wood on the edge of my bed, while the autumn sun wheeled through the sky. Emotions chased each other round and round in my head, like a litter of puppies chasing each other's tails. Anger, contempt, despair, defiance, resignation, and bottomless misery took turns at ruling my feelings. The last was king . . .

Doctor McPhail was brought to examine me, during the afternoon. He did so with great thoroughness. I was first embarrassed, then disgusted, then outraged. He overbore my objections, my tears even, with a sort of harsh professional determination. The examination was personal and humiliating.

His face, when he had finished, was like stone.

'Your denials, Miss Irvine,' he said, 'are themselves given the lie by medical evidence. I must report so to your afflicted uncle. He was – still at this moment is, I daresay – praying that I could in good faith report to him that nothing irretrievably wrong has occurred. You know the truth. I now know it, also. I must make it known to him. Few tasks I have undertaken throughout my professional career have been as distasteful, as distressing, as that which I now contemplate, that of reporting the result of my examination to Mr Dundas and Lady Ravenburn. The vow I made, the oath I took, when I was qualified a physician, obliges me to examine and treat you if I am asked to do so. Otherwise, I would not wish to dirty my hands by touching your degraded body. Good day, Miss Irvine.'

It was the crowning irony.

I had not seen Lady Victoria in the morning. I had not expected to. She was not a person to sit in drawing rooms, or stroll on terraces, or make conversation to other women, I supposed she was writing important letters, to important people, on important topics.

She did not come to see me, after I was shut up in my room. It was impossible that she had not heard what happened. She might despise the gossip of the passages, whispers of the boudoirs, but she would listen to something concerned the honour of her friend. Perhaps she was still busy reforming the public prison system, to visit promiscuous girls locked up in towers. Perhaps she was not allowed come.

risers, because of their abundant energy and busy lives. The low white house looked extraordinarily welcoming, with its big windows, and chimneys beginning to smoke, and the eastern face gilded by the first rays of the sun.

As I waited, I wondered where Killin had gone, after he was sent packing. Perhaps he had the same idea as I. He was an old friend of the Ramsays, from the days when he stayed at Ravenburn with my father. He was always welcome there. He would want to stay in the neighbourhood, surely, in case Tom needed him, and in case I could be helped.

I tried not to let myself become too certain that he would be at Tulloch already, in case I was disappointed.

When the sun had climbed a little, and there was more bustle in the house, I stood up, brushed down my skirt, and marched towards the front door.

I saw only a footman. The Ramsays would not receive me. They would not let me into their house.

I dragged myself back to Ravenburn. I could hardly manage the journey. It was not so much that my legs were feeble, as that my whole being was numb with misery.

My flight had been discovered, of course. Flora Morran had been suspected, questioned, and dismissed out of hand for her disobedience.

I should not get another chance. It was no matter. Another chance was no good to me. There was nowhere I could go. If trusted and trusting friends rejected me, there was no one I could turn to. I did not know where Killin had gone. No one would tell me. If it was more than a few miles away, I could not go there.

I might as well be locked in the tower as not. I was just as much a prisoner out of it as in.

Two weeks dragged by. I heard no news, of Tom and his trial, or of anything else. I was completely out of contact with the outside world. My meals were brought, and thrust in through a door briefly unlocked, A big woman with a wooden face, strange to me, came in to clean. She treated me with a sort of wary kindness, as though she had been told that I was not to be trusted, but that I was weak in the head rather than evil. If anyone wrote to me, I was not given the letters. If anyone enquired after me, I did not hear the enquiries.

The key turned in the lock. My door opened a crack. A voice said I was to come down.

I hoped I should be able to manage the stairs, after so long in a confined space.

Killin was in the great hall, standing full in the light of the sun that streamed in through the open front door. My heart leaped to see him. At the same time, I was consumed by curiosity. He had been ordered peremptorily away, three weeks before, for what had been made out to seem the very best of all possible reasons: yet now he stood, looking more cheerful even than usual, pulling off his dogskin riding gloves.

Uncle Frank came in from the courtyard. His face was very far from its usual placidity. He rushed up to Killin – a small plump sandy man, gesturing furiously to a tall sunburned one. He spoke in a low voice. I could catch the fury of the tone, but at the head of the main stairs I was too far away to distinguish the words.

Killin smiled. He patted Uncle Frank soothingly on the shoulder, and said something.

Uncle Frank's indignation seemed to blow away like thistledown in a gale. Having strutted, he slumped. His shoulders sagged. There was something meek in his air, something anxious and obedient. He looked like a dog over-concerned to please a capricious handler.

I came on down the stairs.

'I trust,' said Killin, 'that Katie has not meanwhile been made to suffer for this misunderstanding?'

'Now that all is clear . . .' said Uncle Frank with difficulty. 'Now that all is explained . . .'

'I took the liberty of sending my man upstairs to let her out. I knew you would do so at once, yourself. I thought I would spare you that trouble, and her another minute of what I suspect she *has* been made to suffer.'

'Of course . . . You did quite right . . .'

'You did *quite* right,' I said, coming to the foot of the stairs.

Uncle Frank looked at me with an expression I had never seen in his eyes before. It was naked terror. Killin smiled, and sedately shook my hand.

'I expect my hostess is in the drawing room,' said Killin. 'I must reassure her about my safe return. You're coming, Katie? And you, Dundas?'

'Oh yes,' I said, 'I'm coming.'

Uncle Frank made a wordless sound; but he followed Killin docilely.

We made a sensation when we entered the drawing room.

I went in first, holding my chin at the angle Killin had always recommended. I expected a mixed reception. I got one. Mamma put her hand to her throat, and stared at me as though I was a snake she had found in her slipper. Malvina screamed, and buried her golden head in Mamma's lap. Mrs Seton sniffed violently, turned bright red, and turned her back on me. Lady Wood echoed both sound and movement. Sir Malcolm Rattray had a coughing fit. Colonel Blair looked close to a fit of another kind.

To Charles Killin's entry, at this moment, there was an almost identical reaction, but intensified. Mamma's hand went from her throat to her mouth. Malvina screamed again, more loudly. The attendant ladies twitched their skirts, as though to prevent any possible defilement by the odious presence of the seducer. Sir Malcolm Rattray's coughing-fit was suddenly cured, as though by shock. Colonel Blair coughed, instead.

Uncle Frank came in behind Killin. Before he came in from the hall, he had contrived to fix a kind of smile on his face. It was a sad, sick apology for the bland smile with which he usually entered the drawing room.

'Frank,' said Mamma piteously, 'we have discussed ... I cannot consent ... You must not subject me ...'

'You must not subject any respectable lady to the company of these profligates,' said Mrs Seton.

'Profligates,' echoed Lady Wood, with unusual sharpness. She was staring at Killin as though he had just made an equivocal suggestion to her.

'Think of Malvina!' said Mamma, with more force than I had ever heard her use. 'Think of me!'

'Think of her!' said Mrs Seton. 'Think of us!'

'Her,' said Lady Wood. 'Us.'

Uncle Frank said, with the same difficulty as in the hall, 'Killin assures me ... Man of reputation ... Honour and integrity ...'

'But the doctor!' cried Mamma.

Malvina screamed a third time.

'Malvina *saw*,' said Mamma with furious intensity.

'Trick of the light,' said Uncle Frank miserably. 'A candle flame, in a draughty passage ... Flickering ... Easy to imagine ...'

'I saw him,' said Malvina shrilly. 'I saw him, I saw him.'

'A dream,' said Uncle Frank, not looking at Mamma or at Malvina, but staring at his feet. 'Overtired. Nervous disposition, as we all know ... My own dreams, when I am overtired, extraordinarily vivid ... Could almost swear, in the morning ...'

'I saw him!' screamed Malvina, hitting at Uncle Frank's chest with her dimpled fists. 'I saw him, I saw him!'

'The doctor—' said Mamma again.

'In short,' aid Uncle Frank in a hoarse voice, 'I do not feel able to take such drastic action ... To take such insulting steps as ... as you require of me, Isabella, on the sole evidence of ...'

Killin smiled, bowed to Mamma, and left the drawing room. Shortly afterwards, I saw his boxes unloaded from a carriage.

My beautiful new clothes came back to my wardrobe. Flora Morran came back too, as dour and self-pitying as ever.

Mrs Seton and Lady Wood overcame their repugnance to living under the same roof as an abandoned wretch like myself.

'We owe it to Isabella to support and comfort her,' said Mrs Seton.

'Comfort and support her,' said Lady Wood, in contrapuntal echo.

It was evident now that nothing whatever would get these two dismal ladies out of Ravenburn. They were living, free of charge, in a palace, the intimates of a very rich peeress. It was paradise for them. A harlot, more or less, in the household, was not enough to shift them.

I was almost sorry for Malvina. She had sworn to seeing Killin creep out of my bedroom at two o'clock in the morning. She could not recant without admitting herself a liar, a most malicious traducer. She had committed herself. She was obliged to persist in the lie, to swear with tempests of sobs that she was telling the truth.

I had supposed that Mamma had put Malvina up to the lie. It was a neat way of disposing of me – of punishing me for daring to emerge from the chrysalis, and of making sure that I was locked back inside it for ever. It was also, perhaps, a neat revenge on Killin, for the enormity of preferring me to herself. Though Killin and I had been intensely discreet, it was possible that she had seen something, or that some tale had been borne to her. I remembered the unfamiliar maidservant, who had looked so interested when Killin and I climbed down from the brougham. She might have glimpsed us, before we climbed down. She might have seen that brief but passionate kiss. She might have told someone, and word got to Mamma, who then had grounds for jealousy and resentment.

So my mind worked, as I think anyone's must have. But I saw Mamma with Malvina, in those highly-charged moments when Malvina swore and swore, through her sobs, that she was telling the truth. I saw Mamma's face – the beseeching, accusing look which she gave Uncle Frank, the angry disgust with which she looked at me. I began to be convinced that Mamma believed Malvina. At the very least, she wanted to believe her so badly that she came to do so. Wanted to believe her, both out of her hatred of me (which she no longer made any attempt to hide), and her reluctance to think Malvina guilty of the smallest fault.

Mamma had no idea, I was sure, why Uncle Frank had folded up before Killin like a house of cards before a seaman's boot. Why was I reinstated, declared guiltless, allowed to flaunt my fine clothes and hold my chin at an arrogant angle? Why was Killin allowed back into Ravenburn, an honoured guest when he should have been ejected summarily by a couple of footmen? I did not think Uncle Frank had ever defied Mamma before in a matter of such importance. I found it deeply puzzling; to Mamma it must have been the collapse of the established order of the universe.

I was almost sorry for Mamma. But she had her toadies, her comfort and support.

I heard nothing from General and Lady Angela Ramsay. Killin, too, stayed away from Tulloch, although he was such an old friend. I found their hostility extremely odd. I was hurt.

Killin said, 'If your friends believe lies about you, dearest, it is better not to have them as friends.'

But, for once, he did not comfort me at all.

There was no fresh news of Tom. He had not been granted bail, which surprised no one. He was held in prison. Killin went to see him, of course. I did not go.

The excitement in the newspapers died down somewhat; it would be fanned into a renewed blaze when the time came for the trial.

The High Court of Justiciary goes on circuit through Scotland, but important cases are tried in the Parliament House in Edinburgh. Tom's was such a case. The Lord Advocate himself would prosecute, because a peer of the Realm was under Indictment on a capital charge. Four judges at least would sit, among whom might be the Lord Justice General himself, Duncan MacNeill of Colonsay.

So much the world knew. It knew, too, that Tom would be defended by Sir Hector McCallum and Fergus Hay as his Senior and Junior Counsel; and it knew from the proceedings of the Pleading Diet in the Sheriff Court in Lochgrannomhead that he would plead self-defence, or alternatively *Chaud Melle*. That was all anybody knew.

'They must have a trick up their sleeve, eh Killin?' said Colonel Blair. 'Hector McCallum is a downy old bird. Young Tom invited arrest, when he could have lain doggo for ever. Wish I'd been there. Odd I wasn't asked to Inverbrake with the rest of you, when I laid myself out to be civil to Lady Aberfeldy here. Not that I should have felt able to go, I daresay. Needed here. Shan't be able to get to the trial, either. I suppose you'll go, eh?'

'Yes,' said Killin.

'Good time of year for it, mid autumn. I believe the courtrooms are as hot as East Bengal in the summer and as cold as the Hindu Kush in winter. Difficult for a jury to concentrate, under those conditions. Used to meet the problem in courtmartial. Man's life might depend on the punkah-wallah, the fellow with the big fan, you know. Too much breeze, the presiding officer gets a chill, puts him in a bad temper, man goes to the firing squad. Too little air, the presiding officer goes to sleep, misses evidence for the defence, man goes to the firing squad. Very much the same in the High Court, no doubt.'

'No doubt,' agreed Killin gravely.

Mamma came into the drawing room, with members of her retinue. The conversation was immediately dropped, as Mamma found the subject repugnant.

A week before the date set for the opening of the trial, Killin went away. I missed him terribly. I was left friendless at Ravenburn. But the magic Killin had wrought survived his departure: I was still free.

The atmosphere was horrible. Mamma looked at me with hatred. Behind Uncle Frank's blandness were always glints of tenseness and suspicion. Malvina moped and whimpered.

Jamie said comfortably. 'Just a few more days now, and everything will be back as it ought to be.'

Uncle Frank went off to Edinburgh for the trial – 'Just in case,' he said, 'I can still be of help to poor Tom.' I heard him tell Mamma, before he left, that there must be no change in the treatment of me, no matter what Malvina had seen.

Mamma found this as difficult to understand as ever, and as bitter to accept.

Two days before the trial, I put on old clothes, and went up the burn behind the Castle. I wanted hard exercise, and I wanted to get clear of the poisoned air of my home. I scrambled up the burn-side, with the grouse complaining all about me, as I had done so many hundred times in an earlier and simpler existence.

A voice behind me called softly, 'Katie!'

I gave a little yelp of surprise, and spun round. A face peeped over a tussock of straggling old heather – a narrow, sour face, with a sneering look. It was Sir George Fraser.

Whose horse had cast a shoe in the Horseshoe Pool of the Chinn, just before Rory Beg was unsuccessfully ambushed, when he himself was supposed to be on an island a hundred miles away.

'What are you doing here?' I asked sharply. I was too angry and disgusted with him to be frightened.

'Hush. You're followed, as you probably know. I've been two days stalking so that I could talk to you without being seen. They tried to kill me once, and they won't mind trying again.'

'When your horse came down?'

'Yes, of course. There was a wire. Now listen closely, Katie, for we haven't much time. I came here, from Tom's lawyers, a fortnight ago—'

'Came where?'

'To Tom's island, to Eilean Fitheach.'

My mind reeled. This was the traitor, and on Eilean Fitheach was . . .

'Someone had to nursemaid that wreck of a man they call Donald McWiddie,' said Sir George in his thin voice. 'I've been giving him a great deal of food, and a diminishing amount of whisky.'

'But . . . You . . . Tom trusts you.'

'Yes, he does. He knows he can.'

'Your horse cast a shoe in the Horseshoe Pool.'

'Yes.' He looked very surprised.

'The day before they fired at us.'

'Two days before. I was taking Tom's message to Rory Beg.'

'Somebody betrayed Rory Beg. I think it was you. And later, you betrayed him again. He was killed.'

'No, Katie.'

He looked at me with such shocked earnestness that I almost began to believe him.

He went on, 'The task now is to get Donald McWiddie to Edinburgh. I tried on my own, but I can't do it. I got a message from Tom, by way of his lawyers, to get help from the governess. By which he meant you, of course. He thinks you will help. You will, won't you?'

'Yes, of course, but . . . I don't trust you!'

He gave a quick, twisted smile, and said, 'People are apt not to. It's my face, I'm afraid. I wouldn't, myself, trust a man with a face like mine.'

'Well, there was the horseshoe, too. I told – Tom about that. He said – he had said, he hoped the Ravenburn farrier would say he had not made the shoe.'

'I know. Something different was in his mind. He knew I'd been to the pool – he sent me there. He was afraid someone else had been there, whom he had not sent.'

'If that is true, then we still don't know who betrayed Rory Beg, that night on the night he was killed.'

'No. One uncomfortable guess turned out to be wrong, thank God. We think it was a friend of Rory Beg's, another poacher, someone Rory Beg trusted, bribed to give away his movements.

It must have been. Now, forget my criminal face, Katie, and forget my unfortunate voice, and listen carefully.'

The moon had waned, waxed, waned, and began to wax again since the last time I had set foot on Eilean Fitheach.

Sir George Fraser rowed me out, in the dark, in my boat, which he had been using. Tom had told him where I hid it, and where to land on the island. I realized that Tom trusted him as much as I had mistrusted him – as much as part of me still mistrusted him.

There was a small carpet-bag between my feet, with a few necessities for a journey. I had left a note for Mamma, telling her that I was going away to stay with friends. She could make what she liked of that.

'Why you, and not Killin?' I asked suddenly.

'Charles can be trusted with some secrets. But not the crucial, basic, central ones. Tom never told him about his home on the island, for instance.'

'But you knew?'

'Two weeks ago, only.'

'*Why* not tell Killin?'

'He – well, the fact's well known, so it's not really disloyal to tell you. It's not in the least disgraceful. Charles sometimes drinks a little too much. Most men do. As a matter of fact, I don't think I could be a great friend of a man who didn't. Well, when Charles has had a glass of port too many, he sometimes talks too much.'

'But – he said that about you!'

'Then he doubtless believes it. Here we are. My camp.'

We had gone inland a little, and away from the end of the island where the ravens' tower stood. In the dying light of the half moon I saw a bed of rough heather under a strip of canvas. Ten yards away there was a snore from beneath another canvas roof.

'I couldn't bear to be any nearer,' murmured Sir George.

'Why didn't you use the tower?'

'For one thing, it's Tom's house. I have been going there, of course, to feed his ridiculous owl, and sometimes to get papers he wanted. But I didn't want to intrude on his hearthstone. He'll be back.'

'Do you truly think so?'

'It depends a good deal on our sleeping friend. He's the other reason I pitched camp here. I thought it best to keep a close eye on him. He sometimes gets the horrors in the night.'

'You have lain hard.'

'I am hard. Tom's father – your father – taught me to look after myself. I've been very well here, in a fine autumn.'

'You must have been bored.'

'Here? With all the wild birds to watch? How could any reasonable man be bored? Now, let's address ourselves to the task of waking Donald McWiddie.'

Donald McWiddie awoke slowly, with much grunting and snorting. But he seemed a little less gross in body, a little less degraded in spirit, than he was the night we brought him from the Choire Odhain Bhig.

'The time has come, Donald McWiddie,' said Sir George very loudly and slowly, 'to put right the wrong you did.'

'Ay . . . ay . . .'

'You shall come with us, with me and Miss Irvine of Ravenburn, to the court in Edinburgh.'

'Embro . . . I canna! I canna! They'll kull me!'

'Come, or there'll never be another drop of whisky on your lips.'

'Wae . . . wae . . .'

'And the ghosts of the Hargues will get you,' I said.

This absurd threat had Donald McWiddie on his feet as though I had jabbed him with a goad.

Sir George glanced at me. I saw his twisted smile in the last of the moonlight.

We took two bottles of whisky from the place where Sir George had them hidden, for stick and carrot were still needed. But it was the threat of the ghosts of the Hargues which got Donald McWiddie into Tom's boat which, since it was bigger, we took in preference to mine.

'I am sorry to have got you involved in this business,' said Sir George, as he rowed us back to the lochside. 'But there was no one else we could call on. No local man, no one from hereabouts, would dare to set foot in that place. Our passenger here has no idea where he has been living. Tom still wants his secret kept, you see, in case he needs his little castle again.'

'But,' I said, 'Tom will either have Ravenburn itself, or . . .'

232

'Or have no need of any castle. Yes, that is quite true. But he might want Daingneach Fitheach also. At least, that is in his mind. He wants the secret kept.'

So that, I thought, he can make love to some other little governess, on the sweet grass sward, in the moonlight. The thought sent a pang like a bayonet into my heart. But he was my brother, my father's son. As I was resolved to forget him in Killin's comforting arms, so I must pray he forget me in some other arms as white and tight round him as mine . . .

Sir George rowed straight to the flight of stone steps near the boathouse. We drove Donald McWiddie out of the boat and up the steps, with the stick of pretending to break a bottle, and the carrot of a promised dram, and the threat of the ghosts of the Hargues.

We went along the boathouse track, until it joined the road to the Castle. We turned along the road away from Ravenburn, and walked for half a mile more. Donald McWiddie did not need support, as he had when I walked with him before. He did not smell as pungently either.

'I gave him a kind of blanket-bath,' explained Sir George, 'when he was too drunk to move. You were a good child, eh, Donald? And I took away his clothes and washed them in the loch.'

Donald McWiddie whimpered at the memory of these indignities.

Presently we came to a closed carriage, with two horses, waiting in the dark on the road. A groom stood by the horses' heads. A coachman sat on the step of the carrriage, smoking a short pipe. He knocked out his pipe as we came up, and greeted Sir George respectfully.

Even in the dark, the question must have been visible on my face, for Sir George said, 'My people. They know nothing, and if they did they'd say nothing. Right, Willie? Right, Duncan?'

They both grunted cheerfully.

Within minutes we were in the carriage, its lamps were lit, and we started.

'I am sorry we had to walk so far,' said Sir George. 'But my men really don't know anything. In deference to Tom's wishes, I have been at these pains to keep it so. If the carriage had been nearer the boathouse, they must have realized we came by

233

water. Ergo, from the island. As it was, we might have come from Ravenburn, or from anywhere.'

'I see all that,' I said. 'And I wish you would stop apologizing.'

'Do you trust me yet, Katie?'

'Almost.'

We drove for two or three hours in the dark. The coachman pushed the horses on quickly. Then, as dawn approached, we stopped at an isolated farmhouse.

We were expected. That is to say, a carriage was expected; I was *not* expected. The farmer's wife looked amazed and a good deal shocked. The people knew Sir George Fraser's name. My name was not mentioned, nor Donald McWiddie's, nor the reason for our having so incongruous a travelling companion, nor the reason for our keeping such strange hours.

We were shown into a little, overstuffed parlour, with an unnecessary fire and a very necessary breakfast. Willie the coachman and Duncan the groom took Donald McWiddie off into the farm kitchen for his breakfast.

'This extemporized staging-post,' said Sir George, 'was arranged in advance by Tom's Edinburgh solicitors. The farmer has been ready for us for three days. Very efficient people, those lawyers. Very discreet, too. I imagine the wife here thinks we're eloping.'

The same thought had occurred to me. 'With Donald McWiddie as a page?' I said.

There was a sadness in Sir George's smile, as we talked lightly about our apparent elopement. I remembered his searching looks at me, a lifetime ago, when he stayed at Ravenburn in May; I remembered being unnerved and unsettled by them.

I realized, with a shock, that he was in love with me. I could not help him. I could offer him no comfort at all. But it made me still nearer to trusting him.

Willie reported that fresh horses were harnessed to the carriage, and Donald McWiddie had breakfasted on oatmeal porridge and a dram of whisky. The farmer's wife was more shocked than ever.

'They're no' the grandest horses in the wurld, Sir George,' said Willie, 'but they'll sairve until Callander.'

'Not the grandest?' said Sir George. 'Then I revise my opinion of the lawyers.'

It was a brilliant autumn morning, the early hint of frost melted by a glorious sun. I was delighted at the chance to see a world that was entirely new to me.

'I'm very sorry,' said Sir George. 'Even if it means apologizing again, I must insist that we have the curtains drawn over these windows. A prying eye now could ruin everything. The enemy will be desperate, you know, with all still to play for. I cannot risk Donald McWiddie. I must get him safe to Edinburgh. I cannot risk you, either.'

'Might they stop the carriage with pistols, like highwaymen fifty years ago?' I asked.

'Yes,' he said seriously.

'Wae . . .' said Donald McWiddie.

He smelled more pungent in the confined space of the carriage, now that the curtains were closed.

'Might they not recognize the carriage, or Willie or Duncan?' I asked.

'The carriage is not mine. It was hired, in Edinburgh, by those same lawyers, in the name of a mythical Mr Alexander Hogg. Willie and Duncan are known as my servants, it's true, but only in Inverness-shire.'

'Oh,' I said, 'between you all, you have thought of everything.'

'We've tried. By God, we've tried. That's why now we must take not the smallest avoidable risk.'

I nodded. But it was a pity that on the first real journey that I had taken since infancy, all I could see of the world was the inside of a shabby velvet curtain.

We went on fast, with many changes of horses, and rattled into Edinburgh about an hour after nightfall. I was allowed to peep between the curtain and the window-frame: and I was speechless at what I saw. I had thought Stirling dauntingly large, from my peeps as we went through it, and Falkirk larger, but I could scarcely believe what Sir George pointed out to me. We came into the city by the Queensferry road, and so to the western end of Princes Street – a mile long, straight as an arrow, with a blaze of tall lamps all along it; with bright-lit buildings lining one side, and a yawning black gulf on the other.

235

'Once a loch, now dry and full of railway lines,' said Sir George.

Beyond the gulf rose tall buildings, tier upon tier, almost on top of each other on the steep hillside. What was startling was that lights blazed from almost every window, of every story, of every one of the tall houses.

'Do they have *very* large families in this city?' I asked dubiously.

Sir George laughed. 'In Edinburgh there is a custom hardly known anywhere else,' he explained, 'for a different family to occupy each floor of a house. Not these houses over here in the New Town, but those you can see under the Castle in the Old Town. The apartments are called "flats" – because, I suppose, once you're at home, you never need stairs. It is an example of Scottish prudence and thrift – half a dozen or a dozen families accommodated on a tract of ground, which in any other city would only sustain one family.'

'I should not like it,' I said, disturbed at the thought of living in a drawer in a tall chest of drawers.

'Nor I,' he agreed.

Donald McWiddie, also peeping out, moaned in terror at what he saw. It was all as new to him as it was to me, and I had at least read about life in cities.

The carriage took us to a house in a quiet street, less brilliantly lit than those we had passed by. Again, we were expected. This time, I too was expected. And Donald McWiddie was particularly expected. A cloak was thrown over his head when he was helped down from the carriage. He was taken at once by a manservant into some underground asylum. I heard the promise of a dram.

I found myself, with Sir George, shaking hands with Mr and Mrs Gilchrist, and accepting from the former a glass of wine, and from the latter a seat by the fire in an elegant little parlour. Mr Gilchrist was Tom's solicitor. It was he who had relayed Tom's messages to Sir George: he who had sent the message asking for my help.

'I know a good deal about you from Lord Ravenburn, Miss Irvine,' he said. 'And I know that if things go well for us in the next few days, it will be very largely thanks to you. Few men have been so lucky in their sisters.'

He was a craggy man in his late fifties, with crinkling iron-grey hair, and a look of tenseness and fatigue round his eyes. He filled me with confidence. I thought Tom had chosen well. Mrs Gilchrist was as round in shape as the Duchess of Bodmin, but infinitely more serious. I could imagine her discussing architecture or astronomy with Miss Anderson. They were kind, and had a late supper ready for us, and told us what would happen in the morning.

thirteen

As a Scottish bookworm, a schoolroom mouse, I knew that the law-courts had been put in the Parliament House, which had been built for the Scots Parliament and the Lords of Session in 1640. I knew that Parliament Square had been laid out over the old churchyard of St Giles, and that John Knox, who thundered against the 'Monstrous Regiment of Women', was thereby buried somewhere beneath the paving stones. Knowing the rich history and antiquity of it all, I expected something grand, but saw something rather muddled. A colonnade masked the old Parliament building; and new extensions, built during the last fifty years, further hid tradition under utility.

The hall in which sat the High Court of Justiciary was in an extension some twenty-five years old. The building had been enlarged the same year it was built, owing to the inadequacy of its design, and enlarged again a few years later, as there had been no room for the advocates and solicitors. It was still, Mrs Gilchrist told me, most inconvenient and uncomfortable. Colonel Blair, in fact, was quite right about it.

There were cells below the Court. Tom was in one of the cells.

There was an immense crowd in Parliament Square, gawping and mumbling – a hundred times bigger than the one in Lochgrannomhead. I had never seen so many people in one place before. It was frightening. Mrs Gilchrist and I went from the carriage to the door along a sort of avenue of policemen, who were holding the crowd back. It was like running a gauntlet.

Mrs Gilchrist was very grand in purple; I was very shabby, in the clothes in which we had fetched Donald McWiddie from Eilean Fitheach.

Donald McWiddie himself had gone off very early, I was told, with Mr Gilchrist and Sir George Fraser.

There were the five judges, awesomely wigged and gowned. In the midst was the President of the High Court of Justiciary (who, when he wore a different gown and sat in the Court of Sessions, was also the Lord Justice General). There were the Lord Advocate and his Junior, Law Officers representing the Crown, and Sir Hector McCallum and Mr Fergus Hay, defending the accused, all wigged and gowned; near the latter were Mr Gilchrist and a colleague.

There were men with staffs, and men with wands, and men in wigs, and policemen.

There were Uncle Frank and Lord Killin, ignoring each other, looking extremely tense. There was Tom, a slight mouse-haired figure in the dock. He wore a neat dark coat and a black cravat. Weeks in prison cells had faded his brow and cheeks to an unfamiliar pallor. He looked well enough, and composed. My heart lurched at the sight of him, my brother, and my hands trembled so that I had to sit on them.

The fifteen jurors had been elected by ballot. Their names and faces were scrutinized by Tom's lawyers, who held a whispered consultation. The Defence could object to as many as five of the fifteen, Mrs Gilchrist told me, by peremptory challenge, giving no reason. If they objected to more, they were obliged to show reasons. In the event, they challenged four, who were replaced by others kept waiting outside the court.

'Why?' I whispered.

'I think Sir Hector and my husband decided that those four looked as though they would like to hang a lord,' Mrs Gilchrist murmured: which was terse and explicit, but scarcely reassuring.

I thought the Lord Advocate might challenge some of the jurors, too, on the grounds that they looked as though they would *not* like to hang a lord. But, although the Crown had this right as well as the defence, it was seldom exercised. The Lord Advocate was content with the jury. I was not sure that I would have been, if I had been a lawyer on either side. Most of the jurors looked completely bewildered – some sullen, some self-important, some lost; they looked like small Edinburgh shopkeepers attending a ceremony conducted in Greek, or Persian.

The Lord Advocate opened the case for the Crown. His Junior called for a witness – Henry Henderson– and to my astonishment the Ravenburn butler came in, very dignified in a black tail-coat, sailing into the anchorage of the witness-box like a respectful battleship. He took the oath loudly and with solemn emphasis (he was a deeply pious butler); he was told to speak clearly, and to address his answers to their Lordships.

'You are Henry Henderson, butler at Ravenburn Castle in Perthshire?'

'Yes, sir.'

(This was not 'leading the witness', because it was merely establishing who Henderson was.)

'How long have you held that post?'

'Fifteen years, sir, come December.'

'And previous to that?'

'I was Head Footman, sir, at the Castle.'

'How long were you in that position?'

'Five years, sir.'

'You have been at Ravenburn, then, for a total of twenty years?'

'Ay, sir, a full score of years.'

It was established that Henderson was at the Castle when my Papa inherited, and arrived there with Tom, and me, and Mamma, and the twins. He saw Tom grow up. He knew him intimately. He saw him the very day before his disappearance. He recognized him in the Courtroom. Thomas Irvine, Lord Ravenburn, was the prisoner standing quietly in the dock.

The reason for this cumbersome business was, I understood, that Tom had used a false name, and a borrowed identity, for many years; it was therefore desirable to remove all possible doubt, and establish that the man in the dock really was the man named on the Indictment.

The defence did not cross-examine Henderson. Sir Hector did not challenge the evidence that Tom was Tom.

The next witness called was Ewan McNair. I recognized, with less surprise, Sir Campbell Stewart's head keeper at Crossmount. He stumped across the Court and up the steps of the witness-box as though through deep mud; he looked very uncomfortable in his black Sabbath clothes; I thought his collar was too tight.

He said who he was; he said he had been a keeper at Crossmount for twenty-six years.

'Your responsibilities, during this long period, have included care of the Crossmount fisheries on the River Chinn?'

'Ay, sir.'

'Which might include dealing with poachers?'

'Ay.'

'Have you, in fact, had trouble with poachers?'

'Ay. Lang syne we haed an unco' plague o' they creeminals.'

'Cast your mind back a dozen years, Mr McNair – did you then have a plague of poachers?'

'Weel – no' a plague, in tairms o' gret numbers. We waur sairly beset by yin in parteec'lar.'

'Beset by one in particular? What was particular about him?'

'He waur aye takin' fush oot o' oor water, sir.'

'He was always taking fish out? You mean salmon?'

'Och, ay, the troots are no' wairth the luftin'.'

'He was always taking salmon. How many salmon did he take?'

'Yon season, he tuk mebbe fufty fush.'

'How did he take them?'

'A' roads! Wi' a leister, wi' a cross-line, wi' a rak'-huk.'

'A leister is a kind of harpoon?'

'Ay, sir.'

'Used by day or night?'

'Baith, but maist the nicht, wi' a torch, ye ken.'

'Is that method a legal way to catch salmon?'

'Nay! The law mad' ut a creeminal act.'

'You are saying that this particular vexatious poacher, known to you, was not merely stealing your master's salmon, but also taking them by a method itself illegal?'

'Ay. An' he waur a ski'fu' leisterer.'

'He was skilful at stealing your laird's fish by his illegal and barbarous methods?'

'Ay. An' wi' the cross-line.'

'Can you tell their Lordships what, exactly, is a cross-line?'

'Ye'll hae twa chiels, sir, yin 'til baith banks o' the water, wi' the line crossit owr.'

'A man on each bank, with the line across the river between them?'

'Ay.'

'This method was practised by the particular poacher to whom you referred?'

'Ay. 'Tis no' creeminal, but 'tis no' sportin'.'

'Not criminal as a method, but he was still poaching Crossmount salmon, and in what you regard as an unsporting way?'

'Ay.'

'The particular poacher to whom you have been referring must therefore have had an accomplice?'

'Ay, for the cross-line.'

'Did you know the identity of the accomplice?'

'Ay, we a' kenned the mannie fine.'

'Who was he?'

'An auld cateran they ca'd Rory Beg.'

'A cateran? You mean a brigand? A bandit?'

'Ay, a creeminal, a poacher.'

'You can testify, Mr McNair, that this Rory Beg was within your knowledge a notorious poacher?'

'Ay. He waur clappit in the jile a whilie syne. We a' kenned the mannie.'

'By "we", you mean you and your fellow keepers at Crossmount?'

'Ilka keeper in the coonty.'

'You can also testify, Mr McNair, that this notorious poacher and convict was, within your knowledge, the accomplice of the particular poacher to whom you referred – the individual who was especially vexatious a dozen years ago?'

'Ay. They waur brithers – brithers in veellainy.'

'You did actually see them together?'

'Mony's the time.'

'As accomplices in poaching?'

'Ay, wi' the cross-line.'

'You mentioned a third method used by the particular poacher to whom you have referred. You mentioned a drag-line.'

'Ay. Yon's a dairty road to luft a saumon. A muckle huk, castit ahint the fush, an' pu'd the lang o' the bottom o' the water.'

'The idea being for this large hook to catch the fish in the side, like a gaff?'

'Ay. 'Tis a creeminal ploy, a verra ill ploy.'

'Thank you. We have then, Mr McNair, a picture from you of a particular and particularly vexatious poacher who, twelve years ago, took a large number of salmon from the Crossmount water on the River Chinn. His methods, as you yourself observed them, were thievish, unsporting, and sometimes actually illegal as methods, quite apart from the illegality of his theft of valuable fish. He was the habitual associate, when he needed another hand, of a notorious poacher, who had been in prison, called Rory Beg. That is correct?'

'Richt enough, sir.'

'Do you, in this Court, recognize the particular poacher to whom you have been referring?'

Ewan McNair nodded. With a face of wood he turned and stared at Tom in the dock. He raised a gnarled hand, and pointed at the dock.

There was a small sensation: but only a very small one: because it had been perfectly obvious to everybody there that Ewan McNair had been talking about Tom.

Mr Fergus Hay (whose wig sat on top of his head like an egg on a pudding) had a brief whispered colloquy with Sir Hector MacCallum. Then he rose to cross-examine Ewan McNair.

'You have been describing, Mr McNair, the events of the spring and summer of 1849?'

'Ay, sir.'

'And you say that you were afflicted not by a plague of many poachers, but by a single poacher?'

'Whiles 'twas twa, sir, him an' Rory Beg.'

'Quite so, when they were cross-lining. Were you out watching, yourself, night after night?'

'Ay, sir, I was.'

'Night after night you saw one particular poacher, alone or with one particular companion?'

'Ay.'

'Some of the nights were dark?'

'Ay, an' mony waur bricht wi' a braw mune.'

'Did you not try to arrest the one particular poacher?'

'Ay, ilka nicht we tried.'

'But you never succeeded?'

'Nae, the mannie was tae soople.'

'Too quick and agile for you?'

'Ay.'

'You mean, he did not let you get near enough to catch him?'

'Whiles he was no' nigh eneuch.'

'Sometimes, if he was cross-lining, he was on the far bank of the river from where you yourself were watching?'

'Ay, certes.'

'I suppose you set traps and ambushes?'

'Ay. He was tae soople.'

'Some of the nights were dark? Some must have been cloudy or rainy?'

'Ay. Braw nichts an' ill nichts.'

'And in those months there were moonless nights?'

'Ay, yince a month a nu mune, an' a fu' mune, an' nae mune at a'.'

'He got clear away from you, on dark nights, because he did not let you get near enough to catch him?'

'Ay.'

'Yet you were near enough, and saw clear enough, to recognize his face beyond any doubt?'

'Weel . . .'

'I put it to you, Mr McNair – you cannot swear that on every single occasion that you saw a lone poacher, it was the accused.'

'Ay, it was him! I ken fine it was him!'

'How, if you were not close enough to catch him on a dark night?'

'I kenned fine it was him!'

'You can see in the dark, like a cat? See far enough, in the pitch darkness, to recognize beyond doubt the face of a man running away from you?'

Ewan McNair frowned unhappily. In a moment Fergus Hay was going to suggest, convincingly, that a score of other poachers besides Tom was plaguing the Crossmount water that summer.

'Well, Mr McNair,' said one of the awesome Judges unexpectedly, 'can you see, let us say thirty yards, or forty, in pitch darkness, well enough to recognize a man's face beyond any reasonable doubt?'

'Beyont ony doot at a', ma Lord! 'Twas the way he esceppit, the way he ren, the way he fushed the water . . .'twas the – the seegnature tae a letter, ma Lord!'

'Ah,' said the Judge. 'You are saying that you recognized the accused by his methods and by his movements.'

'Ay,' said Ewan McNair, with a shade of uncertainty.

Somehow, though, the cross-examination had back-fired. I thought that, strangely enough, Ewan NcNair's evidence was no less convincing for having been shaken. Of course there must have been many nights when he could not truly swear that it was Tom he saw or heard. Yet he had been sure it was Tom. I thought the jury would think he was right. I thought he was right, too.

'There must have been some occasions,' Fergus Hay went on in his soothing voice, 'when you got very near to catching your poacher?'

'Ay, sir, mony eneuch. It was maddenin'!'

'You, or your men, must have come within inches of seizing him?'

'We grippit him, sir, an' he tweestit awa' like a troot.'

'He wriggled free, and ran?'

'Ay.'

'He always did that when he was gripped – just wriggled free, and ran?'

'Ay.'

'He never turned and hit a keeper? He never offered violence?'

'Ay, he did, tae Jock McVie.'

'You yourself were not on the river bank that night, I think?'

'Nay.'

'Why was that?'

'The laird haird a whusper that a geng o' tunkers waur veesitin' the presairves. He telt twa-three o' us tae gaird the wee phaisants.'

'Did a gang of tinkers try to poach the young pheasants?'

'Nay.'

'Meanwhile, you were not on the river-bank, and the events which took place there are not within your personal knowledge.'

'I spied Jock McVie the morn, wi' his puir heid bashit in.'

'On all the nights when you did see the poacher, and narrowly failed to catch him, he never offered the smallest sign of violence?'

'Nay . . .'

'You knew who the poacher was?'

'Ay.'

'Did it not surprise you that a neighbouring laird, a young man of wealth and title, should poach your salmon?'

'Ay. I thocht he was fou. 'Twas no' done for the siller – 'twas deviltry.'

'Deviltry? Defiance? A kind of sport?'

The Lord Advocate was on his feet. He said, in his rasping voice, 'If it please your Lordships, this witness cannot testify as to the motives of the accused in poaching his neighbour's salmon.'

'That is correct,' said the Lord President. 'Please confine your questions to matters on which the witness can testify, Mr Hay.'

'As your Lordship pleases,' said Fergus Hay. 'What I am seeking to establish at this stage is not the motive of the accused in poaching, about which he will himself testify, but the reaction of the Crossmount keepers to the poaching.'

'That may be proper,' said the Lord President.

'Thank you, my Lord. Mr McNair, knowing who your poacher was, you can hardly have regarded him in the same light as an ordinary poacher, a common criminal – in the same light as Rory Beg, for example?'

'Rory Beg ne'er kilt a keeper,' said Ewan McNair.

'Lord Ravenburn has not yet been found guilty of doing so, either. An ordinary poacher, I think, you might have handled roughly?'

'Eneuch tae hauld him, sir.'

'But I suppose you would have been a little cautious about injuring Lor Ravenburn?'

'I'll hae nae wush tae demmage ony mon, sir, mair than needfu' tae hauld him.'

'I cannot at this moment see precisely where this line of questioning is leading you, Mr Hay,' said one of the Judges. 'A gamekeeper in the exercise of his duties is entitled to use such force as is needful to apprehend a poacher. This witness testifies that he endeavoured to use that degree of force, but the agility of the accused prevented him from doing so.'

'I am suggesting to the witness, my Lord, that he and his colleagues would have been most naturally reluctant to use *any* force on Lord Ravenburn of a kind likely to cause him injury. He was – he is – a great landowner with a great name, who in later years might have great local power and influence—'

'Yes, Mr Hay, the implication of your question is clear. But the witness has just testified that he would have used on the accused just so much force as was needful, as he would on any other poacher. The witness has, in fact, already answered your question. Are you now inviting him to reconsider his reply?'

'I will rephrase the question, my Lord. Mr McNair, you presumably reported to Sir Campbell Stewart of Crossmount the identity of the poacher?'

'Ay, sir, I did. He kenned.'

'He already knew that Lord Ravenburn was poaching the water?'

'Ay.'

'Did Sir Campbell give you any special instructions regarding your treatment of the accused?'

'The laird's orders waur the same as aye – "grip the fellie, but I'll hae nae kellin' or wundin' ".'

'Your rephrased question, Mr Hay,' said another Judge, 'has elicited the same response.'

'Yes, my Lord,' said Fergus Hay. 'What I am wondering, Mr McNair, is whether Jock McVie received the same orders as you did, the night of his death?'

'My learned friend may well wonder,' said the Lord Advocate, jumping up. 'But it is not a conundrum with which the witness can assist.'

'That is so,' said the Lord President. 'It is neither proper nor profitable, Mr Hay, to invite this witness to speculate about orders given to another man.'

'As your Lordship pleases. But I would like the witness to share my surprise that the accused, who had always wriggled free when he was gripped, offering no violence whatsoever – that he should on this last tragic occasion have committed an act of such unbridled and murderous violence. That act was, on the testimony of this witness, totally out of character with all previous behaviour of the accused. *Do* you share my surprise, Mr McNair?'

'They grippit him. He cudna tweest awa'. Sae he tuk yon stane an' bashit Jock's heid.'

I thought Fergus Hay was doing Tom more harm than good. He sat down, looking a little glum, saying that he had no further questions.

The Junior Prosecuting Counsel re-examined briefly. Ewan McNair reaffirmed that the Crossmount keepers had strict and permanent orders to catch poachers without killing or maiming them, and that this applied to Tom as much as to any other poacher. Ewan McNair had himself sent Jock McVie to the riverbank the night he died. Jock knew the orders as well as the rest.

Ewan McNair stood down. His evidence had established Tom as an audacious desperado, stealing a great many salmon by cruel and illegal methods, the intimate and accomplice of a notorious criminal. It was horribly easy to see how the jury would be looking at him.

Sir Campbell Stewart was called. He was unusually solemn and unusually overawed. But he looked very solid and trustworthy.

The Lord Advocate himself rose to examine him. Sir Campbell, answering him, said he was not at all surprised that Lord Ravenburn was poaching his water. The lad was, within his knowledge, wild, audacious, resentful of authority.

'Moreover,' said Sir Campbell, 'he sent me a letter early in the year, rather impertinent in tone, promising to poach fifty fish out of my water, and defying my keepers to catch him.'

'How did you react to this threat, Sir Campbell?'

'I was placed in a most awkward position, sir. I was – I still am – a close neighbour and close friend of Lady Ravenburn and her brother. I did not want to be the reason for the public disgrace of her Ladyship's stepson, who was himself approaching his majority, and would shortly take his place as a landowner and proprietor of sporting rights.'

'At the same time, you could not simply allow him to steal fifty fish?'

'No, sir, I could not. For one thing I had an obligation to my visiting rods, my sporting tenants.'

'Who had paid for the right to fish your water?'

'Who had paid or would pay me, yes. I felt that I had an obligation to deal fairly with them. I could not passively allow their sport to be spoiled. Secondly, I hope I have a proper regard for the law. I conceive it the duty of a man placed by Providence in my position to set, as best he may, a good example to those less fortunate. I could not, visibly, connive at audacious contempt of the law even by a close friend and neighbour. I believed I had, as it were, a private obligation, and a public obligation – a private duty and a public duty.'

Sir Campbell was recovering his confidence. I thought he would have a great deal to say. He had. He spoke at length of the struggle in his conscience.

'I concluded,' he said, 'that it was my duty to apprehend that misguided and rebellious young man, to deliver to him myself a sharp lecture, and then to convey him to his home for such correction as his stepmother and uncle saw fit to administer.'

'You did not contemplate calling in the police, even though you had clear evidence that the accused was poaching your water? Nor would you have surrendered him to the police if your keepers had arrested him?'

'I hope their Lordships will not think me contemptuous of the law, in my turn, if I admit, sir, that it was not my intention to surrender the unhappy boy to the police – to the possibility of trial and prison. The scandal, sir! The grief of my old and valued friends, his unfortunate family! I had high hopes that, after sowing these ill-considered wild oats, he might yet outgrow his self-indulgent wilfulness, might yet become a credit to his name and to our country.'

Sir Campbell had accordingly given orders that Tom was to be caught, but not hurt if possible. Jock McVie was given no special or different orders.

Everyone in Court, I think, sympathized with Sir Campbell for the dreadful dilemma he had been in. Everyone thought he had acted wisely, conscientiously, responsibly, and mercifully. Everyone thought Tom's audacious challenge was the act of a spoiled and wilful boy, who had brought untold trouble to everybody out of a naughty whim.

Sir Hector McCallum rose. Answering the Lord President, he said that he would be a considerable time with the witness. The Court was adjourned until the morn, after a day which, although I had sat still and listened throughout it, I found extraordinarily exhausting.

The Court reassembled in the morning, with all the same persons and paraphernalia, and wigs and robes and ceremony, and with Tom pale and composed in the dock.

Sir Campbell Stewart returned to the witness-box, and Sir Hector McCallum rose to cross-examine him.

'You have described the accused as audacious, wilful, rebellious, amongst other adjectives, Sir Campbell?'

248

'Yes, sir.'

'Not evil.'

'I hoped not. For his own sake and his family's, I prayed not.'

'Did he, within your direct knowledge, ever commit an act of violence against any person?'

'Not that I know of, sir, until . . .'

'Did he, within your knowledge, ever wittingly give pain to any person?'

'He must have known that he was giving pain to his family, by his scrapes, and his choice of friends, and his wildness.'

'He caused pain by this thoughtlessness?'

'Yes, sir, I am afraid he certainly did so.'

'But not from deliberate malice? Not from a wish to cause pain for its own sake?'

'I hope not, sir. I should hate to believe that of any man.'

Pressed by Sir Hector, Sir Campbell admitted a difference between wildness and rebelliousness on the one hand, and malicious evil on the other; he agreed that he had seen the former rather than the latter in Tom.

This was all very well, and I thought I could clearly understand what Sir Hector was about; but Jock McVie *was* killed on the river-bank. If this thought occurred to me while Sir Campbell was giving his evidence, it must have occurred to Judges and jury too.

'May we turn,' said Sir Hector, 'to the letter which you received from the accused? You kept it, Sir Campbell?'

'No, sir. After reading it, I threw it in the fire.'

'That is regrettable.'

'Yes, of course I now regret it, in the light of what subsequently happened. But I find it difficult to blame myself.'

'Can you remember with accuracy the contents of the letter?'

'With fair accuracy, sir. The lad disapproved, he said, of my conduct of my affairs, of the management of my estate, and for this reason would make me poorer by fifty salmon.'

'Did the letter state on what grounds the accused disapproved of the management of your estate? With what aspect he disagreed?'

'Ah . . . It is a dozen years ago, sir. If he went into any detail, I am afraid I have forgotten it.'

'You were incensed by the letter?'

'A threat to take fifty salmon, sir? An audacious proposal to defy law and order, to behave with monstrous unneighbourliness?'

'Apart from the value of the salmon and the fishing-rights, the illegality, the unneighbourliness as you term it, were you incensed by the criticism of your estate management?'

'Probably, sir. I don't doubt I was.'

'But you do not actually remember either the substance of the criticism, or your precise reaction to it?'

'Not in any detail.'

'Not at all?'

'No, not at all.'

'You remember some parts of the letter in vivid detail, others not at all?'

'I read the letter in a few seconds, sir, and threw it on the fire. This was a dozen years ago.'

'Yes, of course. And you have remembered with vivid clarity the part which struck and enraged you, the threat to your property, but have not retained in your mind the less immediately interesting part, the reasons given for this bizarre threat.'

Sir Campbell made no reply. Indeed, Sir Hector seemed to expect none.

Sir Hector went on, 'What was your action, on receipt of the letter? One would, I think, expect you to make contact at once with the accused, with his family?'

'Yes, I rode over to Ravenburn immediately.'

'And interviewed . . .?'

'Mr Francis Dundas, brother of her ladyship.'

'Who might be described as *de facto* guardian of the accused, until he attained his majority?'

'Yes . . . He was, he still is, a man of the world, a lawyer, a man of business, an honourable and conscientious man, on whom his widowed sister greatly and properly relied. I spoke to him of the letter and of the threat to my property.'

'With what result?'

'He promised, as I expected, that he would try to control the boy. To dissuade him.'

'No more than that?'

'I do not recall that he undertook to restrain him physically. I did not expect him to.'

'Were you satisfied with the undertaking he did give you?'

'I appreciated that he was doing for me all that he could, without creating a permanent enmity between himself and his sister's stepson.'

'In whose house he lived?'

'Yes.'

'Whose estate he managed?'

'Yes.'

'To whom he was shortly to be answerable for his management, when Lord Ravenburn attained his majority?'

'Yes.'

'Did you speak also to Lord Ravenburn himself?'

'I tried to.'

'To what avail?'

'None. He referred me to his letter, and ran off.'

'Shortly afterwards, the first spring salmon ran up into your water?'

'Yes.'

'And they were poached out of it?'

'Yes.'

'By the accused?'

'Yes.'

'How can you swear to that?'

'There never seemed the smallest doubt. He had threatened to do it.'

'Did you renew your representations at Ravenburn Castle?'

'Yes, sir, I did. To both Mr Francis Dundas and Lord Ravenburn. I felt for Mr Dundas. He was in a position at least as awkward as mine. Was *he* to call in the police, to arrest his own sister's stepson? He again promised to try to dissuade young Ravenburn from the criminal and irresponsible behaviour in which he was indulging. I knew that he would try to do so. I am sure he did try to do so.'

'Did you, in your turn, make any reciprocal promise?'

'Yes, sir. I promised that, if we caught the boy, we would do so without hurting him, and we would bring him back to Ravenburn, in our custody, rather than handing him over to the custody of the County Police.'

'Did you speak also to the accused?'

'He referred me to his letter, and ran off.'

'Salmon continued thereafter to be lifted from your water?'

'Yes, sir.'

'At the commencement of the year, Sir Campbell, you employed how many keepers?'

'Five.'

'To guard how much water?'

'Four miles, effectively, where the salmon lie and can be taken.'

'They were thin on the ground.'

'Yes, sir, too thin.'

'Did you contemplate engaging more keepers, or diverting men from other duties to that of the night-watching?'

'I did both, Poor Jock McVie was one of the new keepers I engaged.'

'Were you not surprised at the continued escape of the accused and his accomplice?'

'Yes, sir. Surprised and annoyed. But he was quick. He was like an eel. He seemed to know in advance where my keepers would be hiding.'

'Do you think he *did* know in advance?'

The Lord Advocate began to stand up. Sir Hector had – as even I could see – asked a question the witness could not give a sworn answer to.

Sir Hector said, having glanced at their Lordships, 'Putting that a different and more correct way, Sir Campbell, the skill and evasiveness of the accused, the way he continually eluded your traps, was consistent with his knowing in advance where your keepers were stationed?'

'Yes, but . . .'

'Did you, Sir Campbell, entirely trust all your keepers?'

'I could not bring myself to mistrust them, sir. I still cannot.'

'All the same, you were, and remain, surprised and annoyed that they did not catch the accused?'

'Well . . . yes.'

'And you were, and remain, surprised that the accused seemed – you said "seemed", and I repeat "seemed" – to have advance knowledge of where the keepers would be waiting in hiding for him?'

'Well . . . yes.'

'Which must have given you the idea – I am asking only about the workings of your own mind – that he did have advance knowledge?'

'An idea which I dismissed,' said Sir Campbell stoutly. 'If

servants owe loyalty to their master, so does, I believe, a master owe loyalty to his servants.'

This was, without doubt, a very popular remark throughout the Courtroom, though perhaps not with Sir Hector McCallum.

'Turning, Sir Campbell,' said Sir Hector, 'to the day before the night of McVie's death. We understand that you heard a whisper that your pheasant preserves were to be poached by a gang of tinkers.'

'Yes.'

'How did you come to hear this whisper?'

'From one of my keepers.'

'Which one?'

'I think it was Jock McVie.'

'May we hear a more certain answer?'

'Yes . . . Yes, it was Jock McVie.'

'What happened, exactly?'

'He came to me about midday. He said that he had heard a whisper about a gang of tinkers.'

'Did he say how or where he had heard this whisper?'

'No, sir, not that I remember.'

'You believed him?'

'I had no reason not to believe him. I had a lot of poults in the preserves.'

'Where?'

'It is called the New Wood. A thirty-acre tract.'

'Called "New" because it was new?'

'Yes, sir. It was a recent plantation.'

'Planted as pheasant preserve?'

'Largely.'

'Planted with what trees?'

'Principally laurel. Some holly. A few pines.'

'Valuable trees?'

'As timber, no.'

'Planted, therefore, purely as pheasant preserve?'

'Largely.'

'Wholly?'

'Well, very largely.'

'To what purpose had this tract of land previously been put?'

'It was farmed.'

'Are these questions, Sir Hector,' asked the Lord President, 'going at last to surprise us by their relevance? They seem, so far, innocent of the smallest relation to the matters into which we are enquiring.'

'I beg your Lordship to bear with me for a moment longer. Sir Campbell, your thirty acres of plantation, of trees useless except as pheasant covert, had previously been farmed. By yourself?'

'No. The land was let.'

'You had a tenant farmer, in a farmhouse?'

'Yes.'

'His tenancy was terminated?'

'He – left, yes.'

'Under what circumstances?'

'I needed his farm.'

'For a pheasant preserve?'

'Partly.'

'Entirely?'

'Very largely.'

'Requiring his land for a pheasant preserve, you evicted him.'

'I terminated his tenancy. It was quite legal, sir!'

'We do not doubt it was legal, Sir Campbell. The farmer had paid rent?'

'Yes.'

'Of what figure?'

'Some twenty-three pounds a year.'

'Which he paid?'

'Not regularly. He was often late.'

'He had difficulty in paying?'

'The holding was too small.'

'The tenant's name was Andrew McQueen, I think?'

'I believe it was he, yes.'

'The McQueens had been tenants of Crossmount, in that farm, for five generations, I think?'

'Some years.'

'Some one hundred and fifty years, Sir Campbell?'

'A good many years.'

'Did Andrew McQueen, at the time you evicted him, have a wife?'

'I believe he did.'

'And children?'

'I – believe so, yes.'

'How many children?'

'I do not know.'

'You never visited his farmhouse, never met his children?'

'I – do not recall doing so.'

'The farmhouse lay how far from your own house?'

'A . . . mile.'

'A bare mile. Will you accept that Andrew McQueen had six children?'

'I do not know.'

'I do know, Sir Campbell, and I ask you to accept that he had six children.'

'Very well.'

'What became of Andrew McQueen after you evicted him?'

'I do not know.'

'What has become of the farmhouse?'

'It is destroyed.'

'You had it pulled down?'

'There was no further use for the buildings.'

'They are now covered by your new pheasant preserves?'

'Yes.'

'Which precisely incorporate the area of Andrew McQueen's farm?'

'Er, yes. I believe it is the approximate area.'

'I believe so, too. I believe, also, that you let your pheasant shooting?'

'Yes.'

'To a group of business gentlemen from Glasgow?'

'Yes.'

'Who come to shoot the covert half a dozen times each winter?'

'Yes.'

'And they pay a rent.'

'Yes.'

'How much do they pay, Sir Campbell?'

'Six . . . six hundred pounds a year.'

There was a large silence in the Courtroom. Sympathy for Sir Campbell Stewart had evaporated, like a shallow puddle of water on a sunbaked rock.

'I put it to you,' said Sir Hector gently, 'that this episode was one of those on which Lord Ravenburn touched in his letter to you.'

'It – may have been.'

'It was?'

'I believe it was.'

'It was this episode, and others like it, which, according to Lord Ravenburn's letter, caused him to take your salmon?'

'I daresay it may have been.'

'But you did not – do not – accept that criticism of your action?'

'It was my land. The tenancy was renewable annually. It was my right to refuse to renew it. I did nothing wrong. Times were not easy.'

'For an evicted tenant farmer with six children – no, times were not easy. It was this covert which, according to Jock McVie, a gang of tinkers was suspected of planning to poach?'

'Yes.'

'How did you react to Jock McVie's report?'

'I ordered my head keeper to guard the covert.'

'Armed?'

'He carries a pistol at night. Many keepers do.'

'But with orders not to kill or wound?'

'Yes.'

'Did you order Jock McVie to the river?'

'No. Ewan McNair, the head keeper, made his own arrangements about the disposition of his men.'

'You were not involved at all in sending Jock McVie, and other keepers, to the river, on that particular night?'

'No. McNair made his own arrangements.'

'In the event, no attempt whatever was made to poach the pheasant preserves?'

'No.'

'Which suggests, does it not, that the gang of tinkers was mythical?'

'They might have changed their minds. They might have seen our precautions, and taken fright.'

'Those are two possibilities. A third possibility, as I think you must agree, is that there was no band of tinkers?'

'I suppose that is possible.'

'Jock McVie had entered your employ, early in the year, after you received the letter from Lord Ravenburn, when you engaged additional keepers?'

'Yes.'

'From whence?'

'I think he came from Ravenburn.'

'You think?'

'He came to me from Ravenburn.'

'Where he had been employed as a keeper?'

'An underkeeper, yes.'

'He came with recommendations? Testimonials?'

'He came with Mr Francis Dundas's recommendation, yes.'

'We cannot ask him why he changed employment from one estate to its neighbour. Did he give you a reason for this slightly surprising move?'

'I expect I did know why he came to me. I must have known. But – a dozen years ago – I am afraid . . .'

'Did you offer McVie a higher salary than that which the Ravenburn estate was paying him?'

'I . . . have no idea, at this date.'

'Can you imagine why he should change his employment, if not for that reason?'

'It may have been that reason. But it is so long ago . . .'

'I think you must accept, Sir Hector,' said a Judge, 'that the witness has forgotten.'

'Yes, my Lord. You told the Lord Advocate, Sir Campbell, that you had an obligation to your sporting tenants in regard to the number of salmon in your water?'

'Yes, sir.'

'A commercial obligation.'

'I should call it a moral obligation.'

'They expected a certain number of fish per annum out of the water which they rented?'

'Yes, sir.'

'The rent, in fact, being calculated on the average number of salmon caught in a season?'

'That is normal.'

'As with the hand-reared birds in your pheasant preserves. The shooting rent and the fishing rent were – still are – both calculated on an average of the bags of the previous few seasons?'

'Yes, sir.'

'Your fishing tenants, like your shooting tenants, were business gentlemen from Glasgow?'

'Yes.'

'How much did they pay to fish for salmon, Sir Campbell?'

'I considered it fair to charge – a pound a day.'

'A pound a day, paid by each of several rods. Six rods, I think?'

'Ah . . . six, usually, for each season, yes.'

'You could get six pounds a day, throughout the fishing season. We can understand, Sir Campbell, your anxiety to preserve your salmon as well as your pheasants.'

Sir Hector had no more questions. I thought, after all this, that he had done very well, and Sir Campbell very badly. Even the prim little Edinburgh shopkeepers of the jury would sympathize with anyone who poached such a man's river, if he did so not out of greed, but out of bravado, and out of disapproval of Sir Campbell Stewart.

But still, but still, Jock McVie, while doing his duty, had had his skull smashed in by a stone at the Horseshoe Pool.

fourteen

Sir Campbell Stewart was re-examined briefly, the Lord Advocate had no questions about evictions, or Andrew McQueen's six children, or shooting rents, or fishing rents. Sir Campbell reaffirmed those parts of his evidence which made him seem a dutiful and conscientious neighbour, land-owner, and sporting proprietor.

Sir Campbell stepped down, having somewhat recovered his confident solemnity.

The Lord Advocate called for Mr Hugh Craigie, who turned out to be the Procurator Fiscal from Lochgrannomhead. Mr Craigie testified (in his raw, hoodie-crow voice) that he had, in July 1849, conducted an investigation into the death of Jock McVie, a keeper in the employ of Sir Campbell Stewart of Crossmount. The most important witness, on whose Precognition the Petition was principally based, was another keeper at Crossmount. The name of the witness was Dickson Carmichael. His Precognition was the essence of the indictment. The Procurator Fiscal had himself taken it down, to Dickson

Carmichael's dictation. The original copy was before him, in his own handwriting.

Dickson Carmichael had been drowned in the August of 1849. Mr Craigie, as the law required, conducted an investigation into that death, too. The body was never recovered, but Mr Craigie was satisfied that the Death Certificate could be issued. There were no suspicious circumstances. It was an unfortunate accident, occurring because the unhappy man fell out of a boat on Loch Chinn when he was drunk.

'Why, in your opinion, did the body of Dickson Carmichael not float to the surface, as bodies usually do, Mr Craigie?'

'I think, from examination of the bottom of the loch at that point, sir, that the body was lodged, or jammed, under a great stone.'

'Attempts were made to recover the body?'

'Oh yes, sir, with the co-operation of Mr Francis Dundas of Ravenburn Castle, and his boatmen and keepers, to whose diligent and public-spirited efforts I take this opportunity of paying tribute. But the loch is very deep at that point, and the water at its greatest depth bitterly cold. No diver could effectively search. The bottom, as appeared by soundings, is composed of a jumble of large rocks, as though in the remote past an avalanche had there descended.'

There was a good deal more evidence, delivered in the Procurator Fiscal's hoodie-crow voice; what it came to was that Dickson Carmichael was the one witness of the actual death of Jock McVie; that he was himself undoubtedly dead; and that the Lochgrannomhead Procurator Fiscal had his account of the murder written down on papers he had with him.

'Little as some of your Lordships like hearsay evidence,' said the Lord Advocate, 'I submit that the late Dickson Carmichael's Precognition is clearly admissible in this case, and is necessary in order to establish the truth concerning the horrible events of that night.'

Sir Hector McCallum was on his feet.

The Lord President looked at him, from under his wig, with some surprise, and even impatience. 'I must warn you, Sir Hector,' he said, 'that we have no alternative in law but to admit the Precognition in evidence.'

'We are in a position, my Lord, to show that Dickson Carmichael is not dead.'

There was first a moment of silence, after this astonishing announcement; then a hum of excitement which sounded like a swarm of bees in a laundress's copper.

Stern men called for silence. It gradually fell.

'The Procurator Fiscal,' Sir Hector went on, 'is not to be blamed for having reached a false conclusion in the matter, since elaborate precautions were taken to simulate a death by drowning in the manner that Mr Craigie has described. Dickson Carmichael was, in fact, taken to a secret place, and there hidden. He is now in this city, and can shortly be brought to this Court.'

There was another buzz of astonishment: and more stern calls for silence.

Blank amazement was stamped on almost every face I noticed – on the Lord Advocate's, and the Procurator Fiscal's; on the faces of the Judges and jurymen; and on Uncle Frank's face.

There was no surprise visible on Tom's face. He looked composed as ever. He even looked contented.

'Why shortly, Sir Hector?' asked the Lord President. 'Why cannot the witness be brought to the Court now?'

'He is indisposed, my Lord. It is hoped that he will be sufficiently recovered by tomorrow to give evidence.'

'Indisposed, Sir Hector?'

'He is drunk, my Lord.'

There was a kind of titter. The intense excitement relaxed. Silence was sternly called for again.

'There are two courses open to us,' said the Lord President, after a pause during which the Judges murmured gravely to each other. 'We can adjourn until Sir Hector has effected sobriety in his alleged witness. This will permit him to establish for us that the unhappy man – or, perhaps, too happy man – is indeed the witness whose Precognition Mr Craigie took. Mr Craigie himself can doubtless give us that identification.'

'Yes, my Lord,' said Sir Hector dubiously, 'but twelve years of the kind of life the man has been living have, I suspect, changed him almost past recognition.'

'Then your task, Sir Hector, becomes more difficult. That admission strengthens, I think, the attraction of the other path open to us. We can proceed with Mr Craigie's evidence on the assumption that the Death Certificate was correctly issued in

August 1849. We have your word for it, Sir Hector, that a drunken man you believe to be Dickson Carmichael is alive and in your care, and will in due course be satisfactorily identified. Against that opinion we have the weighty evidence of the Procurator Fiscal.'

'This particular situation is vexatious and unprecedented,' said another Judge, with gloom. 'There is no precedent for a dead witness returning to life after a dozen years, and to the witness-box in this Court.'

'If your Lordships please,' said the Lord Advocate, 'it could be argued that the Death Certificate, as a legal document in proper form, enables me to introduce the hearsay evidence, and obliges the Court to admit it, in spite of a barely credible and unsupported claim by Sir Hector that a man dead a dozen years is alive and drunk.'

'Sir Hector disagrees with your submission, I fancy?' said the Lord President.

'I do, my Lord. The Court's time may, most regrettably, be wasted by an adjournment until the witness is in a condition to testify; it will be much more severely wasted by the admission of evidence which will, tomorrow or the day after, turn out to be inadmissible. I should respectfully add, for your Lordships' guidance, that the evidence I expect Dickson Carmichael to give here is sharply different from the Precognition which he gave to Mr Craigie.'

The Court adjourned, anyway, for legal argument about the admissibility of the story in Mr Craigie's pocket.

'They simply don't believe Sir Hector,' said Mrs. Gilchrist. 'And I find it difficult to blame them.'

'They are in a quandary, a real one,' said Lord Killin, who had joined us in a crowded granite corridor. 'If they don't admit the hearsay evidence, then there is really no case for the Prosecution. But they know very well there is one, an extremely strong one, in that fellow Craigie's breast pocket.'

'But if . . .' I began, most puzzled and confused.

'Suppose they don't admit the evidence. The Advocate closes his case. Tom is called, and tells whatever story he tells, true or false. Then the drunk is called, and turns out *not* to be the other keeper on the river bank.'

'Then,' said Mrs Gilchrist, 'they revert to the assumption that the witness is dead, and re-admit the hearsay evidence.'

'*After* the Defence has submitted its whole case, ma'am? Would the High Court of Justiciary consent to muddling up its own procedure like that?'

'They would have to recall Lord Ravenburn,' said Mrs Gilchrist, looking as confused as I felt. 'It would be inequitable to give the Prosecution the last word . . .'

'In fact,' said Lord Killin, 'it appears that although a respected advocate has stated that a witness is alive, the High Court has got to go on pretending that he's dead.'

Later, during the same long adjournment of the Court, I saw Uncle Frank at the end of a corridor, talking to a stranger in a black coat. The stranger was a big, hearty-looking man, who looked as out of place in the law-courts as Killin himself. His manner to Uncle Frank, as it appeared from a distance, was that of a prosperous tenant farmer to an indulgent landlord – respectful, yet confident and free-and-easy.

Mrs Gilchrist, standing beside me, saw the two at the same moment as I did. The hearty man, glancing up, saw her also, and waved as though at his oldest friend.

Mrs Gilchrist seemed less than overjoyed at this greeting. She inclined her head a very small way in acknowledgement of the wave.

'Who is that?' I asked, not because I was much interested, but because Mrs Gilchrist and I were in danger of running out of things to say to each other.

'He is called Loudon,' sair Mrs Gilchrist. 'A member of my husband's profession, but not universally regarded as an ornament to it.'

'I wonder what business he has with Uncle Frank,' I said idly.

It was only later that I remembered the most curious conversation I had overheard, between Uncle Frank and Mamma, while I was finding the dress Malvina wanted to wear.

Loudon was Uncle Frank's spy. Loudon had found Dr McAndrew.

Killin was right about the decision the Court would take.

The Lord President told the jury that they might have to dismiss from their minds the evidence they were about to hear, but in the meantime they must attend to it. I thought Mrs

Gilchrist was right, too – the Judges did not believe the jury would have to dismiss the evidence from their minds. They did not believe Dickson Carmichael had come back from the dead, after a dozen years wedged under a rock on the bottom of Loch Chinn.

The Procurator Fiscal testified that what he had by him was a true, exact and verbatim account of the Precognition given to him, in his office in Lochgrannomhead, in July 1839, by Dickson Carmichael.

Then he read the document.

'I, Dickson Carmichael, am employed as a keeper on the Crossmount estate. Early in the evening of the third of July of this present year, I proceeded, according to instructions I had been given, to the Horseshoe Pool of the River Chinn, which is part of the Crossmount water. I was accompanied by Jock McVie. We were instructed, as always, to catch if we could any poacher that we saw, but to use no more force than was strictly necessary. No other keeper was guarding the Horseshoe Pool that night, besides Jock McVie and myself, owing to several men being sent to a different duty elsewhere on the estate.

'At about midnight – I am not sure of the exact hour – we saw an evident poacher. He was alone. He was using a fishing rod with a heavy line. He had a large drag-hook on the line. I recognized him as Lord Ravenburn, whom I knew well by sight. I was not surprised to see Lord Ravenburn poaching the Crossmount water, as I had seen him doing so on many previous occasions. In company with others, I had tried to apprehend him on all those occasions, but without success.

'Jock McVie and I, obedient to our orders, crept towards Lord Ravenburn. Lord Ravenburn was alert and wary, as he always was, listening and looking round. We moved slowly and carefully. When we were fifteen yards from him he hooked a fish. It was a big fish, and fought strongly.'

(I had long stopped believing that this was truly a verbatim version. The words were Mr Craigie's. But it was obviously a faithful account of the sense of what Dickson Carmichael had said.)

The Procurator Fiscal read on: 'To take advantage of Lord Ravenburn's preoccupation with the fish, we crept nearer. As we had arranged, I gave a signal, and we rushed. He heard us in time. He dropped his rod and ran, just evading Jock McVie. I

263

thought he had escaped yet again. Then he fell. I thought he had twisted his ankle on a stone. Jock McVie reached him before I did. By the time Jock McVie reached him, Lord Ravenburn had got to his feet. He could not run. He had picked up a stone the size of a football.

'As I hurried up to assist Jock McVie, I too fell. I twisted my ankle. I got to my feet at once but I was unable to walk. I could not assist Jock McVie in apprehending Lord Ravenburn.

'Jock McVie called to Lord Ravenburn, telling him not to make things worse for himself, but to submit to arrest. I do not remember the precise words he used, but that is an accurate account of their meaning. He added words to the effect that Lord Ravenburn was caught this time, and could not get away, and would do best to go along with us quietly.

'Jock McVie went up to Lord Ravenburn, and put a hand on his arm. I called to him to wait until I could crawl up to assist him. I was still unable to walk, but I could crawl. But Jock McVie kept his hand on Lord Ravenburn's arm. Lord Ravenburn called to him to let him go. He said he was a gentleman, and could not be apprehended by a keeper. Jock McVie said he might be a gentleman, but he was also a poacher. He must submit to being apprehended, and come with us to Crossmount. I do not remember the exact words used by either Lord Ravenburn or Jock McVie, but that is their sense.

'Lord Ravenburn shook Jock McVie's hand from his arm. He took a step backwards. He was limping but he took one or two steps. I am not certain if it was one step or two. Jock McVie hastened to step after him. He stumbled. In recovering himself, he seized hold of Lord Ravenburn round the waist. Lord Ravenburn was still carrying the great stone. He brought it down on Jock McVie's head. I heard the noise of the stone hitting the head. I was some yards away, still trying to crawl towards them. I do not know precisely how many yards away I was. I was not near enough to help Jock McVie, but I was near enough to see the blow struck and to hear it.

'Lord Ravenburn threw the stone into the river. It made a big splash. He saw me crawling towards him. He was better able to walk than I, although he was limping. He recovered his rod. I think he had lost the fish, owing to the line going slack. He went away. I did not see in what direction he went. He was out of my sight at once.

'I crawled to Jock McVie and found that he was dead. I waited by his body until daylight. This was partly to prevent the body being mutilated by foxes, wildcats and the like, and partly because I could not walk on my sprained ankle. Ewan McNair the head keeper came to the pool at first light, and found us.'

The story had had the ring of truth to the Procurator Fiscal, when he wrote it down in 1849. It had had the ring of truth to me, when I read a copy of it at Ravenburn. It still had the ring of truth. The whole scene came to awful life in the mind's eye. It was so horribly probable, so circumstantial.

It was very easy to twist an ankle on that river-bank. It would be easy for two men to do so, running in the dark on wet stones.

The place was littered with stones the size of footballs.

The Procurator Fiscal was thanked. He stepped down.

The Lord Advocate said that his evidence completed the case for the Crown.

'Why did he change his name?' I asked. 'And how did he get at the whisky?'

'As to the first, Miss Irvine,' said Mr Gilchrist in his drawing-room that evening, 'the answer is surely obvious. Does a man go into hiding under his own name? Did Lord Ravenburn?'

'Oh. Yes. It was a silly question.'

'As to the second, I don't know. There's a young kitchenmaid with all too kind a heart, I think. I expect our friend was moaning and sobbing for his dram. "A wee drappie, then," she probably said, and he seized the bottle and emptied it.'

'Will he be fit to give his evidence?'

'We're doing all that can be done with strong coffee, and cold water, and oatmeal porridge. Sir George Fraser is down there now, labouring in the unprepossesssing vineyard of my coal-cellar.'

'Shall I try?'

'With respect, Miss Irvine, what can you do for the man that Sir George can't? I imagine his experience of drunken keepers is more extensive than yours.'

But I persuaded him to take me down.

The gross man looked gross again – a whimpering, degraded, dreadful figure.

'You know what will happen to you, if you don't take hold of yourself,' I said to him, very loudly and cruelly. 'We shall take you to Eilean Fitheach, and leave you there, and the ghosts of the Hargues will get you.'

He shrieked. I thought I had overdone it, and given him the horrors, so that he would never speak rationally on the witness-stand. But Sir George said later that he did take hold of himself, from that moment.

'Still a sister,' said Mr Gilchrist, 'that any man would be lucky to have.'

Still a sister.

I had somehow assumed that the first witness for the Defence would be Dickson Carmichael. In fact, it had to be Tom him-self, which everybody except me had known all along.

The slight figure, neat and composed as ever, was escorted from the dock to the witness-stand, and there sworn.

'You have heard yourself described, Lord Ravenburn,' said Sir Hector McCallum, 'as wilful, audacious, rebellious. Would you accept those words as a fair description of yourself, twelve years ago?'

'Yes, sir,' said Tom mildly.

'It has been suggested in the evidence that you had never, until the fatal night, been known to commit any act of violence. Had you, in fact, ever committed violence against any person?'

'No, sir.'

'It has been further suggested that, although you might cause pain by thoughtlessness, you would not do so deliberately, with malice. Do you think that is, or was, true of yourself?'

'Yes, sir.'

I thought Sir Hector would ask Tom *why* he was wilful and rebellious; but instead he said, 'We have heard much about a letter which you wrote to Sir Campbell Stewart in January or February of 1848. Do you recall the contents of that letter?'

Tom remembered much: not all.

'Will you tell the Court all that you remember?'

'It is a little embarrassing for me to do so, sir, because it was rather – priggish in tone.'

'Priggish?' The word seemed to surprise Sir Hector as much as it surprised everybody else.

'Pretentious. Puppyish would perhaps be the right word. I was a schoolboy, teaching an older man his duty. I said I considered he had an obligation to feed the families he had evicted, many of whom were very long-established tenants of the Crossmount estate, all of whom he had evicted for purely financial reasons, most of whom had no alternative means of livelihood. I said that if Sir Campbell did not fulfil this obligation, I would do it for him.'

'You said you would feed the evicted families?'

'Yes, sir. Some were otherwise in real danger of starving.'

'You would feed them how?'

'With Crossmount salmon.'

'And did you?'

'Yes, sir.'

'How many salmon did you take from Crossmount during that spring and summer?'

'I think it was twenty-three.'

'We have heard the figure fifty.'

'That figure was the one named in my letter, sir, but I did not achieve it. I was not the only poacher active at Crossmount.'

'There was Rory Beg?'

'There were half a dozen, at different times.'

'Known to you?'

'Some. None well.'

'If fifty salmon were taken from the water, you took less than half?'

'If fifty were in truth taken, yes.'

'And every single one of those twenty-three fish . . .?'

'Went to a family evicted during the previous few years by Sir Campbell Stewart.'

'Including the McQueen family?'

'Yes. They had found somewhere to live – a croft made available to them by the generosity of General Ramsay of Tulloch. But there was only a little patch of land with that croft, and General Ramsay could give Andrew McQueen no more without hurt to an existing tenant. The patch did not feed six children, sir. But some twenty-pound salmon in a brine-barrel did.'

'You believed it was morally right to steal from the rich to give to the poor?'

The Lord Advocate was on his feet. 'My learned friend is leading the witness, my Lord.'

'No,' said the Lord President. 'The witness has already given the same answer, in different words, to earlier questions.'

The Lord Advocate sat down, not liking a deliberate comparison between Tom and Robin Hood.

Sir Hector repeated his question.

Tom said, mildly, choosing his words in a way I knew so well, 'My moral position seemed to me a little stronger than that. I was not stealing from any rich man to give to any poor man. I was taking from a particular rich man food, for which he had no need or use as food, but only as money, and giving that food to particular poor men, whose families were hungry because of the rich man's management. Andrew McQueen had fed his family by his own efforts. Sir Campbell Stewart wanted the large rent of a pheasant covert rather than the small rent of a tenant farm. Andrew McQueen could therefore no longer feed his family. I did not and do not deny Sir Campbell's legal right to turn a farm into a wood. But I did and do believe that he should have used some little part of his great new shooting rent to sustain Andrew McQueen's six children. I would have liked to feed that family on pheasants from the New Wood—'

'As a sort of poetic justice?'

'As the new crop from the farm from which no decent landlord would have evicted him. That was not practical however, on any but a very small scale.'

'Why? Was the pheasant covert too difficult to poach?'

'It was not that, sir. But pheasants don't keep in a brine-barrel.'

'Did you, at any time, take any other game from Crossmount than the salmon?'

'Yes, sir. I took a few pheasants.'

'What did you do with them?'

'I gave them to families whom Sir Campbell had evicted.'

'All of them?'

'Yes, sir.'

'Did you take anything else from the Crossmount estate?'

'No, sir.'

'Did you take anything from any other estate than Crossmount?'

'No, sir. The only other sporting estate within easy reach was Tulloch. I would not have touched a fin or feather belonging to General Ramsay.'

'Why?'

'Because he never evicted a tenant who depended for survival on his tenancy.'

Presently Sir Hector turned to Tom's attitude to the Crossmount keepers.

'I knew some of them,' Tom said. 'Ewan McNair best, because I had been deer-stalking with him.'

'Did you know Jock McVie?'

'No.'

'He was a complete stranger to you?'

'As far as I know, I never saw him but once.'

'Yet we have heard that he came from Ravenburn.'

'Yes. That surprised me.'

'You accept that he came from Ravenburn?'

'Oh yes, since Sir Campbell said so. I repeat that I did not know him.'

'I do not understand how a sporting young man like yourself could fail to know a keeper on his own estate?'

'I do not understand it either, sir. I think Jock McVie can only just have been engaged at Ravenburn.'

'And then moved immediately to Crossmount?'

'I can think of no other explanation for my not knowing him.'

'Did you know Dickson Carmichael?'

'I knew him by sight as a Crossmount keeper. I did not know his name.'

'You have said that you never offered violence to any person. That included the Crossmount keepers?'

'Most particularly them, sir, since they were performing an exhausting and exacting duty, as they were ordered.'

'Would you have hit or injured a Crossmount keeper?'

'Only to save my life.'

'Not to resist arrest?'

Tom said slowly, after a pause, 'I do not think so, sir. I hope not. My arrest would have been unpleasant and embarrassing, but I would not have been hanged or deported. I did not think I would be handed over to the police. Also, I took pains that the question should not arise.'

'What pains?'

'Principally, I made it my business to find out before every expedition where the keepers would be.'

'How did you get this information?'

'From one of the keepers.'

'Which one?'

Tom turned, worried, to the awesome bench of Judges. He said, 'Am I obliged to answer that question, my Lord? The man has left Sir Campbell's employ. He is in a responsible position on another estate. I submit that no useful purpose would be served . . .'

'For the moment, Lord Ravenburn,' said the Lord President, 'we may do without the name. But that is without prejudice to our demanding it later, if circumstances so require.'

'Thank you, my Lord.'

Sir Hector said, 'Do you know why this Crossmount keeper betrayed these secrets to you?'

'He agreed with me, sir.'

'He agreed with your – diversion of salmon from Sir Campbell's fishing tenants to families like the McQueens?'

'Yes, sir.' Tom smiled slightly (the smile I knew so very well). 'I would not like to be required to repeat in this Court the terms in which he said so.'

I could just see Sir Campbell Stewart's face. He was purple at what was being said about him. I thought he might have a fit. Almost visible across his features was his furious calculation about which keeper had betrayed his plans, or Ewan McNair's, to Tom.

'May we now turn,' said Sir Hector, 'to the man described in evidence as your accomplice, Rory Beg? First, what has become of him?'

'I believe him to be dead, sir. I believe him to have been killed, but I was not present, and cannot speak with knowledge.'

'He has been described as a notorious criminal. Would you so describe him?'

'Those words are misleading rather than untrue, sir. He was well-known. He did break the law.'

'How did you come to know such a man?'

'We met one night, sir, in the middle of a wood. His leg was in a gin-trap.'

'A man-trap?'

'In effect, sir. It was a big spring, with big jaws. It might have been intended for an animal . . .'

'Where was this?'

'A wood called Aulich, on the Crossmount estate.'

'Why were you there?'

'To set snares for pheasants, sir.'

'And Rory Beg?'

'For the same reason.'

'With the difference that he would have sold his birds, while you gave yours away?'

'With that difference, yes.'

'You found him – what then?'

'I released him from the trap.'

'One would expect him to be grateful?'

'He was grateful, but it was not for that reason that we became friends.'

'For what reason?'

'For no reason. We became friends. We liked each other.'

'You liked him?'

'Yes, sir, very much. He was gentle, honourable, kind. I should say he was typical of the finest type of West Highlander.'

'You are describing a notorious criminal?'

'A celebrated poacher, sir.'

'A West Highlander? You mean from the coast or the islands?'

'He told me he came from Loch Torridon, sir, where his face had become uncomfortably familiar.'

'We have heard that you and he together used a cross-line on the river?'

'Yes, sir. Not often. Sometimes he advised it as the best way to get a fish.'

'Was it successful?'

'When he said it would be, sir, it usually was.'

'When you caught a fish between you, you and Rory Beg, what became of the fish?'

'It went to an evicted family.'

'Rory Beg was agreeable to this arrangement?'

'Yes, sir.'

'But he was a professional poacher?'

'Yes, sir.'

'With no other livelihood?'

'He had been a smuggler.'

'He had been to prison, too?'

'So I believe.'

'This lawless man consented that a salmon, which he had

helped to poach at considerable risk, should be given away to an evicted family, leaving no profit or even food for himself?'

'Yes, sir, indeed he did.'

'He, too, shared your views?'

'Yes, sir, although he usually expressed them in Gaelic. He had himself been born to a tenant crofter family. He knew the misery caused by some great landowners, who deliberately depopulated estates in order to create sheep-walk or deer-forest.'

'Was his own family evicted?'

'No, sir. It was simply too large for the croft. Rory Beg's father had been a tenant of the Duke of Cromarty, who never evicted a tenant unfairly or cruelly.'

'Sir Hector,' said one of the Judges, 'we appreciate that the character and motives of Lord Ravenburn's poaching accomplice are in some measure relevant to his own poaching activities, which led to the events into which we are inquiring. But I hope our patience will not be strained by too protracted an investigation of this man's family and background.'

'As your Lordship pleases,' said Sir Hector. 'I was concerned to bring out that the "notorious criminal accomplice" of whom we have heard could be portrayed in somewhat different colours.'

'The point is made, Sir Hector, and taken. It need not be laboured.'

'No, my Lord, it need not. Lord Ravenburn, may we come to the events of the third of July. Did you receive intelligence of the keepers' movements?'

'Yes, sir.'

'From the usual source?'

'Yes, sir.'

'What did you learn?'

'That Ewan McNair and some other men were to watch the New Wood, because a party of tinkers was rumoured to be nearby with an eye on the pheasant poults.'

'Can you throw any light on this rumour?'

'None, sir.'

'We have heard evidence that Jock McVie reported the rumour. You can throw no light on that?'

'No, sir. Until I heard the evidence here, I had no idea where the whisper had come from.'

'It did not originate with you, as a device to get the keepers away from the river?'

'No, sir.' Tom smiled again (his beloved smile) and added, 'Not that night.'

'Apart from the deployment of some keepers to the New Wood, did you receive other intelligence?'

'I learned that two men only were to be posted to the Horse-shoe Pool.'

'What plan did you make?'

'I knew the Horseshoe Pool was brimming with fish – I had seen them. I expected to be able to elude two keepers. I went there.'

'With what equipment?'

'A rod. A drag-hook.'

'A gaff?'

'No, sir. A gaff is unnecessary when a fish is caught with a drag-hook.'

'A knife?'

'A small pocket-knife.'

'No other weapon?'

'No weapon at all, sir. The knife was a very small one, for cutting my line if that was necessary.'

'Will you please,' said Sir Hector McCallum gently, 'tell us what happened that night, Lord Ravenburn?'

Tom seemed to take a deep breath, to steady himself.

The silence in the Courtroom was absolute. No one knew what Tom was going to say, except his own lawyers.

I found myself praying for him.

Tom said that he reached the pool at about ten minutes to midnight. He crept up to the point on the bank which he had previously picked as the best place to start. It was a place which Rory Beg had recommended. As he went, he searched with eyes and ears for the two keepers he knew would be by the pool. He was not frightened of the keepers, because he was sure he could run faster than they could. He could also take to the water, being a strong swimmer. They would be most unlikely to follow him into the deep fast water of the pool. Even if they did, he was sure he could get away downstream to the loch, and to the place where his boat was hidden. The only danger was that he might literally walk into the arms of the keepers. He was careful not to do such a thing.

He began to fish, casting the big double drag-hook far out across the pool, and bringing it back slowly so that it swam deep. He continued to be alert, watching and listening as he fished.

At the tenth or twelfth cast he hooked a fish. It was a big fish, a bonny fighter. Being foul-hooked in the side, it was much more awkward to bring to the bank than a fish hooked in the jaw. But he had a heavy line, and no fear of breaking or of losing the fish. He was at his most vulnerable to the keepers while he was playing the fish. He wanted to get the fish to the bank as quickly as possible, hoping to do so before the keepers got to him.

He would have done so with a small salmon, but this was a very big one, and the two keepers began to rush him before he had banked the fish. There was a gleam of moonlight and he saw the keepers clearly. One he knew by sight, but not by name, as a Crossmount keeper of some years' service, whom he recently learned to be Dickson Carmichael. The other was a big, swarthy man, strange to him, whom he recently learned to be Jock McVie.

In the moonlight, he saw that Jock McVie had a knife in his hand. It looked like a butcher's knife – a narrow blade, about a foot long. He was surprised. Keepers did not carry butchers' knives. He had never before seen such a knife in the hands of a keeper, at Crossmount or Ravenburn or any other estate. The Crossmount keepers had sticks, heavy cudgels; sometimes shot-guns; sometimes pistols, if they expected a gang of armed poachers. That was normal and correct, in Tom's experience. A butcher's knife was an eccentric thing to carry. In the normal way, a most useless and inconvenient thing.

'Did it frighten you?' asked Sir Hector McCallum.

'At first it merely puzzled me. It did not frighten me, because I was sure I could run faster, and if need be swim faster, than the man who was carrying it. The thought flashed through my mind that he had drawn the knife to cut my line. It did not occur to me that it was intended for me.'

'You remember your thoughts with great clarity, after so long, Lord Ravenburn?'

'Yes, sir. I remember every detail of that night with terrible clarity. I always shall.'

Tom said that he evaded the keepers without difficulty, run-

274

ning downstream towards the loch. He stopped and glanced back, to see if there was a chance of running round them, to retrieve his rod and perhaps catch the fish too. As he stopped, the big man with the knife stopped also. The big man was holding the knife by its blade instead of by its handle. Holding the knife by the blade, between his fingers, he raised his right arm behind his shoulder.

'I realized,' said Tom mildly, 'that he was going to throw the knife.'

'Did he throw it?'

'Yes, sir. Because I had had that moment of warning, from his arm and from the way he was holding the knife, I threw myself onto the ground. The knife went close over me. It hit a rock, and bounced away. I tried to get to my feet. But I found that, in throwing myself to the ground, I had hurt my ankle. I could get to my feet, but I could not move quickly. I saw that the man who had thrown the knife had drawn a second knife.'

'Can you describe the second knife?'

'Not accurately, sir. It appeared to me identical with the first – a knife like a butcher's with a narrow pointed blade not quite a foot long.'

'How far away was the man, when he drew the second knife?'

'Not more than three yards away from me, sir.'

'And the other keeper?'

'Some way behind him.'

'Hurrying towards you?'

'No, sir. My impression was that he was watching, rather than taking part.'

'Did you see him fall?'

'No, sir. At no time did he fall, that I saw.'

'Please go on.'

Tom said the big man with the knife evidently saw that there was no need to throw the knife – that Tom was disabled. He came towards Tom, walking at a moderate pace, holding the knife not by the blade but by the handle.

'You have said,' said Sir Hector, 'that you had nothing with you, with which to defend yourself, except a small pocket-knife.'

'With a blade an inch and a half long. It was in my pocket and closed up. It never occurred to me that it was of any use in this situation. It was not of any use.'

'Since you were unarmed, as the man approached, what did you do?'

'I picked up a stone.'

'Can you describe the stone?'

'No, sir, beyond saying that it was quite large and heavy. I did not have time to examine it before, and I had no wish to examine it after.'

'What then?'

'The man with the knife came close to me, a yard from me, and raised his hand with the knife.'

'With what apparent intention?'

'With the unmistakable intention of killing me.'

'And you?'

'I hit him on the head with the stone.'

'And then?'

'I managed to hobble away.'

'What did you do about the rod?'

'I left it. The other keeper was near it. It was not a moment when I was concerned about a fishing-rod.'

'The other keeper was still on his feet?'

'Yes, sir. Looking in my direction, but making no effort to approach nearer.'

'What did you do with the stone?'

'I threw it in the river.'

'Why?'

'I don't know. It was a horrible object. I suppose it struck me as – more seemly, that it should be washed clean.'

'Did you examine the man you had hit?'

'No, sir.'

'Why not?'

'I was sure he was dead. I did not wish to touch the body of a man I had – just killed.'

'What were your emotions, when you realized that you had just killed a man?'

'Horror. Terror.'

'The horror everyone in this Court can, I think, understand. But why terror, since you had acted in self defence?'

The Lord Advocate started to rise, but sat down again.

'I was seventeen years old, sir,' said Tom mildly. 'I had killed a man by hitting him on the head with a stone. I was terrified of what I had done, of the consequences of what I had done. It is a terrifying thing, to kill a man with a stone, in the dark. It would be terrifying to me now, and I am twelve years older. Also . . .'

'Also, Lord Ravenburn?'

'The man I killed was trying to kill me. But for that stone, he would have killed me. I did not know him. He was not a personal enemy of mine. Therefore, he was acting for another person.' Tom's voice became milder, gentler, more reasonable even than before. He said, 'If that other person wanted me dead so badly, sir, he would try again, with another hired murderer.'

'These thoughts occurred to you immediately, there on the river bank?'

'Yes, sir. When a man tries to kill you with a knife, you ask yourself why.'

'This other person – do you know who he was? Could you – can you – guess who he was?'

'I could, and can, guess. My guess might be utterly false, in which case it would be very wounding and damaging, perhaps.'

Tom said, in answer to Sir Hector's questions, that he knew quite well that he had acted in self defence. He could not have run away from his assailant, because he had hurt his ankle. Even if he could have run, the man with the knife would have thrown the knife. Only by hitting the man with the stone had he saved his own life. But this knowledge did not make him feel safe, even though there was a witness of the whole. That witness had not actively assisted the knife-thrower, but he had not come to Tom's assistance, either. He was an ally of the knife-thrower. Presumably he would lie about the attack; he must do so, or confess himself an accessory to an attempt at murder. Tom had powerful friends, it was true, who would help and advise him, and find him lawyers. But somebody wanted him dead. He would be taking advice perhaps, from someone who was planning to kill him. Right or wrong, that was the way Tom's terrified seventeen-year-old mind had worked, as he hobbled painfully back to his boat on the lochside.

Thus, though knowing himself innocent, he ran away.

He crept back into Ravenburn, to get clothes and a little money, and to say goodbye to his little half-sister, whom he loved better than any other living person. He took a pony of his own from the stable, and rode south the long road towards Loch Lomond. At dawn, he left the exhausted pony in a farm-yard where the animals looked well cared for. He went on, on foot, to Glasgow. He was thoroughly disguised by the time he arrived at the docks, grimy and tattered. He adopted a strong Scots accent, and found a berth on a ship.

He found, when he reached Australia, that he was still a fugitive. He had a famous name, and his case was uniquely sensational. He led a most obscure life, constantly in danger of being unmasked. His life was rough, but he was free, and there was no rope round his neck. And he was not in danger of being murdered. A friend, similar to him in size and age, was tragically killed in a mine. He was able to adopt the identity of his friend. His dead friend adopted his own identity. Dead, he was no longer a fugitive. Now, bearded and not instantly recognizable, he could return to Scotland and perhaps redeem himself. It was many years before he could return, because his friend had been an indentured servant.

All this took a very long time to tell. I could not see that it had much to do with the actual death of Jock McVie. But my friends explained to me during the various adjournments for luncheon and for the night, that Tom's running away had so much the look of an admission of guilt, that his movements and motives must be clearly explained.

Tom told, also at length, of how he had at last come back, and made secret contact with friends of his father's, and with his own old friend Rory Beg. After months of searching, done in great secrecy, they had discovered that Dickson Carmichael, the witness, was not dead. Rory Beg discovered where he was hidden. They fetched him from his hiding-place, and brought him at last to Edinburgh.

The Lord Advocate's cross-examination was almost equally long. He covered, all over again, every bit of the ground – the letter, the decision to poach, Rory Beg, the 'treacherous' keeper, the fatal night. About the events of the night, the Lord Advocate laboured and laboured to break Tom's story down – to trick or compel him into admitting that he was not certain a knife had been thrown, or another raised against him, that he could have evaded the apparent threat by running away. I began to hate the Lord Advocate with furious hatred. But my friends assured me he was doing his duty, as well as he could.

The Lord Advocate was very skilful, and his questions awkward and subtle. But Tom stood firm. It was blindingly obvious

278

to me that he was telling the truth. I could not guess if it was obvious to the jury.

Sir Hector re-examined. This was brief, mercifully, as Tom had been on the witness-stand for three full days already.

Tom stepped down at last, and was escorted back to the dock. Dickson Carmichael was called to the witness stand.

fifteen

Dickson Carmichael, or Donald McWiddie, looked pasty and unhealthy, rather than gross and degraded. They had managed to scrub him clean, and they had brought a barber to him, and found him some decent Edinburgh clothes.

He looked amazingly unlike a West Perthshire gamekeeper or gillie. He looked like an unsuccessful baker, or failed haberdasher.

As well as unhealthy, he looked desperately uneasy and frightened. I wondered if he sensed the ghosts of the Hargues behind his shoulder, as well as the majesty of the law.

His first answers were in so faint and trembling a voice, that he could not be heard by anybody. At last Sir Hector and the Lord President between them induced him to speak up. It was not that he gained courage, but that he was terrified of the Lord President.

He had gone to work on the Crossmount estate some eight years before the death of Jock McVie. He came not from another estate but from Lochgrannomhead, where his father had been a tradesman, a butcher, but bankrupted. He came because he thought he would prefer the life of the countryside to that of the town.

His wages were small, his tastes a little expensive. He liked whisky, more and better whisky than he could afford on what the laird paid him. He began to steal a few things from the sportsmen who visited Crossmount. They were not the laird's friends – they were tenants, paying to shoot and fish. They were rich men, businessmen and bankers from Glasgow. They had expensive rods, guns, spyglasses, silver-mounted flasks. He stole a few of these things, and sold them in Lochgrannomhead. He spent the money on whisky. He was very careful. He was never caught, and never suspected.

On his expeditions to Lochgrannomhead, with the stolen goods, he met Jock McVie. Jock McVie was an idler, a poacher, a thief, a dangerous man. He had been a sailor. In far countries he had learned things which no one in Scotland knew. He had learned to throw knives, to kill a man at thirty paces. He had special knives for throwing. He showed the knives to Dickson Carmichael, in the way of boasting, and demonstrated his skill at throwing them.

One day in the autumn of 1848, Dickson Carmichael was out with a party of the laird's shooting tenants. They were walking partridges in the stubble, on the low ground near the river. Mr Francis Dundas of Ravenburn Castle was one of the shooting party. It seemed he was a friend of the Glasgow bankers who had paid to come to shoot. It was very hot, an early September day, one of the first days of the partridge shooting. Some of the visiting gentlemen took off their coats, owing to the heat of the sun. They were walking after their dogs in their shirtsleeves. Dickson Carmichael was supposed to be far away. He had been posted as a stop, to turn the covey back towards the guns. But he crawled back to the coats, and went through the pockets.

Mr Dundas had not joined the guns, at that point in the afternoon. He was a fair-skinned man, and suffered from heat and bright sunlight. He was resting in the shade, under a hedge, invisible. Dickson Carmichael did not see him, but he saw Dickson going through the pockets of the shooting party. Mr Dundas said Dickson would be arrested, handed over to the authorities, tried, and sent to prison. It was obvious, said Mr Dundas, that he was also responsible for the other unexplained thefts from Sir Campbell Stewart's visitors. Dickson Carmichael would go to prison for a long time, because he was not only stealing, but also abusing a position of trust.

Dickson Carmichael knew that he would go mad and die, in the confinement of a prison cell, deprived of freedom and fresh air and whisky. He begged Mr Dundas to be merciful. He swore that he would never steal again. He offered to do anything for Mr Dundas.

Mr Dundas was merciful. He accepted Dickson Carmichael's

promise that he would never steal again. He said that he would call on Dickson Carmichael for help, whenever he should need it, and Dickson must give that help, whatever form it took.

The following spring, as everybody knew, Sir Campbell Stewart received a letter from Lord Ravenburn. Dickson Carmichael did not see the letter, but he was told its contents. Everybody at Crossmount knew about the letter, and what it said. Because of the letter, the laird began to engage extra keepers, to guard his river and his coverts. Dickson Carmichael understood that he asked his neighbours for recommendations, and for men if the neighbours had more men than they needed.

Mr Francis Dundas sent for Dickson Carmichael. He said that he wanted a man of a particular kind. He wanted a man who could work as a keeper, but would perform other tasks too. Dickson Carmichael understood that Mr Dundas wanted a man who would do violence. He wanted a man who would kill. He did not want to find such a man for Mr Dundas. He did not like the idea of killing. But Mr Dundas reminded him that a word would put him into prison for a long time.

Dickson Carmichael went to Lochgrannomhead, and found Jock McVie, and brought him in a pony-trap to Mr Dundas at Ravenburn. Jock McVie then went from Ravenburn to Crossmount, where he was engaged as an extra keeper. He was engaged at Crossmount about the first of April, having been at Ravenburn for two days.

Dickson Carmichael did not know what Mr Francis Dundas said, on any occasion, to Jock McVie. He was never present at an interview between them.

On the third of July he was surprised to hear, from Jock McVie, about noon, that a company of tinkers had been seen in the neighbourhood, and that they were rumoured to be planning to poach the New Wood for young pheasants. He himself saw and heard nothing of a gang of tinkers. He could not say for certain that Jock McVie invented the gang of tinkers, as a means of getting Ewan McNair and other keepers away from the river. He could say that, as far as he knew, only Jock McVie had word of the gang.

Jock McVie told Dickson Carmichael that the two of them were to go to the Horseshoe Pool that night. He said that Mr Francis Dundas had told Jock to remind Dickson Carmichael of what a word in the right quarter would do. He was to remember that, all during the night. He was not to forget it for a moment, whatever happened. He was to help Jock McVie, in whatever Jock did. He took this as a threat that, if he did not do exactly as he was told, he would go to prison as a thief.

They hid by the Horseshoe Pool. They saw Lord Ravenburn come, and begin to cast a drag-hook. As soon as he was into a fish, they rushed him, on Jock McVie's signal. Jock McVie threw a knife at Lord Ravenburn, but missed him, as Lord Ravenburn threw himself down in the nick of time. Jock McVie drew another knife. He was about to throw it, but evidently saw, as Dickson Carmichael himself saw, that Lord Ravenburn was injured and could not run away. Jock McVie attacked Lord Ravenburn with the second knife. Lord Ravenburn defended himself, by picking up a stone and hitting Jock McVie on the head with it.

Dickson Carmichael was aghast at what happened. He could not bring himself to help Jock McVie, in spite of the threat to himself. But he dared not intervene to help Lord Ravenburn. He was afraid of going to prison, where he knew he would go mad and die. He was afraid of Jock McVie and his knives. He stood watching, too frightened and horrified to move. He made no attempt to give chase to Lord Ravenburn. He could have done so – he had not fallen or twisted his ankle, but he was too frightened and horrified.

The next day he was sent with a message from Crossmount to Ravenburn Castle. He was seen by Mr Francis Dundas. Mr Dundas told him what to say to the Procurator Fiscal. He rehearsed him carefully in his story. He repeated the threat, that Dickson Carmichael would go to prison until he rotted, if he did not do and say exactly as he was told.

He told the Procurator Fiscal what Mr Dundas had told him to say. He had practised the story in his mind, so that he had it quite clear; he could tell the story a hundred times, and it would still be the same story.

Sir Campbell Stewart told him he was to leave his position at Crossmount and go to Ravenburn. This was a few days after he had told his story to the Procurator Fiscal in Lochgrannomhead. He went to Ravenburn, in a cart. He was given a place to sleep in a steading near the Castle. He was given a bottle of whisky. He drank the whisky. He was very drunk. In the middle of the night he was picked up by some men and put across a pony. It may have been a donkey. He did not know how many men there were, or who they were. He was barely conscious. He was taken a long way, by a rough road. He did not know where he was being taken, or by whom. He was given more whisky. He was not frightened. He probably would have been frightened, and have resisted, but for the whisky he was given.

When he came to his senses, during the following day, he found himself in a little isolated croft built into a hillside by a burn. He did not know where he was. It was a very wild and lonely place. It was not a place he had ever seen before. There was food and drink in the croft, and the means of making a fire. When he was well enough, he made a fire, cooked food, and drank the whisky.

A few days later – he did not know how many days – men came in the night. He was too drunk to recognize the men. They left more food and whisky. He was told not to leave the croft, and the burnside immediately near the croft. If he did, he would get no more food or whisky. He would be hunted down and killed. He was to grow his hair and beard. He was to have no scissors or razor. His name was Donald McWiddie. Dickson Carmichael the keeper was dead, drowned in the loch. Donald McWiddie was a crofter, living alone on the charity of the laird.

He did not leave the croft and the burnside. He was content to live there quietly, with a sufficiency of food and of whisky. When his boots got old, new boots were brought to him.

When the weather grew cold, firewood and warm clothes were brought to him. All the things that came, came in the middle of the night. Usually he was drunk when they came, and he did not clearly afterwards remember who had come, or what was said.

At first he was content. Then he grew impatient with his solitude. But he did not dare to go away. He did not know how to go, in what direction. He did not want to go to prison, or to be deprived of food and whisky, or to be hunted down and killed.

He did not know how many years he lived in the solitary croft. He lost count of time. One day was like another. Sometimes he drank more, sometimes less.

His conscience was afflicted by the scene he had witnessed on the river-bank – by the fact that he had not helped Lord Ravenburn. It was afflicted by the fact that he had told a false story to the Procurator Fiscal. But although he was conscience-stricken, he did not dare to go away and tell the truth to the authorities. Part of him wanted to do so, but he was too greedy and frightened. Also he did not know if he could find his way out of the lost corrie where the croft was.

At last he was visited in the night by a man who did not bring food or whisky or boots. He was an old man. He said he was called Clamhan, the Hawk. Dickson Carmichael knew the face, but he did not remember who the old man was. His mind was given to wandering at that time. It was not wandering now, because he had been given little whisky in the last few days. His mind was quite clear now, but it had wandered sometimes when he was still at the croft.

The old man said that Dickson Carmichael must tell the truth about what happened by the Horseshoe Pool, so long before. That, or be deprived of whisky. The old man appealed to his conscience, and at the same time threatened to deprive him of whisky. Dickson Carmichael did not promise to come away, because he was frightened and confused. But his conscience was more sorely afflicted than ever, after what the old man told him.

Some days later, strangers came to the corrie by night. Dickson Carmichael had only a confused memory of them, because he was drunk when they came. He thought two people came, a man and a boy. He thought he knew the man, but he could not remember who he was. They threatened him with eternal thirst, and with other things, and carried him off. They had a very long and arduous journey, on foot and by water. Dickson Carmichael could remember almost nothing of the journey. Afterwards he lay in a new place, in a shelter, where he was given food and whisky. Then he was brought to Edinburgh in a carriage. He met some lawyers. He did not know their names. He told them the story he had just told the Court. He promised to tell the story in Court, even though it meant trouble and punishment for himself. It was the true story of the things he had seen.

He had been threatened, that he should have no more whisky, and that he would be assailed by malevolent ghosts. But he had not been told what story to tell, what evidence to give. He had been instructed to tell the exact truth. All that the lawyers and the others wanted from him was the exact truth. It was the exact truth that he had just told. He was glad to have told the truth, because his conscience had been sorely afflicted, and was now easy.

Dickson Carmichael looked very tired and ill as he stood, shakily, in the witness box. He looked as though he badly wanted and needed a dram of whisky. He looked as though he could hardly stand. Sir Hector asked the judge if the witness might have a chair. A chair was brought, and he sat down. He stumbled as he sat, and nearly fell. His face was grey and sweating. Though cleaner and neater than when I had last seen him, he was a miserable sight.

There was a sort of pathetic dignity about him, when he said he was telling the truth at last.

All eyes had been glued to the witness stand, while Dickson Carmichael was speaking. All eyes now turned to the public gallery, and to Frank Dundas.

Uncle Frank's face wore the most strange expression. It was like a death-mask, made not of flesh but of rough grey plaster, without life or colour, yet wearing the same bland smile that was its most usual expression. There was something dreadful about that bland smile, on a face which looked like a death-mask.

He was utterly disgraced and destroyed, in the eyes of all men and of the law. He had a bland smile on a dead face. He looked like a man who had been suddenly killed, while smiling, so that his smile was still fixed to his face, after his death.

I suddenly felt for him what I had never expected to feel for him – a surge of pity.

He was on his feet. It did not appear to me that he chose to stand up. It was as though his legs straightened without volition on his part.

He was at the front of the public gallery. Before him, waist high, was a stone balustrade. The gallery overhung part of the Courtroom. Thirty feet below him were the granite flagstones of the floor of the Court, the bare central area between bench and witness-box and dock and jury.

He stood up against the balustrade, gripping it with both hands. The bland dead smile never left his face.

He cried out, in a high unfamiliar voice like a child's, 'Isabella understands! No one else can understand! Isabella, and her children . . .'

His voice rose to a shriek as he shouted, 'Isabella understands! Isabella understands!'

A man, I do not know who, rose and put a hand on his shoulder. It might have been equally a gesture of comfort or an arrest. Uncle Frank turned, and hit wildly out at the man. He was still shrieking, but the words now were incoherent.

All the time, even as he shrieked and struggled, the dead bland smile was pinned to the dead grey face.

And then he went over the balustrade, and fell head first to the granite flagstones below.

Afterwards, there were those who said that he fell, and those who said that he deliberately threw himself. I did not then know which it was, and I do not know now.

There was a sickening crash as he landed on the granite floor, clearly audible over the hubbub in the Court. He lay in a heap, like a doll thrown down by a child in a temper. He lay as Rory Beg had lain, on the bank of the burn at midnight. No one could doubt that he was dead.

Though his skull was crushed in, his face still wore in death the mad bland smile of his life.

The Court was immediately adjourned. There was a strange atmosphere – part numbed shock, part a sort of dreadful glee. People were elaborately kind to me. Mrs Gilchrist took me back to her house; she thought I needed hartshorn, or smelling-salts, or burnt feathers, or laudanum, or warm milk; she thought I should go at once to bed. But I wanted none of these things. More than anything, I wanted knowledge. I wanted to understand.

So did others. Therefore Mr Gilchrist assembled in his drawing-room a sort of conference, in the early evening – a curious collection of people, whom I never expected to see together – Lord Killin and Sir George Fraser, Sir Campbell Stewart, and Sir Malcolm Rattray. They all thought I would not wish to join them, after the shock of the morning. But I did wish to. I was most intimately concerned. I was burning with curiosity. At last they reluctantly permitted me to sit in a corner of the room, with my hands demurely in my lap.

'*Why*?' said Sir Malcolm Rattray. '*Why* did he want the lad killed?'

'Surely, because Lord Ravenburn was approaching his majority,' said Mr Gilchrist. 'On his twenty-first birthday, he would have taken over the management of the estate. He would have looked at all the books, and spoken to the lawyers, the bankers, the brokers, the factors. Dundas's reign as Trustee would have been at an end. There was that which Lord Ravenburn must not be permitted to find. It must be so.'

'But what?' said Sir Malcolm. 'Had he stolen money from the estate?'

'No,' said Killin. 'Not for himself. He had no greed for himself. He was rather austere than extravagant. He genuinely wanted little.'

'What we think he had done,' said Sir George Fraser in his whining voice, 'was to have diverted money rightfully Tom's to Isabella and her children. Tom was certain to find this out, as Gilchrist says, the moment he was twenty-one.'

'Dundas must always have known that,' said Sir Malcolm frowning.

'Which means,' said Mr Gilchrist, 'that he must always have intended that Lord Ravenburn should not attain his majority.'

'I am sure that is right,' said Killin. 'By one means or another, he would have contrived to get Tom out of the way before he was twenty-one. In 1849 Providence sent him a perfect opportunity, just such an opportunity as he had been waiting for. He took it.'

'The letter to me. The poaching,' said Sir Campbell Stewart heavily.

'Do you suppose,' asked Sir Malcolm Rattray, with an expression of misery, 'that Lady Ravenburn knew anything about it?'

'No,' said Killin. 'She was not permitted to dirty her hands with theft or murder. She, and her children, were merely to enjoy the fruits.'

'He *was* unselfish,' I broke in suddenly. 'He loved her. He loved her too much. And the twins. He had no life of his own. He lived for them. He did none of it for himself.'

'He tried to kill Tom to save himself,' said Killin dryly.

'Yes,' I said, 'but by his way of it, he was obliged to save himself, to look after Mamma. She needed him. It was not for himself, but for her.'

'You are very forgiving, Katie,' said Killin, 'after what he did to you.'

'Oh, I can forgive that,' I said, 'since I can understand it. There are things I cannot forgive, but I can forgive that.'

'What I do *not* understand,' said Mr Gilchrist, 'is why Dickson Carmichael was kept alive. The simulated death by drowning made the Precognition admissible as evidence in the High Court – that was enough to hang Lord Ravenburn, if he was caught. Why a simulated death? Why not a real one? He did not jib at murder, we know that. Why go to all the trouble and expense to keep that miserable drunkard alive and hidden?'

'I think I can answer that,' said Sir Campbell Stewart.

I looked at him in astonishment. He was staring at his boots.

'I thought you could,' said Sir George Fraser softly. 'That is why I asked Mr Gilchrist to invite you here.'

'I had some slight suspicion of Frank Dundas,' said Sir Campbell. 'Not more than that, but as much as that. I did not like Tom Ravenburn, or approve of him in any way. I still do not. That may shock and anger you, who are his friends, but this is no time for platitudes. I did not like Tom Ravenburn, but I did not think he would kill a man – not without dire necessity, not in that horrible fashion. I was convinced that something strange had happened by my pool. I told Dundas so. I said there must be no more of it. What had happened had happened. An unpleasant man had been killed—'

'A man in your service, Stewart,' said Killin.

'Yes. I took him to oblige Dundas. He was most pressing that I should. There was no reason not to. I needed more keepers. When he was killed, I did not greatly mourn him. Why should I? Ravenburn disappeared. I did not weep for him, either. I was glad to see the last of him. He flouted the law and he flouted me. I was not heartbroken at the result of what had taken place. I can see by your faces that you think my attitude shocking. Well, I do not. Ravenburn had brought all his troubles on his own head. He was a thoroughly bad neighbour. He set a thoroughly bad example to other young men – an example of impudence and lawlessness. I had no sympathy with him. I was glad to see his back. But I could stomach no more of it. I told Dundas so. I made it a condition of my silence that there should be no more of it.'

'Did you think he would have Dickson Carmichael killed?' I asked.

'I don't know, Katharine. It was an obvious possibility. It was obviously the sensible thing, as Mr Gilchrist said, if that evidence was all lies. But I would not have it. I told Dundas so.'

'But,' said Killin, frowning, 'how would you have known if Carmichael was alive or dead?'

'I had the word of one of Dundas's men. He used to go there, to the place, with food. He reported to me from time to time that all was well with Carmichael. I did not know where he was, or seek to know. But I knew that he was alive and well. Dundas knew that I was getting this information. He arranged for me to get it. It was the price of my continued silence.'

'But Uncle Frank did try to kill Dickson Carmichael,' I said.

They all turned to look at me, startled.

'How do you know, Katie?' asked Killin.

'I was there,' I said.

I told them about the avalanche.

'Well, Sir Campbell?' said Mr Gilchrist. 'What would you have done, when you found that Carmichael had been buried under the rocks?'

Almost inaudibly, Sir Campbell said, 'A few days before, Dundas approached me with a proposition. He offered me a Directorship of the new West Highland Railway Company. He offered me a block of shares in the company.'

'Were you to buy the shares?'

'Yes. I was to buy twenty thousand, at a shilling each. The price was preferential. It was to be a secret between us.'

'I, too, was to buy shares and to become a Director,' said Sir Malcolm Rattray. 'I was to pay twenty shillings a share, the par value. I was to pay, on top of that, a substantial premium. My Directorship was conditional on that premium. My continued welcome at Ravenburn was conditional on that premium.'

'You were paying for Sir Campbell's shares as well as your own, Rattray,' said Killin.

'Yes.'

'And would you have done it?'

'Yes. Certainly I would. Of course I would.'

'Because of Isabella,' said Sir George.

'Yes. I would still do it, because of her. What is twenty thousand pounds? I was given grounds to hope, you know. Isabella herself hinted ... Dundas more than hinted, and the child, Malvina ... I *was* given grounds to hope. I am not a poor man. Twenty thousand pounds was well spent, if ... The negotiation, the Directorship, would have brought me closer into the family . . .'

Mr Gilchrist turned to Sir Campbell Stewart, and said with a sort of steely quietness, 'If you had bought twenty thousand shares for twenty thousand shillings, and become a Director of the West Highland Railway Company, would you have kept silent about the death of Dickson Carmichael?'

Sir Campbell made no reply. He looked incapable of speech.

After a long pause, Killin said gently, 'The situation did not arise, so the question is academic.'

I said suddenly, for the question burst into my head, 'Who betrayed Rory Beg?'

'Well,' said Sir George Fraser, 'who, Katie?'

'I wish I knew who,' I said, 'but I know to whom. The man at the head of the band which killed him spoke Scots as though – as though it was not his normal way of speaking. As though it was a way he had learned, and practised.'

'Like an actor?'

'Yes. Like an actor.'

'An accomplished amateur actor, who could imitate the speech of servants?'

'Yes. In *The Rivals,* or on a burnside . . .'

'Rory Beg,' said Sir George, 'was another sacrifice on the altar of Isabella.'

'How many were there?' asked Sir Campbell Stewart, with difficulty.

'There was nearly George Fraser,' said Killin. 'His horse was brought down.'

'There were nearly Katie, and Tom, and Dickson Carmichael,' said Sir George, 'when the mountainside was brought down.'

'There was Uncle Frank himself,' I said sadly. 'Not his death only, but his whole life.'

'I wonder how she feels now?' mused Sir Malcolm Rattray.

'Knowing Isabella,' said Killin, 'I think she feels hard done by. She has lost her manager, her taker of decisions, her smoother of paths. Why, she may even have to interview a house-keeper, or decide on a menu for dinner.'

'No, she will not,' said Sir George Fraser. 'Not at Ravenburn. Tom will do those things.'

'Or perhaps Katharine,' said Sir Campbell Stewart, unexpectedly. 'Perhaps she will keep house for her brother.'

The thought made my heart turn over with joy and with horrified disgust.

The Lord Advocate cross-examined Dickson Carmichael. He was bound to do so. In the interest of truth, he had to test the poor man's story. The case had to proceed, in spite of Uncle Frank's death in its midst. There were questions for the jury to answer, and the questions had to be asked.

In closing, the Lord Advocate quoted Baron Hume's *Commentaries* of 1797. He granted, he said, that there was no premeditated, personal malice behind the fatal blow which Lord Ravenburn had struck. He granted that ill-will, or dole, was a necessary ingredient of the crime of murder. 'Dole,' he quoted, was 'that corrupt and evil intention which is essential (so the light of nature teaches us and so all authorities have said) to the guilt of any crime.' But there were certain circumstances where dole need not be proved. It was murder, without malicious premeditation, if circumstances indicated in the accused 'a corrupt and malignant disposition, a heart contemptuous of order and regardless of social duty'. Those were Baron Hume's words, which the High Court of Justiciary had followed since they were penned. The words specifically covered, and had always been held to cover, the killing of a householder during the act of burglary, the killing of a gamekeeper during the act of poaching. There was no premeditation in such cases, no personal ill-will. But there was clear evidence of 'a corrupt and malignant disposition, a heart contemptuous of order and regardless of social duty'.

Tom had been poaching. He had killed a keeper. It was as simple as that.

Tom, said Sir Hector, was about to be murdered. He had killed to save his own life. It was as simple as that.

The Lord President of the High Court of Justiciary guided the jury as to the law. The evidence was all before them. Questions of fact were entirely for them to decide. There was only one point in dispute. Was or was not the accused obliged to kill in order to save his own life? He was not on trial for poaching. The late Jock McVie was not on trial for attempted murder, nor the late Mr Francis Dundas. Dickson Carmichael was not on trial as an accomplice, or on a charge of perjury.

The jury was out for a short time only. Though a majority of the fifteen was allowed, their verdict was unanimous.

Tom was not guilty, because he had killed in self-defence.

Outside, it was a triumph, a public acclamation. Tom would have been carried shoulder-high all round Parliament Square, had not a party of the Burgh Police bundled him into a carriage.

I did not see Tom's reunion with Mamma. She was in deepest mourning for Uncle Frank. Black suited her colouring, and Malvina's. Lady Wood and Mrs Seton were in deep mourning, too.

The saddest face was that of Master James Irvine, lately known as Lord Ravenburn.

Flora Morran seemed moderately glad to see me again. She complained that she would now have more work. It startled me to remember that she had, without hesitation, thrown away her livelihood, in order to help me. She loved me. One does not choose the people who love one, any more than they choose their own faces. One simply thanks God for them.

It was strange to see Tom in smart clothes as Lord of Ravenburn Castle. It was strange to be in a house where there was at once joy and misery, triumph and tragedy, victory and defeat.

Tom and I scarcely had any dealings with each other. He was busy with the estate, I with Charles Killin. Tom and I hardly met, and avoided meeting when we could.

I was much in the company of Charles, who had come home with us at Tom's request and mine. He made love to me, and I was comforted. There was no longer any secret. He asked me to marry him, and I agreed. Tom gave his approval, most warmly. The betrothal was announced.

I expected some reaction from Mamma – congratulations, if she could bring herself to give them; rage, if she could not hide it. But there was no reaction. She heard conversations on the subject – the inevitable, interminable conversations all round the subject – without seeming to take any of it seriously.

It was as though she knew there was no such betrothal. As though she knew there would be no such marriage. As though none of it was to be taken seriously. As though it was all talk, and no more.

I thought she was in a state of continued numbness, like that after a blow on the head, because of Uncle Frank's death. Or that her placid selfishness had become so totally a habit of mind that she simply excluded, as unreal, things about her which displeased her: that, from disinclination to see them, she was blind to them.

I was wrong. She was neither numb nor blind. Nor had she forgotten certain names which Uncle Frank had told her were important.

Sometimes at night I had troubling dreams of unbearable sweetness, which, when I awoke, filled me with guilt and shame. But by day, and in the evenings, I took refuge from my memories in Killin's arms, and lost myself in his kisses. He was a gentle man. I knew he would be a good husband, and I prayed I would be a good wife. The marriage was arranged for April. We were to be wed in the Chapel at Ravenburn. We were to go afterwards to Paris and Vienna.

Sir George Fraser came, and added his good wishes to all the others we received. He looked at me with misery in his eyes.

Tom never looked at me at all.

The Ramsays of Tulloch never looked at me, either. They refused to dine at Ravenburn while I was there; they refused to admit me to Tulloch.

George Fraser at last asked Lady Angela why they took this stern and unbending line. They said that Victoria Arlington had told them the whole story. I had stolen Charles Killin from her, when I owed her so much gratitude. I repaid her kindness with treachery. I seduced Killin, bewitched him. I played the harlot. I could do it because I was younger than she, and (by their way of it) more beautiful. It was not, they said to George Fraser, the fact of illicit physical congress between Charles Killin and myself which outraged them, though they were much disgusted and astonished by that; it was my treachery to Victoria, who had helped me.

This surprised George Fraser very much; it surprised me equally, when he told me; it surprised Charles, when I told him.

'She loved you – loves you,' I said.

'Angela?'

'Victoria.'

'Nonsense.'

'Yes, I promise you. She told me so – oh, months ago. She told me she would get you, because you would come to realize ... I shouldn't have told you that. It was a – a confidence between women.'

'I suppose you shouldn't have told me. But you shouldn't have any secrets from me, darling Katie. Please tell me everything, now and always.'

'Yes,' I agreed.

But there was one appalling secret I would keep from him and from everyone until the day I died: and I wished I could keep it from God, after I died.

'Victoria,' said Charles thoughtfully, 'goes very vigorously about everything. That is why she is such an effective crusader, in the matter of women's prisons and so forth. She vigorously pulled you out of your chrysalis, and helped you spread your butterfly wings—'

'That is why I understand how the Ramsays feel,' I said. 'I do not understand why Victoria believed Malvina, but I do understand their feelings. I took away from her, they all think, what she most wanted, after she had . . .'

'She created a Galatea more beautiful and desirable than herself,' said Charles. 'I wonder if she went with equal vigour about destroying the butterfly she had helped to liberate?'

'You don't mean,' I said, 'she couldn't have . . .'

'There is a sort of appalling directness about Crusaders,' said Charles. 'A sort of ruthlessness. You don't suppose the Holy Sepulchre was recaptured from the infidels without brutality and bloodshed? Nothing would suit her better than to have you locked up here, and me banished from here.'

'But – even though some people knew the whole story was a lie?'

'A lie, if it was, blamed entirely on Malvina.'

We sought out Malvina. But she stuck to her original story with such bitter tears and screams that we had to give up asking her. The story, it seemed, had become the truth for her. I did not think anything would shake her.

It was desperately unsatisfactory. Charles had much to comfort me about.

'How did you persuade Uncle Frank to let me out?' I asked him. 'And bring back Flora Morran, and Murdo McKenzie, and work those other miracles?'

'I appealed to your uncle's better nature,' said Charles, as he always had before. 'He did have one, you know.'

'Yes, I know, but . . .'

He cut off further questions with his kisses.

But I wondered why he had let Uncle Frank keep me a drab prisoner so long, when it seemed that a simple appeal got me immediately released, and my fine clothes restored to me.

Sir George Fraser surprised me very much by voicing the same question.

Charles Killin had been obliged to leave for a few days. He said that Tom and I, between us, had caused his estate and affairs to be almost wholly unsupervised for most of the year: and that, now that he was getting married, he must fend off bankruptcy. He took a passionate farewell of me, and I a passionate farewell of him. Once again – it had happened so often – I missed him very much.

George Fraser was not much comfort, and Tom no comfort at all.

'Why,' said George, in his thin voice, 'when Charles could have you out of your prison cell, and reinstated as Queen, by the magical snapping of his fingers in Frank Dundas's face – why did he wait so long to snap them? He knew what they were doing to you. It is almost as though . . .'

He must have seen the look on my face; he did not go on to voice suspicions which he knew would enrage me.

Instead he said thoughtfully, 'When my horse came down, just outside Inverness, I was laid up for a few days with a blow on the head, as well as a broken shoulder.'

'I know. I am sorry.'

'I did expect Charles to come to see me.'

'But he did go.'

'No.'

'But – he said he was going, and he said he had been! He had news for you, or wanted news from you, I forget which . . . George, what happened is that the knock on your poor head had you in a daze sometimes, and you don't remember his coming . . .'

I saw the look on his face, this time. I did not go on. Charles had not been to see him.

'Then where *did* he go?' mused George. 'Where *did* the

strange fellow go? Something sent him off in a tearing hurry –
some urgent errand, in some part of Scotland a long way from
Inverness . . .'

'When he came back,' I said slowly, 'he had a long talk to
Uncle Frank. And after that, Uncle Frank did everything
Charles told him to.'

'Yes. He found something out while he was away, something
he told me nothing about. It must be so, mustn't it? But what
sent him away? Something must have happened, or been said,
that sent him racing off, so that he didn't come to see me, even
though we were both deeply engaged in Tom's business. Do you
think he discovered something, just before he left?'

'He failed to,' I said, thinking back carefully, and remembering the curious scene in the library. 'There was talk about an
old family Bible, my father's Bible. Walter Willis was talking
about it, I think, about its being so large and awkward. Charles
said family dates and names might be written in it, as they
usually are, you know – births and baptisms and so forth. He
said nothing was written in it. He said my Papa must have
trusted someone else to do it for him, as he hated pen and ink
himself, but no one else did do it.'

'Your father's Bible. I think I remember it. A monstrous
tome, almost too heavy to carry, in a great black leather binding?'

'Yes.'

'But I think – I think – there were dates written in it.'

'Well, it did seem odd they were not.'

'Very odd. Where is this Bible?'

'In the library.'

'Can you find it?'

'Yes, of course.'

I found it at once, and we opened it on the floor by the
bookshelf.

Inside the binding there was a fly leaf, and inside that a florid
title page. Between the two there was just a suggestion of rough-
ness, in the gutter between the two pages.

'Torn out,' said George. 'Very carefully torn out.'

'Then he did find nothing.'

'Or he found something, and removed it.'

'Why? What are you suggesting?'

'There are so many oddities,' said George, 'that I begin to

wonder if they are not all the same oddity – all linked together, in a way we can't see. Let us speculate a minute, but as logically as possible. Don't fly into a rage, my dear. There *are* oddities here, worrying puzzles. We thought all was solved with Tom's acquittal, but there are questions still unanswered.'

'Such as who betrayed Rory Beg.'

'Yes, that is one of the questions. We start with the clear fact that Charles was highly interested in the fly-leaf of your father's Bible. He wanted to see dates, names. Not of your father's marriage to Isabella, I imagine, or anything to do with the twins, because all that is known to everybody . . .'

'I made some joking remark about my age,' I said. 'I said it was ungallant of Charles to ferret out my exact age in such a way.'

He frowned. 'Is your age a secret? Your birthday? Why should it be? You were born in a small house called Kilcraig, by Loch Torridon, in Wester Ross.'

'On the Duke of Cromarty's land.'

'Yes. He was your father's greatest friend, though some years older. He stood to your father, as your father stood to Charles and me.'

'Rory Beg's father was a tenant of the Duke, by Loch Torridon.'

'Yes, he was. What possible bearing can that have on what has been exercising us?'

'None,' I said, confused.

'I suppose none. And yet . . . I think I must make a journey.'

'To Wester Ross?'

'Yes, of course.'

That afternoon, a stranger arrived at the Castle. I chanced to be in the courtyard, when he climbed down from a hired carriage. He did not at first see me, but stood looking round at our ridiculous Castle, while the coachman unloaded his portmanteaux.

He was a man of about sixty, big and raw-boned, a typical Lowlander of Scandinavian ancestry. He was clean-shaven, and looked as though he shaved with too sharp a razor, scraping painfully over the bony jaw and cheek-bones. He pulled off his gloves as he stared at the Ravenburn battlements; his hands were long and scrubbed, with large knuckles and hairless backs. His clothes were black and respectable, but had a rusty, shiny look, as though he had bought them many years before, and carefully preserved them beyond their usual life.

One leaps to unwarrantable conclusions about strangers, which are not always false. I did so, about this stranger. I thought he was an able and a decent man who, for some reason, had failed in life. I thought he was not resigned to his failure.

He saw me, and cleared his throat. I crossed the courtyard towards him. I saw that, as I approached him, he was looking at me intently, with very hard pale-grey eyes. His scrutiny was not offensive. I had become used to being stared at.

He removed his hat as I neared him, and made a stiff little bow, very brief and reluctant. I thought he was not used to bowing, but the size of Ravenburn had obliged him to bend his back.

I looked at him enquiringly. I think my face was friendly. I was curious about him; and I felt sorry for him, on account of his rusty clothes and his air of failure.

'Have I the honour to address Miss Katharine Irvine?' he said, in a harsh unhappy voice.

I said that he had.

He nodded quickly, continuing to look at me fixedly. He began to ask me questions about the Castle, about the towers and follies my grandfather had raised as a monument to his importance. I answered as best I could. I pointed out this and that, and told him which wing housed which rooms. His questions were intelligent, though the subject was not deeply interesting. The harshness did not leave his voice, nor the intent stare his eyes.

I could not imagine who this person was, pathetic but not without dignity; I could not understand his desire for an extended conversation with me, at the moment of his arrival, about the architecture of the Castle.

A footman came out, and conducted him indoors. He gave me a long backward look as he went. I turned and went away, to walk uphill by the burnside.

'So strange,' said Mrs Seton, 'that dear Isabella should entertain her newest guest in private.'

'Strange,' echoed Lady Wood.

'Professional fellow, I dare say,' said Colonel Blair. 'Matters of business.'

'But to absent herself from the drawing room, to closet herself for two full hours ... Alas, were Mr Dundas still with us, *he* would have protected her from such drudgery.'

'He is called Dr McAndrew,' said George Fraser, 'and he has come all the way from Stirling. That is all I can find out about him.'

'Oh my God,' I said. 'He has. . . He will . . .'

I remembered it all, now – Loudon's report; the doctor who could be compelled to make out any paper, because he had performed an abortion on a servant girl, and the girl had died; Uncle Frank's meeting with Loudon, in the law-courts in Edinburgh; and Mamma's bland refusal to be bothered with my marriage, as though it would never take place.

It never would take place. I should be sent away. Dr McAndrew would send me. He would be made to do so, or go to prison for ever. Probably he had already examined me, as much as he needed to. If Mamma required other weighty and signed opinions, to support Dr McAndrew's, then Loudon would get them for her.

Charles Killin could not save me this time. He had no hold over Mamma; he knew none of her guilty secrets, because she had none. He could not appeal to her better nature, because, where I was concerned, she had none.

I still did not know why Uncle Frank had wanted me hidden away; but I knew very well why Mamma did. A new worm was turning.

'You are going to Wester Ross,' I said to George Fraser.

'Yes. Tomorrow, or the day after.'

'Go now, at once, and take me.'

'But Katie – that is impossible—'

'For the love of God, George, get me away from here!'

'I must ask Tom—'

'Then do it within five minutes, and get me away within ten!'

George Fraser looked at me, as intently as Dr McAndrew had done. Then he nodded briefly, and went to find Tom.

It was a perfectly respectable expedition, though distinctly unorthodox, and planned at hectic speed. Tom gave his permission (though without looking at me, or speaking to me directly). He did not ask where we were going; I did not dare let anyone know, in case doctors followed us. He trusted George Fraser, and he trusted the woman I was taking with me.

I packed, for myself, in two minutes. I carried my own bag downstairs, to save time and to save questions. I drove George out of the Castle and into his carriage, consumed with anxiety about what might happen if we lingered.

'I didn't tell Tom the real reason for our going,' said George. 'The dear fellow has enough on his mind.'

'I know my reason,' I said, 'but what is yours? What do you expect to find?'

'I simply don't know. Answers. There is some key, some single, simple key to all this oddity, something that will answer everything. I'm sure there is. Killin found something out. If he did, we can. It has something, perhaps, to do with the dates in your father's Bible. Therefore Loch Torridon is the place where Killin went, and it's the place where we must go.'

I was safe, in the far west: safe until I went home again.

I saw my mother's grave, a neat grey stone in the churchyard of a tiny Episcopal church near the shore of the sea-loch.

I saw the house where I was born, a low white building with a superb view. The people there were hospitable and kind, but they had only been in the house for five years, and knew nothing of the Irvines a dozen years before that.

George went off on an errand of his own; I stayed and talked to Colonel and Mrs Falconer, and then set off towards the church again, where we had left the carriage.

On the way there was a tiny farmhouse, out of which an old woman came to feed her hens. She was as neat and gay as an Easter bonnet, with a mass of thick white hair caught up in a net, and the brightest petticoat I ever saw. I fell into conversation with her. She was pleased to talk, in her strange West Highland lilt. She looked at me intently, and oddly.

She said, hesitantly, 'Pleass to forgiff me, ma'am, butt there wass a gentleman with a wee picture of a lady. It wass like your face, ma'am.'

A wee picture. A miniature. My miniature, that was stolen from my room at Ravenburn, and never found . . .

I asked her, hardly able to bring the words out, to describe the person who had the picture.

She described – picking her words, in a language she used less often than her native Gaelic – a big, tall, upstanding man, brown-haired, well-dressed, with a gentleman's voice, and laughter in his face. He was asking for any information about the lady of the portrait. He wanted to know when she was married, and when she was brought to bed of a child.

But the old wife had only recently moved to this low-lying farm, from a remoter place, where the life had become too rough for her man and herself. She knew nothing of the lady in the picture.

George Fraser rejoined me. He was visibly full of news, but I told him mine first, for I should have burst if I had tried to keep it bottled up while he talked.

He whistled, and said, 'We are near finding the key, Katie. I have been looking at the parish records. They are very easy to search through, because there are so few people here nowadays. Your baptism is recorded, of course. It was in July. I suppose you were two or three months old at the time, which suggests that your birthday is what you have always supposed.'

'Why shouldn't it be?'

'No reason, but it suggests that something else is odd. Charles Killin certainly thought so. He has been looking at the parish register too.'

'Oh.'

'Yes, that is all the comment I could think of. Incidentally, the Duke of Cromarty stood sponsor as your Godfather, by proxy.'

'Good gracious. That must be why he asked after me, at Ravenburn.'

'And has done no more than that? What a curious Godfather ... Anyway, your parent's marriage is not on the parish register. The minister thinks they were married in the Duke's private chapel, very quietly, I suppose because your father was a widower. I am a little alarmed at the prospect of bearding the Duke, but I think, as a dutiful God-daughter, you can do it?'

'If we must,' I said dubiously: for I was more than a little alarmed.

The Duke's principal seat was sixty miles away, right across the narrow neck of Scotland on the East Coast. But he spent much time at his house in the West, and was in residence there now.

He was out when we presented ourselves respectfully at his door, but was expected home shortly. Meanwhile, an aged steward made us welcome.

He knew my face. He had known my mother, and her family the McNeils of Glennie, of whom now none survived except cousins in Canada. He remembered well when Jean McNeil married William Irvine, in the chapel of this house.

He showed us the chapel, and described the ceremony. He was the only person who attended it besides his master, and the couple, and the housekeeper, and the chaplain.

I wept, as I had not wept at my mother's grave.

The chapel had been very cold the day of the marriage, the old man said, because it was in the week before Christmas.

I put a hand to my head. I knew, I had always known, that my parents were married in June. I was about to burst out with something, but George Fraser restrained me, with a hand on my elbow.

The old man left us alone in a small drawing room, to wait for the Duke.

I said, my voice trembling. 'Of course I don't mind – it is of no consequence – but I was born in May.'

'Yes.'

'The May of 1843. The May immediately after the marriage, not – not seventeen months later. Oh dear.'

'As you say, Katie,' said George as gently as his thin voice allowed, 'it *is* of no consequence. Nobody knows, or need know. I am sorry we had to find out, as I hardly think it can be the revelation we're looking for ...'

The old steward returned, and was tactfully questioned by George. He was quite happy to talk, owing to my face and his memories of my parents. Information gushed from him. He said that Mr Irvine, as he then was, had had to go away from June to October of the year before the marriage, 1842, far away, on business connected with his father's estate, maybe as far as Edinburgh, or even England. His Grace, out of friendship, kept an eye on Miss McNeil of Glennie while Mr Irvine was away. His Grace was very kind to the young lady. She spent many days at the house here.

The Duke returned, old, erect, stately, formidable.

He looked at me with absolute amazement, then took both my hands in his.

He said, 'I know those eyes.'
I knew his eyes, too. They were my green eyes.

sixteen

The Duke was tall and thin, with a pale clean-shaven face. He seemed to me very old, though I suppose he was no more than seventy. He had thick white hair, worn long, beautifully brushed. His face was hard and hawk-like, with a thin mouth and angular chin, high cheek-bones and a high-bridged nose. He was dressed in simple country tweeds, but the stateliness of his bearing made them seem like Coronation robes.

Below heavy white eyebrows, bright green eyes – like a cat's, like my own – stared into my eyes, while he held both my hands in both his.

'You are Katharine,' he said softly. 'I am so happy to meet you, child. You are . . .'

'Who am I, sir?' I asked, in a voice I could not keep steady.

He did not answer at once, but sent the old steward for wine, and pressed us to stay with him. He said he was tired, and would rest until dinner at six; he said he would tell me, after dinner, about himself and about myself.

I had to be content with this. He did look tired. There were lines of fatigue about his mouth and eyes. He was an old man. But it was not easy to wait.

Servants infinitely defter and quieter than those of Ravenburn looked after us. I had not expected, when I came away, to be dining and staying with a Duke, so I had brought no amazing gowns with me. I had brought only one evening dress, chosen because it packed conveniently. It was of grass-green silk, severely simple, cut low over my shoulders and bosom. I was glad this dress had chosen itself for the journey, because it matched the Duke's eyes and my own.

I held my chin at a properly arrogant angle, when I went into the drawing room.

Though the Duke looked so stiff and formidable, his

manners were very easy. When he smiled, his green eyes filled with warmth and humour. Yet it was unnerving, as we chatted in the drawing room, waiting for dinner to be announced, because he could not take his eyes off me.

George Fraser was thoughtful, and said almost nothing.

All during dinner, the Duke and I talked of a thousand things. Though I was bursting with curiosity about what he was going to tell us afterwards, he was so amusing and interesting, on so many different subjects, that I almost forgot why we were there. He induced me to talk far too much, especially about myself, and drew me out with the shrewdest and most probing questions.

Well, I had no secrets from him, or from anyone, except one.

We talked of birds and animals. He had had a tame otter, years before (and my heart lurched when he described its bewitching friendliness and playfulness). He had spent many hours watching a raven's nest (and my heart lurched again, so that I could hardly eat).

We talked of Ravenburn, and Mamma and Uncle Frank and the twins. We talked of the trial; of Tom, whom the Duke knew well as a little boy at Kilcraig; of Rory Beg, whom he also knew.

'There was nothing that fellow did not know,' said the Duke, smiling with a sort of irritated affection at the memory. 'He had eyes and ears everywhere. He knew where my keepers were, when we tried to catch him. He knew everything that went on in this house, and every other house.'

'People told him, sir?' suggested George.

'Yes, I think so. Girls, especially. There was something deceptively gentle and frail about him, you know, a sort of waiflike quality they took pity on.'

'Men liked him, too,' I said.

'Yes. I did myself, in spite of the vexation he caused me. That is why I persuaded him to go away, to start afresh in a new place. He had made things too hot for himself hereabouts, in this very thinly populated place. He went to West Perthshire, did he? A sensible choice. Rich men with fine estates, pheasant-preserves and salmon fisheries, fat stags on the hill and fat fallow-deer in the parks.'

After dinner we went not to a drawing room, but to a small, cluttered study, with a peat fire and a lot of books and sporting pictures. I almost disappeared into a huge leather armchair. The Duke sat stiffly in another. George Fraser, restless, perched here and there, on a stool and on the edge of a desk.

The Duke turned to George, and said, 'I think you have found me out. But why did you want to?'

'We did not come here to find you out, sir,' said George. 'We did not know what we should find. We came here because Charles Killin had come, and found something which it seemed important for us to know, too. Especially important, because he did not tell us – because he pretended there was nothing, when plainly there was something.'

'I understand. He was using knowledge. Knowledge is power, and he was using power. But you did not know what it was.'

'Or why he was using it, or where it was leading him to, or leading us all to. You told him, sir?'

'I had no need to,' said the Duke. 'He knew, as you did, before I spoke to him. But, since he knew, I was frank with him. Why not? He was a close friend of my old friend. He is a close friend of my old friend's son. I trusted him. I liked him. He was asking his questions on Tom's behalf, and on Katie's ... At least, I took it that he was. There was no advantage to himself in learning an ancient story in which he was not concerned. At least, I took it that there was none ...'

'The secret was not very closely guarded, sir,' said George, 'Killin found it all out quite easily and quickly. He needed only William Ravenburn's Bible, and the parish register here. He showed Katie's mother's miniature to local people hereabouts. He spoke to your steward. It was not difficult for him, once he knew what to look for, from the Bible. It was not difficult for us, once we knew he had found something here.'

'No,' said the Duke. 'We buried it tolerably deep, but not deep enough. There were more precautions we could have taken, to baffle future prying. But those very precautions might have given rise to suspicion, don't you think? A page torn from the parish register, or a line blotted out, would have cried out that there was something to hide ... In any case, we never anticipated that, eighteen years later, a pack of sleuth-hounds would be peeping here and searching there. Why should we expect such a thing? The fiction was accepted. The legality was absolute. Katie was provided for.'

'Amply? Munificently?' asked George. 'Forgive the question, sir, but I think I suddenly understand . . .'

'Yes,' said the Duke, 'Katie had, and I am assured still has, a large estate of her own, with a substantial income from it.'

'Which would have reverted . . .?'

'To the donor, in the event that she predeceased me.'

'There were Trustees?'

'Of course, as she was unborn when the arrangement was made. William Irvine was Trustee, naturally. After his death, Katie's estate was administered by Francis Dundas, naturally.'

'You told Killin this?'

'Yes. Why not?'

'This answers so much,' said George. 'It explains why Katie is alive. Why she was not – smothered or poisoned years ago. Why she was not killed when Rory Beg was killed. Why Dundas tried to have Tom killed. And the power that Charles had over Dundas.'

'I follow you almost all the way, Fraser,' said the Duke. 'But not in your last point. What power did Killin have over Dundas?'

'He knew from you, sir, that Katie was rich. He knew from her and from his own observation that she had not a penny.'

'Dundas took the whole?'

'For his sister and her children. We thought it was Tom he was cheating. It was not. It was Katie. It was no less criminal. It was no less a stick, for Killin to lift against Dundas. It was no less certain to be discovered by Tom, the moment he attained his majority.'

I digested all this. It was true, as George said, that it answered many questions. But it did not answer the question which had now become uppermost in my mind.

I said to the Duke, from the depths of my chair, 'Will you tell me the story?'

'Yes,' said the Duke.

He turned to stare into the dull red glow of the peat-bricks in the grate, which gave off the most haunting aroma in the world, and filled the pleasant little room with gentle warmth.

After a long silence, the Duke began to speak softly, still staring into the fire as though he saw there the events of long before.

He said, 'My youth had flown by. I was almost fifty. I had

been a sportsman and naturalist. I was a politician, too, spending most of each year at Westminster, a Minister with a succession of portfolios in a succession of governments. I was respected, even eminent. I was tired and disillusioned. I was bored. I was married – had been, for a quarter of a century. My wife was a perfectly worthy woman. I respect her memory. We had no children. She has been dead these ten years. She had many virtues, among which was not humour. She was a good wife for an ambitious politician, but not a good companion for a man. She was miserable in Scotland, in this remote place. There was nothing here for her to do – no levées, no assemblies, no card-parties, no political intrigue.

'In the early summer of 1842 I was very tired, having overworked for two years as a member of the government. On the urgent instructions of my physicians, I resigned from the administration, and came here for a long holiday. I had been half-promised an appointment I craved – the Governor Generalship of Canada. I was fascinated by the growth of a new world there, and believed I could contribute to its development. A new country was, and is, the most fascinating and demanding of all challenges. But my acceptance of this tremendous honour, the following spring, was conditional on my full return to health, the full recovery of my strength and energy. I knew that this was the right place.

'My wife, very sensibly, elected to remain in London until the end of the season, and then to go to her sister in Kent, and other places where she would have society congenial to her. I applauded this decision, and was thankful for it.

'The first person I saw here, of course, was William Irvine, who had taken my little house at Kilcraig after his wife died. His little boy was with him, learning far more about birds and beasts than about the Greek poets or the Roman emperors. I was very happy to have those two as neighbours. They were a tonic to me, after the intrigue and overstrain of London. I can hardly pay sufficient tribute to William Irvine. He was not faultless. In some ways he was casual, careless. But he was kind and honourable to a degree unknown among the cleverer, more ambitious men with whom I had been spending my life.

'We had a new neighbour, also, a very young lady called Jean McNeil, a McNeil of Glennie. Her father was dead, her mother bedridden. An elderly great-aunt kept house for them. They were very poor. They had once had a considerable estate, and a small castle on the sea-shore; but the estate had been broken up, and the castle had fallen into the sea from neglect. McNeil, Jean's father, had been in the service of the East India Company. He died in Madras. The widow and the child came home, to live in a small house in a place where they had once been great.

'William brought Miss McNeil to visit me, one afternoon towards the end of May. I shall never forget my first sight of her. I saw her way of moving, before I saw her face. I saw her simply step down out of a carriage, and walk towards the door. She had the agility of a cat, of my pet otter, and the grace and lightness of a bird. As she neared the window where I was standing, the afternoon sun was behind her. I still could not see her face, but I marvelled at the slim and supple elegance of her figure. I was intensely curious about this last survivor of an ancient line.

'Her face was beautiful. It was unusual. Though young, it was strong. Though intelligent, it was full of sweetness. Her voice was most attractive, shy and hesitant, but musical.

'Of course she was frightened of me at first. I was nearly fifty, a Duke, until recently a cabinet minister. I treated her as one would treat a nice child, laughing, flattering a little, reassuring, asking questions. I treated her as one would treat a young animal, gently, patiently, to give courage, to create trust.

'William had been, continued to be, extraordinarily kind to her. This conveyed nothing special to me. William was extraordinarily kind to everyone.

'In the days that followed, the four of us – William, little Tom, Jean McNeil, myself – spent nearly all our time together. We went fishing, and scrambling. We went on long expeditions, in a donkey-cart or on ponies, taking picnics, or catching our own supper. They were golden days. My fatigue and disillusion fell away from me. Because William was all the time busy teaching Tom, I took to teaching Jean. I taught her to catch trout, and to recognize birds by their cry. I loved teaching her. She was wonderfully responsive, and eager and quick to learn. Her fear of me left her. She trusted me. She admired me. She seemed to enjoy my company as much as I enjoyed hers. Sometimes she was grave, but usually gay. My youth, which had left me, came back. She gave it back. I had never been so happy in my life.

'Then William's father sent for him. There were all kinds of decisions that had to be taken about the Ravenburn estate, and about railways and coalmines and investments. Old Lord Ravenburn's health was failing. He wanted William to know what dispositions he was making; he wanted William to approve the dispositions. He trusted and esteemed his son, you see, as everyone who knew him trusted and esteemed him.

'William went away into Perthshire, and to Edinburgh and to London. He took Tom, so that the boy should get to know his grandfather. I saw more of Jean than ever. Both of us missed both of them, because we loved them and enjoyed their company, yet we were very happy to be just the two of us together. There were endless things to do. There was an infinity of things she wanted to learn, which I could teach her.

'I found that, at the end of each of our days together, her lovely little face lingered in my mind's eye, and the sound of her voice lingered in my mind's ear. I should have realized what was happening to me, to us, but I never thought – I never thought. Day succeeded golden day, and I never thought. I had a playmate for the first time since my childhood, and I never thought.

'One day, starting early, we took the pony-trap far up into the hills, to find a little burn I remembered. We left the trap, and the groom, and the two of us went on on foot, far up, to a lovely lonely place, which we shared only with the whaup and the raven, with the burn and the little trout in the burn. Jean crossed the burn by stepping-stones. She was laughing, and talking to me, not taking care. She slipped, and would have fallen into the water. I sprang forward, and caught her. My arms were about her, to save her from a wetting. My arms were about her, and hers were about my neck, and her cheek was pressed to mine.

'We were bewitched. The place and the moment were magical. We loved each other wildly and completely. If such passionate love-making was new to her, an innocent young girl, it was just as new to me, who was nearing fifty, and experienced and worldly. If she wept and cried out, so did I. If she clung, and sobbed with happiness, so did I.

'It could be said, it would be said, that I was a cynical older man taking advantage of a young girl's ignorance, of the respect and admiration she must feel for me, of a situation of my devising. It could be made to sound evil and callous in the last degree. It did not strike me in that light then, and has never done so since. Such beauty, such kindness, such happiness, such love, must be divine, not sinful. So I thought then. So I still think.

'The weeks slid by in golden succession. I was truly happy for the first time in my life. So, I think, was she. The weather changed. Rain beat on the windows of this room, and winds howled in the towers. Still we were together, always together, cocooned in happiness, forgetting everything except ourselves, and each other, and our love.

'Jean told me that she was to have a baby.

'At first I was transported with joy. The child of a love such as ours must be blessed beyond ordinary mortals. I prayed that the child might have the mother's beauty of face and form, her goodness and gentleness and strength.

'There came a message to me from London, from the Prime Minister. He asked after my health. He said that he must immediately announce to the Canadians the name of their next Governor General, because they clamoured to know, and had a right to know. Was I strong enough, recovered enough? Would I accept the appointment?

'With this, the outside world blew cold through cracks in the walls of our warm little kingdom. Horrible problems gibbered at me, like half-seen beasts in the shadows. I could not give Jean my name. My wife was a strictly virtuous woman, who demanded from others the standards of moral conduct she set herself. She would not condone, forgive. Divorce was impossible, unthinkable. The world's judgement would destroy my reputation, my career, my usefulness. Above all, Jean's youth and inexperience would be held most violently against me, and my name would be odious everywhere.

'I tried to keep the turmoil and misery of my thoughts from Jean. But she loved me far too well, knew me far too well, not to see into my heart. And then she showed a strength greater by far than mine. When I should have been helping her, supporting and sustaining her, it was she who sustained me. I have never met such courage, such gaiety, in the face of disgrace and disaster.

310

'She was content to be abandoned, so that I should not be ruined. I could not abandon her, an unmarried girl of gentle birth, carrying my child, in the midst of grim and censorious Highlanders ...

'William Irvine came back, in November, with his little son. He came at once to see me here. He had completed all his business with his father and the estate. All was very well with him. He saw at once that I was fully restored to health. He saw at once that I was eaten by misery and worry. He asked, most earnestly, after Jean McNeil. He said that, while he had been away, he found he missed her more and more, longed for her, wanted and needed her. Like me, he had seen the strength and courage behind the kindness and loveliness. Like me, he had been bewitched by her beauty of face and soul.

'He wanted to make her his wife. I told him all. He understood.

'Nothing I had done in my life had made me worthy to have such a man for a friend. He did not the less want to marry Jean, after he knew the truth. He wanted the more to marry her. He had found that he needed her for his happiness. Now he found that she needed him.

'He went to her. I do not know what they said to each other. But they agreed. They were married here, very quietly, by my Chaplain, in the week before Christmas. Jean went with William to Kilcraig. Though this was a most happy and providential outcome to all our despair, I could not bear to see her as his wife, in his house. I went, as I should have done long before, to London. My appointment was announced.

'I made arrangements that the child should have a fortune of his own, or her own. William Irvine was sole Trustee, so that the secret should be kept. Also, I trusted him as I trusted no one else.

'I was already in Canada when the child was born in May.'

For a long time there was silence in the little room. The Duke – my father – stared still into the fire. He turned towards me at last, and held out his arms towards me. I flew from my chair and knelt on the hearthrug before him.

He said softly, 'You are very like your mother, my darling child.'

He embraced and kissed me. I was weeping. So was he.

*

Later I said, trying not to sound reproachful, 'You did not come to see me often.'

'No,' said my father. 'It seemed best to abide by the arrangements we had made. I did not wish it to be evident that I was – extraordinarily interested in William's daughter. I came to Ravenburn occasionally, as though casually. I saw you as a young child, Katie, while William was alive. By various chances I did not see you thereafter. I could not make too great a point of wishing to see you.'

'They were not chances, that prevented you seeing me,' I said. 'I was sent away or hidden, when you were expected.'

'Yes. I might have guessed that. I might have guessed the reason. But I trusted Dundas, because William had done so. He sent me regular accounts of your health, the progress of your studies, and so forth. He reported also on his stewardship of your estate and fortune.'

'Falsely,' said George.

'Yes, falsely. Of yourself, Katie, he said that you were painfully shy, and in danger of nervous complaints. He said the doctors had advised a very quiet and withdrawn life for you.'

'That,' said George, 'was so that no one should ask why the beautiful Katharine Irvine had everything except money.'

'Yes,' agreed my father. 'It was adroitly done. I did not suspect. Even if I had suspected, there was not much I could do, without making a public display of my interest.'

'I understand,' I said. 'You couldn't have done more than you did.'

'Oh, yes, dearest child, I could have and should have. But I was still obsessed by the need to keep the secret.'

'Are you now?' I asked.

'No. You are so beautiful, and so delightful, that I intend to boast to the world about a daughter, a FitzCromarty, that any father would be proud of.'

This made me cry again. I could not have looked beautiful, or, sniffing and hiccoughing, appeared delightful. Most of my tears fell on his chin and his waistcoat.

'Rory Beg knew,' said George Fraser.

'Yes,' said my father. 'I don't know how he knew, but he knew everything. It was another reason for me to send him far away.'

312

'Did you tell Charles Killin that Rory Beg knew?'

'Yes. Killin was anxious to find out if anyone else knew. He said it was important to find out, for Katie's sake. I told him that, as far as I was aware, the knowledge was restricted to himself and myself, Dundas, probably his sister, a few of my old servants, and Rory Beg.'

'Why,' I asked, 'did Uncle Frank, I mean Mr Dundas, not have Charles killed?'

'Charles is a shrewd man,' said George. 'My guess is that he had left a letter with a lawyer, to be opened if he died suddenly or in suspicious circumstances. The letter incriminated Dundas, and gave evidence. Charles told Dundas about the letter, warning him to do nothing which would cause it to be opened.'

I nodded. This seemed entirely probable. I said, 'Why did Charles let me stay a prisoner, after that story of Malvina's? Why did he not have me let out at once? Why did he go away, knowing I was in disgrace, knowing how I would be treated, without doing anything to help me?'

'Because,' said George, 'if you were a free agent, there was a danger of your learning the truth.'

'From me?' suggested my father.

'From you, sir. You must have assumed Charles Killin would tell Katie about her parentage.'

'Yes, of course. That was why I was surprised that you arrived as you did, asking questions as you did.'

'It was highly likely that you would be in touch with Katie. If you wrote—'

'I did write.'

'The letter was intercepted, sir, like all Katie's letters.'

'Then Dundas knew—'

'What Killin had already told him, sir. At any rate, while Katie was under Killin's eye, he could keep her in ignorance. She trusted him. But he had to go away from Ravenburn, so he – he contrived to have her put on ice, until he got back. Once he was back, she could safely be let out, because she was under his eye again.'

'*He* contrived . . .?' I said.

'Yes,' said George. 'I'm nearly sure he engineered the entire episode of Malvina's night vision. He somehow arranged for Malvina to be on the stairs, and he *did* come out of your room at two in the morning.'

'But he never came to my room!' I said.

'How do you know? You were asleep.'

'Oh. Yes. Malvina was telling the truth, then. How very extraordinary.'

'I think she was. That is why Victoria believed her. Victoria was anxious to believe her, but she would not have done so dishonestly. She would certainly not have spread that dreadful account, if she had not honestly believed it.'

'I am glad to think that,' I said. 'I hope we can put things right between us.'

'I wonder if she will still want Charles?' George murmured.

'I wonder if anyone will,' I said. 'He went to great lengths, didn't he, to keep the secret to himself?'

'Great lengths,' agreed George. 'Remember Rory Beg.'

'My God, he – he betrayed Rory Beg to Uncle Frank – to Frank Dundas?'

'He must have. He had a powerful motive to do so. Rory Beg knew you, and knew Tom very well. There was every possibility that his ancient loyalty to Tom would cause him, one day, to tell Tom the story.'

'He ought to be tried and hanged!' I cried.

George shrugged. 'He has committed no crime known to the lawyers.'

'He should have told me who I was, after he found it out.'

'But that is the very last thing he would do, Katie. The very last.'

'Why?' my father asked. 'Your theories about Killin are horribly convincing, Fraser, but why did he go to such lengths to keep my secret? Why did he send Rory Beg to his death, so that Tom should not know? Why did he not tell Katie about herself?'

'He knew Tom loved Katie,' said George. 'He probably knew Katie loved Tom. As long as they thought they were brother and sister, he could have Katie for himself. As soon as they knew the truth, he would lose her. That is why he did it, all of it. He very nearly got away with it, you know. What started me thinking was one thing only – that he did not come to see me, after my horse was brought down. Even then I might not have suspected. But he told Katie he did come. It was the one mistake he made. Otherwise, I think he would have got away with

314

it.' George's face twisted into his curious, bitter smile. 'I wish I'd thought of it myself,' he added.

I jumped up and kissed him. As I did so, I remembered my father's words about William Irvine – nothing I had ever done made me worthy of such a friend.

My father pressed me to stay with him – and George too, if he could – because he said he did not want to lose the child he had found.

'I will come back,' I said. 'But I must go away first. There is someone I must talk to.'

But, to my bitter disappointment, Tom was away from Ravenburn. He had business of some kind.

The Castle was in deep mourning. As long as Mamma was there – I mean, Isabella Lady Ravenburn – it always would be.

Sir Malcolm Rattray had gone home to Lanarkshire. He knew, I suppose, that he could do no good at Ravenburn, neither as railway-director nor as suitor. Staying could only make him more miserable. I was a little glad for him that he had gone away, and more glad for myself.

Colonel Blair had gone away, with his glossy hats and his fine cigars. Perhaps Tom had seen, without help from Loudon, that he was a fraud and a sponger, and sent him away. Or perhaps he had begun to repeat too many of his stories, and Isabella had at last grown tired of him.

Still nothing would dislodge Lady Wood and Mrs Seton.

Within an hour of my return, they faced me with Dr McAndrew's written opinion. It was handed to me by Miss Maitland, Malvina's governess, who did not mind being Isabella's ambassador in such a business.

In the old days, Isabella had had legal authority over me. Now she had none. A doctor consulted and paid by her could, in the old days, have put me into a padded cell, and no power in Scotland could have stopped him. Now he could not oblige me to take a headache powder.

I sighed, and glanced at the paper. Dr McAndrew wrote that he had examined me minutely and at length; he concluded that I should without delay be committed to an institution, for my own sake and that of others; that I should never marry; that I should never be permitted to control my own affairs; that my memory was not to be trusted, or anything I said believed.

I tore the paper slowly across, and handed it back to Miss Maitland.

Lady Victoria Arlington arrived in a carriage, from Tulloch, with General and Lady Angela Ramsay.

Victoria threw herself at me, with the impetuosity I had loved about her.

She cried, 'Katie, I beg your forgiveness. I have spoken to George Fraser. He was very cross with me. He was right. I am so ashamed. I did believe that dreadful child, and I believed Charles when he told me that you had – that you had—'

'Seduced him?'

'Well, yes, that was what he told me. I was mad with anger and jealousy. Forgive me, if you possibly can.'

I kissed her.

The Ramsays spoke in similar terms, most generously and kindly, and made the most handsome apology. Lady Angela kissed me. I think the General did also, although there was no need for such a gesture.

We were all happy to be friends again. But we were not so happy when we turned to discussion of Lord Killin. He had lied to us all, which was cynical and evil. He had suppressed a truth vital to my happiness and Tom's, which was worse. He had sent Rory Beg to his death, which was by far worst of all.

'Everybody will know a little of this,' said Lady Angela at last. 'But nobody will know all of it. He won't be absolutely ostracized, but he won't be absolutely trusted.'

'I agree,' said the General. 'He'll survive as a man of fashion, but he's dead as a man of honour. I don't envy him the rest of his life. People will stop talking suddenly when he comes into a room, and he'll know they were talking about him, and he'll know what they were saying.'

'I know that feeling,' I said. 'I used to have that feeling, when they made me think I was mad, and made other people think it too.'

'They made you think so, Katie,' said Victoria. 'But Charles really was mad. He was mad with love for you. *I* know *that* feeling, unfortunately. I can understand how a – how a once decent man could go to such appalling lengths.'

316

' "To understand all is to forgive all",' murmured Lady Angela. 'Or not, Victoria?'

'No,' said Victoria slowly. ' "To err is human, to forgive divine." I'm not as divine as that.'

I had put off the moment, because I half dreaded it: but at last I went to find Isabella in her boudoir. I asked her abruptly if she had known the truth about me, about my parentage, about my fortune.

'I left everything to my dearest Frank,' she said, with a sort of hesitant misery. 'I relied on him so much for everything . . . I do not know how I shall manage without him . . .'

'You managed Dr McAndrew without him,' I said.

She looked at me, blinking, and made a little meaningless gesture with her hand.

'I shall go away,' she whispered presently, 'with my babies. We no longer feel . . . Now that poor Frank . . . Jamie does not think he will be happy, in a place where he was once . . . Now that Tom . . . We shall go back to Edinburgh, perhaps, where once . . . But how I shall manage, with so little, now that I no longer . . .'

'Now that you no longer have my money,' I said.

I had come into the room full of anger, full of contempt. I had rehearsed brave and cutting phrases. They died in my throat. Isabella was wretched enough, with the ruins of her world about her. My insults were needless. Not even her toadies, at their most insincere, could have said now that she looked like Malvina's sister.

'I will give you what money you need,' I said, 'now that I have money to give. You can buy a house in Edinburgh, or wherever you like. You can do what you like, where you like.'

'Thank you, Katharine. I always . . . You were always, to me . . .'

I did not like her, but I pitied her. I had no more to say to her. I turned, and left the room.

I was sick with longing to see Tom. He was still away.

I put on old clothes, and walked along the lochside to the spur from which I could see Eilean Fitheach. I took Tom's spyglass, and looked at the half ruined tower of Daigneach Fitheach, of

Castle Raven. The birds were there, black and sinister and fascinating.

Then, as I watched, I saw one of the birds cock its great head, and stare downwards.

I wondered idly what it had seen.

The truth blossomed in my head like a flower.

My boat was still on the island, where George and I had left it when we fetched Donald McWiddie, who was Dickson Carmichael. Well, I could use what boats I liked.

I flew to the boathouse. It was still open and in use, although the season was well advanced into autumn. Surrounded by the astonished disapproval of the boathouse-men, I jumped into a boat, and started rowing.

It was a glorious autumn day. After a brisk bright morning, the noonday sun was hot. So was I, after a few minutes' rowing. I took off my hat, and my jacket. I was thankful I was wearing no stays. I wished I was wearing no stockings.

The island was silent, and seemed deserted from the water, except for the autumn crowds of titmice and finches busy in the trees.

I landed, and went inland. I walked slowly, somehow nervously, towards the tower.

Tom was crouched, in his shirtsleeves, beside a fire he was making. My heart jumped. He did not see me, because he was blowing at the fire, and concentrating on it. He did not hear me approach over the turf and pine needles.

My heart bounced in my throat, choking me. I felt such a wave of love that my knees almost buckled.

Tom had recovered some of the colour in his cheeks and brow, after the pallor of his weeks in prison. He looked very well, but tired.

I stood watching him. I made no effort to approach him because, now that I could see him, I was not sure that my legs would carry me. I made no effort to speak because, now that it was time to speak, I was not sure that I could utter a word.

His fire was burning. He sat back on his heels, flushed from the flames and from blowing at them. He looked up. He saw me. I tried to smile, but my face was frozen. I tried to speak, but no sound came.

Tom rose slowly to his feet. His clothes were untidy and his hands muddy; there was a smear of soot on his brow; his hair was dishevelled. To me he looked more beautiful than anything I had ever seen.

He stared at me with misery in his eyes. He made a little despairing gesture with his mud-stained hands. It was oddly like the gesture Isabella had used.

'We were wrong,' I said, in a sort of hoarse squeak, which was the best I could do for a voice.

He nodded dumbly.

'I mean,' I tried to explain myself better, 'we were *not* wrong, because we were wrong!'

He looked at me blankly. The misery did not leave his eyes.

I began to explain, breathless, the words tumbling out.

Very slowly, Tom's face changed, as he began to make sense of the confused and garbled story I was telling him. Misery left his face. A smile grew, like sunrise.

'So, you see . . .' I said, and suddenly burst into tears.

He held out his arms to me, and I collapsed into them. He held me so tight that I almost felt my ribs crack. I clung to him, and pressed myself against his dear body.

Into his neck I said, with the greatest difficulty, 'I must tell you the whole story. It is very complicated, and long, about Killin, and Isabella, and so forth.'

'Do,' murmured Tom, 'later.'

I drowned in his kisses, and in his words of love.

He said, into my cheek. 'I was going to climb the tower at last, to look at the ravens' nest. Shall we do that?'

'Yes,' I said. 'Later.'

E. V. Thompson
Harvest of the Sun £1.25

A magnificent saga of passion and conflict in Africa a century ago ...
The ship was bound for Australia. Aboard, Josh Retallick and Miriam
Thackeray, prisoners destined for the convict settlements – until their
vessel was wrecked on the Skeleton Coast of South West Africa. Far
from their Cornwall origins, the two strangers in a hostile land meet
Bushmen and Hereros, foraging Boers and greedy traders in an alien
world of ivory tusks and smuggled guns.

Elizabeth Byrd
The Flowers of the Forest £1.50

Edinburgh in the year 1513 – the bloodstreaked year of Flodden Field.
Against the setting of the teeming capital of Scotland, plague-ridden and
aflow with riches and squalor, this vivid novel follows the fortunes of
two women: Bess Andersen, the spirited country girl, seduced and
scorned, turning to prostitution and wedlock to a weakling; and
Margaret Tudor, the princess who became Queen of James IV, seeking
in vain for love and affection ...

'Full-blooded stuff' SCOTSMAN

You can buy these and other Pan books from booksellers and
newsagents; or direct from the following address:
Pan Books, Sales Office, Cavaye Place, London SW10 9PG
Send purchase price plus 20p for the first book and 10p for
each additional book, to allow for postage and packing
Prices quoted are applicable in the UK

While every effort is made to keep prices low, it is sometimes
necessary to increase prices at short notice. Pan Books reserve
the right to show on covers and charge new retail prices which
may differ from those advertised in the text or elsewhere